Praise for Jo Ann Brown

"Jo Ann Brown writes with an eye for conflict and a heart filled with love."

—Charlotte Hubbard, author of *Christmas Comes to Morning Star*

"Jo Ann Brown's *A Promise of Forgiveness* is a heartfelt story of second chances, reminding us that a pursuit of grace includes grace toward ourselves. In a measured unfolding of individual limitations, the resilience of community rises to flourish in a circle of unexpected love, gleaming hope, and a truthful future. Fans of Amish fiction can step into a layered story with timely themes that lead them into their own hearts."

—Olivia Newport, author of the Amish Turns of Time series

"*A Promise of Forgiveness* is a beautiful story of faith, forgiveness, and family. Naomi and Samuel's journey back to each other is emotional, yet delightful, and readers will fall in love with them and their families."

—Kathleen Fuller, *USA TODAY* bestselling author

"A poignant tale of betrayal, secrets and love. A lovely story about the importance of family and forgiveness! A must read by author Jo Ann Brown."

—Rebecca Kertz, Love Inspired and *Publishers Weekly* bestselling author

"Brimming with richly layered characters, newly discovered secrets and startling twists, *A Promise of Forgiveness* will have readers holding their breath and dabbing their eyes right up until the very last page."

—Carrie Lighte, *Publishers Weekly* bestselling author

"Wholesome romance that pulls on the heartstrings. Jo Ann Brown never disappoints."

—Katy Lee, bestselling and award-winning author

"Jo Ann Brown's expertise in numerous areas is evident as she weaves a tale of hope, forgiveness and enticing surprises. Intriguing characters abound, including an adorable set of twins."

—Jocelyn McClay, *Publishers Weekly* bestselling author

"*A Promise of Forgiveness* by Jo Ann Brown is charged with emotion. It's a delightful blend of courage, hope and faith. The tension and multi-layered twists will put you on the edge of your seat from start to end. A must read that will leave you feeling thrilled and satisfied."

—Leigh Bale, *Publishers Weekly* bestselling author

Also available from Jo Ann Brown
and Love Inspired

Secrets of Bliss Valley

A Wish for Home
A Promise of Forgiveness

Visit the Author Profile page at LoveInspired.com for more titles.

A
SEARCH FOR
REDEMPTION

Jo Ann Brown

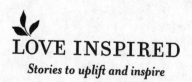

LOVE INSPIRED

Stories to uplift and inspire

LOVE INSPIRED®

Stories to uplift and inspire

ISBN-13: 978-1-335-53003-5

A Search for Redemption

Love Inspired
22 Adelaide St. West, 41st Floor
Toronto, Ontario M5H 4E3, Canada
www.LoveInspired.com

Printed in U.S.A.

Recycling programs for this product may not exist in your area.

To my dear friends on the Faith, Hope & Love Christian Writers Board.
We made it through all the changes!
Loved serving with you:
Nancy, Terri, Martha, Renee, Judy and Robin.

And be ye kind one to another, tenderhearted, forgiving one another, even as God for Christ's sake hath forgiven you.

—*Ephesians* 4:32

A
SEARCH FOR
REDEMPTION

Chapter One

If it hadn't been for the rain, Joel Beachy never would have gone into The Amish Quilt Emporium on the southwest corner of Main Street and Decatur in the center of Strasburg, Pennsylvania. Not only was it raining hard enough to flood the road, the water rushing through the intersection, but the lightning had barely faded before monstrous claps of thunder echoed among the brick buildings.

He could have gone into the Creamery if he'd been on the other side of the street. Dozens of *Englisch* tourists—and it was astounding how the *Deitsch* words he'd used in his youth had sprung into his mind as soon as he entered Lancaster County—had sought shelter inside and on the front porch of the inn next door. Others huddled under the drive-through at the bank across the road. Facing it, a pizza parlor offered both a sanctuary from the storm and a chance for a delicious slice. But he'd been on the southwest corner of Main Street where a single porch offered haven from nature's fury.

One part of him was grateful for the storm. All day, the late

August air had been heavy and rides nonexistent. Not many people stopped for a hitchhiker on busy Route 30, the major thoroughfare through the heart of Lancaster County. Even fewer would stop on the back roads that led into farming country in the southern half of the county. Most drivers—whether in a car, a pickup or a buggy—were traveling a short distance. They didn't see any reason to give him a ride for a mile when they believed someone else would come by and take him farther.

Nobody had.

So Joel had continued tramping on through the countryside in shoes that had raised one blister on his left heel and another on the ball of his left foot three days ago. That he limped, looking a bit like Frankenstein's monster lurching along the road, had kept more than a few kindhearted folks from offering him a ride.

Now he was running through the rain, his knapsack banging on his back. He tried to ignore the bitter scent of ozone that warned a lightning bolt had struck not far from him.

"This way!" called a woman, standing in a doorway. She motioned for him and an elderly couple behind him to come into the shop. "Hurry!"

He barely could make out her form in the sudden cloudburst. Water ran from his hair down into his eyes, blinding him. Wind abruptly whipped around him. He winced when something hit him on the shoulder, once, then another time. Hail! Just pea-sized, but he knew the danger after years of working in the fields and having a furious late-summer storm erupt over him.

A muffled cry behind him made him spin around. The elderly man had come to a halt as he folded at the waist. The woman beside him had her arm around his shoulders as she leaned in to speak to him. Her body was tense, and she flinched when lightning danced across the sky overhead.

Rushing to them, Joel said, "Let me help."

The woman, bedraggled in the downpour, nodded, but the man waved him away, saying, "Give me a minute to catch my breath."

Another onslaught of hail struck them.

"We don't have a minute!" Joel took the man's left arm and draped it over his shoulders, shifting his worn knapsack to his other side. Straightening the man, Joel remained bent because he was much taller than the gray-haired man who wore a soaked T-shirt with the words *Amish Country* emblazoned on a bright red background. "C'mon! Let's go!"

"I can get there on my own," argued the old man.

"I'm sure you can." Joel lowered his voice to a conspiratorial whisper, trying not to grunt with pain as each icy pellet battered his head and back. "But we need to get your wife out of the storm."

He'd found the right words because the gray-haired man nodded and began shuffling forward. The man's wife reached for his other arm, but Joel shook his head. If the old guy realized he needed help more than she did, he might refuse to cooperate.

Assisting them to the porch, Joel urged them up the steps and toward the door. He was about to follow when the wife exclaimed she'd left her purse in the middle of the street.

"Go inside!" he ordered. "I'll get it. No problem."

As if in reply to his boast, the wind rose, rattling tree branches against each other. Twigs fell from the lone tree in front of the shop, cracking on the sidewalk and littering the road. Somewhere in the distance, the faint cry of a siren was distorted with the storm. He couldn't tell if it was a fire truck or an ambulance or a cop car. Hoping it was as far away as it sounded, he ran toward the woman's purse. He scooped it up and turned, his foot sliding on the wet asphalt. Pain riveted his right ankle as he pivoted.

Great! Now both feet would complain while he tried to get a ride once the storm had passed.

He winced, but didn't slow as more bolts split the sky. The siren sounded closer in the wake of the thunder.

Ducking his head against a gust of wind, he ran toward the front porch. His hope that he'd found shelter vanished as soon as he jumped up on it, not bothering to go around to the steps. Rain and wind continued to batter him and tried to pull his knapsack off his shoulder. Even beneath the porch roof, he might as well have been standing in a bathroom shower with the water turned up to max.

Someone gave him a shove forward, and he scrambled up the four stone steps to the door where the woman had called to him moments ago. He opened it, going in and edging aside to let the person behind him come in, too. Seeing the crowd packed into the narrow spaces between tables covered with merchandise and racks of quilts in every possible shade was enough to make him almost turn around and head outside. He felt abruptly claustrophobic.

With a half smile at his own foolish reaction, he calmed his instinctive yearning to flee. He'd had plenty of experience with fighting the need to escape from a confined area with too many people. Through hard lessons, he'd learned to hold his elbows in tight to his body and make himself as small as possible—a challenge for a man who was more than six feet tall—in order to avoid bumping into one of the volatile prisoners who was looking for any excuse to start a fight. Being raised Amish had put him at a distinct disadvantage when confronted by someone who'd used his fists his whole life to get what he wanted...or to prove a point.

But he was out of prison. After almost six long, long years, he was out. No more mornings of waking up and looking out at a wall topped by razor wire. No more hearing shouts born more of frustration and boredom than anger. No more smells of too many bodies crammed into too small a space.

He was out.

And he wasn't going back.

No matter what, he wasn't going back.

Joel sighed, knowing that was an empty pledge. If he didn't find a job before the few dollars in his pocket were gone, he'd have the choice of begging or resorting to the crimes he'd been accused of committing. No, he'd starve before he gave his parole officer the satisfaction of putting him back in prison. Roland Shriver had made it clear he'd be more than happy to see Joel behind bars with the key tossed away.

"The world doesn't owe you a living," Shriver had said to him during their most recent meeting. "With that chip you've got on your shoulder, I don't have much hope you'll stay clean."

Wanting to say—again—that he'd never done drugs, though he'd drunk an ocean of alcohol since he'd left Bliss Valley, he hadn't bothered to argue. Shriver wouldn't have believed him. Nobody had. And if he had a chip on his shoulder, he deserved it after having his *daed* consider him a worthless failure most of his life. Not that anyone could have been the paragon Wyman Beachy expected his only son to be.

Odd... *Daed* was the only word he'd never stopped using from his years of living plain. He put aside *Deitsch* years ago, but that one word lingered. How ironic! The person whom he'd worked hardest to forget had created a connection to the past that he'd tried to get rid of.

Pushing those thoughts aside, he saw the elderly couple now was perched on a bench with peeling paint. He knew it was a style *Englischers* liked, but he couldn't imagine why anyone would want furniture that looked worn-out, especially at the prices he'd seen in antique shops where he'd stopped to get out of the heat. The wife gave him a grateful smile when he stretched past several other people to hand her the purse.

"God bless you, young man," she said.

He nodded, but didn't reply. God's blessings were few and far between. He'd shunted God aside years ago when he'd asked himself why he wanted another *daed*. The one he had on Earth had been tough enough to be around because Joel could never meet his expectations or toe the line with rules that had seemed arbitrary. God had even more rules, and Joel had broken many of them. Too many to ask for forgiveness now, even if God would offer it to him. Maybe it would have been different if he'd been the typical prodigal son, seeking a different way in the world and trying to be a success. All he'd done was make a mess of himself and everything around him.

A sharp crack of thunder helped him push aside the dreary thoughts. He brushed his too-long hair out of his eyes and stared at the puddle beneath his feet. His eyes jerked up when someone let out a screech and pointed out the window.

He looked past the display of quilts just in time to see lightning bounce off the metal roof of a cupola on a nearby roof. All around him, people reached for their cell phones, ready to call 911. Sparks fell to the road like spent fireworks. On the roof, there was no sign of fire or smoke. Then he saw the broken globe on one corner. The ancient lightning rod with its glass globe had redirected the lightning toward the ground, saving the building.

Others had seen that, too, and conversation buzzed through the store. Some people were focused on the storm, but others were interested in the products for sale.

While rain slashed at the window, sending sheets of water

along the uneven glass, Joel saw what appeared to be several familiar faces. He hunched into himself and, holding his knapsack close, eased into a space not far from the right-hand window. A wall of folded quilts was in front of him, but he paid no attention to the beautiful handiwork.

Had anyone recognized him?

There was a plain woman at the back of the shop near the register, but the rest seemed to be *Englischers*. That didn't mean anything. Nor did it matter that more than a decade had passed since he'd last been so close to Bliss Valley, a few miles south of Strasburg. He'd grown four inches and wasn't the skinny kid he'd been then. He wore a mustache and goatee, the complete opposite of the jawline beard a plain man grew once he was married.

But that might not be enough to keep someone from identifying him. There had been plenty of people beyond the plain communities who'd been the focus of the pranks he'd pulled years ago with his best friends Adam and Samuel. None of them would be happy to learn Joel Beachy was back, and there would be quite a few who felt they had scores to settle with him.

He pulled out his handkerchief and wiped rain off his face. More ran out of his hair, so he kept dabbing at it. He glanced again around the room, but stuck to the shadows.

He hadn't intended to return to Lancaster County. When he'd gotten out of jail, he'd planned to go anywhere else, but during the past four months, he'd found out that the "anywhere elses" he'd tried didn't want an ex-con in their backyards. The news that a Las Vegas–style casino was being built along Route 30 suggested there might be a job he could get. Not in the casino. His criminal record would preclude any chance to be hired there. However, there would be new hotels and other businesses being developed to take advantage of the crowds coming to the casino. One of them might be interested in hiring him. The carpentry skills he'd learned on a plain farm had been refined before he got caught up in the mess that sent him to prison.

"Sorry," he said when someone else coming into the shop pushed him against a man between him and a table where a variety of tchotchkes, most made to look like Amish buggies pulled by a single horse or chubby hand-painted plain men and women, awaited tourists.

Set as it was along the road that connected many of the plain districts to the north in Bird-in-Hand and Intercourse to the southern ones in Bliss Valley, Strasburg offered plenty of ways to spend money. Visitors came to visit Amish venues and the steam train museum outside the village and left with silly knickknacks and loud T-shirts. He looked around the shop at the opulent array of quilts mixed with other handicrafts and toy trains, and T-shirts with a variety of designs and sayings. Some, under different circumstances, would have made him smile at their puns, but right now, all he wanted was to get out of the shop and on his way...

To where?

One problem at a time, he reminded himself as he had so often in his cell. Anything could be handled if he didn't let himself get overwhelmed by the challenges ahead of him.

"You've g-g-got to move," said a woman from behind him. "Right n-n-now!"

At the quavering voice that was trying to sound as stern as the guards who liked to order the inmates around, he looked over his shoulder, guilt suffusing him. The woman behind him was about as far from one of those detestable sadists as summer was from winter. In front of her heart-shaped *kapp*, her red hair caught fire from the large lights hanging from the building's vaulted ceiling. Her plain dress in the perfect dark green to match her eyes was covered by a black apron that couldn't hide her slender form. He guessed she was in her midtwenties, a few years younger than he was, because her pink cheeks were unlined and teased his fingers to caress them.

He clamped his hands to his sides before he couldn't resist touching her skin to see if it was as soft as it appeared. Had he lost his mind? She was a plain woman, probably married with several *kinder*. He was a convicted felon. Even a hint of impropriety—Where had that phrase come from? It sounded like some boring, historical romcom—would give Shriver the excuse he needed to put Joel back in prison, this time with no hope of parole until his full sentence was served.

No matter how enticing a plain woman was, she couldn't be for him. He had jumped the fence from the Amish world to the *Englisch* one many years ago. Others had been welcomed back once they confessed their sins, but those people hadn't done the things Joel Beachy had.

And now, when he was trying to walk the straight and narrow to hold on to his precious freedom, he was causing trouble.

As he started to apologize, the plain woman went on, "You're d-d-dripping on the f-f-fabric, ma'am."

She wasn't talking to him. He looked to his right and saw a well-dressed, middle-aged *Englisch* woman aiming a frown at her.

"I am not," the *Englischer* said in a tone that suggested the woman working at the store was not even worthy of her contempt.

The Amish woman's fingers tightened as she clasped her hands in front of her, but her voice remained serene. "Could you please take a step to your left, ma'am? That will solve the problem."

"Are you calling me a problem, young lady?"

"Of course not!" The flattering pink in the Amish woman's face deepened toward a blush. "You aren't a problem, ma'am. It's the water dripping off your sleeve. If you'd take a step to your left, everything will be fine."

"There's no room." The older woman's voice boomed through the shop, drawing attention.

That wasn't true. There was a four feet between her and a table holding stacks of quilted potholders. The woman was being cantankerous for no reason.

He glanced at the Amish woman. She now was rubbing her palms together so hard he was surprised a flame didn't pop out from between them. Yet she was attempting to smile. Like any plain person, she must be hoping to ease the situation without creating more conflict.

Swallowing the bitter laugh bubbling in his throat, he thought of how often his *daed*—his adoptive *daed*—had derided him for not being a *gut* plain person. Joel was supposed to have been Wyman Beachy's exemplary son, the one who got the best marks in school as well as being skilled at sports. He needed to prove he was such a hard worker he kept laboring long after others had called it a day. Mistakes? For others, to err was human, but not for Joel. He was supposed to do everything right the first time and never slip up.

"Please, ma'am," the Amish woman said, trying to squeeze past him. When he didn't move, she aimed her green gaze at him for a second, but it was enough for him to discover how distressed she was.

Hoping he wasn't being foolish by stepping out of the shadows and giving others a chance to notice him, he couldn't stand there and do nothing. He'd watched too many people do that too often while in prison. The pretty Amish woman wasn't being beat up, at least not physically. However, a bully, no matter whether they lived behind bars or not, was something he couldn't tolerate.

In the back of his mind, he heard disbelieving laughter. Young girls' laughter, and he knew neither Laurene Nolt nor Naomi Gingerich would have believed his thoughts were sincere. Why should they? He'd made their lives miserable by bullying them for years before he'd turned to making his own a disaster. He wasn't that angry kid anymore, whether anyone would believe it or not.

Joel cleared his throat once, then a second time. When both women looked at him, he said, "I'd be glad to move. That way, ma'am, you can have my spot here by the door." He motioned for the *Englisch* woman to step past him.

The *Englisch* woman gave him a derisive sniff. "Then I won't be able to look at the quilts on the big rack."

Refraining from mentioning that, as she was more than a foot shorter than he was, she couldn't see the largest rack from where she stood, he put on his best smile. It felt rusty, because he hadn't had much of a reason to smile in years. Hoping it didn't look macabre, he gestured again toward his spot.

"But you'll have an excellent view of the quilts in the window." He spoke quietly as if sharing a special secret with her. "You know, don't you, that owners of these shops put the best ones in the window to entice buyers in?" The lie tumbled off his lips. After all, lying was something he'd had plenty of practice with.

The woman blinked as she considered his words. Glancing around, she must have realized how almost every person in the shop, except for two other women who were in earnest discussion about which of three possible quilts they should purchase, was focused on her. Not wanting to appear stupid, she said, "Of course I know the best ones are in the window. Everyone knows that, young man."

Now he had to work to keep from laughing. What a shame that, when for the first time he'd felt like laughing in years, he mustn't. He couldn't annoy the woman so much she'd refuse to move until her feet took root in the wooden floor.

Don't be fanciful, boy. You've got too many ideas in your head and not enough work on your hands.

The echo of his *daed*'s voice dampened his amusement. Wyman Beachy's words, though he'd repeated them often, hadn't always made sense. However, Joel had understood the meaning. Joel had—yet again—disappointed his *daed*. His adoptive *daed*, as Wyman had taken pains to correct everyone soon after Joel started getting into mischief when he was seven or eight old. From that point on, there had been a clear division in their family. Joel the adopted kid versus his *daed*, his *mamm* who'd never gone against Wyman's dictates, and his three younger sisters. Rosemary had been born six years after him followed by Alta and Erma. He'd wondered often, since he'd left Bliss Valley, if anyone had sensed the ugly undercurrents swirling beneath their image as a happy plain family.

Realizing he needed to say something to the matronly woman, Joel smiled again. "All right. We'll change places, ma'am."

She edged past him, pulling her purse in tight to her. He almost told her she didn't have to worry about him stealing it. He wasn't a pickpocket. He was a convicted drug dealer.

As he moved away from the window, he looked over her head, pretending to be interested in watching the rain bounce off the deserted street.

"*Danki*… I mean thank you," said a soft voice from next to his right shoulder.

He wasn't surprised to discover the Amish woman had edged forward to begin wiping water off the display table next to him. Her face, unembellished with makeup, was the epitome of sweetness. She wore a shy smile, and when she lowered her eyes, her red lashes were lush against her cheeks where scattered freckles accented her high cheekbones.

"You're welcome," he said. Like her, he didn't want to chance starting another confrontation with the *Englisch* woman. "Is this your shop?"

"No. I work here." Her stutter had vanished, and he guessed she'd been uneasy about giving an order to a customer. "It belongs to Tiffany Spanner, but she's not here right now. Did you want to speak with her?"

No, I want to speak with you when we aren't surrounded by so many people. The thought burst out of his mind so strongly he hoped he hadn't said the words aloud. This woman wasn't like the ones he'd spent time with after he left Bliss Valley. They'd been out for a *gut* time, and he'd been glad to give them one. Or as much of one as he could afford, which was why each of them moved on as soon as his money ran out.

"I was curious," he said, again curtailing his thoughts before they sucked him into the past, "when you were quick to protect the items for sale."

"That's part of my job." Her tentative smile returned. "Making sure what we have for sale isn't damaged or stolen."

He flinched. He couldn't help himself. Was she trying in a roundabout way to make sure *he* hadn't slipped something in his pocket? Not that he would have any interest in the bric-a-brac on the table, even when he'd been a kid and had considered shoplifting a fun and exciting way to spend an afternoon.

"It's a big job for one person."

Her laugh was hushed. "We don't usually have more than one or two customers at a time."

His reply was halted by a clap of thunder so loud it shook the windows. The *Englisch* woman jumped back, and he put out his arm to halt her from running over the Amish woman.

"That was close." The *Englisch* woman glowered at him and the redhead as if it were all their faults. "Step aside. It's too dangerous where I am."

"There's a place," the other woman said, again with a timid smile, "on the other bench by the counter. If you can get to it—"

"Step aside." Without a further word, the woman pushed her way past the people who were talking about the storm. She seemed impervious to the glowers shot in her direction.

"That was kind of you," he said to the red-haired woman. "Especially when she hasn't been kind to you."

"That's what the Bible teaches us."

"You mean turning the other cheek?"

She smiled. "*Ja,* but I prefer the final verse in Ephesians 4. *'And be ye kind one to another, tenderhearted, forgiving one another, even as God for Christ's sake hath forgiven you.'* She's frightened of the storm, so I would be wrong to judge her actions as anything but fear."

When someone called out, "Grace!", she excused herself and wove through the crowd toward the rear of the store. He should have been grateful he didn't have to reply. He wasn't sure what he would have said. He *was* sure of one thing, though. Grace was a warmhearted person with goodness at her core.

The complete opposite of Joel Beachy.

Chapter Two

Ten minutes after Grace Coffman had been called to the rear of the shop where rain had been leaking past one of the windows overlooking the road leading south to Bliss Valley, the storm lost its fury. She'd handled the problem by stuffing paper towels around the edges of the window, and then returned to the center of the store where she nodded and smiled at the people who'd sought shelter. They thanked her before they drifted out as the storm continued east across the railroad tracks and into the farm fields.

She wasn't sure how she missed when the man who'd been so helpful had left. She'd wanted to thank him again and maybe offer him a cup of *kaffi*. He'd looked exhausted, as worn as his light brown knapsack, and she wondered if he was on one of the tours that took people from one Amish site to the next without giving them a chance to catch their breaths.

No, he hadn't seemed to know any of the other people in the shop. She'd heard some whispers among the women about what a nice guy he was for stepping aside so that "old biddy"—as several had described the *Englisch* woman who'd refused to believe she was dripping on the table—could move.

That Grace had to agree with. Whoever the man had been, Grace was grateful she hadn't had to calm the woman herself. In tense situations like that, Grace tended to stumble over her words and make a complete *dummkopf* of herself.

But the man was gone, and she needed to get the shop cleaned before any more damage could be done. The refugees from the rain hadn't gotten much water on the quilts. A few were damp, but she'd spread them out in the back room and give them a chance to dry. A few motes of dust or even a damp fingerprint could leave a spot on a quilt and diminish its value.

She was relieved to see the biggest puddles of water from her impromptu guests had gathered among the silly souvenirs her boss thought were adorable. Grace considered them junk being sold at inflated prices. She'd realized within days of starting at The Amish Quilt Emporium that she and her boss, Tiffany Spanner, wouldn't see eye to eye. She admired Tiffany's agile business sense, but not her single-minded determination to squeeze every penny out of the pocket of anyone who came into the shop. When Grace had begun there almost five years ago, Tiffany had offered her below what Grace knew was a fair starting pay. Every year since, Tiffany had tried to find ways to avoid giving her a raise. Grace knew she needed to ask for one soon, and she dreaded doing that. Each time she tried to bring up the subject, Tiffany would walk away muttering about how plain people were supposed to avoid confrontations.

That was true, but Grace needed to earn more money. She'd worked at the shop a long time and been a faithful employee. Tiffany appreciated her devotion and her knowledge about quilting. However, her boss hated how many customers came in asking for Grace's help. Tiffany wanted to be the center of attention as well as the acknowledged conduit between the local seamstresses and the buyers who were searching for the perfect quilt. Yet she didn't have the patience to assist customers who had trouble making up their minds about which beautiful quilt to purchase. Tiffany pushed the most expensive ones where she would garner the most profit.

Grace appreciated days like this when Tiffany was somewhere else. Today, her boss was busy searching for a location for a second shop about a half hour drive to the northwest in Lititz, and Grace was grateful she could postpone asking for a raise. She couldn't wait any longer to ask for that raise, but it wouldn't have to be today.

If she hadn't become the sole support for her *daed* and *mamm*, she wouldn't have pushed for the pay increase she deserved. She was the youngest of four siblings. Her three older brothers had married and moved away from Bliss Valley during the past six or seven years. Two brothers, Duane and Alphus, had found homes in Colorado and the oldest, Fritz, had settled in Montana. She'd been left behind to take over the farm with her future husband so she could assure their parents were provided for.

That had been the plan, but it'd all fallen apart when her fiancé, Lamar Mullett, died after being trampled by a bull. His sudden death had sent her spiraling into herself, leaving her living on autopilot. She'd worked and attended church. She'd tended to her *daed*, helping him when his Parkinson's disease flared up and left him able to do little more than stay in bed or sit in a chair in the living room. She'd watched over her *mamm* and her medications after the *doktors* had diagnosed her with coronary artery disease. Getting them to their medical appointments and stepping up when they couldn't do things for themselves had become the focus of her life, but it'd been the outer husk of herself going through those motions. Inside, she'd curled up in unspeakable grief for a year. Even God's comfort hadn't been able to reach through her anguish as she tried to pick up the pieces of her life.

All of that had happened four years ago, and Grace had struggled to work her way from beneath the heavy blanket of sorrow. Lamar had been the first person beyond her family and a handful of friends to *see* her. Everyone else had left her to loiter in the shadows. Lamar hadn't let her hide. He'd insisted she was worthy of his attention and his life, and she'd begun to believe it, too.

But once she'd come out of her deepest mourning, it had seemed as if the world had moved on without her. Friends were now married, and some even had *kinder*. None of them had lost a fiancé, which made it hard for her to talk to them or them to her. The memory of Lamar hung between her and everyone else, snatching what once would have been simple words right out of her mouth.

It had become easier to interact with strangers than with the *Leit*. That was why she hadn't stuttered while talking with the man who'd helped with the *Englisch* woman. Like everyone in the shop, he'd come and stayed a short time and probably wouldn't return. He didn't know about her painful past, and she liked keeping it that way. She didn't want pitying glances and whispers and sighs like the ones she'd gotten from too many of her neighbors after Lamar's death. Only a few close friends had insisted she let them past the walls she'd raised, and she asked God to bless them for their persistence.

"Do you have any more paper towels?" called her dearest friend, Pepper Underwood, from the tiny bathroom under the stairs that led up to the apartment where Tiffany once had lived. Now her boss had a beautiful, expensive brick home— as she bragged—on Main Street in Lititz.

"More?" Grace asked. "I thought I'd gotten everything mopped up."

"You did, but there's a new lake growing on the floor by the back door." She rolled her eyes and shook her head, making her small Mennonite *kapp* bounce on her ebony hair. "Tiffany's going to have to part with some of her precious money and do repairs on this place before it crumbles right in front of our eyes."

"Fixing up this shop isn't going to happen. She's only interested in the new place that's going to be—"

"'A showcase for the highest quality quilts,'" Pepper quoted along with Grace, then laughed. "I've lost count of the number of times I've heard her announce that as if she plans to carve the words over the front door. I can't imagine how many times *you've* had to listen to the whole spiel."

"I didn't keep track."

"You wouldn't. You're a nicer person than I am." Not giving Grace a chance to protest, she asked, "Where are the paper towels stored?"

"In the gray metal cupboard in the storage room by the back door."

"Got it!" With a wave and a smile that made her dark brown eyes crinkle, Pepper vanished.

Grace smiled. Pepper was one of the seamstresses who provided beautiful quilts for the shop. Sending up a quick prayer of gratitude that Pepper had been dropping off her latest creation as the storm had struck and had agreed to stay to help clean up after the rush of wet people into the shop, she wondered how many of the tourists had guessed that Pepper was a skilled quilter. Not many knew the nimble fingers of seamstresses who had immigrated from Southeast Asia and their daughters and granddaughters had helped create the quilts that sold throughout Lancaster County.

Pepper Underwood had been born Paj Maiv Vang, but

she'd been called Pepper for as long as Grace had known her. It seemed the perfect name because of her spicy nature. She wasn't *gut* about keeping her opinions or her temper to herself. She'd married a Mennonite, despite ardent objections from her parents. In the past year, after almost three years of her marriage to Cameron Underwood, her *mamm* and *daed* were accepting the inevitable.

Or it could have been their *kins-kind*, an adorable infant granddaughter with dark brown eyes and a full head of curly hair, who'd changed their minds.

In the early 1970s, many Hmong exiles who had fled Laos to settle in Thailand before being sent on to the United States had found a home in Lancaster County, supported by local churches, including the Mennonites. Their existence, at first, had been hand-to-mouth. A chance article in a home design magazine had put a spotlight on Amish quilts in Lancaster County, including one with appliqué. A rush exploded to find and buy plain quilts. More than a few families had been able to pay off their farm mortgages with the tens of thousands of dollars paid for an antique quilt in *gut* condition. However, most plain women hadn't known how to appliqué a quilt.

The Hmong women did. Their traditional style of needlework had long included the intricate techniques of appliqué. A few business-savvy Amish women contacted their Hmong neighbors and hired them to do the appliqué work on a quilt top before the plain women handled the quilting of the layers of backing and batts. It was a venture that had worked out well for everyone involved for several years, bringing the two communities—both outsiders among the mainstream American culture—together.

But greed had interfered when demand far outstripped supply. Some quilters, both Hmong and plain, had started contracting with villages in Thailand to hire people to do the work that couldn't be done in Lancaster County. When the truth had come out, it had been a local scandal.

Now a handful of the original Hmong quilters and their *kinder* remained involved in making high-quality quilts sold in shops like The Amish Quilt Emporium. Pepper was one along with her *mamm* and her *grossmammi*.

Gathering up the two quilts she needed to make sure were dried, Grace went to the front door and locked it before going into the back room. It was near enough to closing time, and the street outside was deserted. Nobody was going to come in to buy a quilt when more clouds were building in the west. Even so, she shot a guilty glance over her shoulder. Tiffany would have a hissy fit of epic proportions if she learned Grace had closed one second before five.

Grace spread the quilts on the racks and opened them with care. Draping clean cloth over them to absorb any dampness, she looked past the refrigerator and microwave Tiffany used to heat her lunch. She grimaced when she saw the large puddle Pepper had found. Another was beneath the window beside it. Her friend was right. If Tiffany didn't repair the old building, it would continue to fall apart. No customers wanted to come into a place that looked like it might tumble down on their heads.

From the rear of the shop, Pepper's lyrical soprano rose in a song Grace didn't recognize. Pepper belonged to a liberal Mennonite church, and she could listen to the radio, though there wasn't a television in the small house Cameron had built for them on a lot given to them by his parents. It was an adorable dollhouse with elements of both plain and Hmong in its decor, an amalgamation of two cultures…as Pepper was.

Grace had to admit her friend was everything she wasn't. Pepper spoke her mind with ease, too much ease for a Mennonite wife as Pepper had mentioned her husband lamenting. Whenever she walked into a room, heads turned. Not because she was beautiful, though her features were pleasant and her cheeks always a rosy color because she seemed to have one speed—lightning fast! However, there was a light within her that warmed everyone who encountered it.

"All set," Pepper said, carrying a roll of paper towels that she put in front of some boxes. Her nose wrinkled as she read the words on the cardboard sides. "More junk? How many more cheap dust collectors does Tiffany have here?"

"A lot. She ordered a whole pallet of water globes and knickknacks and T-shirts a few months ago."

"Has she sold many?"

Grace arched her brows. "More than I would have guessed she would. Whatever else you can say about Tiffany—"

"And I could say a lot, but I'll be nice."

"Whatever else you can say about Tiffany," Grace began again, smiling at her friend's sarcasm, "she knows what her customers will buy."

"I wish she knew as much about how her suppliers would like to be paid on time."

Grace's face fell. "She's late again?"

"Months late this time."

"She pays thirty days after the sale, remember." She hated having to defend her boss, but a bizarre sense of loyalty pushed the words past her lips.

Pepper gave her a sympathetic smile. "I know you have to spout the company line, Grace, but the end of those thirty days was two months ago."

"I'll talk to her if you'd like."

"That's like talking to a wall, and you know it!" Pepper sighed. "I'm sorry to yell, Grace. It's not your fault she keeps every penny for as long as she can. It bothers me how she holds us freelancers hostage. I was speaking with Alta, and she said she and the other Beachy sisters have been discussing whether they want to make quilts for the shop any longer."

An icy frisson slipped down Grace's spine. If the quilters stopped providing quilts, the shop would close, and then what would she do? There weren't many jobs near to her family's farm. She could find work as a waitress in a kitchen at one of the smorgasbord restaurants that catered to tourists, but most of them were an hour away by buggy. She couldn't walk that distance. It would have been close to three hours each way. In comparison, she could walk to the quilt shop in fifteen minutes, and the hours she worked allowed her time to make a hot breakfast for her parents before she left as well as being home in time to prepare the evening meal.

"I hope the Beachy sisters will keep working for us!" Grace clasped her hands in front of her chest as she spoke from the heart. "Their quilts and yours are the best ones in the shop, and they sell as soon as I put them out on the racks."

"I know *you* appreciate us, Grace. The others know that, too, but you don't control the purse strings here."

"Tiffany realizes how much our customers love your work." Grace did, too. She was amazed at how unique each quilt was and how she could tell by looking at the patterns and choices of colors which seamstress had made each quilt. Pepper and her family sewed vibrant quilts that lit up any room just as she did. The Beachy sisters' quilts were more subdued, but the quilting stitches were tinier and more complex than Pepper's exquisite quilts.

Pepper said with a sigh, "She seems to forget we work on consignment. When one of our quilts sells, she's supposed to take her third and pay us the rest within thirty days."

"I'm hoping when she opens the other shop—"

"You mean…" Pepper struck a pose with both her hand

and her nose in the air. "'A showcase for the highest quality quilts'?"

"*Ja*, that one." Relieved her friend was jesting again, Grace allowed herself a smile. "I'm hoping while she's focused on that, she'll put me in charge here, including purchasing and accounts."

"That would be a true gift from God. I'm going to set my prayer circle to praying for that. *Niam* and *Pog* will add theirs, I know."

Grace was always amused by how her friend mixed Hmong words with *Deitsch* and English. She nodded as she walked with Pepper out into the shop's main space. "I know your *mamm* and *grossmammi* have been anxious about being paid, too."

"They want to buy things to spoil Christiana. That child is going to be impossible if they keep heaping gifts on her." She glanced out the window. "I should get going now that the rain has stopped. But I've got another question. What's bugging you?"

"Nothing much." *Other than needing a raise and making sure you and the others are paid and feeling guilty I didn't thank that guy properly.*

"Then *who* is bugging you?"

Instead of answering, Grace hurried to the front of the shop and pulled down the yellowed shade to protect the quilts from tomorrow's morning sun. She glanced out at the street where a few cars were edging around huge puddles as she said, "Nobody in particular."

"Uh-huh." She eyed Grace up and down with a stern expression. "I thought you Amish didn't lie."

"I'm not lying."

"You aren't telling the truth either. I saw you giving the eye to that good-looking guy who came in with the lady's purse." Pepper held up her hands in a pose of surrender. "Don't shoot the messenger. I call 'em as I see 'em."

"He had every eye on him when he convinced that stubborn woman to move aside so she didn't damage the quilts."

"But you lingered over there by him after Her Royal Highness deigned to move."

Grace laughed. She couldn't help herself each time Pepper awarded someone a new nickname. Most of those monikers were as incisive as a scalpel cutting through a pompous facade.

"I'm relieved she agreed to switch places with him," Grace replied. "Her voice carried enough so everyone became aware of how her sleeves were dripping. He may have saved the quilts."

"You're avoiding the subject."

"Which is?"

"You know what it is. Or who it is, I should say. The guy you talked with over by the window. Mr. Tall, Not Too Dark and Handsome." Her nose wrinkled. "Nope, that won't work. Too long and too much of a cliché. Let me think about some other name for him."

"While you're doing that, I'm going to do the end-of-day accounting."

"No way! I'm not letting you escape until you share what you and Mr. Good Guy were talking about for so long." She smiled. "Now that name I like. He helped that old lady with her purse, and he helped you with Her Royal Highness. So he's a good guy."

"He helped defuse the situation, and, before you ask again, that's what we were talking about. I thanked him for being helpful." *Briefly.* "He—"

A knock on the front door startled her. Looking toward it, she gasped, surprised to see Mr. Good Guy standing on the other side. No, she couldn't fall into the habit of thinking of him that way. She might slip and say the name aloud.

His caramel brown hair was a few shades lighter than his mustache and goatee. Through the glass, the planes of his sculptured face were emphasized by shadows cast by the sun reappearing from behind the clouds. It was a face that made her want to look once, then again and linger while her gaze traced those implacable lines.

"What's he doing back here?" she asked.

"Go to the door and find out." Pepper made shooing motions. "Maybe he couldn't live another hour without the sight of your face."

"Shhh!" she ordered with rare fervor. "He'll hear you."

Pepper giggled, sounding no older than her *boppli*.

Grace hurried to the door. She twisted the lock and opened it a handsbreadth.

"Can I come in?" he asked.

"*Ja*." She stepped back, bringing the door with her. She hoped Pepper was right about him being Mr. Good Guy. Otherwise, she might be welcoming in more trouble than she needed now.

Joel wasn't sure what silent message had passed in a glance between Grace and the other woman in the quilt shop as he walked in, but he had no doubt it'd been about him. They couldn't be more surprised than he was that he'd returned. He'd intended to hightail it out of Strasburg and away from Bliss Valley.

Instead, he was at The Amish Quilt Emporium talking to pretty, warmhearted Grace. Behind her was an Asian woman with the round doily-like *kapp* worn by Mennonites. He hid his shock at the unexpected sight.

"I'm sorry to disturb you after you're closed," he said into the silence.

"You haven't," Grace replied with a cool smile. "It's ten to five. We don't close until five. Can I help you with something?"

The Asian woman answered before he could. "I'll see you soon, Grace. Let me know what Tiffany has to say."

"I will." Her voice trembled on the two words. Because she was upset about what she'd agreed to do or because the other woman was leaving her alone with him?

He locked his hands together behind his back as the Asian woman slipped by him, turning in the doorway to give him a look that suggested he'd better behave himself. He would. He had no intention of going back to prison, and the slightest slipup would let his parole officer send him there.

"Talk to you soon," the woman said. "Bye, Grace."

"Bye, Pepper."

Pepper? His lips twitched, but he clamped them closed before either woman could notice.

As soon as the door closed, Grace asked, using the pleasant voice he guessed she did with potential customers, "How can I help you?"

"I think I lost something when I was here."

"I'd be glad to help you look for it."

"Thanks." He found himself unable to look away from her warm green eyes. There was such genuine kindness in them, something he'd forgotten existed.

"What is it?"

"What is what?"

She smiled. "What you lost. What is it? I can't help you look for it, if I don't know what I'm looking for."

"Oh, yeah. Sure." He felt like a fool. "It's the cover for a pocket watch."

"Gold?"

"It was, but most of the color has been scraped off."

She edged by him, and he caught a lilac scent. From her shampoo or soap. Plain women didn't use perfume. She went to where he'd stood by the window and scanned the floor.

"How big?" she asked.

"About the size of a half dollar, but shaped like a bowl so it can fit over the watch's face."

Squatting, she looked under the rack holding a dozen quilts. She bumped against one of the supports. It wobbled.

He leaped toward the rack, holding it in place before it collapsed. "I've got it!"

"Danki." She remained under the quilts for a few moments longer, then backed out. "Not under there." She straightened her *kapp*, which was askew on her head.

He was fascinated to see curls pinned to her head where they'd been concealed by the organdy. As she stood, he shifted his eyes away. He shouldn't be gawking at a sight only her husband should see. He realized he was assuming she was married. But why shouldn't he? She was past the age when most plain women wed, and she had such a pleasant personality. She must have had boys swarming around her during youth events.

Not that he was familiar with what happened during a singing or an evening gathered in someone's living room. He'd never attended a single event when, at sixteen, he was considered the right age to participate. He had been disdainful of the whole idea of *rumspringa.*

Rumspringa? *Why would I want to run around when I can run away from this stupid, boring life?*

The words played through his memory as clearly as if he spoke them. He and his friends Adam and Samuel had taken advantage of every opportunity to poke fun at the plain life they hated. Adam might not have been sincere because he never jumped the fence, and Joel had no idea what Samuel thought because he'd been a willing participant, not a leader in their plans to go into the *Englisch* world. Only too late had Joel come to realize what it had cost him to flee his plain life.

"Look under the table behind you," Grace said as she squeezed into a small space on the far side of the rack. "You were there for a while, too."

He bent, wishing he had a flashlight. As if he'd said that aloud, she said he could find one in the topmost drawer behind the counter where the register sat. She continued searching the floor, and he took a single step toward the counter. If she had any idea where he'd been, would she have let him go unwatched to the register?

It was a question he didn't have to answer, because she exclaimed, "Here it is!" Edging out from between the rack and the window platform where the display was set, she added, "At least I think it is what you're looking for." She held up her hand. "Is this it?"

The cover for the pocket watch looked oversize on her slender palm. Making sure his fingers didn't brush her skin, he lifted the cover out of her hand. "That's it. Where was it?"

"On the edge of the window, leaning against the wall as if you'd placed it there."

"It must have fallen out of my pocket when I got my handkerchief to wipe my face." He curled his fingers around the cover. "The watch belonged to my grandfather, and so it's more about sentimental value than anything else."

"I'm glad you found it."

He chuckled. "I'm glad *you* found it, Grace."

She waved aside his words as he'd guessed she would. No proper Amish person would take credit for any deed. She said, as he'd expected her to, "We both looked, and I happened to be in the right place first."

"I don't think I could have squeezed in there."

Her lips tilted in another of her shy smiles. "You're right…"

"Joel," he said when he realized while he knew her given name, she didn't have any idea what his was.

"You're right, Joel." She took a step back, then another. "I'm sorry, but I need to finish closing the shop so I can get home."

"I'm the one who should apologize for not realizing I'm keeping you from your husband and family."

"Just family," she said, then flushed.

Again he wanted to apologize. He hadn't been fishing to try to find out if she was married. Or had he? Why else would he have probed to discover her marital status? If she knew the truth about how he'd spent the past ten years, she'd know he didn't have any right to think about her as anything other than a shopkeeper.

He stuck the watch cover in his pocket. Groping for the doorknob, he fumbled to open the door.

As he opened it, she said, "Have a nice evening."

"*Danki.*"

Her eyes widened, and he wanted to take back the single word that had betrayed too much. He'd been so focused on escaping without another mistake that he'd put his foot in his mouth with the next thing he said.

"You're Amish?" she choked out.

Joel nodded. "I was raised that way."

"In Lancaster County?"

Again he nodded.

"But you left." She didn't make it a question.

"I did." He held his breath, waiting for her kindness to turn to cool disdain or a fervent determination to point out the error of his ways. He knew the mistakes he'd made. He didn't need anyone else pointing them out.

"Then welcome back, and enjoy your visit to Bliss Valley." She'd switched to *Deitsch*, the language of the plain folk.

An odd sensation bubbled deep within him, something he couldn't name. He nodded as he rushed out of the shop. Hearing her lock the door behind him, he almost laughed. Not in humor, but something that was the utter opposite.

Enjoy your visit to Bliss Valley?

Not likely.

Chapter Three

That night, Joel would have slept in his car…if he'd had one. A vehicle was the first thing he intended to buy once he got a job. A real roof over his head would have to come later.

Instead, he found a house that looked as if the owners were out of town. The sun porch wasn't locked, and the cushions on the glider were pretty comfortable, though his legs hung over one end so far his toes could almost touch the floor. He didn't have anything to eat, but he'd been hungry plenty of times before, and he knew skipping a meal—or two—wouldn't kill him. Tonight, he'd get a decent night's sleep. In the morning, if he couldn't get a ride into the city of Lancaster, he'd head back to Strasburg. Either way, he'd splurge on something caffeinated and something sweet for breakfast. He'd ignore his stomach's growling until then.

He eased off his shoes and sighed as he wiggled his toes. He could see two of them on his right foot and one on his left through his thin socks. He had another pair in his knapsack but a few more days of walking would leave them as torn as

the ones he wore. Sometime soon, he needed to find a place
to get a shower. There must be homeless shelters in Lancaster,
and one of them might allow former felons to have a chance
to clean up and get something to eat.

Before he settled in for the night, he stared out at the few
stars he could see in the small area of clear sky. Clouds were
rising again, and he guessed it would rain before dawn. A
quick check of the wind's direction told him that he could
open a couple of windows on the far side of the porch to allow
in some air without getting the floor wet. He raised them only
an inch or two. He didn't want anyone passing by to notice
they weren't shut.

Lying on the glider, he stuffed his knapsack under his head.
It was lumpy pillow, but was better than nothing. Barely.

He sighed as he recalled how he once would have said his
prayers before he went to sleep. He couldn't remember the last
time he'd done that. He also couldn't remember the last time
he'd had anything to be thankful for...before today.

He drew out the pocket-watch cover he'd lost at the quilt
shop. Grace had been eager to help him find it. Probably so
he'd get out.

No, that wasn't fair. She'd been nothing but kind to him,
but he wasn't able to trust any plain folk who expected him
to be something he couldn't be. What he'd never been able to
be. She most likely was, if he'd gotten to know her, as short-
sighted and hidebound as the rest of the Amish.

Yet as his thoughts ran through his head, he chided himself for assuming the worst. When he'd slipped up and spoken in *Deitsch*, she hadn't turned her back on him. She wished
him the best on his journey without prying into where he
was bound.

One thing he couldn't get out of his mind was how happy
she'd been to find the watch's cover. He needed to figure out

a way to stop looking for dark motives in everyone's actions and begin to trust people. He didn't know how.

Look and listen, boy. That's the only way anyone learns anything new. That voice didn't belong to his conscious. It belonged to his grandfather—his brain filled in the word as *grossdawdi.*

He spun the watch's cover between his fingers. It was his last connection to his *grossdawdi* and the life he'd had as a kid. *Grossdawdi* Beachy had given him the watch for his eighth birthday. Joel hadn't guessed the old man, who'd treated him like the other *kinder* in the family, would die before Joel's next birthday. The watch itself had vanished after he'd jumped the fence with Samuel. For years, he'd suspected his friend had hocked it, but even if Samuel had in an effort to get money for food, it wouldn't have been worth much. The cover had broken off after falling out of Joel's pocket when he was about twelve.

What would his *grossdawdi* think of him now? Convicted of a serious crime, a jailbird who now was hiding out on some unsuspecting person's back porch.

Rolling onto his side so he faced the door, in case someone came to check the house, Joel didn't bother to answer that question as he surrendered to sleep.

He didn't have to. He knew what his *grossdawdi* would have thought of him. Just what *Daed* had called him the day before Joel had made his decision to leave.

Loser.

From the moment Grace stepped into The Amish Quilt Emporium the next morning, she knew it was going to be one of *those* days. Not because the sky and the hot, still air warned another storm would crash down on Strasburg soon, but because the second Grace walked in the door, her boss pounced. Tiffany didn't give Grace a chance to put her lunch in the refrigerator or take off her bonnet.

"What's the meaning of the mess in the back room?" demanded Tiffany, who wore a simple dress not that different from Grace's. It was a costume to her, because Tiffany had shown off dozens of photos on her cell phone with her dressed in elegant *Englisch* fashions along with shoes with skyscraper heels. "There are damp paper towels everywhere, and two quilts are uncovered."

"W-w-we had some water c-c-come in during the storm yesterday af-af-afternoon." Grace hated how she stuttered whenever her boss raised her voice. She tried edging past the other woman. If she didn't react to Tiffany's tantrums, they'd sometimes fade away. She hoped today would be one of those days because she was exhausted. Both of her parents had had difficulty sleeping last night. Pain had plagued them, and they needed help with their medicines.

Tiffany wasn't to be denied. Grace's boss trailed after her into the back room. With her hands on her narrow hips and her painted lips curled in a sneer, she tossed her hair that was bleached to an ashen blond.

"What about these quilts?" Tiffany pointed a red fingernail at the racks.

"I d-d-did cover them before I l-l-locked up. The cloth must have sl-sl-slipped off." She bent to pick up the fabric pooled by the racks. "I'll be more careful next—"

"Don't put that filthy stuff on my quilts!" Her voice rose to a shriek. "What are you thinking?"

Thinking that after five years you don't know a thing about me. The retort was only in Grace's mind. Having an argument with her boss wouldn't get her anywhere. Not when she needed to find a way to remind Tiffany she was long past due a raise. She should have gotten it five months ago. She couldn't wait any longer. Not when *Daed* had lamented this morning that one of his medicines was going to double in price the next time he had it refilled. It already cost three hundred dollars each month.

The *Leit* would have stepped up to help, she knew, but other families in the district were also dealing with high medical costs. If she could get the raise she'd been promised and used her paltry savings, they'd get by.

Barely.

"I'll be more careful," Grace said as she folded the fabric and put it on top of a box of horse-and-buggy pencil sharpeners. Not looking at Tiffany allowed her to stop stuttering. "I'll check the quilts to make sure there aren't any spots on them. If there are, I'll clean them before I put them out front."

"There had better not be any spots." She waved an imperious hand. "And get rid of this mess! I can't have my shop looking like this."

"I'll take care of it." Remembering what she'd told Pepper she'd do, she added, "Pepper Underwood helped me keep the rain out."

"Uh-huh." Tiffany walked around the room, her nose wrinkling with disgust.

"I figured you'd w-w-want to thank her for helping the n-n-next time she came in." She grimaced as her stutter returned.

"Uh-huh."

It wasn't going well. Not that Grace had expected it to, but she'd agreed to push for the payment due to her friend. Taking a deep breath, she said, "Pepper mentioned she's been w-w-waiting for p-p-payment for the most recent quilts you've sold."

"She'll get it. In thirty days like it says in our agreement."

"Those thirty days were up t-t-two months ago."

"I'm sure that's not correct. I'll have to check my records."

Grace sighed. *Checking my records* was Tiffany's go-to excuse whenever she didn't want to talk about something. Tiffany's records were a joke, and Grace knew her boss liked them that way. It allowed her to avoid any blame for late payments or missed deadlines. After she'd started at the shop, Grace had offered to organize the shop's paperwork. Tiffany's fury at what she declared was an insult and a desire to snoop had seared Grace's ears.

"Look at this mess!" Tiffany tried to tug a paper towel out from between a window and its frame. With a curse, she jerked her hand back and stared at her index finger. "Look at this! I just had these nails done, and the best one broke! Why did you stuff paper into the windows? What were you thinking?"

Grace didn't bother explaining again. Tiffany hadn't listened the first time, and she wouldn't now.

"Do you want me to get the towels out?" she asked.

"No, you're too short. I'll need to do it."

"I'll get the step stool."

Tiffany nodded and flicked her fingers at Grace as if she were a queen ordering a worthless servant. Grace brought the bright red folding step stool to where her boss was scowling at the window, then got out of Tiffany's way.

After hanging up her bonnet and putting away her lunch, she carried the two quilts to a nearby table where the light was better. She examined them, pretending not to hear her boss's stream of colorful phrases as she tried to clear out the paper. If the windows had been in proper repair, they could have been lowered and the towels removed, but most of the windows were painted shut.

She smiled when she realized the quilts were fine. She folded them as she carried them into the shop. After putting them on the table where the quilts were stacked, she raised the clear yellow shade so the quilts in all their beauty would be visible to passersby. Her fingers became motionless on the strings connected to the shades.

She'd been standing where she was now when she found

Joel's watch cover. Mr. Good Guy, as Pepper had dubbed him. She hadn't been able to get him out of her head last night as she wondered why he'd left the plain world. She'd thought about asking her parents, but Joel was a common Amish name. She had no idea where he was from, but she'd sensed his underlying unhappiness. Because he was away from the life he'd been raised to have or because talking with her reminded him of the reasons he'd left?

Not many plain people had left Bliss Valley. There had been a family that vanished in the middle of the night when she was a youngster, and two teenage boys had jumped the fence a few years later. But most of them had returned to Bliss Valley at least for a visit. The connections created between members of the *Leit* were strong. Had they been more tenuous where Joel had lived? Going out into the *Englisch* world wasn't an easy decision for any plain person, and there had to be repercussions that echoed through someone's life.

A *kind*, who was skipping past, waved, and Grace waved back with a smile. Several others passing by copied the little boy's motion. She responded to each, recognizing other shop owners and people who lived along the street.

Her hand froze when her gaze was caught by a man standing on the porch of the ice cream shop across the street. Joel didn't wave, but he held her with his compelling eyes as if his broad hands gripped her shoulders.

"Grace! Help! Grace!" Tiffany's frantic voice tattered the fragile thread connecting her to him.

Grace ran into the back room.

Her boss was standing on tiptoe on the step stool, her palms thrust under the upper edge of the top pane of a tall window. She'd lowered it about halfway. "The sash cord broke. It'll drop and shatter into a million pieces if I let go. Help me!"

"How? We don't have another stool."

"Then get someone tall to help! My arms are breaking!" For once, Tiffany didn't seem to be exaggerating. Sweat beads glittered on her forehead, and her teeth were set. "Hurry!"

Grace threw open the door and raced onto the porch. Humidity struck her like a blow, but she ignored it and the clouds thickening overhead. She looked across the street. Joel wasn't there. Had he gone inside or...? She risked a glance along the road.

There! On the other side of the intersection.

Jumping off the porch, she paid no attention to the twinge in her knee as she sped to the corner. The light was against her, and cars rushed past. She shouted Joel's name.

About a dozen heads turned as she yelled, and she was grateful when one of them was his.

"*Danki*, Lord," she breathed as the light changed. She didn't pause as she rushed into the street. A car's horn bellowed when she kept it from turning right on red. "We need help!" she cried as she skidded to a stop in front of Joel. "My boss lowered one of the windows. The sash cord broke and—"

"I get the picture. Let's go."

Grace had no hope of keeping up with his longer legs. By the time she reached the shop, he was already through it and almost to the back room. She paused long enough to lock the door behind her so no customers came in while Tiffany let loose another string of words that would curl a sailor's hair.

When Grace paused in the doorway between the two rooms, Tiffany's voice had softened to a purr as she smiled at Joel. Grace clenched her hands by her sides when she heard Tiffany say, "She stuffed paper in the windows. Can you believe it? I didn't hire that girl for her brains, that's for sure."

"Can you edge over on the stool?" Joel asked as he tossed his knapsack onto the nearby table. "I want to get a better grip on the frame."

"I'll do my best." She batted her eyes at him, then leaned in a pose that offered him a *gut* look at her curves. "How's this?"

He shoved his larger hands against the window. "I've got it. You can move now."

Tiffany looked disappointed he wasn't responding to her flirting. With a grumble, she stepped off the stool as he took her place.

"Where did you find *him*?" she muttered as she pushed past Grace to answer the ringing phone. Picking it up, she smiled. "Oh, Nat. I was hoping to hear from you. Do you have any more of the trivets with the puns about Amish and electricity? I…"

Grace went into the back room. "Can I help, Joel?"

"Do you have a pallet around here?"

"Out back."

"Can you break off a couple of narrow pieces and bring them in?"

"For shims?"

He glanced over his shoulder and smiled. "I should have known you'd get it right away."

Grabbing a couple of oven mitts from the drawer beneath the microwave, she threw open the door. She pulled on the mitts to protect her hands from splinters as she tore a couple of pieces off the already broken pallets at the edge of the parking lot. She brought them inside.

"Will these work?" she asked as she pulled off the oven mitts.

"Temporarily." He toed off one of his shoes. "Hand me that, will you, so I can use it to jam the wood into place."

She picked up the shoe and passed it to him, noticing the holes in his socks.

He ordered her up on the step stool as he slid the window

into place. "Can you reach the top of the window to hold it while I get the shim in place?"

She tried. Her fingers missed by inches, even when she stood on tiptoe. The motion sent a renewed ache across the knee she'd jarred jumping off the porch. Again she paid it no mind.

"Okay, I'll have to hold the window, and you can knock it into place," he said.

"But I can't reach—"

"The shims don't have to go in at the top. This window is so loose they can go in anywhere above the other window frame."

Taking his shoe, she positioned the strip of wood. She followed his instructions and with a couple of sharp whacks with the heel of his shoe, drove the wood into the narrow space between the frame and the molding.

"Now the other," he said.

She did the same on the opposite side before climbing down. Stepping out of his way, she watched as he eased one hand away from the frame. The window shifted but less than a quarter inch. He gave it a shove up again before drawing back both hands. This time, the window locked into place.

"It worked!" Grace clapped her hands.

"It's working," he corrected her with another wry smile. "I suggest you or the other lady—"

"That's my boss. Tiffany Spanner."

"I suggest you or Tiffany hire a carpenter right away. I'm not sure how long that will hold, and the other windows don't look much better."

"I'll tell her." Grace knew it would be a waste of her breath because Tiffany wasn't going to spend a penny more than necessary on the building. "*Danki* for your help."

The wrong thing to say, she realized when he winced as

she used the *Deitsch* word that had revealed a secret he clearly would have preferred not to have come out. But she had to thank him, and he'd hear plenty more *Deitsch* speakers if he stayed in the area.

Tiffany called from the front for Grace to tend to the shop while she ran some errands. When Grace stepped into the main room, she saw Tiffany had her purse and her coat and her umbrella. She guessed her boss's errands would take the rest of the day.

"Tiffany," she began, "I need to talk to you about my—"

"We'll talk as soon as I get back. Promise." Blowing a kiss as if they were the best of friends, her boss reached for the door. Her smile faded when she realized it was locked. Again she muttered something about Grace not having the sense God gave a goose before she unlocked it and left.

"She's an E-ticket ride, isn't she?" asked Joel from behind her.

"A what?"

He smiled as he settled the strap of his battered knapsack over his shoulder again. "Sorry. It's a reference to a roller coaster ride. I don't suppose you know it."

"No, but you're right. It's a roller coaster around here most of the time." Realizing she shouldn't be speaking of her boss like that even when she was annoyed Tiffany hadn't given her a chance to talk about her delayed raise, she asked, "How about a cup of fresh *kaffi* or a glass of iced tea? I can make *kaffi*, and we've got the tea in the fridge. It's not much to show how grateful I am for your help."

"You helped me yesterday, so let's call it even." He glanced toward the windows where the thinning sunshine warned the storm was barreling toward town. "I need to get going."

"All right." Disappointment flared in her, surprising her at its intensity.

The door opened, and several people came in at the same time. Joel bid her farewell before leaving her to her customers. Though she wanted to watch him go and maybe figure out a way to convince him to stay a bit longer so she could get to know him better, she turned to the ladies who were twittering like excited birds over the items for sale.

Her arm was grasped, tugging her away from the customers. Grace stared in disbelief at her friend Rosemary Mishler. Rosemary's calm face was distorted with shock that made her mouth and brown eyes identical circles. The oldest of the three Beachy daughters, dark-haired Rosemary had provided the shop with exquisitely made quilts.

"What's wrong, Rosemary?" Grace asked.

She pointed to the door. "Do you know that man's name?"

"Joel. He helped me fix a window in the back room."

"His name is Joel?"

"*Ja.*" She put her hand over Rosemary's on her sleeve. "What's wrong?"

"I think… That is…" She gulped hard. "I think he's my brother who's been gone for more than ten years."

Grace opened her mouth, but no sound came out. That man who'd put up with Tiffany's flirting and had helped save the window, the man who'd stepped in to defuse that *Englisch* woman's anger yesterday, the man Pepper had labeled Mr. Good Guy. *He* was Rosemary's missing brother?

Everyone had heard about Joel Beachy. He was the kid who'd jumped the fence, abandoned his friend who'd almost died in a car accident and then—if rumor was to be believed— gone to jail.

No, it was impossible.

It couldn't be.

Could it?

Chapter Four

The buggy stopped under a sycamore tree not far from the farmhouse that followed the contour of the ridge. Grace wondered if her *daed* had pulled back on the reins or if Pearl had halted on his own. The white horse had been pulling her family's buggy for more than ten years, and it soon would be time to retire him to a life in the pasture. She hoped they could delay that day for as long as *Daed* insisted on handling the reins. A younger horse, or one that didn't know the family's routine as Pearl did, would be more difficult for *Daed* to handle.

Grace couldn't help noticing how her *daed*'s whole arm shook as he lowered the reins to his lap and climbed out of the buggy. She exchanged a worried glance with her *mamm*, but neither of them spoke as he gripped the side of the buggy door so hard that she feared he'd put his fingers right through it.

Both of her parents were elderly. Nobody had expected another *boppli* in the Coffman household so long after her brothers were born. Younger than her next older sibling by more than a decade, Grace had grown up with her brothers as well as her parents overseeing everything she'd done. Now her big brothers lived far away, and she didn't want to think about the day when she'd be alone in the rambling farmhouse.

Neither of her parents was much taller than she was. She remembered when she'd thought *Daed* could touch the moon, but both he and *Mamm* had shrunk as she'd grown. Their hair was thin and turning from gray to a pure white, especially *Daed*'s beard dropping to the third button on his light blue shirt.

"Harold," her *mamm* said in her quiet, no-nonsense way, "let Grace tend to Pearl. I could use a hand out."

His jaw worked, but he said, "Of course, Saretta."

Sliding out on his side, Grace urged, "You go into the house, and I'll unhitch Pearl."

"I can handle the horse," her *daed* argued, but without much vehemence as he reached for his wife's hand and missed it because his own vibrated with the tremors he couldn't control.

"Let her do it, Harold," *Mamm* said with a strained smile. "You know how she dotes on Pearl."

Not giving her *daed* a chance to argue, Grace smiled. "There's lemonade in the fridge. I'll fix us a nice supper of leftovers."

"*Ja.*" *Mamm* stepped from the buggy. "It's been a long time since lunch."

"I'm not that hungry." *Daed* frowned.

"You know you can always eat some of Grace's cheesy potato casserole." *Mamm* patted his arm as if it weren't shaking like a sapling in a storm.

Grace made shooing motions before she went to release Pearl from the buggy. Only when her parents had turned toward the house did her smile fade.

Harold Coffman would have been piqued if she chided him for *hochmut*, but her *daed* was too proud to eat when others were present, so he seldom had anything after a church service. She wasn't sure why he was so resistant when his Parkinson's was common knowledge in the district. Nobody would be offended by his splattering soup or dropping his sandwich as he often did at home.

Turning out the horse into the field to enjoy the rest of the sunny day, Grace walked past her garden as she returned to the house. The rows were burgeoning with vegetables, proof of the care she'd lavished on them. Every weed had been dug up during the few hours she could find to work in the garden each week. She knew the weeds would be back within days, but, for now, the garden looked lush and ready to harvest. She was grateful that the hail in Strasburg hadn't fallen on her vegetables and ruined them. She guessed by next week, she'd been canning the last of the tomatoes and sweet corn. *Mamm* would be eager to help, so Grace needed to figure out ways her *mamm* could be involved without stressing her weak heart. Standing over steaming jars on a hot, humid day could be a challenge for *Mamm*.

She glanced toward the house. It was a fine line she had to walk with her parents. She helped them whenever they needed it, but had to discern when they would accept her assistance. The *doktor* had urged them to speak with a social worker who could teach them how to establish boundaries in their home, but her parents had refused. When Dr. Underwood had suggested Grace meet with the social worker by herself, she'd declined, not wanting to go against their wishes.

But what would the social worker have suggested? She wished she knew. A few ideas to add to the ones she'd devised on her own would help.

Dr. Underwood had reassured them a social worker was there to make suggestions, not change their ways. "They help in all sorts of situations," he'd said from his side of his simple desk at the family clinic in Strasburg. "And they help people connect to services beyond their families. Part of their job is to help you discover what services are out there."

"Our community takes care of us," *Daed* had argued. "It's always been that way."

"Others in your community have used social workers. Those with children who need medical help or educational help, for example. Social workers help with everything from finding physical therapists to tutors. They assist in finding medical assistance, too. There are social workers who focus on assisting with houses or jobs." He'd smiled. "Not something you need, I realize, but I want you to know taking advantage of their knowledge is a good thing."

"*Gut* or not, it's not anything we need." *Daed* had been adamant, unwilling to be shifted from his opinions.

Grace sighed as she bent to pull a green bean off its stem and take a bite while she continued toward the back porch. She hadn't argued with *Daed* at the clinic. Her attempts later to bring up the subject had been futile. *Daed* refused even to consider speaking with a social worker. Others had spoken to them. The *doktor* had said so.

Had Joel Beachy?

She was startled when his face popped into her mind as it had far too often since she'd spoken with Rosemary Mishler yesterday at the quilt shop. Too many questions about Joel taunted her. She'd assumed he was a down-on-his-luck *Englischer* passing through Strasburg.

He wasn't.

He'd been born and raised plain. He'd jumped the fence, and if rumor was true, he'd spent time in jail. For what? Nobody had ever said.

So why was he back in Bliss Valley? Did he want to reconcile with his family or was there another reason for him to return?

To the scene of the crime.

The words appeared, unbidden, in her head, but she pushed

them away. If Joel Beachy had committed his crimes in Bliss Valley, she would have heard about them long ago. She couldn't recall his family saying anything about him in years. Either they hadn't missed him, or they wanted to pretend he'd never been part of their family.

Her breath caught because she couldn't imagine anything sadder than that. Too many people around her acted as if Lamar hadn't ever existed. How she longed for someone to speak about Lamar and the *wunderbaar* man he'd been! Each time his name was spoken, people looked askance as if fearing she would burst into tears at the mere mention of his name.

She tried to ignore those thoughts as she reached for more beans. The wrong thing to do. As soon as she'd banished Lamar from her thoughts, Joel's face returned along with the question that confused her most.

Why was he back in Bliss Valley?

Rather than trying to find an answer she didn't have, she hurried into the house.

The comfortable kitchen wasn't large because it was part of the original house that had been built by *Daed*'s *grossdawdi*'s *grossdawdi*. There was enough space in the off-white room for a table, stove and sink, but the refrigerator didn't fit. It was set in the next room that served as larder and laundry and general storeroom. Which was just as well because it was as loud as the washer that was connected to a diesel engine outside the house.

She set the handful of beans on the long oak table covered by a blue-and-white-checkered oilcloth. With a wink at her *mamm*, she grabbed one and took a generous bite.

Daed hurried into the kitchen. Grace hid her smile, but she'd guessed the crunch would bring him to check out what she'd brought in from the garden. As he sat in his usual chair at the head of the table that was too big for the three of them, he snagged a bean on his first attempt. It took him two tries, however, to get it to his mouth.

"Delicious," he pronounced. "Are there many ready?"

"*Ja,*" she replied, going into the larder to get the pitcher of lemonade she'd made yesterday. "I'm going to pick some more tomorrow before I head into work. It's easier to pick when the rows aren't clogged with weeds."

"I used to wield a mean hoe." He chuckled, his whole body shaking with his amusement as his left hand did. His diagnosis of Parkinson's disease had come almost three years ago, and the tremors that inflicted his hand had begun to make his left foot tap as if he were listening to a quick-tempo song. Some days, his head rocked as well, and he had trouble forming words, but his voice was clear today.

He'd lost more than control of parts of his body. For a few months after his diagnosis, he'd tried to keep up with the farm chores, but it became obvious he couldn't. It wouldn't have been a problem if Lamar hadn't died, because, as Grace's husband, he would have taken responsibility for the farm while her parents moved into the *dawdi haus* and enjoyed a quieter life.

Her parents continued to live in the main house with her because she wanted to keep a close eye on them. Her *mamm*'s health wasn't *gut* either. Her heart didn't always maintain a steady beat, but *Mamm* was as stubborn as *Daed*. With them in the main house, Grace could make sure they ate and took their medications.

"I remember," she replied, not wanting him to discover what she was thinking. "I learned everything I need to know about weeds from you."

He laughed. "What a legacy to leave my only daughter! A broad knowledge of broad-leaf weeds."

Pouring three glasses of lemonade, she said, "And narrow ones, too."

"*Danki,*" *Mamm* said when Grace brought the glasses to the table. She sat next to her husband, her voice heavy with fatigue. Church Sundays were difficult, despite her parents being given comfortable lawn chairs so they didn't have to sit for three hours on the backless benches.

Grace started to answer, but paused, looking out as she caught a motion near her garden. A neighbor's dog had dug up several pepper plants in the spring. It made a few more attempts to bury a bone or whatever it had in the garden, and she'd chased it away each time.

Hurrying toward the door, she threw it open. Her shout shriveled up in her throat as she stared at the intruder. It wasn't a dog.

It was…

Joel Beachy!

He wasn't looking to the left or the right. Why was he skulking around their house? He opened his knapsack as he reached for the beans. Was he stealing her vegetables?

She wondered if she'd asked that aloud as he paused in midstep. Their gazes collided. He looked astonished to see her. Taking a deep breath, he continued forward.

She'd forgotten how to breathe.

Or so it seemed.

"Grace?" Joel frowned. "Isn't this the Coffman farm?"

"*Ja.*"

His eyes narrowed. "You're a Coffman?"

"*Ja,*" she said as she had before.

"Duane's little sister?"

"*Ja.*" When a smile tugged at his lips, she knew she sounded ridiculous repeating the same word over and over. "What are you doing in my garden?"

"Collecting the vegetables I paid for."

"What?"

He gestured toward the road. "I left money in the honor box on your stand by the road, even though there weren't any vegetables there. By the way, when I passed your phone shack, I saw the light was blinking on your answering machine. You may want to check it."

"I will. Later." She came to the edge of the porch, which allowed her to look him straight in the eye. Was that why Joel was here? To buy garden vegetables? The sign out by the road announced, No Sunday Sales, but when had he followed the rules?

She scolded herself. She had no idea where he was living or if he had any place to keep food. Many of the grocery shops and restaurants in the area were closed on Sundays. The stores closer to where *Englischers* lived had Sunday hours, but he'd need a vehicle to get there. Every time she'd seen him in the past few days, he'd been on foot.

"We don't sell vegetables on Sunday," she added when he didn't speak. "Didn't you see the sign?"

"I saw it, but..." He looked uncomfortable for the first time.

But what? *But* he'd thought she wouldn't mind? *But* he hadn't thought anyone was at home? Her heart contracted as she wondered if he was too hungry to care.

The door opened behind her. *Daed* called, "Is everything all right, Grace?" Before she could reply, he asked, "Who are you?"

"*Daed*," she said, "this is Joel Beachy."

His brows lowered as he stared at Joel. Grace had expected *Daed* to greet him, but *Daed* turned on his heel and walked with unsteady steps toward the barn. He didn't slam the door as he went inside, but he didn't need to. The straight, stern line of his back made his opinions clear.

Heat scoured Grace's face. She didn't have to ask why *Daed* had been so rude. His whole posture had altered the moment she'd told him Joel's name.

She babbled into the smothering silence, desperate to say something—*anything*—to fill it. "I'm sorry. My *daed* is usually the friendliest guy in Bliss Valley."

"You don't need to apologize." Joel's shoulders sagged. "It's not as if you did or said anything wrong."

"But I wanted you to know *Daed* doesn't usually act like this."

"I know. I remember your *daed* from when I was a kid." When she opened her mouth, he waved aside her words. "Don't worry about it. To tell you the truth, I've been seeing the same response a lot since I came back here. Too many people remember what I was like as a kid." His mouth became a straight line. "And they whisper about how I got what I deserved when I was thrown in prison."

"Prison?" The word exploded out of her because she hadn't expected him to be so forthright.

"For the past six years, more or less."

"More or less?" She couldn't believe he was being so cavalier.

"I was arrested six months after Samuel and I got into a car accident, and I was convicted."

"You were arrested and sent to jail for six years because of a car accident?"

"No." He stuffed his hands in his pockets, but she could see they were clenched into fists. "I was arrested and charged with drug possession and the intent to distribute."

She could almost sense him holding his breath, waiting to see what her reaction would be. A dozen questions appeared in her mind, but she pushed each one aside as she tried to guess what she should say next.

What would you want him to say to you if your situations were reversed?

She asked, "Did you do what they accused you of doing?"

"What does it matter?" His sharp laugh was filled with so much pain her own knees threatened to buckle beneath its weight. "I was arrested. I was tried and found guilty. I was sent to prison and got out a couple of weeks ago. Whether I did the crime or not doesn't matter now. I've got a record that's going to follow me the rest of my life."

"It matters to you, ain't so?"

He stared at her for a long minute, and astonishment blossomed in his eyes, replacing his puzzlement. Was he used to being able to daunt someone with a glare? If so, he needed to learn such tactics wouldn't work with her.

She knew what people's first impressions of her were. She was short and young and a *maedel* who'd been left a widow even before she married. With her round face and bright red hair that couldn't be trained not to wisp along her cheeks, others considered her not much more than a *kind*. Her stutter, which came and went without warning, as well as her efforts to get along with everyone, even someone as difficult as her boss, labeled her timid and shy.

But she'd grown up with older brothers who never gave her a break because she was so much younger. If she wanted to spend time with them, she was expected to do anything they did. Her oldest brother, Fritz, had demonstrated how to put a worm on a hook the first time she joined them fishing, but after that, she was on her own. When she asked to play baseball with them when she was six, she didn't even make contact between the bat and the ball for more than three years.

Warmth filled her as she remembered that moment. She'd caught a piece of the ball and had sent it foul in front of third base, but her big brothers had acted as if she'd hit a grand slam, cheering and lifting her high on their shoulders to parade her around the bases before returning her to the batter's box. Duane, the brother who was next in age to her, had handed her the bat before walking to the pitcher's mound where he proceeded to throw two strikes to send her to the sidelines.

When Joel didn't answer her, she asked, "It—it—it…" She grimaced. Thinking about stuttering shouldn't bring it on. Pausing for a moment to compose herself, she said, "What happened… It does matter to you, ain't so?"

Joel wasn't going to answer Grace's insightful question. There was more to this woman than her cute smile and delightful voice. A lot more. He'd be a fool to give her an honest answer. How many times had the Amish grapevine spread rumors about him and his friends so fast they'd barely gotten themselves out of a jam before reports of it—some true, many exaggerated, others outright lies—had spread from farm to farm as if on a tornado wind?

He didn't know Grace well enough to accuse her of gossiping, but his sense of self-preservation, well-honed in prison, warned him to change the subject.

So he asked a probing question of his own. "Why are you being kind to me?" If she refused to answer, that would put them on a nice, steady plane as strangers. That's how they should remain. Strangers.

Even as he thought that, a small part of his brain was arguing she was a unique woman and that it'd be fun to get to know her better.

No, he argued with his own thoughts. *She's plain, and I'm* Englisch *now.*

Are you?

He ignored the annoying small voice that plagued him with doubt. That same whisper at the back of his mind had warned him not to trust the attorney the court had appointed for him. It'd been right then, but not now. He'd left a plain life behind, and he'd be happy to do so again once he had a decent job. He'd use the construction work up along Route 30 as a stepping-stone to a job far away from Bliss Valley.

62 *A Search for Redemption*

Grace's soft answer brought him back to the moment. "Because I was taught—"

He raised a hand to warn her to stop. "Don't quote me some Bible verse about the importance of being kind to a stranger."

"You mean like the second verse of Hebrews 13. 'Be not forgetful to entertain strangers: for thereby—'"

He interrupted her again. "'—some have entertained angels unawares.' Trust me, Grace. I'm no angel."

"None of us are."

He quirked his eyebrow.

Annoyance lashed through her voice. "Your family is part of our district. Your sisters have been making quilts for the shop during the past three years. I went to school with them, so I've known them most of my life."

"You were in our school?"

"Ja." She looked away, but not before her face revealed her thoughts.

He needed to end this conversation. His question had bothered her, and he understood why. Nobody wanted to think of themselves as forgettable. But he'd worked for years to forget about everything about Bliss Valley. He'd succeeded with most things and people.

He shifted uncomfortably. "Sorry, Grace." Knowing he must be honest to try to assuage her hurt feelings, he added, "I don't remember much about school the last few years I was supposed to be there other than trying to figure out ways to avoid going."

"That was obvious. You were absent more often than you were there." She frowned. "But we're not scholars any longer."

"No, we're not."

"Are you planning to stay in Bliss Valley?"

Her question was direct, and he appreciated that, even as he wished she hadn't asked it. Other people had beaten around the bush when he revealed he'd been raised in an Amish community. He'd wished they would have come out and peppered him with questions to satisfy their curiosity.

"It depends," he answered. "I'm applying for a job at a construction site by the new casino tomorrow morning. I'll stay as long as I have a job."

"I'll pray it works out for you."

It wasn't easy when she spoke with easy confidence about God listening to her prayers. Once upon a time, he'd believed that was true, too. Now...

Exhaustion rolled over him, threatening to iron him as flat as the wooden steps. It was definitely time to end this conversation.

He was about to ask her if he could take some vegetables and be on his way. He didn't want to show up for an interview tomorrow with his stomach growling. He had enough in his pockets for a bus to the construction site, but he was hoarding the rest of his money because he needed something to eat later. He could have walked to the interview and have enough for another meal or two, if he was thrifty. But he needed to be practical. The air was thick with humidity. Showing up sweaty after hoofing it for two hours in the August heat would suggest he didn't care enough about the job.

Joel clamped his lips closed as a buggy rolled up the driveway and came to a stop not far from where they stood. He watched as a tall, thin man emerged. His beard was sparse, a sign he hadn't been married long. While the man walked toward them, his long legs ate the distance at a surprising rate.

The man stopped about an arm's length from Joel. From under his black Sunday church hat, the man's brown eyes appraised Joel and then dismissed him before the man turned to Grace.

"Sorry to interrupt," he said. "Are you busy with your customer?"

"It's Sunday, Eddie," Grace replied with a grin that appeared far more comfortable than any she'd given him.

The man she'd called Eddie chuckled. "*Ja*. I know that." He glanced at Joel, as if curious what an *Englischer* was doing in the backyard. "Is Harold around?"

"He's in the barn."

"*Gut*. I'll go and talk with him." He paused and appraised Joel from head to foot. "I'm Eddie Mishler. You are?"

"Joel."

Eddie waited for Joel to give his surname, then asked, "Have we met? You look kind of familiar."

"I don't think so." He wanted to ask whom Eddie thought he resembled. It wasn't as if he had any blood relatives in Bliss Valley. He had no idea where he'd been born or how he'd come to be adopted by the Beachys. *Daed* had dictated that nobody speak of Joel's life before he was adopted. When Joel first spoke of jumping the fence into the *Englisch* world, *Daed* had threatened that if Joel left, he would never be spoken of within the family again.

But Joel had left anyhow, or maybe because it was the best way he could guarantee never again having to meet his *Daed*'s impossible expectations.

Before Eddie spoke again, Joel moved closer to the porch. He took Grace's hand and turned it palm up. Her slender fingers trembled in his, and he wished he could run his own along her tantalizingly silken skin. Before he couldn't resist letting his fingertips explore the gentle curve of her palm, he dropped the beans he'd picked onto it and walked away without another word.

The sooner he got out of Bliss Valley the better.

Chapter Five

Grace stared after Joel as he strode down the lane toward the main road. He hadn't given her time to introduce Eddie as his brother-in-law. Joel must not be aware of the truth. Was Eddie?

Would it have made any difference? She couldn't help remembering how shaken Rosemary had been at the shop about discovering her brother was in Lancaster County.

"You know who that was, ain't so?" Grace asked Eddie who was checking the row of sweet corn she'd planted.

"No." He fingered the top of the husk on one ear, pulling aside the silk to look at the kernels. "This looks about ready to pick. Our corn—"

She interrupted, "Eddie, that man was Joel Beachy, Rosemary's brother."

His head jerked up, and his eyes threatened to pop out of his head. "You're joking."

"No." She swallowed her sadness that Eddie hadn't recognized his own brother-in-law. Though she'd never seen her brother Fritz's sons who lived in northwestern Montana, she was sure she would recognize them from the descriptions in the letters her sister-in-law sent each week.

Odd... They hadn't gotten Flossie's regular letter this week. It usually arrived on Tuesday. It wasn't like her sister-in-law to miss a week. In fact, Grace couldn't remember a single time she had.

Realizing Eddie was waiting for her to go on, Grace paid no more attention to her abrupt uneasiness. There could be any of a dozen reasons why the letter hadn't arrived.

"You knew Joel was in the area, ain't so?" she asked.

"*Ja.* Rosemary mentioned she might have seen him, but she's said that before when she thought some stranger was her brother."

"This time she was right." Realizing she held the green beans Joel had plucked, she stuffed them into her pocket.

Eddie shook his head as he tugged a bean off a vine near the edge of the row. He examined it, then took a bite. As he chewed, he said, "I don't trust a man who's not willing to give his full name."

"He's leery of how people will react to him."

"He should be." His eyes narrowed. "Why are you coming to his defense, Grace?"

"I'm not."

"Rosemary told me a lot about her wayward brother's behavior. He's charming, like a snake is charming to a mouse." He wiped his hands on his trousers. "You shouldn't trust him."

"What makes you think I trust him?"

Eddie's laugh was as sharp as a whetted blade. "Because you believe the best about everyone, Grace. Nobody else would have put up with your boss for as long as you have. You defend her, even when you know she's wrong. You need to be careful before you make a bad name for yourself by defending Tiffany."

She flushed. Had Rosemary been complaining about Grace to her husband? Grace had been certain Rosemary and the other quilters understood she was trying to be their best advocate to loosen Tiffany's purse strings and get them paid on time.

"You can't," Eddie continued when she didn't answer, "let an ex-con convince you to trust him."

"I don't trust him. He admitted he's been in prison."

Eddie shook his head. "Don't fool yourself, Grace. If he's told you a few things, it doesn't mean he's told you *everything*. Every man has secrets he's hoping the rest of the world won't guess." He looked at the ground as he added, "Keep away from Joel Beachy. He's not someone a nice woman like you should spend time with."

"He's been nothing but helpful so far."

"Even when he was helping himself to your garden?" He took a deep breath as if he were about to add something more, but he turned on his heel and walked toward the barn. Pausing, he faced her. "Be careful, Grace. No *gut* will come from him. You know that as well as I do. Don't let him run roughshod over you like you've let Tiffany do."

Astonished, she stared after him. It wasn't like him to denigrate others or accuse them without proof. She'd always believed she knew Eddie Mishler well. Now she wasn't so sure.

About anything.

Joel's image invaded her mind again. She pulled the green beans out of her pocket and sighed. If he was so hungry he was raiding her garden...

Grace strode into the kitchen. It was empty, and she heard her *mamm*'s slow footsteps upstairs. She sighed again. She wished *Mamm* would let her run up and down the stairs to get whatever *Mamm* wanted. The stairs were such a challenge for both her parents. Perhaps it was time—again!—to bring up the idea of her parents moving their bedroom furniture to the main floor. It would be useless—again!—but she had to keep trying. Or should she involve her siblings? Would *Daed* and *Mamm* listen to one of Grace's brothers?

Even as she wondered which sibling to approach first or if she should send a letter to each of them, she gathered food and put it in a basket. She threw a paper napkin over the top, grabbed the handle and rushed out the front door, letting the screen door slam behind her. Cutting across the yard, she ran toward the road. Was she being foolish?

Probably, but she hated the idea of someone going hungry. She'd give Joel the basket and hope it would tide him over until he got a job. It was the least she could do for her friend's brother.

Putting one weary foot in front of the other, Joel didn't hurry along the road connected with one that would take him north. Somewhere along the way, he'd find a place to sleep. He hoped that would take his mind off his empty stomach and the bugs whining around his head. He hadn't had anything but a cup of coffee for breakfast and nothing for lunch. It looked like he'd be enjoying the same nothing for supper.

Stop being a wimp, he told himself as he paused beneath a tree to enjoy its shadow that cut the strength of the relentless sun. He'd gone without eating after the car accident that had sent his friend Samuel to the hospital and his own life into a downward spiral. The pain of three broken fingers and a throbbing headache that hadn't let up for almost a month had banished his appetite.

"Joel? Wait up!"

At the call from behind him, he looked over his shoulder.

Grace? Why was she running after him?

Hope danced for a single beat in his heart. He tamped it down as she slowed to a walk, continuing toward him. She wasn't chasing after him to tell him she wanted to throw her door open wide for him so he'd have a place to stay tonight. Disappointment washed over him. Along with guilt that he'd spent the past two nights sleeping on someone else's porch. Going there tonight was too much of a risk, because the family might come home on a Sunday evening so they were ready for another workweek.

Grace stopped beside him and held out a basket. "Here."

Joel didn't reach to take it, though scents of strawberry jam and apple butter wafted from it. Two of his favorite foods. There had been strawberry jam in prison, but it hadn't tasted like what his *mamm* had made each summer.

"What's that?" he asked, even though he knew. Perhaps keeping the conversation going a few minutes more would allow him to stop thinking about how dire his current situation was.

It'll be fine tomorrow when you get a job. He longed to believe that, but knew he'd somehow have to find a way to survive until he got his first paycheck. He looked over her head toward the barn behind her family's house. There were plenty of barns that would be deserted after the evening milking was done. Sleeping in a haymow at this time of year would be stuffy and hot and inviting wasps to sting him, but his only other choice might be trying to find a spot under a tree where he wouldn't be noticed. Farmers were spending more time in their fields now than in their barns.

"It's for you if you want it." Uncertainty tainted Grace's voice. "For your supper. If you want it."

He felt bad for forcing her to say the obvious. She was trying to be nice, and he was acting as if she had hidden something in the basket that would leap out and bite him.

He shuddered. Once burned, twice shy. The drugs found in the car he'd been driving the night he'd been arrested hadn't been his. He hadn't even known they were there. He'd had no idea that night why the police had decided to stop him. The car had been in working order, and he was always conscientious about using turn signals. He hadn't been speeding, something he'd avoided doing since the night Samuel had slammed their car into a tree. And Joel hadn't imagined the police would decide to search his car.

At that point, he hadn't had any record, and he'd cooperated with the officer who stopped him and asked for his license and registration. The woman had taken the forms to her patrol car as he'd expected she would. But when she returned, she ordered him out of the car. Two more police cars, one unmarked, sped toward them and screeched to a stop before he could ask what was wrong. Two days later, when his head no longer was spinning from the night's events, he realized someone must have set him up.

But Grace hadn't been the one to put the drugs in his car and then call the cops. She was trying to be kind by offering him something for his supper.

As a friend would do.

A soul-deep craving riveted him. When was the last time he'd had a friend? He'd been alone for the past six years, leery of those around him because any offer of friendship could become a betrayal.

"Don't you want it?" she asked with a frown. "I can't stand here all night waiting for you to make up your mind. *Daed* and *Mamm* are waiting for their supper."

He matched her expression with a scowl of his own. "You still live with your parents?"

"*Ja.* I was going to be married, but…" Color fled from her face, leaving it the color of ice.

"You were? What happened?"

Her face became a rigid mask, and he wished he'd thought before blurting out the questions. Her voice was as stiff as her features. "He died before our wedding day."

He stared, shocked. How could he have forgotten that, while he'd been suffering from his mistakes, others' lives had gone on, laced with joy and grief? But he hadn't guessed Grace's life was anything but happy. She always had a smile for everyone, even for those who didn't deserve one, like the irritating woman who'd caused such a ruckus at the quilt shop.

And one for you, even when you're being irritating, too. Oh, how he hated the honest voice that refused to be silenced.

He should be as honest as his conscience. "I'm sorry, Grace."

"I appreciate that," she replied in the same clipped voice, "but I've come to acceptance about Lamar's death in the past four years."

"Really?"

"*Ja.*"

He arched his brows. "My *grossdawdi* has been gone for more than twenty years, and I miss him every day."

"You do?"

He put his hand into his left pocket and fingered the cover of the pocket watch that was his sole connection with *Grossdawdi* Beachy who had accepted him as he was. That had been such a precious gift. Though he wished he had the watch itself, he was grateful he had a part of it.

"*Ja.*"

"I never knew my grandparents. They died before I was born." Her face softened as her lips tilted with a wry smile. "That's what I get for being the surprise *boppli* who came long after all the others."

"I'm sorry you didn't get to know your grandparents. I had a special relationship with *Grossdawdi* Beachy. He taught me so much my *daed* didn't."

"That's important."

"It is, and I'm grateful every day he wasn't alive when I was arrested. It would have broken his heart."

"As well as your parents'."

"Naw. They expected I'd end up in jail sooner or later." When he gave a terse laugh, he saw her astonishment. What was it about this woman that teased him to show his true feelings, even the ugliest ones? With others, he'd been able to pretend he was covered with some nonstick substance that let his pain and bitterness slide off and away. Not with Grace.

"What are you going to do now?" she asked.

"Look for a job. I hear they're hiring up by the new casino."

"I've heard that, too." She held out the basket to him again. "Take it."

"I can't believe you packed me supper when you wouldn't let me buy a few vegetables."

"Because it's Sunday." She pushed the basket into his hand. "Wait here."

"I shouldn't—"

"Wait here." Her gaze rose to meet his. "Please."

He knew he could give her dozens of reasons why he should get out of her life, but he nodded. He couldn't ignore the entreaty in her eyes that were almost the same color as the leaves shading the road.

Joel watched as she walked toward the farm stand at the end of her family's lane. Her bare feet didn't flinch from the heat wafting up from the asphalt road, and her skirts swayed with a rhythm that captured his gaze. Looking at her, he wouldn't have guessed how much grief she kept concealed within her.

He stayed where he was while she went to the farm stand,

which was a simple shack, almost identical to the phone shack a dozen yards away, with a few shelves inside. She lifted a metal box off an empty shelf and opened it. Reaching in, she pulled out the five-dollar bill he'd put in there.

His last five-dollar bill. Only two singles remained in his pocket, money he'd saved for coffee in the morning.

Without a word, she came back and held it out to him.

He didn't take it.

"Go ahead," she urged. "It's yours."

"The basket—"

"Is a gift. We don't do business on Sundays." She offered him the bill again.

"That's splitting hairs, Grace."

"Maybe it is for you, but not for me."

He realized she wasn't going to be budged on this. He'd be a fool not to take the money. She didn't want it, and he needed it. More than she could guess.

Or did she realize how dire his situation was? Though she was cocooned in her plain world, she must realize how difficult it would be for someone to start over after being convicted of a felony. Her bringing him the basket of food for his supper was proof of that.

"All right," he said as he took the money.

"*Danki.*"

How weird that she was thanking him for returning the five-dollar bill! But nothing had been as he'd thought since he returned to Bliss Valley. Tomorrow, he'd apply for a job. Once he had it, he'd get his life under control. His first call would be to Roland Shriver, so he could show his parole officer he wasn't the loser Shriver had labeled him.

"I should get going," Joel said, though he didn't have any place to go. He just wanted to put an end to this unsettling conversation.

"All right." She met his eyes. "Do you know who Eddie Mishler is?"

"Should I?"

"*Ja.* He's your brother-in-law."

The ground seemed to shake beneath his feet. Grace's simple comment was a reminder of the hideous cost of his decision to leave.

"My brother-in-law?" he managed to choke out. "Which of my sisters married him?"

"Rosemary."

He tried to imagine his oldest sister with that curt man. It was impossible. Rosemary had always been the take-charge sibling. Just like him. Why had she selected such an officious man? "Do they have kids?"

"Not yet. They've only been married since January. They had to wait because it was a busy wedding season last fall."

His head was spinning. What else had he missed? His *mamm* had sent him a daily letter during his first six months away from Bliss Valley. She'd pleaded with him to return, expressing how much the family missed him and feared he'd turned his back on them and God. He'd never heard a single word from his *daed.*

Grace grew serious again. "Eddie isn't happy you're back."

"He won't be the only one."

"I'm sorry."

He waved aside her words. "Don't be. I made the decisions I did, and I've paid the price. All I want now is to restart my life and leave the past in the past."

His stomach growled, and Grace laughed. "And have some supper, ain't so?"

"True." He patted his belly.

"You've got apple butter and strawberry jam—"

"I know from the luscious scents."

"—as well as bread and some cookies that *Mamm* made." Her smile grew sad. "It's a *gut* batch. Sometimes she forgets to put in one or two of the ingredients, and I have to sneak the batch down the road to a neighbor's pigs."

"Are your parents well?"

She looked away. He recognized the dodge. He used it himself when a question delved into the painful, unhealed parts of his soul.

"I saw," he said when she didn't answer, "how your dad's hand was shaking. Does he have Parkinson's?"

"*Ja.*" She raised her head and met his gaze again. "He's doing as well as can be expected."

"And your mother?"

"She's been slowing down, and she's having to learn to deal with both the *gut* days and the ones that aren't *gut.*" A smile spread sunny warmth across her face. "She makes amazing apple butter, though."

"I'm glad."

"You're a big fan of apple butter?"

"More than a fan. The thought of apple butter makes my mouth water." His shoulders eased from their stiff pose. There was something about Grace that allowed him to relax as he hadn't in more years than he wanted to count. "One time about a year after I jumped the fence, I went to Yoder's Country Market to get a jar of apple butter."

"You could have run into someone you know there."

He nodded. Plain people shopped at the grocery store in New Holland. "I went there on a Saturday night just before closing time. I figured anyone who'd recognize me would be home by that time."

"That's too bad."

"Too bad?" he repeated, astonished.

Grace had been so empathetic. She'd listened to him and hadn't been judgmental.

Until now.

"If someone had seen you," she said, "they might have found a way to convince you to return to Bliss Valley before your life took such a horrible turn."

"Nobody could have convinced me to come back then."

"Or now?" Her gaze riveted on his mustache and goatee.

Was she right? Had he grown his facial hair to show outward rebellion against the plain people and his *daed*? Yet he still used the *Deitsch* word he'd never been able to put aside.

Just as he'd never been able to put aside his regrets that his stubborn nature had kept him away from his mother and sisters for more than ten years.

So whom was he trying to fool? Everyone else...or himself?

Chapter Six

"You look pensive, *liebling*. Is everything okay?"

Grace smiled at her *mamm*. It amazed her each time she realized she could look over her *mamm*'s head without raising her eyes. The older woman must have shrunk at least two inches in the past decade because Grace had stopped growing around the time she finished school.

"Praying, *Mamm*," she replied.

"A *gut* way to spend your time, but you've been washing that same bowl for the past five minutes. You're going to scrub the pattern right off it." She chuckled. "That tells me you've got a lot on your mind."

"One thing today," she said, though that wasn't true.

"That handsome young man who was here yesterday?"

"*Ja*. He told me he's applying for a job today. I've been praying God leads him in the direction he needs to go."

"I will, too."

"*Danki, Mamm*."

"Your *daed* tells me that young man is one of the ones who caused such trouble around here years ago."

"He was. Are you upset with me for helping him?"

Mamm shook her head. "Of course not, Grace. We always should help our neighbors, even when they've done others wrong. It's not our place to judge. It's God's. We've got to give Him a chance to do His work on Joel as He has on Adam Hershberger and Samuel King. Those two have turned their lives around."

"I think Joel wishes to do the same."

"That would make his *mamm* happy. Though she never speaks of him, I've seen her sorrow when others mention *kinder* who are far from them. She grieves for him every day."

"Don't take this the wrong way, *Mamm*, but I'm glad to hear that. Joel has said enough that I think he believes his family doesn't want anything to do with him."

"He may be right about his *daed*. Wyman washed his hands of his son years ago, and he refuses to speak of Joel. That causes Sharon even more grief because she'd love to have her husband and son get along."

Grace listened as *Mamm* continued to lament the sorry situation in the Beachy family. Talking about Joel would keep *Mamm* from guessing how Joel wasn't the only person on Grace's mind. She was also worried about what would happen at the quilt shop today. Payments were due to two quilters, and she guessed she'd be making excuses for why Tiffany was late yet again.

The quilters had been patient. Too patient, in Grace's opinion, while Tiffany established her shop and built its reputation. However, since Tiffany had announced plans to open the second shop in Lititz, that patience had worn paper-thin. The quilters thought Tiffany should rectify her problems with late payments before investing everyone's money into a new shop.

Grace agreed.

So why haven't you said something? Why haven't you stood up for your friends or yourself and demanded fair and timely payment?

She sighed as she put the bowl in the drainer on the counter. The answer was always the same. As she glanced over her shoulder to see her *mamm* lean on the table and take shallow breaths, she knew she must keep her job. Her parents had lost their *gut* health. She couldn't be the one who caused them to lose the home they'd had purchased a year after they married. Her income wasn't much, but it was enough to cover the taxes on the farm. Not the upkeep, for every building including the house needed repair.

Taking a deep breath of her own, Grace turned to finish the dishes. She made sandwiches for herself and for her parents. She set the platter in the refrigerator, stuffed her own roast beef sandwich in an insulated cooler and grabbed her bonnet. Calling to her parents to enjoy the day, she opened the back door.

God, please make this day a gut *one for them and for Joel.*

She didn't add a prayer for herself. She already knew it was going to be a horrid day, another day when she had to kowtow to Tiffany's absurd demands while placating the quilters. She wished the situation would change, but she didn't see how.

What a waste of a day!

Joel jammed his thumbs in the back pockets of his jeans as he strode along a road leading to the southeast. His feet hit the asphalt as hard as if he wanted to drive them right through to the ground underneath. What would it matter? He couldn't get any more stuck than he was now.

Everyone in prison had cautioned him how bad it'd be when he was on the outside again. He'd thought it'd be different for him, that he'd be the one to get a break. It wasn't as if he'd ever gotten one, so he'd figured it was about time for positive things to come his way.

He'd been wrong.

Could he have done anything today to reach a different outcome? He'd been up at dawn, sneaking out of the garage where he'd slept after enjoying the delicious food Grace had packed in the basket. He'd headed up to Route 30 and the construction area surrounding the casino that was already being built, washing his face in the water from someone's hose before slipping into a gas station restroom to shave. He'd nicked himself in two spots, but a small piece of toilet paper blotted the blood. Finding the money to buy a new blade for his razor wouldn't happen until he landed a job, and he couldn't go for interviews without a decent shave. He could have stopped shaving and let his beard fill in, but he refused to do that. Some unexpected resistance from his past life remained. Only married men among the Amish grew their beards along their jawlines, and he didn't want to look like one of them.

Why hadn't he headed toward Philadelphia or Scranton as soon as he'd gotten out of prison? Coming to Lancaster County had been the stupidest thing he'd done since getting caught with drugs in his car.

But he'd come to Lancaster County because everyone had told him the expansion around the casino site would be the best place to look for a job. He'd assumed the construction companies would be eager to hire anyone who could swing a hammer or lay concrete block.

Even when he'd reached the dusty construction trailer where job interviews were being done, he hadn't been discouraged by the long line of people waiting to interview. The line had moved far faster than he'd expected. When he'd reached the front, gone into the trailer and was directed to one of the desks lined up inside, he'd found out why. The employment service hired to interview workers had set up a website where forms were to be completed before prospective employees came in person to the site.

The blond woman who'd told Joel that had rolled her overly made-up eyes at his apparent flouting of the rules before she'd pointed to a terminal on the other side of the trailer where he could fill out the form. In a bored and condescending tone, she'd asked if he needed help with the computer.

He hadn't, but once Joel had filled out the form—or what parts he could because he hadn't been employed in the past six years by anyone other than the prison system of the Commonwealth of Pennsylvania—he was sent to wait with a few other people who had been relegated to the corner for not following procedures. No one had spoken to him, and he hadn't said anything to the others waiting, though the younger of the two women sitting there had given him a sympathetic smile.

Or maybe not as much sympathetic as pitying. He knew he looked like a homeless bum. He was homeless, but he was trying to turn his life around. He would...as soon as he could get a job. With his first paycheck, he'd find a room to rent and make a visit to a Laundromat to clean his clothes better than he could by rinsing them in a creek or walking in the rain.

So he'd sat.

And sat.

And sat.

All morning, people around him came and left after having their names called by one of the men or women who popped up from among a bank of work cubes. Nobody called his name. His stomach began to rumble, but he remained where he was. He ignored the sounds and concentrated on listening for his name.

"Joel Beachy!" A woman looked over the top of a cube. Instead of motioning for him to come toward her desk as others had, she walked around the end of the temporary wall. Without meeting his eyes, she said, "Thank you for coming in today. We'll call you if we need to speak further."

Coming to his feet, he bit back his response that they hadn't spoken yet, so how could they speak more? Instead, he'd nodded, understanding what she'd avoided saying. His application had been sent to the bottom of the pile because of his incarceration. Or maybe it'd already been filed in the trash. Guys he'd met in prison had warned him.

Even so, Joel struggled to hold in his fury as he strode along the country road, heading south and east. All his plans had been focused on getting a job at one of the projects near the casino. What was his plan B?

He didn't have one. A social worker who'd spoken with him before he left prison had suggested he contact Goodwill or another social service organization that might help him. He didn't like the idea of charity, but he wasn't going to have much choice any longer.

Joel's steps faltered when he saw something move on the other side of the road. Right at the edge of the asphalt before the road vanished into grass. Was it an animal? Had something been hit by a car and tried to crawl away?

Be careful. A hurt animal is a dangerous one.

As he did so often, he ignored the common sense flickering through his head and inched across the road. He didn't want to leave an animal to suffer.

It wasn't an animal.

Joel gasped as he stared down at several twenty-dollar bills. Were they real? He glanced in both directions. The road was empty. As he took a step toward the money, a car zoomed past. The bills fluttered. He bent and grabbed them before they could fly away. Counting the money, he whistled.

One hundred and twenty dollars.

The twenties looked authentic to him. It wasn't a *kind*'s play money. The serial numbers weren't in any sort of order, and the pictures and symbols seemed right.

The cash had to belong to someone. Who?

There was nobody nearby. On the top of the next ridgeline, nearly a half mile away, he saw both a tractor and a team of five mules working in different fields. Neither field opened onto the road where he stood.

Leaving the money on the road would be stupid. Someone else would come along and find it. Most likely, not the rightful owner.

Even so, a twinge of guilt taunted him as he stuffed the bills in his pocket. He knew what Grace would tell him. God had put the money in his path for some reason he must discern while he put the money to the use God intended.

He wasn't in the mood to play guessing games with God.

"If Your plan is to keep me alive so I'm miserable longer, God, You've succeeded," he said to the empty road.

He regretted the ungrateful words. He should be relieved he could eat for a few more days while he looked for work.

Glancing at the men working in the fields, he sighed. He hated doing field work. If he could have found a farm where he spent all his time taking care of stock, he'd hire on as a farmhand in a split second. He'd have to keep an eye out for Help Wanted signs when he reached Strasburg. Some of the businesses must be looking for employees. He had some kitchen experience to go along with the construction skills he'd picked up since he'd left Bliss Valley.

He wished he could figure out the way he was supposed to go.

With a sigh, Joel kept walking. He passed the Bliss Valley covered bridge. The creek below it was so low that it wasn't more than a trickle. Even the recent storms hadn't helped.

He didn't stop, though he wasn't sure where he was bound. He followed the road until it ended and then turned right because there was a buggy coming from the opposite direction, and he didn't want to see someone's reproachful expression when they realized he was Joel Beachy. Glancing at the storm clouds building in the west, he hoped he could find shelter before the rain broke over him.

Grace would take you in.

He almost laughed aloud at the thought. He was sure it was right, but he was as sure Harold Coffman would have something to say about letting a convicted felon stay on his farm.

A sudden, bright flash followed by an ear-threatening crack of thunder, both uncomfortably close, halted Joel in midstep. He looked ahead of him, and his eyes widened. He wasn't far from a farm lane leading to a place he knew well. Ephraim Weaver's farm and the home of one of his two best friends. He couldn't count the number of times he'd visited Adam Hershberger there.

The barn was still white like the house. The chicken coop still leaned to the right, looking as if a stiff breeze would knock it to the ground. Two horses, both black, grazed in the meadow in front of the house and a herd of Holsteins waited by the barn door to be milked.

He didn't recall a picnic table under a tree or the house having so many flowers growing in front of the porch. Both suggested a female touch in a house that had been filled with men and boys.

"Things change," he reminded himself as he turned to walk up the lane as two more flashes of lightning followed in quick succession. The wind shoved him along the lane.

This meeting was one he'd been dreading, so he might as well get it over with on a day when nothing was going right already. It was time to see if some bridges could be mended.

He fingered the bills in his pocket. It would pay for bus fare to the far side of the state, but then how would he eat? It wasn't like he could get away from his criminal record and walk onto another construction site and land a decent job. That wasn't going to happen.

A man walked from the barn toward the house, and Joel stared. He recognized the aged man. "*Grossdawdi* Ephraim, you're alive!" The words burst out of him before he realized how they'd sound.

The old man was Joel's friend's great-*grossdawdi* and had raised Adam after his parents died. However, everyone called him *Grossdawdi* Ephraim, even those close to his age.

"I am." *Grossdawdi* Ephraim squinted at him. "Barely."

"It's great to see you!"

He eyed Joel up and down. "I'd say the same thing to you if I had any idea who you are."

"Joel."

"Joel?" His rheumy eyes narrowed beneath his bushy brows. "Which Joel?"

"Joel Beachy, Adam's friend."

His voice became clipped. "Oh, I see."

"Is Adam here?"

"In the barn." The old man walked away without another word. He didn't need to say anything. Disgust oozed from every pore.

Joel sighed. *Grossdawdi* Ephraim's reaction was what he'd expected in Bliss Valley...until he'd met Grace Coffman. She'd asked probing questions, some which he would have preferred not to face, but her curiosity had been laced with kindness.

Kindness. His hands shook at the thought of the word he'd begun to believe described something that didn't exist except in his earliest memories. In the days before he realized he couldn't meet his *daed*'s highest expectations, so he aimed for *Daed*'s lowest ones.

"Joel?"

He looked over his shoulder at the voice that sounded familiar. It should. Though a decade had passed since the last time he'd seen the boy he'd once called one of his two best friends, he guessed the man standing behind him was a grown-up version of the gangly teenager. Adam Hershberger wore a beard, marking him as a married man who'd embraced the plain life he'd once been eager to escape.

Right up until the moment he and Joel and Samuel were supposed to leave that fateful night. Adam had stayed behind while Joel and Samuel had driven away in Adam's car. A car all three of them had worked to fix while they planned their escape. At the last minute, Adam had backed out, and Joel and Samuel had vanished into the night.

"Wie geht's?" Joel intentionally used *Deitsch*. Back when they'd been teens, they'd spoken to each other in English. Getting ready for jumping the fence was what they'd called it.

"I heard you were back," Adam said in English. "Why haven't you stopped by the farm before now?"

"I wasn't sure if I'd be welcome."

His one-time friend didn't lower his eyes. "You're always welcome here."

"I wasn't before, so why would I be now?"

Adam's face hardened. "Does your family know you're home?"

Joel shook his head.

"If you're going to stay here, Joel, you need to seek your family's forgiveness."

"You know that's not going to happen. My *daed* won't want me under his roof. He regrets the day he adopted me." When Adam started to retort, Joel hurried to add, "Don't tell me I'm exaggerating. He's said those exact words to me for as long as I can remember."

"I know. I—" A stream of light flickered across the sky. "Let's get out of the storm." He motioned for Joel to follow him.

Joel hesitated, then hurried to catch up as thunder exploded overhead. He stepped into a small building that wasn't much bigger than an oversize shed. It was filled with odors of oil and gasoline mixed with dust and a hint of mildew. Engine parts were set on shelves hung on every wall between the door and the windows. A large table in the middle of the room held an engine broken down into pieces. Beyond it was the outer skeleton of a riding lawn mower, so Joel guessed Adam was rebuilding it. His friend had been happiest when his fingers were blackened with grease and he was finding the source of an engine's problem.

Wind whipped through the space before Adam closed the door, leaving them in a weird half-twilight amid more frequent flashes of lightning. Rain began to splatter against the dust on the windows.

"Nick of time," Adam said with a smile.

"Thanks for inviting me in." Joel stuffed his hands into his pockets as he watched the trees whipped by the rising wind. "This is your shop, I'm assuming."

"It is. I was working on this engine when I saw you coming up the lane."

"*Grossdawdi* Ephraim told me you were in the barn."

"This used to be a barn, so *Grossdawdi* Ephraim didn't lie."

"He always hated lying."

"Still does." Adam picked up a greasy towel and tossed it on top of the engine. "What do you want, Joel?"

He had expected that, out of all the doors in Bliss Valley,

Adam's was the one most likely to remain open to him. His friend's cool tone told him he could have been wrong.

"Right now, I want to stay out of the storm."

"I'm not going to throw you out."

"I didn't think you would." Joel sighed. Once he could have depended on Adam. Now they were strangers, separated by more than a decade of choices. Mostly bad choices, though Adam looked like he was happy in the life he'd once denounced. Searching for something to say to ease the tension, he asked, "Have you seen Samuel King? I hear he's back."

Adam's face remained taut. "He is. Came back quite a few years ago. Right after the accident you two had." He paused as if trying to decide whether or not to go on. "Samuel suffered a lot after that accident, Joel. I know he was the one driving, but you abandoned him when he was at his lowest. He could have used a *gut* friend while he recovered and went through physical therapy."

"But I wasn't his friend," he argued, trying to ignore the guilt striking him like the rain on the windows. "By the time of the accident, Samuel and I were barely talking. Both of us were miserable and took out our frustrations on each other. In fact, before he hit the telephone pole, we were arguing about whether he'd move out of our place or if I would."

"Even so, you could have—"

The door opening silenced Adam. Though Joel wondered what Adam thought he could have done to help Samuel when he was such a mess himself, he didn't ask. All he could do was stare as the friend they'd been discussing walked into the shop.

"Hey, Adam. Any chance you could look at…?" Samuel's voice faded as his eyes riveted on Joel.

Staring back, Joel saw the uneven scar over Samuel's left eyebrow as his onetime friend shook rain off his straw hat. Memories of blood running along his friend's face turned his stomach, and he swallowed hard to keep from being sick. He also noticed how Samuel's right arm was pressed close to his body, and he held a cane in his left hand.

"*Komm* in," Adam urged as thunder cracked overhead.

Samuel did, limping as he leaned on the cane.

Joel's throat closed with grief. He'd walked away from the accident with three broken fingers. To look at him now, nobody would ever guess he'd survived an appalling crash. Samuel had had the cost of their foolishness dropped on his shoulders, and now he was dealing with the consequences every day for the rest of his life.

"Joel?" Samuel asked, as disbelieving as Adam had been. "You're back! Are you staying?"

"I don't know."

Samuel startled him by putting a hand on his arm. "Things aren't the same. We're not the same."

"Maybe you two have changed, but you know as well as I do that the whole valley will soon be buzzing with stories about Joel Beachy and what he's done and how he's back with his tail between his legs."

"Are you angry at the gossips or yourself?"

Joel scowled. "That's not the point. You've been welcomed back. That's not going to happen to me."

"I wasn't welcomed back with open arms. It took me more than five years to find a decent job. In fact, I got hired to work in the buggy shop because Elvin Gingerich thought I was someone else. By the time he learned I was one of the boys who'd harassed his daughter, he'd come to know me enough to see I'd changed."

"Five years?" Joel bit back a groan. If it'd taken Samuel so long, what hope did he have? Samuel hadn't been in jail. "Adam, you were the smartest one. How were you able to see into the future when we couldn't?"

"I'd planned to go." Adam came around the table to stand beside them. His face was patterned by the reflection of the rain falling against the glass. "I was planning to go right up to the point of putting my hand on the knob to open the door and walk out."

"But you didn't."

"I intended to meet you as we'd planned. As I was getting ready to walk away from everything I'd ever known, I realized I couldn't. Leaving would be like slicing off a part of myself that couldn't ever be replaced."

Samuel nodded. "I get that. Now. It took me longer to learn that lesson."

Both of them looked at Joel. Were they expecting him to say that he'd come to the same conclusion? He hadn't. As far as he could see, there was no place for him in the plain community of Bliss Valley.

Grace has welcomed you.

Oh, how he despised the voice of his conscience! He'd been able to quell it during his teen years, but it'd gotten louder and more insistent in the past couple of years.

"You said," Adam added as if there hadn't been any break in the conversation, "you aren't sure if you're staying here, Joel. If you're looking for work, I could use a hand at the shop."

"I don't know the first thing about working on small engines."

"I know. I don't expect you to rebuild one from scratch on your first day, but I could use help." He rubbed the back of his neck. "I can't pay you more than meals and a roof over your head."

Joel savored the warmth that spread through him as he realized what Adam was doing. Adam didn't need a helper, but he was extending the offer to assist Joel through a tough time. Before he could do something stupid, like letting pride convince him to say no, Joel nodded and thanked his friend.

Both Adam and Samuel smiled, but the tension didn't ease. Joel couldn't read the glance his friends shared, and he felt like an outsider.

Wanting to find a way to reconnect with his friends, he reached in his pocket and pulled out the money he'd found. Putting it on the table beside the engine block, he said, "Someone must be missing this."

His one-time friends shared another glance. This one, he could read. They were wondering how he had the money as well as why he was showing it to them.

Not waiting for them to ask, he said, "I found this out on the road."

"Is it real?" Samuel yanked his finger back as if he feared getting his fingerprints on the bills.

"It's not counterfeit, if that's what you mean." Realizing there was too much anger in his voice, Joel hurried to add, "Maybe it is. I don't know how to tell if it's real or not. Like I said, I found it beside the road. I was walking along, and there it was like…like…"

"Like a gift from God?" Adam asked in such an unemotional tone Joel turned to stare at him.

"I don't think God gives gifts to felons. It must have dropped out of a vehicle, but I don't know how to find the rightful owner."

"You want to give it back?" Samuel sighed. "Sorry. You do, and I didn't mean to insult you by suggesting otherwise."

Adam leaned forward to rest his hands on the table. "I can't see any way you could find the rightful owner. If you put out the word you've found the money, you'll get a bunch of people claiming it's theirs. How would you figure out which one is telling you the truth? It's not like you're Solomon and you're trying to determine which woman was the *boppli's* true *mamm*."

"Money is easier to divide." Joel smiled, glad he could talk with his friends about the unexpected windfall.

"Only if you don't have a swarm of people stepping forward. You could be facing the challenge of dividing up a single cent." Adam motioned for Joel to pick up the money. "Hold on to it for now. I'll talk to Jonas to get his advice."

"Jonas?"

"Our bishop."

Joel should have guessed. The bishop was the community leader for plain folks in matters both spiritual and everyday. Anything out of the ordinary should be taken to him for his advice.

As Joel gathered up the bills and put them in his pocket, Adam added, "But if you need some of the money to get by now, Joel, go ahead and use it. Nobody would want you to go hungry."

"I thought you wanted to talk to Jonas first."

"I will talk to him tomorrow, but I know him well enough to guess what he'll say."

"That sounds like a plan," Joel said. "I'll keep track of any money I use so I can replace it, if necessary. Thanks, my friends."

"*Danki,*" Adam replied.

Puzzled, Joel asked, "What are you thanking me for?"

"Not thanking you. Correcting you," Adam said. "You haven't forgotten *Deitsch*, ain't so? You greeted me in it."

"I do remember it."

"Then you should use it when you're with your plain brothers and sisters."

"I'm not sure anyone else would appreciate that."

"Because you don't know whether you're returning to our life?" Samuel asked.

"There's that, but also there are plenty of people who don't want me back."

Adam stood straighter. "That isn't for the *Leit* to decide. It's your decision, Joel. Yours and God's."

"What I've done—"

"That's between you and God. When you're ready to seek forgiveness, all you need to do is ask."

Joel didn't answer. It wouldn't be that easy, no matter what Adam said. If it had been, Joel wouldn't have stopped asking for forgiveness years ago. Now, he believed it was too late.

Chapter Seven

On that Monday morning, Grace arrived at work right on time. She must have glanced at the clock on the wall a thousand times before noon and even more times as the afternoon wore on. Though she was curious how Joel had fared with his job interview, she shouldn't have been so disappointed when he hadn't come and told her about it.

Had she lost her *gut* sense? Joel had been in jail, and she should be glad that he was out of her life.

There was the possibility, too, she'd reminded herself over and over, that he'd been hired on the spot and put to work. She'd heard other people talking about that happening because the construction companies were in such serious need of experienced employees. Did Joel have experience with construction? He hadn't said, and she hadn't thought to ask.

The day had otherwise gone well, and she'd found time to eat her lunch during a lull at midday. Some days she didn't have a chance to wolf down a sandwich. She'd sold four large quilts, a remarkable feat for a Monday in late August when the tourist surge was waning. By the end of October, most of the tourists would be gone for another year, and visitors to the shop would be locals and avid quilt collectors.

But it was impossible to keep her mind on work. She tried to halt herself from glancing at the clock, but it was difficult. She shouldn't be curious about how Joel had fared at the job interview. He wasn't her responsibility. God must have made their paths cross so she could help him before their lives went in different directions again. She had to focus on taking care of her parents, not on Joel and whether he'd gotten a job.

"Either way, he's someone else's problem now," Grace murmured as she refolded a quilt and put it back on a table. Looking around the shop as she went to lock the front door, draw down the shades and turn over the Closed sign, she nodded to her own silent appraisal. Everything was ready for reopening the doors in the morning.

But she *was* sorry Joel hadn't stopped by to share the news.

The phone rang. It was an old-fashioned, pale turquoise rotary phone that Tiffany displayed on the counter beside the brass cash register. Grace rushed to answer it, then grimaced as she realized she'd reached across the counter—again—and would be restricted by the short cord connecting the phone to the receiver. It wouldn't stretch far enough for her to go around the end of the counter to reach the drawers in the back.

But she didn't have to worry. It wasn't an order. It was Missy Garnier, and Grace wondered when she'd get to say another word after "hello." Chatty Missy led group tours for Heart of the Amishlands. The company's large, bright green-and-yellow buses were a familiar sight along the twisting country roads in Lancaster County.

"Oh, Grace, so glad I caught you. I wanted to let you know I'll be arriving in Strasburg tomorrow morning around ten with more than fifty ladies who are interested in purchasing

Amish quilts," Missy said without pausing to take a breath. Missy was accustomed to a running monologue while leading her tours, and she approached every conversation with Grace the same way. "The ladies are eager to see *real* Amish quilts. None of those questionable ones made in Southeast Asia. You don't sell those, right? My ladies want quilts made by real, live plain women. I don't want to disappoint them. My—our reputation depends on—"

"Missy, all our quilts are made in Lancaster County by plain quilters," Grace interjected. "That's one of the reasons we work on consignment with quilters. We interact with each and every one of the people who provide quilts for our store."

"Will you guarantee that?"

"Like I said, I've met each of our quilters, and I'll vouch for them."

"You know them? Hmm..."

Grace wasn't sure what the other woman meant with her pause. It wasn't like Missy to allow for even a moment's silence. Grace hurried to say, "I—I—I kn-kn-know—" She halted herself from stuttering on each word by taking a deep breath before beginning over. "I know our quilters well. Many of them my whole life."

"I don't doubt that, Grace, but after the stories I've heard..."

Gritting her teeth so she didn't ask how many more times she needed to repeat the same thing, Grace managed to say, "I've heard the stories as well, Missy. We all have. That's why Tiffany and I inspect every quilt that comes to us, even from a trusted quilter."

"You can understand why I'm concerned, can't you?"

"I can," she said with a sigh, wondering how something that had happened decades before still hung like a dark cloud over Lancaster County quilt shops.

The scandal had begun before she was born. When some

quilters and quilt shops in Lancaster County had come to realize how skilled the Southeast Asian seamstresses were, they began shipping material and thread and patterns to the refugee camps and small villages throughout Laos and Thailand. The quilts that were returned were beautiful, but they hadn't been made by plain quilters. Some of the people selling the quilts had neglected to mention that fact, and residents of the county talked about how a quilt sewn in Thailand was passed off as a genuine Amish quilt at a mud sale for a local volunteer fire department. Now quilt tops pieced together in Southeast Asia and shipped across the Pacific to be quilted in the county were labeled as "Quilted in Lancaster County."

When Grace had started at The Amish Quilt Emporium, Tiffany had been selling those quilts. Grace had changed that, and Tiffany had agreed once she realized how much more money she could make by selling genuine Amish and Mennonite quilts.

Knowing she must do something to keep Missy from taking her clients to another shop, Grace asked, "Would your ladies like to meet some of our quilters in the future?"

Missy's delighted squeal was so loud Grace pulled the phone away from her ear. Wincing, she brought the receiver back toward her in time to hear Missy say, "...arrange such a meeting? We would be willing to compensate the quilters for their time. Speak to them as soon as possible, Grace. This would be such a coup for Heart of the Amishlands."

"I can't promise I'll have anyone here tomorrow, because it's too late to try to contact someone now, but if you can give me a few days' notice before you bring your next group, I'm sure I can arrange to have at least one plain quilter here."

"A real, live one? Not someone pretending to be plain like at some of the tourist places?"

For a moment, a silly part of Grace almost said that she

couldn't guarantee both real and alive, but she kept that response to herself. Instead, she soothed Missy again.

Hanging up the phone after Missy babbled a little longer, Grace hoped she hadn't promised more than she could deliver. Having a plain quilter present when the bus arrived was sure to increase sales for both the shop and the bus tour company. Would that be the way to convince Tiffany to pay her quilters on time? And would this be the project that would show Tiffany how vital Grace was to the shop? If so, Tiffany might give Grace the raise she needed to provide for her family without Grace having to harass her for it.

Someone rapped on the front door. She hurried across the shop. Grabbing the knob, she opened the door without raising the shade to see who was there.

"Joel!" She took a step forward, then two back. "What are you doing here now? We're closed. I thought—"

"That I'd be at work?" He shook his head. "Do you mind if I bend your ear for a moment? You've been so helpful, Grace, though you don't have any reason to be."

"I've known your sisters for years." She frowned. "I told you that a couple of days ago."

"You did."

"Because you're my friends' brother and a member of our *Leit*, I would be wrong not to help you as I can."

His mouth tightened into a straight line. "I'm not a member of the plain community. Not any longer. I can't live the life you all expect me to."

"No one expects you to do anything, Joel. How can they? Other than Rosemary, nobody else in your family has seen you, ain't so?"

"No."

She wasn't sure if she heard regret or relief in his voice. Maybe a combination of both.

Before she could ask another question, the sound of stiletto heels against the old floorboards rang through the shop.

"Who was on the phone?" called Tiffany as she came into the front of the store. She was dressed in what she claimed was the highest style. Her sleeveless top was eye-searingly bright, and she wore it over a pair of skintight jeans. She glanced at Joel, and her brows rose. "I didn't expect to see *you* back here. What can *I* do for you?"

Grace clasped her hands and lowered her eyes before either her boss or Joel could gauge her reaction to Tiffany's flirtatious words. She was shocked by how annoyance mixed with some stronger emotion that came from deep in her middle. She wasn't sure what it was, but she was sure she didn't like how her boss looked at him as if he were a fine stallion on the auction block. From under her lowered eyelashes, she saw the shock on Joel's face. He was a *gut*-looking man, so other women must have offered him a coy smile.

Surprised how he stumbled over his words as he tried to form a reply, Grace took pity on him. She raised her head and said, "Tiffany, the call was from Missy Garnier."

"Missy?" Tiffany asked, her eyes giving Joel a blatant appraisal.

"*Ja.* From Heart of the Amishlands tours. She wants to bring her next tour—"

"Yeah, yeah, fine. I'm glad she listened to me about quilt quality." Tiffany wafted her fingers in Grace's direction. "You take care of it."

"I already have."

Impatience filled Tiffany's voice. "Good. Good. What about those calls I asked you to make?"

"I made them first thing this morning. I—"

"This morning?" Tiffany's voice rose in volume and pitch with each word. Had she forgotten that—for once—there was a witness in addition to Grace to her temper? "I told you to make those calls on Saturday. Why didn't you make them then?"

Grace bit the inside of her cheek to keep from retorting. When she was sure she could control her tone, she said, "I told you I wouldn't have time because I needed to inventory the new quilts and put them on display."

"Nonsense. Making the calls would have taken five minutes. You should have made them."

"But you said it was okay to wait until today when I explained—"

"I needed those calls made Saturday. You should have known how important they were."

Again Grace had to restrain herself from reminding her boss that Tiffany had been fine on Saturday with Grace making the calls this morning. "I know every call you ask me to make is important." Would her calm words placate Tiffany? Sometimes they did. Other times, nothing would.

Tiffany glared at her and opened her mouth to retort. Wanting to apologize to Joel for what he was having to watch, Grace cut her eyes to him for a second.

It was enough to startle Tiffany. She gasped, then smoothed her blouse down over her silver belt. A simpering smile seemed forced, and her voice became sugary-sweet. "No matter. I'll forgive you, Grace. This time. But you need to keep in mind what's important. Your job."

Grace stared at her in astonishment. Tiffany was offering forgiveness as if Grace had failed her. How could that be? Grace had explained in advance why she wouldn't be able to do as her boss had requested and had been told it was all right to wait.

"You never said," Tiffany cooed as she gazed at Joel, "why you're here."

"I wanted to speak with Grace." He didn't elaborate further.

Tiffany recoiled as if he'd slapped her across the face. Lifting her chin, she looked down her nose at him. "I've got an important meeting I can't be late for." She turned to go into the back room. "Don't forget to lock *all* the doors." Pausing in the door between the spaces, she added, "And henceforth, handle your private business on your own time, Grace." She vanished into the back room seconds before a door slammed.

In the silence that followed, Joel asked, "Does she always speak to you like that?"

"It's nothing."

He frowned, his narrowed eyes focused on the door leading to the back room. "It's not nothing, Grace."

"Let it go, Joel." Not wanting to give him a chance to continue, she asked, "How did your job interview go?"

Joel should have been prepared for that question, but Grace's outrageous boss had fazed him more than he'd guessed. Not her flirty words, but how she'd lambasted Grace for what hadn't seemed like a big deal. Grace had brushed aside his concerns, but he hated the idea of her having to work with such ludicrous expectations.

Running his fingers along his goatee, he said, "I applied, but never got an interview. They didn't want an ex-convict."

Her heart deflated like a balloon stuck with a pin. "Oh, Joel, I'm so sorry. I thought they were desperate for help."

"They are, but not desperate enough to hire me." He raised his hand to halt her from speaking. "I don't need sympathy or pity, Grace. Sympathy is useless, and I'm feeling pitiful enough already. What I need is a job. Can you keep your ears open? If someone is hiring, will you let me know? I'm going to be staying at Ephraim Weaver's farm and helping there."

"Why there?" She answered the question before he could.

"Oh, that's right. Adam is your friend. Doesn't he run a small engine repair business in addition to being our deacon?"

"Adam is a deacon?" His shocked voice sounded as high-pitched as it had when he was a boy. Clearing his throat, he asked in a more normal tone, "How did Adam ever get put into the lot after all the trouble we caused when we were kids? The deacon's the guy who's supposed to make sure everyone keeps on the straight and narrow."

Quiet dignity filled her answer. "Adam made a true effort to straighten out his life. Just as you're doing."

"If I'm ever allowed to…" He sighed and again waved aside her response. "Don't bother telling me to stop feeling sorry for myself."

"I wasn't going to say that. Do you like the work you'll be doing with Adam?"

"Not really." He grimaced. "But beggars can't be choosers."

"That's the attitude that will win over a boss."

Chuckling, he replied, "Adam knows I would prefer to call him friend than boss. I doubt I'll be able to do more than sweep up around the shop."

"It'll give you a chance to reconnect."

"I hope so. It was tense when I talked to him and Samuel. They've made lives in Bliss Valley."

Grace went to lock the front door, and he guessed she didn't want to let a late customer sneak in.

Guilt filled him. She must need to get home to fix supper for her parents. He shouldn't be delaying her.

He was about to say that, but before he could, she said, "*Ja*, they've made lives here. *Gut* ones. Did you have a chance to speak with Laurene and Naomi, too? You were all scholars together, ain't so?"

"Laurene? Naomi?" His eyes widened. "You mean Laurene

Nolt and Naomi Gingerich? They were best friends back in school, but Laurene left Bliss Valley years ago."

"She's back, and she and Naomi have discovered they're twin sisters."

"What?"

"It's a long story, but they were adopted. As you were. It's only recently they learned that and that they're sisters."

He couldn't wrap his mind around what Grace was telling him. It was astonishing enough Laurene had returned to Bliss Valley, too, but it seemed impossible she and Naomi had discovered they were twins.

Knowing he sounded stupid, he asked, "Why would they have been at Adam's?"

"Because Naomi married Samuel a couple of months ago, and Laurene is, I've heard, marrying Adam later this fall once she's baptized."

He put a hand against the wall as his knees threatened to fail him. The whole world tilted sideways, as it had the day he'd arrived at the prison and everything he'd believed was ripped away. Somehow he managed to ask, "The two of them have married Adam and Samuel? Laurene Nolt and Naomi Gingerich have married Adam Hershberger and Samuel King?"

"Laurene and Adam aren't married yet, but everyone knows it's coming. She spends a lot of time at the Weaver farm taking care of Adam's daughter."

Daughter? Adam hadn't said anything about a daughter. That must mean his friend had been married before, and his previous wife had died. So many questions erupted through his head, but each was shadowed by the realization how much his mistakes had cost him. He'd lost his best friends, his family and so many events in their lives. How could he ever find common ground with them again?

As he had before, he thought about walking out of the shop

and going as far from Bliss Valley as he could and still remain in Pennsylvania. Once more, Grace's sweet voice drew him back from the edge of running away. Not from his past, but from everyone else's.

"Mary Beth is so cute," Grace said. "Laurene's brought her in here a couple of times, and she has a ton of questions. She's interested in everything like all four-year-olds, and she and Laurene adore each other."

He shook his head. "I can't believe it. Adam and Laurene. Samuel and Naomi. Who would have guessed?" He shook his head as if coming out of a trance. "Sorry. It's so unbelievable. The three of us bullied those girls who didn't do anything other than try to be our friends."

Grace stared as if he'd sprouted wings and a tail. "You bullied them?"

"I assumed—"

The phone rang, and she held up a finger to halt him. Going to the counter, she reached across and picked up the phone he'd assumed was a decoration.

"Hello," she said. "You've reached The Amish Quilt Emporium. This is Grace. May I help you?"

A pause.

"*Ja*, I'm Grace Coffman," she replied to a question he hadn't heard. "How can I help you?"

The phone fell from her fingers. She dropped to her knees, paying no attention to the phone that dangled from its cord, swinging in a slow arc while a voice squawked out of it. The woman on the other end was calling Grace's name.

She hid her face in her hands and cried out as if in pain.

He knelt beside her, ignoring the phone. Putting his hands on her slender shoulders, he asked, "Grace, what's wrong?"

"F-F-Fr..." She shuddered, then whispered, "My brother and his wife..."

He put his hands on her shoulders. "Grace, what is it? What's wrong?"

She kept shaking her head.

She acted as if she couldn't hear him or the woman yelling her name into the phone. Would she listen to him if he spoke in *Deitsch*? He had to try.

"*Was iss letz*, Grace? What's wrong? *Was iss letz?*"

She raised her eyes, and he saw unspeakable agony filling them. "My brother and his wife..."

"What about your brother and his wife?" He gave her a gentle shake, then hated himself when she groaned. "Grace, *was iss letz*? Tell me. Please."

"My brother and his wife..." She shivered so hard he thought she would crumble in front of him. He understood why when she whispered, "They're dead."

Chapter Eight

Joel stared at Grace, not wanting to believe what she'd said. She curled away from him, leaning against the counter and weeping. He reached for her, but halted when the swinging phone almost struck his nose.

He grabbed it and reached to put it on the counter. He stopped when he heard a woman's voice coming from it, shouting Grace's name. Putting it to his ear, he said, "Hello?"

"Who is this?" asked a woman in a strained tone.

"Joel Beachy. What's going on?" He looked at Grace. Sobs wracked her body.

"Are you a member of the Coffman family?"

"*Ja.*" He made sure he used the *Deitsch* word.

He didn't regret the lie for a moment when the woman replied, "I've been trying to get in touch with your family for the past three days. I'm Bailey Lightfoot from the Child and Family Services Division of the Montana Department of Public Health and Human Services."

He thought about the blinking light on the answering machine in the phone shack. "There's been an accident?"

"Yes. I'm sorry to tell you that Fritz Coffman and his wife Flossie were both drowned in Lake Koocanusa last week. You didn't hear from the local authorities?"

"Oh. No." He wasn't sure what else to say. "*Danki* for letting us know." Thanking Bailey didn't seem like the right response, but he wanted to get off the call and do what he could to help Grace. She done so much for him. He wasn't sure how he could help her, but he couldn't let her cry on the floor. "Goodbye."

He lowered the phone away from his ear, but heard Bailey shout his name along with "Wait! Don't hang up!"

"*Ja?*" he asked into the phone.

"I didn't call you to let you know about the Coffmans' deaths. They have two sons."

"Two sons?" he repeated in shock.

He could almost see Bailey frown, even though he had no idea what she looked like. Suspicion seeped into her voice as she asked, "Aren't you a member of the family?"

"I am." He couldn't let the lie catch up with him now. "I'm j-j-just overwhelmed with the news. About the boys…?"

"Okay," she answered, but he guessed she wasn't sure about telling him more. After a hesitation, she went on, "Brandon and Wesley have no family here in Montana. Because so many of the Amish families in the Rexford area don't have relatives nearby, the bishop has spent time with each family asking about plans for their children. The Coffmans told him that if anything ever happened to them, the boys would be taken care of by their grandparents." He heard papers rattle.

"Harold and Saretta Coffman," he supplied.

As he spoke her parents' names, Grace's head jerked up.

Tears ran along her face, but she ignored them as she gathered her feet beneath her to stand.

He offered his hand. When she put her fingers on it, sensation zinged through him as if he'd grasped the prongs on an electric plug. But instead of yanking his fingers away, he wanted to hold on. He'd always been averse to dangerous situations, and he'd become even more so in prison, but there was something about her touch that urged him to risk everything to experience it a second longer.

She drew her hand away, and he silenced the sigh he didn't want her to hear. When she held out her hand, he gave her the phone and backed away a single step. He didn't want to go far. In case she needed him.

But what could he do to alleviate even a smidgen of her pain? Tell her that he understood? She didn't have any reason to believe him when his own family had disowned him and he hadn't had contact with them for almost a decade. He hadn't even recognized his own brother-in-law.

So he stood in silence as Grace grabbed a notepad and wrote down a telephone number that he guessed was Bailey Lightfoot's. She nodded, before talking in such a hushed voice he wondered how the other woman could hear her. He couldn't pick out more than a few words.

Boys.

When.

Okay.

The rest was a jumble to him. It didn't help that his heart was sending his pulse thundering through his head, muting every other sound around him.

Grace hung up the phone, but didn't turn to face him. A deep shudder ran along her before she squared her shoulders and pushed herself away from the counter.

"Grace…"

"I need to get home and let my parents know," she said in a voice that could have belonged to a robot.

"All right. I'll drive you."

She looked at him and nodded. That told him more than anything else how devastated she was.

Grace knew she should thank Joel for handling the reins on the way to the farm. She was sure there were words to express her gratitude. *Gut* words that would convey her relief she hadn't had to drive when her head was spinning.

But she couldn't find a single one.

She reached for the knob on the kitchen door, but her fingers closed in front of it. Shutting her eyes, she took a deep breath as she offered up a wordless prayer. She didn't know what to pray for when there was so much she didn't want to face inside the house.

"Let me—" Joel began, stretching past her.

"I've got it." She snapped out the words.

When he drew his arm back, she knew she should apologize. She'd add it to her long list of to-dos. She'd get to that list after she broke the terrible news to her parents. Oh, how she wished she didn't have to be the one to tell them about Fritz and Flossie!

Memories slashed at her like a hundred different blades as she remembered telling them about Lamar's death. It had changed everything *Daed* and *Mamm* had planned for their retirement. Instead of moving into the *dawdi haus* and spending their time doing what they wanted to do or bouncing a *kins-kind* on their knees, they'd had to keep working on the farm as they had for the past forty years.

Now she had to tell them about their eldest son's death and how two young boys they'd never seen were going to be sent to live with them.

She grasped the knob and opened the door. Neither *Mamm* nor *Daed* was in the kitchen. That was odd for the late afternoon. Usually one or both of them were there when she came home from work. They didn't get out as they used to, so they were eager to hear news from around the world which was broadcast on the radio Tiffany had on when she was in the shop. They also liked hearing gossip that had sped across the Amish grapevine about new *bopplin* or accidents or upcoming events to raise money for those who needed help. Every tidbit was welcome, though they had both *The Budget* newspaper and the monthly magazine, *The Diary*, delivered to the house.

"*Mamm?*" she called. "*Daed?*"

When she got no answer, she frowned, her fatigue forgotten as she rushed into the front room. It was empty. She whirled, growing frantic. Where had they gone? They never left the house without putting a note on the fridge. Maybe she'd missed it.

She ran back into the kitchen and stared at the refrigerator. None of the magnets advertising local businesses held a piece of the bright orange notepaper *Mamm* kept in a nearby drawer. She scanned the room, seeing a pile of unopened mail on the table. That wasn't a surprise. Since he'd accidentally ripped an invoice from the gas company in half, *Daed* left the mail for her to open. Lately, she'd begun reading the mail to both her parents. Nobody had said anything about why, but her *mamm* spent far less time sewing, a sure sign her eyes weren't as strong as they'd been.

Her parents should be retired and living simpler lives. Instead, they were going to be responsible for two young boys. With a start, Grace realized she didn't even know how old the boys were now.

"Are you looking for this?" Joel asked, picking up a piece of paper from in front of the sink.

She took it and read the words in her *mamm*'s unsteady scrawl. *Mamm* had to write it, even though she hated her penmanship. *Daed* couldn't control his tremors to put a pen to paper.

"They're having supper with friends." She lowered the page. "I can drive you—"

"No. Let them enjoy this one last meal before they hear the news." She crumpled the page and threw it in the wastebasket. The paper bounced out and rolled along the floor to stop between the toes of Joel's worn shoes.

He bent again to scoop it up. With a quick flex of his wrist, he sent the paper into the wastebasket. This time, it didn't pop out again.

Pushing himself away from the counter, he said, "Sit. How about a cup of *kaffi*? Or tea?"

"I don't want anything. I've got a lot to do before my nephews get here."

"It can wait." He put his hands on her shoulders. "You've had a big shock. I know you want to have everything ready for the boys, but they aren't here yet. You need to take this time to take care of yourself, too."

She shrugged off his fingers before she could be enticed to step closer and beg him to hold her until the hurt vanished. How long would that take? Months? Years? She still hurt each time she thought of Lamar. That pain had lost its serrated edges at some point. She couldn't pinpoint the exact moment, but she'd begun to think of him without her breath clogging in her throat.

Now...

"Joel, *danki* for driving me home. I'm sorry if I sound rude, but I need to..."

He didn't speak as her voice faded. The hush in the kitchen was broken by the faint sound of birds singing.

Grace was torn between stamping out, not wanting to play whatever ludicrous game he was trying to draw her into, or grabbing the dishcloth and cleaning every flat surface. Once word of the tragedy reached the community, every family in their district as well as some beyond it would appear at their door with offers of food and assistance. She didn't want them to see a messy kitchen. Her parents always left crumbs on the counter and the table during dinner, in spite of *Mamm*'s attempts to clean up all of them.

Again she chose the less confrontational route. She grabbed the dishcloth, soaked it under the faucet and wrung it out. Without a word, she went to the table and began cleaning the oilcloth on top of it. She waited to hear the door open and close to announce Joel had left.

And waited as she rubbed a stain she knew wouldn't come out. She kept scrubbing and scrubbing until the whole table shook.

Gentle hands lifted hers away from the table. Looking up, she saw Joel's grim face.

"Go ahead," she snarled.

"Go ahead with what?" His voice was as tender as his touch as he withdrew the cloth from her hand and carried it to the sink.

"Go ahead and tell me I'm acting like I've lost my mind."

"Why wouldn't you be acting like you've lost your mind? Your brother and his wife are dead, and you're going to be responsible for two boys you don't know as well as taking care of your parents."

Ice wedged in her lungs, making it impossible to draw a breath. Joel was right. How was she going to oversee two boys and her parents and the farm and her work at the quilt shop? Tiffany was after her to work more hours while the other store was getting ready to open. Grace should, because there would be two more mouths to feed. But how was she going to do that when she had to watch over her nephews?

"I know," Grace moaned. "What do I know about taking care of boys? My brothers were almost grown by the time I came along."

"You can ask for help from other members of the district. They're going to offer it anyhow."

"I can't ask when I don't know what I need."

Joel's eyes narrowed. "Why are you acting as if you're useless?"

"I'm not."

"You are." He folded his arms over his chest and leaned back against the sink cabinet. "You're as skittish as a barn cat, and you won't look at me. Either you're mad at yourself or at me. As far as I know, I haven't done anything to tick you off."

"No, *you've* been *wunderbaar.*" She clamped her lips closed before she said something else stupid. She didn't need to sound like a teenager gushing over a cute boy.

"And you will be great, Grace. As far as I've seen, you're great at everything you do."

"You don't even know me." She slammed her fist on the table, sending the napkin holder and the mail flying.

Joel stepped forward to gather it up, but she waved him away.

Grace stuffed the napkins into the wicker holder, then reached for the mail. She set it on the table. Her eyes were caught by the return address on a larger manila envelope.

Child and Family Services Division of the Montana Department of Public Health and Human Services.

Ripping it open, she pulled out the pages inside. The letter on top was long, and she choked back another gasp as she read the letter that had been sent as another attempt to contact the grandparents of Brandon and Wesley Coffman. The two boys were aged ten and eight. Searching her memory, she tried to remember stories about what her own brothers had been like at that age.

She shunted aside those thoughts. Too many memories of Fritz exploded out. Not when he was the same age as his sons, but when he was a young man. She was assaulted by images of him playing ball with his friends, washing his buggy before he went to a youth event so he could offer a girl a ride home in it, the day he and Flossie had been married before leaving for their new home in Montana. That was the last memory she had of them other than their letters, which had arrived like clockwork for the past eleven years.

Now their sons, whom she'd never seen, were coming to Bliss Valley. Neither *Daed* nor *Mamm* was able to look after two young boys. They couldn't take care of themselves some days.

Again self-doubts rushed in. What did she know about young boys? What would she talk to them about? How could she make them feel at home? How could she help them heal their hearts when she hadn't figured out how to patch her own?

How would she even know them when…

"Oh, my!" She stared at the letter. "They're going to be here tomorrow."

Joel took the letter and scanned it as if he were looking for words to refute her. Lowering it, he said, "You're right. A social worker is bringing the boys here. They're arriving tomorrow afternoon, bringing their things with them. What things?"

"I would guess they're bringing their clothes and favorite toys." She gazed at the envelope. "I hope they've got their *mamm*'s Bible. It has come down through Flossie's family for generations. Fritz wrote how he used to read it to his sons each evening. They'll want that."

"Something you can worry about later. Now you need to focus on these two boys arriving tomorrow." He looked over the letter to her. "Didn't Bailey tell you they were coming?"

"No… Yes… I don't remember."

"She didn't say anything to me about it, but it doesn't matter." He folded the page and handed it to her.

She stuffed it and the other pages into the envelope. "No, it doesn't. We need to be there when the bus pulls in."

"I'll drive you."

Grace's fingers clutched the envelope until the paper creaked. "You can't. *Daed* will—"

"Will he despise having me drive him more than the idea of you having an accident because you're too upset to drive?"

"You didn't let me finish. *Daed* will hire a van. It's too far to go by buggy."

He looked sheepish. "Sorry. I've gotten too used to thinking about distances based on using a car."

"I know." She smoothed out the envelope on the table as she asked, "Do you want to come with us to pick up the boys?"

Shock raced through his eyes. "Are you sure? Won't your *daed* be upset?"

"I may need your help in supporting him so he doesn't fall, Joel. His tremors become worse when he's stressed."

"I'll help, and I'll see if Adam or one of his cousins can come as well. In case your *mamm* needs help, too." He started to add more, but halted and glanced out the window.

She followed his gaze. Her parents had returned home and were walking toward the house.

"I can stay," he said.

"Go. We need to be alone now."

"Being alone is never the answer, Grace. I learned that the hard way in our small apartment after the car accident sent

Samuel to the hospital and during the days I'd sat by myself in a jail cell."

"But I won't be alone. I'll be with my family."

He recoiled, astonishing her. What could be wrong? She hated having to break the horrific news to her parents, but they'd find a way to share the grief and seek comfort together.

The truth blared through her head like a wild trumpet blast. A scorching pain burned deep into her heart as she'd realized how alone he was. When he'd been suffering, he'd had no one to turn to. He'd thrown away the very thing Grace needed most tonight.

A family.

Chapter Nine

The next afternoon, Joel glanced at his watch as he emerged from *Grossdawdi* Ephraim's barn. It was already past two, and the bus bringing the Coffman boys was scheduled to arrive just past four. He couldn't be late getting to the Coffman farm. He'd told Grace he'd go with her in the van to meet her nephews, and he didn't want to cause the Coffmans to be delayed going to the bus station.

Looking around, he saw Adam coming out of his shop. Joel waved to him, and his friend strode toward him. "Ready?" Joel asked as soon as Adam was within earshot.

"I can't go."

"What?"

"I have to run over to my friend Frank's auto shop. He's got an emergency repair coming in, and he needs another set of hands. I'm sorry, Joel. I don't like letting you down again."

"Again?"

"Well, I didn't do as I told you I would when you and Samuel left."

Joel gave a humorless laugh. "I'm trying to let go of my past, and I don't need everyone reminding me of it every time I turn around."

"I wanted to apologize for bailing on you that night."

"Don't."

"But—"

"Don't say you're sorry when you made the right decision for yourself." Joel kicked a pebble across the dirt yard. "It took me a lot of years to see that, but I've come around to understand why you remained in Bliss Valley."

Adam's face relaxed along with his shoulders. "It was where God meant me to be."

"I don't know about God, but it was what your heart was telling you."

"He talks to me from deep within my heart."

Joel nodded, not wanting to get into a discussion of faith with his friend. Being unsure about his relationship with God made him feel inadequate when Adam spoke of how God was guiding his life, helping him avoid the pitfalls.

"It's just as well you aren't going to the bus station," Joel said to change the subject. "I don't need to hear more mumbling about the hypocrisy of the deacon working with the jailbird."

"Nobody's mumbling," said Eddie Mishler as he rounded a corner of the house. How long had his brother-in-law been eavesdropping? What had his sister seen in this slimy guy? He must be different around Rosemary and the rest of the family than he was when talking to Joel.

Astonishment struck Joel like a fist to the nose. *Daed* was the same, having two faces. The scowling, disappointed one he showed his only son and the jovial, nice guy one he displayed for everyone else. Could that be why Rosemary had married this jerk? Because he reminded her of *Daed*?

"That's right," Adam said, coming to Joel's defense. "Folks aren't mumbling anything."

"*Ja.*" Eddie squared his shoulders and shifted on his feet. "Some folks are saying it right out loud."

"Like you?" Joel almost laughed. Did Eddie think his pugnacious pose with his jutting chin and his hands fisted on his waist was going to intimidate Joel after the men he'd encountered in prison?

"*Ja,* like me."

"Everyone has a right to their opinion," Adam said before Joel could laugh at the insipid comeback, "but they don't have the right to share it wherever and whenever they wish. Did you come to see me, Eddie?"

Eddie frowned at Joel. "No, him."

"Say what you need to. Joel has something important to do."

"All right. I'll make it short and to the point." His scowl furrowed his brow. "Stay away from our farm. I don't want Rosemary upset because you're hanging around, looking to cause trouble."

Joel released a half laugh, though he found Eddie's attitude amusing. If he showed that, he'd make the man more irate. Not that Joel wouldn't have minded giving Eddie a lesson in minding his manners, but that would upset Adam and Rosemary. He'd caused enough unhappiness for his friends and his sisters. He didn't want to create more, though it was tempting. "I haven't been hanging around your farm. I'm not even sure where it is."

"Don't spread your filthy lies around me, Joel Beachy. You've been seen near the house."

Astonished, he struggled to keep his voice steady. "You're wrong. I haven't been there. Like I said, I don't know where you and Rosemary live."

"Stay away." He jabbed a finger toward Joel, shocking him. It wasn't like most plain men to be in someone's face. Then he understood. Eddie was scared for Rosemary's safety. He believed if her brother—and his fellow felons—started loitering near the house, there would be trouble.

"Eddie—"

Adam interrupted, "I've known Joel most of my life, Eddie, and I know he loves his sisters and wouldn't do anything to endanger them."

"Really? Then why did he come back at all? It would have been better if he'd..." He clamped his lips closed.

Too late, because Joel heard what his brother-in-law had intended to say. *It would have been better if he'd stayed in jail. It would have been better if he'd never come back. It would be better if he were dead and they could forget him.*

Not that it mattered what Eddie had been going to say. Whatever it had been, the meaning was the same. He didn't want Joel near his family.

Adam sighed. "Anger will get us nowhere."

Was he speaking to Eddie or to Joel? Again it didn't matter.

Eddie glowered at them before turning on his heel and stamping away.

In his wake, Adam said, "Eddie is a *gut* guy, but too often, he forgets to think before he talks."

"Like when he's upset?"

Adam nodded with another sigh. "I'll talk to him. He might listen to me."

"Or he might continue to listen to my *daed*."

"You don't know if Wyman—"

"Of course, I know, Adam!" He lowered his voice, which had risen sharply. "Where else would he have gotten the idea that I'm dangerous to my own sister?"

"Lots of people are talking. You know that."

Joel turned and walked toward the road, knowing he already risked being late. He wanted to escape the truth, though it was impossible. If his sisters believed the worst of him, who would give him a second chance?

Grace will.

He almost laughed at the insipid little voice in his head. It was ridiculously optimistic, acting as if he could pick up his life where he'd left it the night he drove away from Bliss Valley. *Why is everything this hard? When are You going to send a break my way, Lord?*

The prayer that burst out of his heart startled him so much, he almost stumbled over his own feet. The plea had been instinctive, but part of an instinct he'd submerged years ago. Even in jail, he hadn't turned to God, not wanting to be disappointed when his prayers were ignored…again.

When Adam fell in step with him, Joel said, "I don't want a sermon, Deacon."

"I'm not going to give you one."

"I know I can't keep people from talking, and I deserve to be distrusted by everyone around here. But I don't know how anyone can expect me to redeem myself when they begin tallying up a list of my mistakes every time they see me. I know I can't expect forgiveness, but I thought at least they'd be willing to give me a chance to show I'm not the boy who left Bliss Valley."

"It would be great if the *Leit* would forgive you like that." He snapped his fingers. "But people aren't like that. You must give them some time, Joel."

"I get that I don't have any right to forgiveness."

"You don't need to search for redemption, Joel. God has already forgiven you."

"How do you know?" he growled, wondering if he should

remind his friend that Adam had said he wasn't going to give him a sermon.

"Because He knows our sins from before we are born, and yet He forgives us. His son gave His life on the cross to absolve us of our sins. You know that."

"Of course I do. I haven't forgotten everything about this life."

Adam stopped as they reached the end of the lane. Putting his hand on Joel's shoulder, he said, "Then my best advice to you is to pray, my friend. Listen to the guidance of that small voice from deep within your soul. It won't steer you wrong."

Again Joel couldn't find the words to answer. Adam's small voice had guided him along a *gut* path, but Joel's had goaded him into trying ever more outrageous things to prove he was as useless as his *daed* had labeled him. How could he explain that to Adam who'd turned his life around while Joel's was spinning in place, going nowhere?

He couldn't, so he wished Adam success with the project at the auto repair shop and turned in the opposite direction to head toward the Coffmans' farm. He reached it as the large white transport van was pulling into the lane.

"Your timing is perfect." Grace edged toward the back seat and sat beside him. "You didn't give my folks a chance to argue about you joining us."

Her parents claimed the seat right behind the driver, leaving an empty bench between them and where he and Grace sat in the cramped last row. He kept his face serene when Mr. Coffman aimed a vexed glance over his shoulder.

"I can see that," Joel said, speaking as softly as Grace had. "Are you sure you want me around?"

"I asked you to come with us, ain't so?"

"Because you thought I could help your parents." He chose his words with care, not wanting to let anyone else hear them.

Grace nodded, and, for a moment, he was surprised. Then he reminded himself that Grace was always honest. As long as he didn't want to talk about her late fiancé. That subject closed her up faster than a flower pulling in its petals to protect itself against the cold.

"And," she said, "I don't know how the boys will be when they get here. They've suffered such a loss, and now they're thousands of miles from the only home they've ever known. It's got to be like coming to another planet to move from mountainous Montana to the hills around here."

"If you're expecting I can help, I don't know if I can. I've been beyond Pennsylvania, but just to New Jersey and New York."

"That's farther than I've been. I'd hoped to see the Grand Canyon, but that didn't work out."

He didn't ask her to explain. He guessed she and her fiancé had spoken about going out West for their honeymoon. More couples were copying the *Englisch* way of taking a trip after their weddings.

The van turned in the barnyard, then drove down the farm lane. It was astonishing to be traveling in a motorized vehicle again, and he was grateful Grace's *daed* had arranged for the van.

"Did you have trouble getting a van at the last minute?" he asked, trying to peer around the brim of Mr. Coffman's hat to see if he recognized the older man behind the wheel. Retired *Englischers* often drove the vans, giving them a small income and the chance to get out of the house.

"No," Grace replied. "Morris Transport always has extra drivers on standby."

"Morris?"

She looked around the edge of her bonnet. "What's wrong?"

He grinned. "I'm going to keep my face averted so it's not

visible in the rearview mirror. The driver might recall when Adam, Samuel and I covered their vans' windows with soap every night for over two weeks."

"You didn't!" She put her hand over her mouth to muffle her laughter.

"We did. They had the cleanest vans around for those two weeks."

"You three were such *gut* friends."

His smile fell away. "We were. I keep hoping we can be again, but it's not the same. *We*'re not the same."

"Is staying at Adam's putting a strain on your reconciliation?"

"It's not helping. Is it that obvious?"

"You seem on edge." Her gaze slid toward her hands, which were folded on the black apron she wore over her pine green dress. "Or maybe I'm so on edge myself, the whole world feels off-kilter."

The van bounced into a pothole, and she reached out to grab the seat in front of her. He did the same, and their smallest fingers touched. It was the lightest of caresses, his skin against hers, but the jolt was more powerful than the van wheels hitting the hole.

She pulled her hand away and laced her fingers together again. "I'm sorry to hear it's not great for you at *Grossdawdi* Ephraim's."

"I feel useless. I don't know much about engines, and I'd be more apt to break one than mend one."

"I don't know if you'd be interested in working on our farm, but—"

"I'll take the job." Hope flooded him, startling him with its power.

She stared at him in astonishment. "But you don't even know what the job is."

"Will it include a place to live?"

"*Ja.* The *dawdi haus* is empty, and *Daed* agreed last night to let me find someone to help when we realized how much our lives are going to change. He said if I could find a hired hand, I should offer to let him live in the *dawdi haus.*"

"Did you mention you were thinking of hiring me?"

"I wouldn't go behind his back, if that's what you're asking. He told me to find someone who's not afraid of work and isn't interested in being paid much. To me, that sounds like you."

He chuckled, unable to curb his relief at moving his life forward. Not far, he had to admit, because he didn't want to spend his whole life being someone's hired man. Yet, he'd be doing work he was familiar with and helping Grace and her family. It wouldn't be make-work like with Adam.

"The job sounds like what I need right now," he said. "What will you want me to do? I can milk cows. I used to be able to milk faster than any of my friends."

"We sold the herd after *Daed*'s diagnosis." A flash of sorrow flicked through her eyes. Because of her *daed*'s prognosis or because she was thinking about her late fiancé who would have taken over the husbandry of the farm from Mr. Coffman?

Or maybe both.

"I can plow fields."

"It's a bit late in the year for that," she replied. "It's harvest time, not planting time."

He grinned. "True, but I can bale hay. It's not too late for a final cutting."

"We rent out the pasture to our neighbors."

He rested his shoulder against the van's wall and half turned to look at her. "Okay, guessing isn't getting me anywhere. What would you need me to do?"

"Paint and repairs. That's what the farm needs. Basic maintenance. I figured if you were interested in doing construction work, you'd know how to do repairs."

"There's a big difference between pouring concrete and putting on a new roof."

"I know that. I'm not a fool." She gave him what he guessed she meant to be a daunting glare.

He fought his own lips, which yearned to twitch. He would insult her if he was honest and said her expression was closer to cute than contemptuous. Speaking about the dangerous scowls he'd witnessed in prison might cause her to renege on her job offer.

That couldn't happen. If he hadn't found that money along the road and Adam hadn't gotten the district's bishop to agree the day after it was found that Joel could keep the cash, he would have gone hungry days ago. Adam had offered to bring him food from the house, but Joel had declined, not wanting to cause trouble between his friend and *Grossdawdi* Ephraim.

"So do you want the job?" Grace asked, her voice serious. "It won't be easy for you to live in a place where you're not welcomed by everyone."

"I'm already living like that." Knowing he was risking so much, he reached over and put his hand on top of her clenched fingers. "But it'll be easier, Grace, knowing I have an ally in you."

"A friend," she corrected him. "Allies are something you have in a battle. Friends are what you need in life."

"That's true." He didn't say more as she moved her hands from beneath his at the same time she leaned forward to answer a question from Saretta.

A friend. Grace considered him a friend. He knew he should be grateful, because he had so few, but he wasn't. From the sensations that raced through him each time he touched her, even by chance, he knew friendship with Grace would never be enough for him.

But, he reminded himself, he'd be a fool to hope for more when it could ruin her life as he'd already ruined his.

Grace craned her neck to see around the crowd gathered along the circular drive where the buses pulled in and out of the station. She hadn't guessed there would be so many people at the bus terminal, but the boys' bus was late, so maybe others were, too. She glanced at Joel and saw his mouth was set in a straight line. He obviously didn't like crowded spaces either. Did it remind him of the cell where he'd lived?

"We can wait over there, too," Grace said, pointing to an overhang that opened onto the street. She'd already moved her parents into the shade because the heat coming off the road and sidewalk was ferocious. She'd given them bottles of half-frozen water to keep them cool and hydrated, and she had several more in the tote bag hanging from her arm.

"Will you be able to see when they arrive if we stand there?" Joel asked.

"The social worker traveling with them has instructions to look for us." She rubbed her hands together. "I gave her a description of me when she called last night. Look for where there's a vertical dent in the crowd. That's where I am, trying to look past the people who are taller than I am." She tried to smile.

"It's going to be okay," he said.

"Only God knows what lies ahead for us."

"He knows if there's anyone up to this challenge, it's you."

"You've got more faith in me, Joel, than I've got in myself."

"I could say the same thing about you."

Unsure how to reply to his candid words, she looked toward the street, wondering where the bus was. Cars rushed past, but there weren't any pedestrians challenging the day's heat. Worrying about the bus's delay kept her from wondering if she'd been too quick to offer Joel a job on the farm. *Daed* had told her to find someone, but had he guessed she'd ask Joel? In so many ways, though she oversaw the house and the farm, *Daed* considered her a *kind*.

Somehow, she would find a way to get *Daed* to see Joel was the logical choice. He needed a job and a place to live, and he wasn't fussy about what they could afford to pay him.

Grace pushed aside her thoughts as a bus pulled up to the entrance of the bus station. Its brakes made a whooshing sound before it took the sharp turn from the one-way street into the station. She searched each window as it passed, though she had no idea what the boys looked like.

"They're probably sitting on the other side," Joel said as the bus went past.

She flashed him a smile, but grew serious again as she watched her parents go toward where the bus had stopped. Hurrying to make sure neither of them needed help, she wiped sweat off her forehead. Another slimy drop slid down her spine. Her parents looked ready to collapse in the heat.

Joel vanished into the bus station. Where was he going?

Grace focused on her parents. Pulling another bottle of water from her tote bag, she opened it and handed it to *Mamm*, whose face was an unhealthy crimson. *Daed* waved aside her offer of more water. The bottle she'd given him before was barely tasted. She understood why when she saw the fading marks of water dripped down the front of his shirt. He didn't want his *kins-kinder*'s first sight of him to be marred by his Parkinson's tremors.

Joel reappeared by her side and held something out to *Mamm*. In amazement, Grace saw it was a large, black umbrella. He was stuffing a receipt in his back pocket as *Mamm* stared in confusion.

"It's not raining," she said, her voice as unsteady as *Daed*'s shaking hand.

"Think of it as a parasol," Joel said, "instead of an umbrella."

"*Ach!* What a *wunderbaar* idea!" *Mamm* held it over her head and motioned for *Daed* to step under its shade.

"*Danki,*" Grace said as her parents went toward where the bus door was opening. "That was kind of you, Joel."

"I do have my moments, y'know."

"I do know." She didn't add more as a subtle flush climbed his neck toward his goatee. She didn't want to embarrass him by adding that she was glad he'd agreed to come to the bus station. She guessed she'd need to depend on him again before the day was done.

She took a deep breath and followed her parents who'd reached the rear of the bus as the driver emerged to open the storage space underneath the seats. Sending up a quick, fervent prayer, she hoped God would grant them the strength and patience they would need in the days to come. The boys would be seeking to understand why this tragedy had happened to them, and she didn't have an answer.

Help me so I can help them.

Chapter Ten

Joel said nothing as he walked beside Grace to the front of the bus where the passengers were disembarking and claiming their luggage. Each step she took was as uneven as Mr. Coffman's. She looked as if she were swimming, and he guessed she was fighting not to drown in her anxiety. He wanted to put his arm around her to keep her steady, but he knew she'd be horrified by him doing that in public.

It would be better to stand to the side and be silent unless he was needed to help her parents, but Joel had seldom chosen the wiser path. That was a bad habit he needed to break. He would try...after he made sure Grace was all right.

"Things aren't as bad as our imaginations suggest," he whispered.

She looked at him, her expression easing for a single moment, before a woman called out, "Are the Coffmans here?"

Grace raised her hand and stepped forward to greet a woman who looked as if she hadn't slept in days. The woman's clothing was mussed, a sure sign any catnaps she'd gotten had been while dressed. Dark crescents underlined her eyes that were the same brown as her hair, and she carried a shoulder bag he assumed held her laptop and other paperwork.

Joel stepped aside to allow Grace's parents room beside her on the sidewalk. He wondered if any of them had, while identifying themselves to the woman, paid attention to the two boys standing on the bus's steps.

With hair as bright red as Grace's, they looked younger than their ages...and at the same time so much older because their faces were long with the painful emotions of losing their parents so suddenly. They held hands, the younger boy having a death grip on the older one's hand. The younger boy's lower lip trembled, but the other one kept his head high in defiance of the circumstances that had brought them across the continent, far from home and friends.

Trouble, Joel thought as he recognized the older boy's expression. *They're scared, and they don't think they've got anything left to lose because they don't have anyone but each other.*

"I'm Rhonda Thorne from the Child and Family Services Division of the Montana Department of Public Health and Human Services," the woman was saying with a tired smile. "All that long title means is that I'm the social worker assigned to Brandon and Wesley Coffman." She motioned for the boys to step out of the bus.

For a moment, Joel thought they were going to refuse. He understood that reaction all too well. When he'd been taken to prison, he'd been reluctant to leave the van, knowing once he did, his life was going to change in ways he couldn't imagine, but already feared.

Rhonda said, "It's okay, boys. This is our stop."

The boys edged down one step at a time, their freckles becoming more visible as they emerged into the sunlight. Joel wished he could tell them it would be all right, but he knew the last thing the boys needed were empty platitudes. How could everything be all right when their lives had been up-ended?

Either the social worker hadn't read the boys' reactions, or she was trying her best to make the situation as comfortable as possible. She put an arm around the taller boy's shoulders, which he shrugged off. "This is Brandon." She didn't try to embrace the younger boy who'd stepped closer to his brother. "And this is Wesley. Boys, these are your grandparents and your aunt. Don't you want to say 'hi'?"

Wesley said, "H-h-hi" before looking at his brother guiltily.

Joel wondered if the brothers had made a pact to act as if they didn't care so nobody could guess how scared they were. Such an agreement would make everything more difficult. That was something he'd learned the hard way after he and Samuel had followed the plans they'd made with Adam to flee Bliss Valley. Acting like something or someone you aren't was a recipe for disaster.

Saretta reached to give the boys a hug, but they edged aside. Her lined face crumbled, and Joel had to bite back the words burning on his tongue. Didn't the boys realize how much they needed their grandparents and how much their grandparents needed them as they shared mutual grief?

He wasn't surprised when Grace stuttered with her strong emotion as she said, "I'm your *a-a-aenti* Gr-Gr-Grace."

"She talks funny. Like you, Wesley. Remember?" Brandon shot Grace a superior smile. "*Daed* said she couldn't get out two words in a row when she's upset, and she's upset we got dumped on her."

Color flashed up Grace's face, and Wesley hung his head again.

Joel stepped forward, driven by his annoyance at how Brandon had thrown Grace's welcome into her face. "Congratulations, Brandon."

"Congratulations?" the boy repeated. "For what?"

"Being able to insult and hurt two people who care about you at the same time."

Brandon stared at him, shocked, while his brother raised his eyes enough to meet Joel's before looking away. In that moment, Joel caught the sight of Wesley's gratitude that someone had defended him against his brother's harsh words.

Grace said softly, "Joel, it's all right. They're tired."

Her parents glowered at him. Had he ruined his chance to get a decent job because he'd come to Grace's and Wesley's defense against the boy's overbearing brother?

When no one else spoke, Grace asked the boys to point out their bags. She then asked Joel to help them with the two backpacks and large suitcase while she handled the paperwork with the social worker.

Both boys looked at him with suspicion as he lifted their heavy suitcase.

"I'll be extra careful with it," he said.

"You'd better be." Brandon's voice was taut. "*Mamm*'s Bible is in there. It's ours to take care of now."

"We'll put that suitcase," Grace said quietly, "where you can keep your eyes on it on the way back to the farm. All right?"

Reluctantly, the boy said, "All right."

Motioning with his head toward the street where the transport van had been waiting, Joel said, "This way."

He was relieved when Brandon and Wesley followed him without comment. Shooting a glance over his shoulder, he saw Grace's parents trailing after them as Saretta tried to keep the umbrella over both their heads and Mr. Coffman edged away until the heat drove him back under it. The whole parade would have been amusing if the situation wasn't so tense.

Helping Wesley and Saretta into the van, Joel wasn't offended when neither Brandon nor Mr. Coffman wanted his assistance. He stood to one side where he could jump forward to catch them if they stumbled while climbing into the van. The boys claimed the back, and their grandparents selected the middle bench. That left the seat behind the driver for him and Grace.

Joel sighed. They'd had a bit of privacy on the way into Lancaster, but on the way to Bliss Valley, four pairs of eyes would be focused on them, keeping them from having any opportunity to talk honestly.

"All set," Grace said in a cheerful chirp as she let him hand her into the van. She carried a sheaf of papers that she stuffed into her tote after emptying it of water bottles and handing them to the others. When she held one out to him, she asked, "Aren't you getting in?"

"The social worker isn't coming with us?"

"No. I invited her." She turned to smile at her parents and her nephews. "But she needs to get to the airport and catch a flight back..." Her words faded along with her smile.

Joel saw the boys' faces work as they struggled to keep their sudden tears from falling. Grace looked as ready to cry because her commonplace comment had hurt her nephews. He thought of how homesick he'd been during the first weeks after he and Samuel had fled from Bliss Valley. Not that he would have admitted it, but he'd missed *Mamm* and his sisters so much he suffered a physical ache each time he'd thought of them.

The ride to the Coffmans' farm consisted of Grace trying to begin a conversation, and each attempt failing after one or two responses. Joel knew he wasn't the only one to be relieved when the van pulled into their farm lane. He was surprised, however, when after they'd emerged from the van, Mr. Coffman asked him to take the big suitcase into the house.

"Then," the old man said, his hand shaking so hard by his side it was almost a blur, "have Grace show you the *dawdi haus* while we get the boys settled."

"All right," he said, wondering when Grace had told her father that she'd offered him the job and he'd accepted.

Joel carried the bag to an upstairs bedroom where two double beds were covered with bright quilts. Two dressers were set on either side of a mounted deer head with a large array of antlers. Rag rugs were scattered across the glistening hardwood floor. He wondered if the boys' *daed* used to sleep in the room.

Not wanting to be in the way when the Coffmans introduced the boys to the house, he hurried down to the kitchen. Grace was waiting there. Without a word, she turned and walked toward a door leading into a combined larder and laundry. Another door was at the far end of the long, narrow room. When she opened it, he followed her through, not bothering to pause and check out the cans of vegetables and fruit on the shelves running the length of the larder.

On the far side of a breezeway, Grace pushed aside another door. "Here's the *dawdi haus*."

He didn't go in. "How did your father know you'd hired me?"

"Apparently his hearing is as *gut* as ever. Age and Parkinson's hasn't affected that." She gave him a quick grin. "We never were able to slip anything past him."

"And he's okay with you hiring me?"

"He must be if he told me to show you the *dawdi haus*." She gestured for him to enter, then walked into the shadowed space. She opened the dark green shades on two windows.

Sunlight washed into the room and onto an ancient brown-plaid sofa covered with a blue afghan. Another chair with the same tired looking upholstery faced it across a low table. A propane lamp hung from the ceiling, and a picture of a bluebird done in a childish hand hung on the wall. Next to the windows was a simple kitchen with a refrigerator, a two-burner stove and sink even older than the furniture.

"This is nice," he said.

"It is. *Mamm* was beginning to fix it so she and *Daed* could move in after I married." She sighed, then went on, "I know *Daed*'s worried *Mamm* will be overwhelmed by having two young boys in the house, especially two young boys who've lost their parents."

"And he's worried about you, too."

"I know."

"And everyone's worried about having me around." He wanted to take back the words as soon as they left his mouth because Grace's brows shot up in astonishment.

"What do you mean?"

Deciding he might as well explain, he said, "Eddie Mishler told me to stay away from his farm. He's gotten it in his head that I've been skulking around it and am a danger to my sister."

"Eddie Mishler needs to think before he opens his mouth." She clapped her palm over her own mouth.

He reached over and took her wrist, lowering her hand. He cradled it for a moment in his hand, then released it before he couldn't keep his fingers from exploring the soft skin on the inside of her wrist. "You shouldn't ever keep yourself from speaking the truth."

Though she looked ready to disagree with him, she nodded before saying as if there hadn't been any break in their conversation about the *dawdi haus*, "The bedroom and bath are through there." She pointed at the only other door in the room. "The sheets and towels are in a cupboard inside. I've tried to keep them aired out, so they should be ready."

"I'll move in tomorrow. I can see you're going to need some help."

"Danki."

He hesitated, then asked, "Is it okay that I move in?"

"Of course it is. I can see Wesley likes you already." She sighed as she opened a window to let fresh air into the space. "More than he does the rest of us."

"The rest of you remind him of the family he's lost." He glanced down at himself. "He thinks I'm an *Englischer*, so he sees me differently."

"No. It was because you stood up for him."

"An *Englisch* thing to do."

With a sigh, she nodded. "That's true, but it's not easy being the youngest when your older siblings think they can boss you around and assume they know more than you ever will." She wrapped her arms around herself. "I hope Brandon isn't a bully."

"I think he's a scared kid."

"But aren't most bullies scared kids who don't want others to know they're afraid?"

Was she talking about Brandon, or was she talking about him? Joel didn't want to ask because he wasn't sure he'd like the answer. Had he and his friends been scared kids when they started bullying Laurene and Naomi? He hadn't considered that. If anyone had asked him, he would have said they were just boys being boys.

But what if it hadn't been?

Grace's sweet voice explaining how he'd need to strike a match to start the kitchen stove broke into his disconcerting thoughts. He listened to her, but the idea she'd planted in his mind wasn't one he could forget.

After she'd finished, Joel said, "I owe you and the rest of

your family an apology. I shouldn't have scolded Brandon as I did."

"No, you shouldn't have." The faintest hint of a smile played along her lips. "Though he deserved it for picking on Wesley." She became somber again. "I can't help wondering if Brandon always treats his little brother so...poorly."

"Cruelly is the word you're looking for."

She shook her head. "Cruel is too harsh a word to describe a boy who has suffered as much as Brandon has in the past few weeks. He's lost his *daed* and his *mamm*, and now he's lost the only home he's ever known. He's angry and he's afraid. Who can blame him?"

Joel shrugged. Anger was something he understood too well. In fact, he couldn't think of a time when he hadn't been angry. First at his *daed*, then the whole world. He'd thought he'd put that rage in the past, but it'd seeped out today to lash at Brandon.

As Wyman Beachy had at him.

I don't want to be like my daed. *I don't want to become him.* The words clanged through his head, a death knell for his assumption that he would be a better man than Wyman Beachy.

Lord, help me.

Long after Joel had returned to *Grossdawdi* Ephraim's farm for one last night and everyone else had gone to bed, Grace dropped into a chair in the living room. Her parents had gone to their room as soon as the boys had quieted down. Were any of them asleep? She was exhausted, but if she got into bed, she doubted she'd be able to close her eyes for more than a few seconds. Too many thoughts raced through her head, bumping into each other and sending some careening off in unexpected directions.

Supper had alternated between strained silence and frenetic attempts by the whole family, including the boys, to act as if their visit was a normal one. *Mamm* seemed overpowered by the idea of having two youngsters in the house. More than once while the boys were brushing their teeth, she'd told Grace she wasn't sure if she was up to handling two such spirited *kinder*.

Grace had resisted replying she thought her nephews were being subdued. *Mamm*—and *Daed*—must recall how uproarious her older brothers had been. The walls had rung with the sounds of laughter and their teasing. She could remember several times when they'd wrestled like a litter of gigantic puppies in the living room, threatening the furniture and even the propane lamp that hung from the ceiling.

She closed her eyes as she sank into the chair. Maybe those memories were plaguing *Mamm* more than her *kins-kinder*'s volatile mood shifts. Fritz had always been in the midst of the fun, goading on his brothers to join him. If none of them took the bait, he'd drawn Grace into his games. He'd been gentler with her, but they'd always ended up laughing and covered with grass stains from running around the yard.

Tears seeped from the corners of her eyes, and she wiped them away. She missed all her siblings, but Fritz had always held a special place in her heart.

"I'll make sure they laugh, too, Fritz," she whispered. "I'll find a way to do that as you did with me."

A knock kept her from having to determine how she would follow through on that pledge. She glanced at the clock on the kitchen stove. It was almost ten o'clock. Who was calling at such an hour?

She shuddered as she jumped to her feet even as she was praying it wasn't someone bringing more bad news. She wasn't sure she could handle any more this week.

Opening the door, Grace felt her dread slip from her shoulders as she exclaimed, "Pepper! What are you doing here so late?"

"I figured you could use someone to talk to about now, and it took me longer than usual to get Christiana to sleep tonight. She decided she'd rather play with me and Cameron all night. He'll deal with her if she wakes up, but I think she's good for the night." She stepped into the kitchen and held out a covered bowl. "For you and your family. So you don't have to cook tomorrow."

"*Danki.*" She raised the lid and took a sniff. Aromas of chicken and garlic delighted her senses. "Oh, that smells amazing. Is it *ko-pia*?"

"I know how your dad adores *Pog*'s chicken noodle soup." She smiled as Grace motioned for her to sit at the table. "I hope your nephews will, too. How are they doing?"

"So far, they've eaten everything put in front of them." She carried the bowl to the refrigerator and shifted things inside to make room for the gift from Pepper's *grossmammi*. "But they're so sad I don't think we've seen a hint of their real personalities yet."

"Give them time. *Pog* talks about how strange it was when she first arrived here as a child. Everything was different, even the weather. She didn't recognize anything but the grass and the stones. She prepared meals like she had in the refugee camp. They didn't taste right because the ingredients weren't the same. She felt like she'd gone to another planet until the day she met Hli. Hli was also Hmong and trying to find something or someone familiar, too. They became best friends and saw each other every day until Hli died about fifteen years ago."

"But the boys," she argued, careful not to say their names in case they weren't asleep, "are with family. It shouldn't seem as strange to them as it did to your *grossmammi*."

"Really?" Pepper leaned her elbows on the table and propped her chin on her palms. "I know you're related, but when was the last time you saw them?"

Grace poured two glasses of cold *millich*. "Today was the *first* time. They don't know any of us, and Bliss Valley doesn't look like Rexford, Montana. Tiffany showed me pictures on her phone one time when I mentioned my brother and his family lived there."

"Tiffany, ugh!"

"Is she giving you trouble again?"

Pepper leaned her elbows on the table. "She's insisting our quilts should be priced for less because they aren't plain quilts."

"Not plain? Has she ever looked at you and the *kapp* you wear?" She put the *millich* in the fridge.

"You know she doesn't pay any attention to anything but the bottom line." She sighed. "What do you think, Grace? Should we change our quilts?"

"No. Your quilts are popular with our customers, especially those who want something a bit different." She set the glasses on the table. "Tiffany is complaining about everything because she's wrapped up in her plans for the second store. Don't pay her any attention."

"I wish I could." Pepper picked up one glass and took a reflective sip. "Okay, I'll try. God tells us to think the best of each other, and I need to try to do that with Tiffany."

"That's what I try to do, too." She sat.

"How's it working out for you?"

Grace laughed. "Don't ask."

"I won't." After another sip, she said, "So tell me about Montana."

"The pictures showed big mountains and a huge lake and trees everywhere."

"So for the boys, Bliss Valley feels as different as it did when

Pog came here. And, like *Pog*, the boys must be exhausted from the long trip."

"They've left so much of their lives behind in Montana." Lifting her own glass, she set it down untasted. "How can we ever fill the empty places in their lives?"

"You can't. Nothing can, but you can help them build new connections here. You can't find those connections for them. Just make sure they take advantage of any connections when they become available, as *Pog* and Hli did."

"They were blessed to find each other."

Pepper reached across the table and took Grace's hands in hers. "As your nephews are blessed to have you. God asks us to treat one another as we pray we'll be treated. Tend to them and love them and be there for them as if God brought them first to you instead of your brother and his wife. They are *yours* now, Grace, brought into your life by tragedy. You know about tragedy, so share with them what you've learned."

"I haven't learned much. I don't know how to handle it." Her voice was barely a squeak.

"You've learned enough to know grief isn't a simple one-two-three step process down a straight path. It moves backward and forward and to the side. I discovered that when *Yawg* died."

Grace nodded. Pepper had been close to her *grossdawdi*, and the old man, who had been almost blind and nearly deaf when he died, had been kind to everyone he met. "I remember how sad you were. He was a *gut* man."

"I thought the worst of my grief was gone within a year, but it keeps coming back again and again." A sad smile raced across her lips before she took a deep drink of her *millich* and then wiped its white remnants off her upper lip. "When Christiana was born and I saw her head was bald as *Yawg*'s had been, I wept. I told Cameron they were tears of joy because

I didn't want to ruin his excitement with his new daughter. But I was wishing *Yawg* could be there to love and spoil her as he loved and spoiled me."

"Little things sneak up on us and bring back our grief, ain't so?"

"You understand, so you can help your nephews, too."

"You make it sound simple."

"It's simple." Pepper's smile returned. "It just isn't easy."

"I get that."

Standing, her friend said, "I know you do. Don't forget you're not alone. You can reach out and let us know when you need a shoulder to lean on." Giving Grace a quick hug, she said, "Don't forget that! You're great about helping others, but you're lousy about accepting others' help. One of these days, you're going to figure out you don't have to do it all by yourself."

Pepper didn't give Grace a chance to argue before, with a quick wave, she hurried out the door.

It was just as well, because Grace couldn't have said anything other than her friend was right and Grace had no idea how to change when so many people depended on her.

Chapter Eleven

Putting Pepper's *gut* advice to practical use the next morning wasn't simple. Brandon had woken in an uncooperative mood. He would have argued with her or her parents if any of them had said the sun rose in the east. On top of him being disagreeable, he made sure his brother didn't consent to anything she or her parents suggested. Even when Grace offered them cinnamon buns that she'd made last night before going to bed, Brandon had refused and then complained how the oven had made the kitchen unbearably hot.

Wesley had licked his lips when his gaze focused on the icing sliding down the sides of the buns. She slipped him one when his brother wasn't looking before they went to explore the barns and the garden.

"He's really a *gut* boy," *Daed* said as he sat in the chair she'd brought onto the back porch so he could keep an eye on his *kins-kinder*.

"They both are."

"I hope they will be." *Daed* closed his eyes and ran his fingers through his long beard. "Fritz was such a well-behaved boy."

Grace bit her lip to keep from reminding him of all the times years ago when he'd lamented how her oldest brother would turn his hair gray with his mischief. School was starting later in the week, and that would give Brandon and Wesley something to think about other than their horrendous loss. *Daed* had already alerted the school board that the boys would be joining the other scholars at the schoolhouse that was less than a half mile along the road.

Uneasy about going to work when her parents would be left with the boys who didn't know them, Grace didn't have any choice. Tiffany had insisted she must come in that morning.

"I'm asking for only a day off," Grace had said when she asked for time to get the boys settled.

"No." Tiffany had replied with her most uppity tone, the one she used whenever Grace made sense, but her boss didn't want to admit it. "You're asking for a day and a half off. You know how thin I'm stretched right now, Grace. It's selfish of you to ask."

Grace hadn't been able to figure out then—or now—what was selfish about wanting to help her family, but she'd given up. If the conversation had continued, Tiffany would pull out one of her threats that she'd happily find someone more reliable to take Grace's job. Though Grace doubted Tiffany would be able to replace her quickly, she knew Tiffany would fire her.

Losing her job would be disastrous. Instead of three mouths to feed, she had six, including Joel. Why hadn't she considered the ramifications when she offered him the job? Having him work at the farm locked her more tightly into Tiffany's snare where even the most reasonable request was met with a sneer and derision along with the suggestion that Grace soon would be applying for unemployment. Reminding Tiffany the

Amish didn't ask for any sort of government stipend might make matters worse, because Grace suspected from Tiffany's grumbling about the costs of the second shop that her boss kept her on because she didn't want her unemployment insurance costs to go higher. She left instructions for her parents to call the quilt shop if they needed her help with their *kins-kinder*.

Pondering how complicated her life had gotten in such a short time, Grace was in a grim mood by the time she parked the buggy behind The Amish Quilt Emporium. She went in through the back door and stood, drinking in the quiet and the serenity of a place filled with beauty and creativity.

She always liked the minutes before the quilt shop opened, but today she was especially grateful Tiffany had decided to focus on her new shop. Nobody was in the Strasburg shop, where Grace was surrounded by beautiful colors and patterns. The scent of ironed cotton lingered in the air, fresh and clean and filled with possibilities.

"I need possibilities," she said to herself. Saying her thoughts aloud was another reason she enjoyed the peace that would end when people came in to look through the quilts and ask questions about how they were made.

Grace left her lunch in the small fridge, her bonnet on a peg and turned on the lights. She checked the cash register and counted the cash to make sure it was the same as the amount Tiffany had written on a slip and put inside. Many mornings, the numbers weren't the same because often Tiffany didn't bother to double-check her math, so Grace was grateful they matched.

After running a dust cloth over the counter and the shelves behind it, she checked that the quilts were displayed properly. Those were tasks she usually handled after closing. With having to leave early yesterday to pick up the boys, she didn't trust Tiffany had paid attention to details.

Glad she'd taken the time to make sure everything was where it should be, Grace moved two quilts from the sales rack at the rear of the store to the rack at the front where they should be displayed as the latest arrivals. She recognized them both as the quilts Pepper had brought in the day Joel first came into the shop. They had the unique swirls in the quilting Pepper said the Hmong called a snail-shell pattern.

Policy was that quilts were given sixty days to sell before they were discounted. These had been here only a few days. She checked other quilts on the discount rail, but nothing else had been put there by mistake. Why had Tiffany set them on the sales rack?

Grace grimaced. Most likely, a customer had returned them to the wrong spot. Tiffany hated checking the merchandise at the end of each day to make sure everything was in the proper place. In fact, Tiffany hated everything about running a shop except the chance to be the gracious hostess to the customers who were willing to pay through the nose for handstitched quilts. She must expect to sell more of the higher priced ones in Lititz, because she'd leased space among the fancy boutiques and antique shops on Main Street, not far from the Bulls Head Public House where tourists liked to congregate.

As she rolled up the shades on the front windows, Grace saw Rosemary Mishler pause on the street, then walk toward the door. Grace threw it open and stepped back to let Joel's sister enter.

"Rosemary, I didn't expect to see you. You dropped off your latest quilt last week." She went to the counter and reached under it for the consignment ledger. "We haven't sold any more of your quilts, but let me check—"

"Don't bother." Rosemary set her black purse on the counter, then leaned her hands on the edge. "I'm not here about quilts. I'm here about Joel."

Closing the consignment ledger, Grace folded her hands on top of it. It was the only way to keep them from shaking as she asked, "What about him?"

"I'd like to see him, but he's avoiding me."

"I don't think he is."

"If he's not avoiding me, why hasn't he visited me at our farm?"

Grace kept her eyes on the quilts in front of her. "Maybe because he's listened to what your husband had to say after Joel came back."

"Eddie? You know he jokes around a lot."

"I don't think he was joking and I doubt Joel was laughing when Eddie told him to stay far away from your farm."

"That can't be."

She nodded. "*Ja.* Joel told me about it yesterday after we went to Lancaster to pick up my nephews. He was upset about what Eddie said."

Rosemary sighed. "I was afraid of this. Eddie's been on edge since he found out Joel had come back. He's trying to protect me."

"From your own brother?"

"*Ja.* We've had arguments about it every day since I told him that I'd seen Joel here. I want to talk to my brother. We used to be close, but I haven't heard a single word from him since he jumped the fence. When Samuel returned, I asked him about what their lives had been like and where I might be able to contact Joel. Samuel couldn't tell me much because he had no idea where Joel was by then. He did say they'd had a hard time adjusting to the *Englisch* world and he was worried about how Joel would do on his own."

Grace glanced past Rosemary as two women peered into the window. She didn't want to cut their discussion short, but if customers came in, she would have to interrupt Rosemary.

She was relieved when the women turned and pushed the button to activate the walk signal at the intersection.

She started to speak, but Rosemary kept talking. "It's clear now Samuel was right to worry. Joel messed up his life, and it's affecting all of us. Eddie has insisted no jailbird—that's what he keeps calling my brother—will step as much as a toe on our farm. He keeps saying Joel must be hiding plenty of things he hasn't told us, things he's done that are far worse than what he admits he did."

"What could be worse than being sent to prison?" She leaned her hands on the counter and frowned. "You know your brother, Rosemary. He made a mistake, and he's paid for it. To keep punishing him is wrong, and to assume he's done other crimes is to judge him. That's God's job, not ours."

With a shrug, Rosemary spread her fingers across the counter, stretching them out as far as they could reach before drawing them closed in a frustrated fist. "I don't know what Eddie's talking about, but whenever I say that we need to talk to my brother, he keeps saying Joel has to be hiding things he doesn't want us to know."

"Sounds like Eddie might be hiding something and is putting his guilt on your brother."

"I thought about that, too, but Eddie's always been honest with me. He's worried if I let Joel back into my life, I'm going to end up hurt more than I was when he left."

Grace reached across the counter and put her hand on her friend's. Rosemary was almost two years younger than she was, but they'd been friends when they were scholars. That had changed after Grace left school at fourteen. Since then, they'd chatted each time they ran into each other. Yet it hadn't been the same as when they'd gone to school together, especially since Rosemary married Eddie. Like too many others, Rosemary had acted as if Grace must begrudge other newlyweds their happiness because hers had been snatched from her when Lamar died.

Never would Grace have done that. She loved seeing those she cared about happy. She prayed for the same for her battered heart.

"Why don't you meet him here?" Grace asked. "If you don't want anyone else around, I can arrange for you to use the back room either before the shop opens or after we close."

Her lips tightened. "I can't."

"Why not?" She was startled because she'd thought her idea would solve the problem of Eddie refusing to let his wife speak with her brother at home.

"Don't ask, Grace. It's not your business. It's Joel's."

"Maybe you haven't heard, but I hired him to help at our farm. Would any of Joel's *business* keep him from doing a *gut* job for us?" She regretted the sarcastic emphasis she'd put on the single word. Rosemary was a friend...or she had been until she'd seen her brother leaving the shop.

Rosemary drew back at Grace's tone. Before Grace could apologize, Rosemary did. "I'm sorry. You're asking reasonable questions, Grace. The situation hasn't been reasonable for as long as I can remember."

"I'm sorry, too."

"You gave Joel a job?" Rosemary had regained her composure. "Why? I'd heard he was working with Adam Hershberger."

"He was, but he felt like Adam was giving him a handout instead of real work. Not knowing anything about repairing engines, Joel was pretty much consigned to sweeping up the place at the end of the day. He wants a real job. He'd tried to get work at the construction up on Route 30, but as soon as he reached the question about being convicted for a crime, the interview was over."

"So he's working for you now? How is that different from Adam giving him a job?"

Grace explained how, with the arrival of the boys, they needed more help on the farm. She didn't go into details about her parents' health. Rosemary saw them on church Sundays, so she was familiar with their slow deterioration.

"Okay," Rosemary said, "I see now. *Danki* for offering Joel the chance to work on your farm. It solves two problems. You need help, and I need Joel to stay in Bliss Valley until..."

"Until?" prompted Grace when her friend's voice drifted away.

"Until we work things out." She cleared her throat, then said, "With our family."

"Do you think you can?"

Again Rosemary sighed. "I think I can come to a compromise that will allow me to talk to my brother again, but I don't know if either Joel or Eddie can." Her voice dropped to almost a whisper. "Or if *Daed* will be interested in trying."

"Is it because Joel is adopted?"

She shook her head. "I don't think so. From what *Mamm* says, *Daed* and Joel were close when we were small, but things changed soon after Joel began school. *Daed* pushed him to do better than everyone else, and *Daed* never hid when he was disappointed in Joel's work."

"So nothing Joel did pleased him?"

"It got to that point. I'm not sure why. At first, from what *Mamm*'s said, Joel did well in school and was well-behaved. That changed. Joel changed. *Daed* changed. So much anger must have altered them, though I can't understand why they didn't work out their differences." Her mouth twisted into a caricature of a smile. "*Daed* and Joel are both stubborn." Her smile disappeared. "Y'know one thing, Grace?"

"What's that?" she asked, her heart aching for the whole Beachy family who'd let harsh words drive them apart.

"I can't believe Joel was selling drugs. *Ja*, he got himself in trouble when he was a kid. Mischief types of things, not real crimes. Nothing that would hurt anyone. Why would he turn to a crime that ruins people's lives?"

"I don't know." She didn't add it was a piece of the puzzle she couldn't reconcile with the man she'd come to know. No matter how she looked at Joel and his past, his being a drug dealer—albeit a reformed one—didn't fit.

Eddie Mishler might be right. There were things Joel hadn't told about that part of his life. She'd tried to look past them, but she wondered if she could any longer.

Joel had caught a ride with Adam into Strasburg to go to the hardware store about a mile north of the town center. He needed to pick up some white exterior paint to begin painting the fence and the smaller outbuildings on the Coffmans' farm. It was too late in the year to tackle a massive paint job like the main barn or the house. That would have to wait until spring.

Carrying the paint and the supplies he'd need, he walked toward the center of the town. Clouds were building up to the west, and he wondered if it would rain every time he came into Strasburg. Chuckling to himself, he crossed the road by the ice cream shop and went around to the back of the quilt shop. He was pleased to see Grace's buggy there with Pearl waiting in the shade in a small paddock. After putting the cans of paint and the bag of brushes in the back of the buggy, he reached over the wood fence to give the horse a pat and make sure there was plenty of water in the trough.

The shop was busy when he walked through the front door. Grace was the eye of the storm, a serene spot while a dozen customers swirled around her, calling out questions to each other and to her. She answered with a smile as she returned quilts that had been viewed but not bought to their proper places. When a customer selected a quilt, she rang up the sale without any hint of hurry, taking time to talk to the customer about how to clean her new quilt and sharing information about the pattern and the woman who'd made it.

Stepping into the spot near the window where he'd stood the first time he entered The Amish Quilt Emporium, he watched her orchestrate a beautiful symphony of warmth and competence. Ten minutes after he'd come in, the last of the women were rushing out the door to join the rest of their tour group in an extended van. He closed the door behind them, but they were so busy talking about their purchases they didn't notice him.

"Is it always like this?" Joel asked as he crossed the store to where Grace was rehanging two quilts in bright shades of reds and blues complemented by darker bindings along the edges.

"*Ja*, when we get a tour group." She smiled as she held up a quilt, but he saw the shadows in her eyes and guessed her thoughts were on her nephews and her parents. He couldn't blame her. They'd claimed too much space in his head all day. "Grab the other end, will you?"

He did and helped as she folded it. Taking it from her, he followed her instructions on how to hang it over a wooden dowel sticking out from the wall.

"*Danki*. The king-size quilts are a challenge," she said as she put a pair of wall hangings onto a shelf with others. Without a pause, she asked, "Are you all moved into the *dawdi haus*?"

"It doesn't take long to unpack when you don't have much." He grimaced. "Sorry. I didn't mean that the way it sounded. I'm not complaining. The *dawdi haus* is nicer than anywhere I've lived in years."

"It's not much. Three rooms."

"It feels like a castle to me."

She laughed while she returned to the counter and began sorting the receipts from the afternoon's sales. "You have low expectations for a castle. I didn't expect to see you in town this afternoon. I assumed *Daed* would put you to work."

"I needed to pick up paint and brushes." He motioned toward the back of the shop. "I left them in the buggy."

"What about clothes while you're painting?"

He shrugged. "I hadn't thought about that. I guess I should go to a thrift store and buy some clothes to wear."

"*Mamm* told me this morning she p-p-plans to make you some p-p-plain clothing." She gripped the edge of the counter, a sure sign that she was uneasy about what she was saying.

He wondered if she'd always worried more about other people's feelings than her own. No wonder she stuttered when she was anxious. If she fretted that every word she said could hurt someone else, she'd have to fight to get each one out.

"She doesn't need to."

"Sh-sh-she wants to." She took a deep breath and got her voice under control. "But you don't have to wear them if it makes you uncomfortable."

"Plain clothing is sensible for the work I'm doing, but wearing it might give people the wrong idea."

"Like you're thinking of returning?"

He nodded.

"Are you?"

"You never ask the easy questions, do you?"

She folded her arms in front of her and arched her brows. "No, because nobody ever asks me the easy questions."

"And do you like it when they ask you the tough ones?"

"You're trying to change the subject. Are you thinking of returning?"

"Thinking? I've always thought about it, but I've never

considered doing it. You know as well as I do that it would cause an uproar in the district and beyond. Everyone would be talking about the district that welcomed a felon back among them."

"Do you care what others say? You caused trouble throughout the community and among *Englischers*. You left your plain life and Bliss Valley despite knowing it would w-w-wound your f-f-family."

He frowned at the subtle shift in her voice. "My family? What about them?"

Color flashed up her cheeks. "Your sister was in here today."

"Which one?"

"Rosemary. She wants to see you."

"Her husband—"

"She knows what he's said, but that doesn't change anything." She met his eyes steadily. "She misses you, Joel. I think she told me that because she was hoping I'd tell you."

He was shocked at how glad he was to hear that. He and Rosemary had been close before he jumped the fence. Though she was almost six years younger, as soon as she could toddle, Rosemary had tagged along after him like a faithful puppy. They'd shared taking care of their younger sisters and other chores around the farm. When *Daed* had said something outrageous and hurtful to Joel, Rosemary was always the first one to comfort him with a hug or a silly story that got him to smile again. As horrid as his childhood had been, it would have been worse if his sister hadn't been there.

"There's one more thing," Grace said when he didn't answer. "I need to ask you something I should have a long time ago. Talking with Rosemary reminded me."

He went on high alert. "What have you been intending to ask me? Was it if I did do what the cops said I did? Is that what you're going to ask?"

"No."

"No?" he repeated dumbfounded, his automatic defenses shattering as she went on in a hurt voice. Hurt because he'd thought the worst of her, he realized.

"Do you think I would have asked you to come to work on our farm, knowing you'll be spending time with my nephews if I thought you'd be a bad influence on them?"

"As you've told me, you're in dire straits balancing your job at the quilt shop and with your parents depending on you. Now you've got two kids to take care of as well." He sighed and glanced around the shop before returning his gaze to her pretty face. "Desperate people do desperate things. How many times have we heard people say that? Are you desperate enough to hire a former jailbird when you can't find anyone else who can step in to help?"

"Are you done?"

He frowned. He hadn't expected *that* question either. After the cold shoulder he'd gotten from the construction companies, he'd assumed she would have demanded some sort of reassurance he'd be on his best behavior.

No, Grace never demanded anything. She quietly found ways for those around her to do as she needed them to.

When he didn't answer, she said, "If I didn't know better, I'd believe you're doing everything you can to talk me into firing you. I thought you were excited about the job."

"I am."

"So why are you acting as if *you* are the desperate one? Desperate to find a way not to take the job on our farm. If you don't want to work there any longer, just say so." She drew a ledger from beneath the counter and turned it to an empty page, but she didn't pick up a pen to enter the sales into it.

How had the conversation taken such a ridiculous turn? He wanted the job. He was grateful for it and for Grace and her family—despite their reluctance, or maybe *because* of it—giving him the chance to prove he was more than his reputation.

Then he realized she was confused and trying to find an explanation about his ludicrous behavior and words for one reason.

He'd never told her the truth.

"Grace?"

"Ja?" She didn't look up from the ledger. Was she reading it or hoping he'd take a hint and leave?

A pang was sharp against his heart at the thought. Everyone in Bliss Valley seemed eager for him to move along. Everyone but Grace. She'd taken the time to listen to him, to get to know him, to let him be himself instead of the criminal everybody considered him to be. Her kindness could have endangered her as Eddie believed it would Rosemary and his other sisters, but she hadn't hesitated. She'd looked inside him, her clear eyes seeing into his heart and discovering the man he might have been if he'd made different decisions.

"I didn't do it."

"What?" She looked up at him. "What didn't you do?"

"Sell drugs."

"You didn't?"

He gasped aloud. She'd been so kind to him, making sure he had enough to eat and bringing him into her home by offering him a job, and she hadn't been sure if he was guilty or not. He was overpowered by an emotion he couldn't name, but it was a mixture of disbelief and gratitude and determination to make sure he paid her back somehow. He didn't have the slightest idea how, and he guessed she would urge him to put his faith in someone else as she had in him.

Could he? He wasn't sure. While he had faith in God, though he stayed distant, having faith in other human beings was impossible after what he'd seen and experienced.

But she lost her fiancé and her brother and sister-in-law, and she still has faith everything will turn out for the best.

He marveled again at the strength compacted into her petite form. If he could have been half as strong and stood up to *Daed*'s preposterous demands, how differently would his life have turned out? It was too late now to wonder about that.

"Grace," he said, "I didn't sell drugs as they said I did. I never would have used other people's misery to make money. I did some low things, Grace, but nothing like that."

"So why were you arrested?"

"Because there were drugs in the car. They weren't mine. I didn't even know they were there." He took a deep breath and admitted aloud what he never had before. "I should have known the guys I was with had drugs on them, but at that point, I didn't care. Not about them. Not about myself. Not about anything."

"And now?" She faced him, her expression neutral. He noticed how her fingers shook almost as hard as her *daed*'s did, a sure sign she was trying to stay calm so she didn't upset him further.

When was the last time someone had cared about his feelings? It was sad to realize he didn't know the answer to that question.

"Now," he said, knowing he needed to be honest with her, "I'm trying to relearn how to care."

"But you do care. At least for others. You wouldn't have chided Brandon at the bus station, if you hadn't cared about Wesley's feelings."

"And yours."

"I've heard worse." There weren't any accusations in her voice. She spoke as if it was an irrefutable fact. "Brandon was scared, so he lashed out."

"I get that. I've done the same."

"We all have." She closed the book and stored it under the counter. "We've all said the wrong thing at the wrong time."

"And the right thing at the wrong time."

"Exactly." Walking past him to turn the lock on the front door, she closed the shades before she faced him again. "You already care about others, Joel. The question is if you can care about your own feelings." She met his gaze as her voice dropped to a whisper. "How can you ask for others to respect you when you don't have any respect left for yourself?"

He wished he had an answer to give her. He wished it with all the broken shards of his heart.

Chapter Twelve

Joel stood by the fence that ran the length of the farm lane. It separated the road from the meadow. It was an excellent pasture, lush with grass and slanted enough so the water didn't gather and turn it into a mire. He imagined it with a herd of rusty-red-and-white Hereford beef cattle scattered across it, grazing.

His rusty-red-and-white Hereford beef cattle.

How many times had he sat in his cell, staring at the block walls, while he envisioned such a scene? The cattle were his, a herd he'd bought through the results of his hard work, and he spent his time taking care of them, making sure they were fed and healthy, while he enjoyed being outside in the fresh air. No matter the weather, whether it was sunny or cold and rainy or even with knee-deep snow on the ground, he'd tend to them.

It hadn't happened yet, but he had to believe it was possible. The promise of what could come had kept him sane in prison amid the ongoing insanity surrounding him.

Now he was back in Bliss Valley, and he was wearing the broadfall trousers Grace's *mamm* had had waiting in the *dawdi haus* last night. His fingers had fumbled buttoning them closed. Before he'd left home, he would have buttoned them up without thinking. He'd become too accustomed to zippers. His cotton shirt in a purple that he would never have chosen himself was looser and allowed more air circulation than the T-shirts he was used to. At first, he'd disdained the suspenders lying next to them, but after having to hold on to the waist of his trousers to keep them from dropping, he'd hooked them in place.

Setting the paint can on the ground, he touched his goatee. Did he look as if he was straddling two worlds that had little in common? Like he felt?

He'd waited in the *dawdi haus* until Grace had left for the shop. He wasn't sure if she'd be amused or appalled to see him in such clothing. He'd been astonished how important it had become for her to think well of him. For a moment, he allowed himself the special delight of thinking about her. Her pretty smile, her sparkling green eyes, her fiery hair that he longed to see loose along her back as he let his fingers sift through its rich silk.

Two things hadn't changed since the first time he'd seen her. He still yearned to draw her close and sample her soft lips. Yet, even if he hadn't been a convicted felon, she was plain and he was… He wasn't sure what he was any longer, but even a single kiss would mean something different to Grace than it did to an *Englisch* woman. For an Amish woman, a kiss was a pledge of one's heart.

His fingers tightened around the paintbrush he held as he took a deep, deep breath of the fragrant air. Smells from the neighboring farms and the heat off the asphalt road flavored it.

Cheerful voices reached him, and he noticed a group of scholars walking toward the school building that was hidden by a sharp corner in the road. The same school he'd attended in what seemed like someone else's life. He must once have sounded as carefree as the *kinder* passing this farm on his way to school, but he couldn't recall now. By cutting his connections to Bliss Valley, he'd ripped away so much of his childhood.

Joel pried open the can and stirred its contents before dipping his brush in the thick, white paint. He'd already washed the fence with a dripping sponge, getting rid of spiderwebs as well as debris. It hadn't taken long for the wood to dry in the hot sunshine. The calendar might have turned over to September, but summer wasn't ready to give them any surcease from the heat and humidity.

He hoped it wouldn't be too hot in the small schoolhouse. Grace had driven the boys there today, and Joel was supposed to walk over and meet them at the end of the school day. That was the plan for the next few days, so Brandon and Wesley could get accustomed to going to and from the school. He'd heard Grace talking to her parents last night about buying the boys scooters, so they could use them to get to school as the other *kinder* did.

For the first time he wondered how the Coffmans would afford the costs of raising two boys. Grace had mentioned her brother farmed in Montana, so once the property was sold, there would be money to help. Yet, knowing Grace, he suspected she would try to keep as much in trust for the boys so they would have a nest egg when they were old enough to look for land or a skill of their own. She considered it more than a duty to take care of her family. She considered it a privilege.

It was going to take him some time to adjust to such selflessness. In prison, the motto had seemed to be to get yours before someone else took it away.

"How's the painting going?" asked Grace's *daed* as he came to stand beside Joel.

Trying not to stare at how the old man's body quivered as if he were a metronome counting the tempo for a silent song, Joel said, "It's a fine day for painting. Hot, but not too hot, so the paint should dry quickly, Mr. Coffman."

"Have you forgotten how we do things?" The older man slanted against his cane, holding it with both hands because his left one was shaking so hard.

Joel looked down at the paintbrush he held. Was there a plain way to paint a fence that he'd forgotten? Since he'd returned to Lancaster County, he'd discovered how many small details of plain life had escaped his brain. He'd recalled how it was expected that everyone at the table express their gratitude to God at the beginning of each meal, but he'd forgotten that the same was done at the meal's end.

Another reason to be glad Grace was in his life. When he'd been about to rise from the table to put his dishes in the sink last night, she'd said, "*Mamm* and I always clear the table after we say our prayers to thank God for enjoying this meal together." Her smile had not even looked forced when she added in a playful tone, "You'll get used to the way we do things around here soon enough."

He'd nodded, settling back on the bench beside Wesley. From across the table, Brandon had flashed him a superior look, but Wesley had patted his knee in silent commiseration.

"What way is that?" Joel asked, bending to dip the brush into the can again. It allowed him to hide his disquiet at making yet another mistake.

"We don't use titles. Call me Harold, not Mr. Coffman."

Joel was relieved he'd made such a simple mistake, though he'd made the opposite error when first living among *Englischers*. He'd addressed a lady by her first name and received a stern lecture about the importance of respecting one's elders. "I should have remembered that."

"*Ja*, you should have." His bushy brows lowered. "How long are you planning to stay?"

"I told Grace I would—"

"Not here on the farm. How long are you staying in Bliss Valley?"

"I haven't thought about it."

"Why not?"

Joel wondered if Grace's father had always been so plain-spoken or if his Parkinson's disease had removed any filters he'd once possessed. Grace chose her words with care, eager not to offend anyone, but that might have been a habit she got from her *mamm*. He couldn't recall Saretta ever speaking a negative word about anyone or anything.

"To be honest, I've had other things on my mind," Joel said because he knew the old man expected an answer.

"Like?"

"Finding a job and a place to live."

"You've got both now."

Spreading more paint across the top board of the fence, Joel noted he'd have to cut the grass and weeds that had overgrown the lowest board before he could paint it. He wondered what kind of landscaping tools the Coffmans possessed. Most likely a push mower, but maybe they were among the growing number of plain families in the area who owned a battery-operated mower.

"I do, thanks to your daughter," he replied, smoothing out where a rough spot had caught his brush.

"And now what?"

"I'm painting this fence."

Harold's white brows lowered, and his whole beard seemed to jut in Joel's direction. "Don't give me lip, boy!"

"Sorry." Hadn't he learned that firing back didn't work when he was cornered by someone asking a question he didn't want to answer? Harold had been pleasant to him up until now. A nice surprise, and Joel had ruined it with his answer that sounded as if he were no older than Brandon. "I should have said I'm going to use the time while I'm painting this fence to do some soul-searching."

"Drifting through life means you could end up where the current takes you, and that may be somewhere you don't want to go."

Joel flinched. He knew the older man's words were true. After all, if he hadn't been drifting years ago, he might never have been in the wrong place at the wrong time with the wrong people. If he'd come to his senses and not let his stubborn determination to prove his *daed* was right about his uselessness control him, he would have returned to Bliss Valley when Samuel had.

Could his life have turned out as well as his friends' if he'd come back then? Both Adam and Samuel were happy with their work, their families, the women they loved. They'd turned their lives around while he'd continued to seek ever more ways to destroy his life and self-respect.

He hoped he hadn't lost his one chance to get his life back on even footing. It didn't work that way...or did it? He'd heard sermons over and over about following the path God set out for him, about how there would appear to be forks in that path and how important it was to select the one that would allow him to continue to walk with God. Nobody had ever said what would happen if he chose the wrong way or how to find his way back once he'd left the path God had created for him.

"I know that look," Harold said quietly. "You're playing the what-if game. What if I'd made this decision rather than that one?"

"I didn't realize it was so obvious."

"Only to everyone who's seen that expression in his or her

mirror." Harold folded his arms on a part of the fence that hadn't been painted. "We all have dreams. We all see some of those dreams dashed." He held up one shaking hand. "And there's nothing we can do but to hold on to the dreams within our grasp and be grateful God has given us opportunities and choices."

"Even when we make the wrong choices?"

"Especially when we do." He smiled. "So, Joel, after ten years among *Englischers*, what's your dream now?"

Joel answered with hesitation. "I want to raise beef cattle."

"There's a field." Harold gestured toward the meadow beyond the fence. "It's big enough for a few head."

"You use it for your horse."

"*Ja*, but Pearl's been lonely since we sold our *millich* cows." The old man's voice was so sad that Joel guessed the horse missed the cows far less than Harold did. "There's an auction at the New Holland Sales Stables on Mondays and Thursdays for cattle."

"I should go."

"You should."

Again he thought he heard something beyond what Harold was saying. "Would you like to go, too? You could introduce me to other farmers, so I could pick their brains."

"*Ja*, that would be *gut*. I could let you know which of the men know what they're talking about. Others?" He raised his eyes skyward. "Some like to talk more than they like to learn. Life is about learning something new every day." Cutting his eyes toward Joel, he added, "Like learning that you're not as bad as rumor suggests."

"Nobody can ever be as bad as rumor suggests." He couldn't keep the bitterness out of his voice.

"Maybe."

"Why are you okay with me working here?" He didn't

add he also wanted to ask why Harold had agreed to go with him to the cattle auction, but he assumed the old man was so eager to attend himself he'd use any excuse and any companion to get there.

"Grace says you will work hard because you want to rebuild your life."

"She's right."

"She usually is." He tapped his temple. "That girl has a fine head on her shoulders. Gets her smarts from her *mamm*. Saretta would never tell you this herself, but she was the top scholar in our school every year she attended. I decided if I had any intelligence at all, I should marry the smartest girl. Of course, it didn't hurt she was the prettiest girl, too."

Joel grinned. He almost said Grace resembled her *mamm* in that as well, but wasn't sure how Harold would take his words. Harold had done a complete switch in his opinion of him, and it could revert to his previous distrust as quickly.

"That shows how smart you are," he said, earning another grin from the older man.

"I know you're no fool. Grace wouldn't be trying to help you if she thought you were. God has given you a second chance to come home and redeem your mistakes."

He dunked his brush into the bucket again. "I hope I can. One thing I know for sure is that I need to make wise decisions from now on."

"You don't have to depend on yourself to make decisions. God's always willing to listen when we stand at a crossroads."

"I know," he said, hoping Grace's *daed* didn't guess he was lying. He hadn't stopped reaching out to God because he was ashamed of the turns his life had taken. He'd stopped reaching out because he hadn't seen any sign God was listening to his abject prayers as his life spiraled out of his control.

"You don't sound certain."

Joel was startled. In prison, nobody had cared about him. If he said something, it was either accepted or ignored. Looking beneath someone's words to discern the truth was a skill he'd forgotten, but it was one the Coffmans had honed to an art form, stripping aside his layers of protection to get a clear view of what he tried to keep hidden.

"I'm not," he said. "But I'm trying."

He wasn't sure if Grace's *daed* heard him because Harold said, "You're wearing plain clothing, Joel, but you don't look like a plain man."

"I'm not a plain man."

"You are as God made you. He decided what you'll be before your heart beat for the first time." He grasped Joel's shoulder in a surprisingly strong grip. "It's your choice whether you acquiesce or fight Him every moment of your life. Why would you spend all your days fighting the One who is omnipotent? You can try to hide behind anger and distrust or even a mustache, but what *gut* will it do you when God sees all?" Without another word, he walked away with unsteady steps as he leaned on his cane.

Joel looked from him to his dripping paintbrush. Sticking it in the can, he strode toward the *dawdi haus* and went inside. It took him only moments to splash water on his face and soap up a lather. He rinsed his razor over and over as he ran it along his chin and upper lip. Once he'd cleaned out the sink, he looked into the mirror again and touched his shaven face. He was tired of hiding who he was.

Why would you spend all your days fighting the One who is omnipotent? Harold's wise words filled his mind as he stared at his unfamiliar countenance in the mirror.

He prayed that this decision had been a *gut* one...finally.

★ ★ ★

When Joel walked into the kitchen for their evening meal, Grace almost dropped the plate of sliced bread she was carrying to the table. She'd never imagined he'd look so different without his small beard and the mustache. How could she have let herself be so distracted by his facial hair that she'd failed to notice the square strength of his jaw?

She ducked her head as Brandon said, "Well, look at him! He doesn't have a cat's tail wrapped around his mouth any longer."

"Be nice," *Mamm* chided, but she patted Brandon's shoulder before she set a bowl of apple butter beside the sliced turkey and ham that would fill their sandwiches.

The boy flinched as if she'd struck him, and a hungry expression filled his eyes. Not for the food Grace and *Mamm* had prepared but for something else.

Wesley sidled closer to her and whispered, "That's what *Mamm* used to say to him, too."

Grace took a chance and put her arm around the little boy's narrow shoulders. When he leaned against her—only for a moment—her heart ached with both grief and love. She couldn't imagine the weight of the grief the boys carried. *Ja*, she'd stood by Lamar's coffin and bid him farewell, but she'd been a woman grown. She couldn't imagine suffering such a loss—times two—when she'd been a *kind*.

Joel fingered his face as if he couldn't quite believe he'd shaved off his beard. "I thought I looked rather dashing."

"What's that?" asked Wesley.

"It means he thinks the ladies should fall all over themselves telling him he looks *gut*," Grace replied as she motioned the boys to take their seats on either side of the table.

"Oooo," Brandon said, "you're so pretty."

"So are you." Joel reached across the table and fluffed the boy's hair until it stood straight up. "Now!"

Grace held her breath. How would Brandon react? When her nephews chuckled, she did as well. Lines eased on her parents' faces as they took their seats at the table. The lighter spirits remained with them through the meal, as if everyone was ready to make an effort to push the reality of their shared sorrow away for a few minutes.

God, danki *for touching our hearts with joy when we need it so much.* The prayer rose through her like the trill of the first robin of spring.

She clung to that happiness through the rest of the meal and while she cleaned the kitchen, leaving *Mamm* and *Daed* to chat in the front room. When she came into the living room, she looked around for Joel and the boys.

"They're outside." *Mamm* wore a tired smile, but there was a lightness about her that Grace hadn't seen since the news came of Fritz's and Flossie's deaths.

Grace went onto the porch to find Joel sitting on the rail and the boys playing catch with a large ball at the edge of the shadows growing out from beneath the trees. The sun was setting earlier with each passing day, a sign summer was waning. She frowned when she heard Brandon shout at his brother after Wesley didn't catch the ball and had to chase it.

"Don't worry about everything they do and say," Joel said. "I'm sure you quarreled with your siblings."

"Not that often. I'm so much younger they treated me more like a pet than a sister."

He chuckled. "You don't know what you missed. One time my sisters got so irritated at me that they dumped a whole basket of wet clothes over my head." He gave a fake shiver. "That was a cold dose of reality."

Grace smiled as she walked to the front of the porch and

put her hand on the upright supporting the roof. "I'm happy I missed that." Glancing at him from the corners of her eyes, she said, "But I've noticed something else missing."

He rubbed his chin and said with feigned seriousness. "You're observant."

"It's hard to miss. What made you decide to shave off your mustache and beard?"

"Harold. He got me thinking."

"He has a way of doing that." She sat on the step and watched the boys. "I can't count how many nights during my childhood when I lost hours of sleep because he'd asked me a question I didn't know how to answer. Things like whether it was more important to use your eyes to see the truth or your heart." She laughed before going on. "It took me years before I could think as clearly as he did and could answer one of his questions without having to debate it with myself and with God."

As Wesley chased the ball again, Joel said, "Excuse me." He cleared the porch railing with a single smooth motion. Crossing the yard, he spoke to the boys. Brandon backed away, but Wesley nodded.

Grace locked her fingers around her knee and watched him show Wesley how to hold the ball so he could throw it where he wanted it to go. Neither Joel nor Wesley seemed to notice as Brandon inched closer, wanting to learn the secrets, too. When, as if it were no big deal, Joel tossed Brandon the ball and told him how to throw so the ball would reach his brother, she smiled, relieved.

The sharp words Joel had said to Brandon at the bus station had been heavy on Joel's heart. Now he was encouraging the boys and acting as if the exchange had never happened. For the first time, her nephews were acting like regular kids, enjoying a game of toss and kicking the ball around as they would have with other scholars during recess.

When *Mamm* came out to announce it was time for baths, prayers and bed, both boys grumbled, but grinned when Joel said they'd play catch with a baseball the next evening. They ran past her, Wesley pausing to give her a kiss on the cheek but Brandon never slowing. She knew she should be grateful for sweet favors, though she wished Brandon would trust her a bit more.

Why should he? she asked herself. He didn't know her other than what Fritz might have mentioned about her, and Fritz had seen her as a silly teen the last time he'd been in Bliss Valley.

Joel sat beside her, bouncing the ball on the ground and catching it with ease.

"*Danki* for helping them," she said, trying to pretend as if she wasn't aware of the heat swarming off him after his exertions. It created a responsive warmth within her that urged her to lean her cheek on his shoulder. To cover her own thoughts, she said, "They miss their *mamm* and *daed*."

"I get that."

"Do you?"

"*Ja.*" His brows lowered with his frown. "Of course I miss my family."

"Then why don't you go and see them?"

His fingers tightened on the ball until she feared he'd pop it. "They won't want to see me."

"Are you sure of that?"

His smile held no humor. "Absolutely. My parents aren't like yours, Grace. They don't forget or forgive. Or I should say, my *daed* doesn't."

"Rosemary is eager to see you, but she's not sure how."

"Coming between her and her husband wouldn't be a *gut* idea."

She nodded. "I agree. I wanted you to know she's spoken to me more than once about how she wishes she could speak with you."

His brows lowered even more. "Don't, Grace. Don't get in the middle of something that could blow up in your face."

"Rosemary is my friend. I don't like seeing her upset."

"She chose her side a long time ago." He pushed himself to his feet. Without another word, he went to the door. As he opened it, light spilled out to reveal the regret carved into his face.

She didn't move when he went in and closed the door. That one sight of his face was enough for her to know that, despite his calm words, he longed to return to his family.

There had to be a way to bring his family back together. She wasn't sure how, but she couldn't let him waste more time before reconnecting with his sisters. She'd learned through hard lessons how things could change and everything she'd thought would be hers was snatched away.

She wasn't going to let him make the same mistakes she had.

Chapter Thirteen

Grace found her answer to her problem about how to reunite the Beachy siblings three days later when Laurene Nolt brought a sign into the quilt shop and asked if it could be hung in the window.

"What is it?" Grace asked, knowing how Tiffany didn't like anything in the window that might distract from at the quilts for sale.

"We're having a bone marrow donation event at the church up the street." She handed one of the sheets to Grace, then shoved her too-short hair back beneath her *kapp*. While Laurene had lived among *Englischers*, she'd cut and layered her light brown hair, and now she waited for it to grow enough to stay under her *kapp* without dozens of bobby pins. "Naomi and I have been working to get it set up."

"What is it?"

"You know Naomi and I are twins, ain't so?"

"*Ja*. Everyone knows that." *Everyone but Joel who was so shocked when he learned.* He hadn't said a word about that since.

Neither had she, caught up in the aftermath of her brother's death and his sons' arrival.

"Our birth *mamm*, Gina Marie, started looking for us when she realized she needed a bone marrow transplant to defeat her cancer. She hadn't wanted to barge into our lives before that. However, neither of us is a match, and we're hoping someone who comes in to offer a sample to be tested is."

"Isn't that a long shot?"

"A very, very, *very* long shot, but a nonrelative donor is her sole hope now."

"I'll pray the perfect donor walks through the door."

"Even if we don't find a match for Gina Marie, maybe we'll find one who can save someone else."

"What can I do to help?"

Laurene smiled. "You are so kind to offer, Grace, but you have more than enough on your plate at the moment. Rosemary Beachy and her sisters have offered to help during the event, so we have more than enough volunteers. But if you want to stop by and provide a sample, we'd be grateful."

"I'll do that."

As Laurene thanked her and hurried out the door, Grace looked at the paper she'd put on the counter. Convincing Tiffany to let her hang the sign in the window would be easy because she'd remind Tiffany how much *gut* will that would create in Strasburg.

What would be more difficult would be convincing Joel he needed to attend. She must be careful not to push too hard because he'd become suspicious about why it was so important to her. Even mentioning Laurene and Naomi could make him decide to stay away.

But if she could persuade him to go with her, it might be the best—and perhaps only—chance he had to reconnect with his sisters. She couldn't let him miss it.

★ ★ ★

Joel stood by the fence he'd painted earlier in the week, flipping the pocket-watch cover in the air and catching it in a steady rhythm. Looking across the field, he imagined how it'd look when he had a half dozen heifers grazing there. That wouldn't happen soon, but he'd go to the next auction at the New Holland Sales Stables with Harold and get a feeling for how far the few dollars he had would stretch. He'd start with calves because he couldn't afford to buy anything older. Taking care of such young animals would require a lot of his time, but it'd be worth it once they were old enough to be bred.

"What's that?" asked Brandon.

He saw the boys with the small coolers they used to take their lunch to school. So lost in his thoughts of the future, he hadn't heard them coming up the lane. "Weren't you supposed to wait for Grace to pick you up today?"

Brandon waved aside his words. "We're not *bopplin*. We can find our way home now."

Wesley's eyes were focused on Joel's hand. "What do you have?"

"My *grossdawdi*'s pocket watch." He tossed it and caught it one more time before holding out his hand toward the boys.

The smaller stood on tiptoe to peer into Joel's palm. "That's the skinniest watch I've ever seen."

"That's because," Joel said with a smile, "it's just the cover."

"Where's the rest of it?" the boy asked.

Joel shrugged. "I don't know. It was lost years ago. Would you like to see it?"

Wesley reached toward it, but pulled his hand back when his older brother asked, "Who wants to look at a broken old watch cover?"

"I do." Joel shoved it into his pocket, trying not to be vexed by Brandon's attitude.

The boy had lost everything he'd known and loved—his parents, his home and his friends. Grace was right to say they needed to be patient with the boys, but Brandon's attitude was too familiar. Joel had acted the same when he was the boy's age, pretending he knew everything and nobody could tell him anything.

When Brandon called to his brother to come with him, Wesley glanced at Joel's pocket. Joel almost asked the boy again if he wanted to examine the watch cover. He halted himself when Brandon shouted to Wesley to hurry up.

How he wished he could tell Brandon he was treading a path that led to more pain and grief! No, how he wished Brandon would heed him when he said it. Joel had thought he'd made a breakthrough with the boy when they played ball the night after Joel had shaved off his beard. It had been an aberration because Brandon had been his usual, surly self the next morning at breakfast and ever since.

God, can You show me a way to reach the boy before he commits himself to the wrong path? The prayer unfolded in his mind with an ease that amazed him. He'd been seeking God's guidance more in the past few days as he worked on the fences and imagined his herd grazing in the meadow. So far, he hadn't seen any sign of a response, but one thing he'd learned in prison was the need for patience.

"Joel Beachy?"

At the question in a voice much deeper than Harold's, Joel pushed aside his thoughts and pulled himself back to reality. Way back to reality, he realized, when he turned to see two men standing behind him. He didn't know the Pennsylvania state trooper's name, but he knew the dark gray uniform with the darker tie. The other man, shorter and stockier and with an icy smile on his face, was his parole officer. Roland Shriver stood with his arms crossed over his chest, but balanced on his feet as if he expected he'd have to stop Joel from fleeing.

Joel kept his voice even. "What can I do for you gentlemen?"

"You're Joel Beachy?" asked the trooper.

"I am."

"We need to ask you some questions."

"Go ahead." He motioned toward the house. "We can talk here or over there."

Shriver said in a low, menacing tone, "I don't think you want others to overhear our questions."

"All right. Ask away."

He wasn't surprised the trooper—who identified himself as Alex Reyes—read him his rights before the questioning began. He wanted to say he was familiar with them and how little they'd done for him when he was arrested. But he played along, nodding that he understood.

"You need to speak your agreement," Shriver said.

"I understand that, and I understand what my rights are supposed to be." Hearing how his answer had taken on Brandon's snide tone, he added in his usual voice, "Go ahead. What can I help you with?"

Joel listened and replied to each question. He guessed Shriver was disappointed he couldn't pin something on Joel that would mean revoking his parole right then and there and tossing him back in prison. Shriver's frown got tauter with each question. Trooper Reyes kept a stony face, offering no hint to what he thought of Joel's answers as he transcribed them into a handheld computer. They must have passed some sort of muster because after what seemed to be an eternity, but was only fifteen or twenty minutes, the two men paused.

When they looked toward the road, Joel realized they'd heard an approaching buggy. His heart had been thudding so hard in his chest he hadn't noticed. He wanted to groan when he recognized Pearl and knew Grace was holding the reins.

How he'd longed to keep this nasty, messy part of his past away from her! When she reined in the horse and jumped out of the buggy as soon as it'd stopped moving, he opened his mouth to explain.

She didn't give him a chance as she called, "Have you seen the boys?"

"They're in the house," he said. "They walked home from school."

Closing her eyes, she released a pent-up breath in a deep sigh. "I'm glad to hear they're home and safe, but they were supposed to wait for me to pick them up."

"Brandon said when I asked him—and I quote—'We're not *bopplin*.'"

She opened her eyes, then widened them. He realized she'd been so worried about her nephews she hadn't paid any attention to the car or the trooper and Shriver standing beside him. "Hello. I'm sorry. Can I help you?"

"You live here?" asked Trooper Reyes.

It took every bit of Joel's strength not to bristle at the question. Grace hadn't done anything to merit an interrogation. Then he warned himself to calm down. The trooper wanted to make sure she was on the farm for legitimate reasons.

"Ja," she replied, glancing at each of them. "I'm G-G-Grace C-C-Coffman." A blush rose up her cheeks as she added, "How can I help you?"

"Would you confirm something for us, Ms. Coffman?"

"Call me Grace. What do you need to know?"

Joel bit his lip not to smile when she chided the trooper far more gently than Harold had done when scolding him about using a title for a plain person.

"Do you know this man?" He pointed at Joel.

"*Ja*. He's Joel Beachy. He's our hired man."

"Thank you, Ms.— Grace." He closed the handheld, nodded to her, then motioned for Shriver to come with him to the police car.

Shriver shot another scowl at Joel before he followed like a little duckling going after its parent. Again, Joel had to bite his lip—harder this time—to keep from smiling as he thought of Shriver's reaction if Joel had shared that comparison with him.

Grace edged closer to him as the men got in the car, started it and drove away. "What was all of that about?" she asked.

"Apparently there are rumors flying around the county that I'm the go-to guy for all sorts of drugs."

"What?" Her eyes grew wide. "Why would anyone think that?"

He wasn't sure whether to hug her for having such belief in him or to remind her he'd been in prison for selling drugs, so any drug activity would point an accusing finger in his direction. "Though you've accepted my assertion of innocence, neither the police nor my parole officer has."

"Maybe if you talked to him."

"Talked to who?"

"Your parole officer."

He gave a curt laugh. "He was the guy with the trooper."

"Oh." Her slender fingers curled around his arm, sending that special warmth through him. "I'm sorry, Joel. He seems like a grim man."

"He is." Not wanting to let Shriver stain their conversation more, he added, "I don't know who would have started those rumors. Or why."

"You need to speak with Adam and Jonas."

"Jonas?"

She tightened her grip on his arm. "Jonas Gundy. He's our bishop. You should talk with him and Adam. Right away."

She tugged. "*Komm mol.* We can take the buggy over to the far side of the Bliss Valley Covered Bridge and talk with Jonas. We can pick up Adam on the way. *Komm mol!* If we go now, I can be back in time to help *Mamm* with supper."

He smiled in spite of himself. "Always practical, aren't you, Grace?"

"I find it hurries things along." She walked toward the buggy and looked over her shoulder. The shy, quiet Grace had been replaced by a woman who was determined to do whatever she could to help him. She was about as unstoppable as a bolt of lightning. "Are you coming?"

"I wouldn't miss it for the world."

Grace waited in the doorway to Jonas's woodworking shop, wanting to give Joel a chance to speak with the bishop without her listening in. They'd stopped at *Grossdawdi* Ephraim's farm, but Adam hadn't been there, so they'd continued on to the far side of the creek and up the hill to the bishop's farm.

If Jonas had been surprised to see them, he hadn't mentioned it. Instead, he'd listened as Grace introduced him to Joel and explained the situation. Jonas had motioned for Joel to join him inside the small barn.

The bishop was quite a bit shorter than Joel, and he didn't have a spare ounce of flesh on him. His face above his black beard appeared gaunt. Grace knew he was well-fed because his wife, Myrtle, was renowned throughout both of his districts as a superb cook. On every occasion, whether it was joyous like a birth or hopeful like a fundraiser to garner money to pay a hospital bill, she arrived with one of her meat and pasta casseroles. Her food always was scooped up first, the dishes empty before some of the others had even been touched.

"Aren't you joining us, Grace?" Jonas called.

"I thought… That is, if Joel—"

"Join us." Joel's voice was subdued.

She inched around a planer and took the chair Jonas pointed to. She perched on the edge. Her hands clutched both sides as if she feared it was about to be pulled out from beneath her.

Was that how Joel was feeling? As if some sort of rug had been yanked out from beneath him? He'd been settling in at the farm, even making some progress with getting the boys to trust him. Not Brandon, but her older nephew didn't trust anyone at the moment.

Pulling up another chair, Jonas had Joel explain the whole situation all over again. Joel's voice was strained as he told the bishop how he'd been talking to the boys one minute and the next the state police car had rolled up the lane. He went through the questions he'd been asked and the answers he'd given.

Only when he was finished did Jonas ask, "You can understand why they came to you, ain't so?"

"Of course, I know that. It's part of any cop's job to follow up on tips." Joel rubbed his palms together, and she guessed he was far more nervous about the situation than he wanted anyone else to think. And why wouldn't he be? A single misstep could land him back in jail with little or no hope for early release again.

In a quietly dignified tone, Joel added, "I hated when my fellow inmates ranted on and on about the people they believed had snitched on them."

"'Snitches get stitches,'" Grace murmured.

Both men looked at her, and she saw their astonishment.

"Where did you hear *that*?" Joel asked, speaking first.

"I don't remember. Probably when I was grocery shopping. You know how while they're going up and down the aisles at the grocery store, people talk as if nobody else is around. I don't mean to eavesdrop," she added with a guilty glance at Jonas, "but it's impossible not to hear."

The bishop chuckled. "I know. I've overheard some strange things, too, which have gotten stuck in my brain. One day I was waiting to check out behind two young men who gave me an education on how to pick football players for a fantasy team on a computer. Not that I'll ever need it, but I heard enough to know how to do it." He grew serious again. "Joel, if you'd like, I'll speak with Trooper Reyes. He's a *gut* man and a fair one. I think you saw that today."

"Because he didn't slap handcuffs on me?"

"*Ja.*"

She watched as Joel drew a deep breath. She prayed it would cleanse him of the anger that had suffused him when he was questioned by the trooper and his parole officer. Such rage was like battery acid, eating away at one's heart and soul. Powerful emotions that had no outlet. She'd learned that after Lamar died, and she'd suffered in silence, not wanting to inflict her pain on anyone else.

"I guess you're right," Joel drawled, then shook himself and sat straighter. "No, Jonas, I know you're right. I can't blame Reyes for what happened in the past when he wasn't part of that."

Jonas came to his feet and offered Joel his hand. "I'll be praying for you, Joel, as I'll be praying that the person who is selling is caught so his drugs can't hurt anyone."

"I appreciate that," Joel said.

"Grace?"

She realized both men were standing and looking at her. She rose and took the bishop's hand and Joel's. She bent her head while Jonas asked God's blessing on those who loved Him and pleaded for Him to intercede with the drug dealer and touch his heart. It wasn't easy to concentrate on the bishop's words when her fingers tingled within the warmth of Joel's hand. She hoped nobody noticed how unsteady her voice was as she said, "Amen."

Once she was back in the buggy with Joel, Grace waited for him to speak. She didn't want to break into his thoughts, guessing he was wrestling with his reaction to the unexpected visit from the state police and his parole officer as well as the bishop's comments.

It wasn't until they'd gone through the Bliss Valley Covered Bridge, its boards resounding beneath the metal wheels of the buggy, that he spoke.

"Can we stop?" he asked.

"Here?"

"Yeah. I'd like a few minutes to clear my mind."

"All right." She drew Pearl in and slowed the buggy alongside the stone walls that radiated out from each end of the bridge.

She expected him to hop out, but he asked, "Come with me?"

"I thought you wanted to be alone."

"No. I've had enough time alone to last me a lifetime." He climbed out, then came around to help her get down. Taking the reins, he lashed them to a bush before he walked toward the grass edging the road.

When she didn't follow, unsure what he intended, he came back and held out his hand.

"Please, Grace."

Without a word, she put her hand in his. The touch of his rough skin felt thrilling and familiar at the same time. It was as if her hand had been made to be in his, and she was where she was meant to be.

High grass swished against her skirt and apron as she walked with him toward the creek. Again he was silent. Was he focused as she was on where their hands were linked, connecting them? She should draw away because anyone going past would see her holding his hand, but she didn't lift her fingers out of his. He kept her close as they came to stand beside the creek that was low within its banks. Pebbles cluttered the sides of the languid water.

He reached out one foot and kicked a small stone toward the water. He sighed when it tumbled in, and concentric circles rippled outward from the spot.

"Danki," he said.

"For what?"

"For believing me when I said the rumors aren't true." He paused as a car whipped past on the road, but didn't release her hand. "Nobody else has."

"The trooper must have because you aren't in jail."

"He doesn't have enough evidence to arrest me. That's not the same as believing I'm being honest when I say I'm not selling drugs. Don't think the cops have given up because they're gone for now."

"But you cooperated with them."

"I did when I was arrested, too, and it didn't help me."

"That must have been terrible."

He gave a shrug of indifference she didn't believe before he picked up a stone and tossed it in the water. She noticed he didn't throw it where a school of minnows were swirling in a dance that sparkled against the water.

"To be honest," he said, "I was in such a state of shock, most of my memories of that time aren't much more than a blur."

"I'm sorry." She put her hand on his arm again as she said, "But I think you're wrong, Joel."

"What do you know of cops and crime and anything beyond this quiet world you've wrapped around yourself?" He shoved her hand away as if it'd grown spikes.

She refused to let his abrupt anger daunt her. He'd done it before, putting an end to a conversation he didn't want to have. Making sure her own voice was even, she said, "Roland Shriver would have searched the *dawdi haus* if he'd believed you had drugs there. He must not have believed it."

"Or he didn't bring the proper search warrant."

"My parents wouldn't have required him to have a search warrant. We have nothing to hide, and neither do you."

"But Shriver would have expected he needed a search warrant."

"You're making my point. He knew you didn't have the drugs. He was there to make sure you were given a fair hearing by the state trooper."

"You're wrong. He'd like nothing better than to put me back in a cell and throw away the key. He's said so a bunch of times."

"But he didn't today. For that, you should be thanking God for blessing you with His love."

"Have you?"

She pulled her gaze from the stream and looked at him. "Have I what?"

"Have you thanked God for your blessings?"

"I try to. Every day." She chuckled. "Even when my so-called blessings head home and leave me waiting for them at school."

"Do you think they had a reason for doing that?"

"Other than Brandon not wanting to look like a *boppli*, as he put it, because his *aenti* is picking him up, I don't know. They don't tell me how they're feeling and what they're thinking." She wondered if Joel could guess how much pride she had to swallow to make that simple statement.

"Wesley may speak to you, Grace, if he knows you're willing to listen."

"I've tried. I've tried to talk to them about their lives in Rexford and with their parents." Now it was her turn to pick up a stone and fling it into the water. "They don't say anything about their parents. I know they're grieving, and I can see how it's eating them up inside. A few times, Wesley has tried to talk to me, but Brandon interrupts every time with some comment that starts a fight." She folded her hands in front of her so she didn't seize a handful of stones and hurl them. "I know both boys are afraid of showing they're weak. I know my brother. He would have been telling them since they were little that if anything happened to him, that they would have to step up and be the men of the family. I can recall my *daed* saying much the same to my brothers."

Joel put a consoling hand on her shoulder. "*Gut* intentions don't always lead in the direction we want them to take us and those we love. So Brandon and Wesley believe they must be *men*. Not real men who know there's a time and a place to grieve, but their impressions of what a man is. Someone stoic who swallows pain like it's a handful of potato chips."

She put her fingers over his and looked up at him. Her breath caught over her rapidly beating heart as she imagined tracing the line of his strong jaw and slipping across his volatile lips.

"It's hurting them," she whispered. "I want to reach them. I want to help them."

"I know you do, but they've got to be willing to accept help." His mouth hardened. "I grew up with a *daed* like theirs, demanding and expecting too much from a young boy. I couldn't help myself, but I hope I can help them."

"If anyone can, you will."

His gaze softened as it caressed her face. "Your faith in me continues to be surprising."

"I know we each give what we can."

"You give too much."

She shook her head and stepped back, turning toward the buggy. "I give what I can. It's the way I want to live."

"It's a great way to live."

Realizing he was giving her the opening she wasn't sure she'd get, she paused and faced him. She was standing higher on the bank than he was so their eyes were level.

"Do you think so? Really think so?"

"*Ja.*" He gave her a crooked grin as he used the *Deitsch* word.

"Then come with me on Saturday. There's going to be an event to find possible donors for sick people who need bone marrow transplants. I thought we both should go."

"Jonas wouldn't have a problem with it?"

"No."

"Who's it for?"

The question she had dreaded. The last time she'd brought up these names, Joel had been shocked...and then she'd gotten the call about Fritz. Speaking the names of his friends and his victims from when he used to live in Bliss Valley was like tiptoeing through a minefield.

"Laurene and Naomi's birth *mamm.*"

"They want to do this after she gave them away when they were *bopplin*? Why would they want to do that?"

She frowned at him. "What's wrong, Joel? It's not like you to make such cruel comments."

"It's just like me." He swept a hand toward the buggy. "Didn't you hear what I said to Brandon at the bus station?"

"I heard, and I heard you apologize for it as well."

"I don't understand why they'd want to do this when she abandoned them."

"What if it were your birth *mamm* or your adopted *mamm*

who needed the transplant? Would you deny either of them a few ounces of your blood?"

"Or a pound of flesh?"

She regarded him with bafflement. "I don't know what you mean."

"It's a saying among the *Englischers*. Something from Shakespeare. He wrote plays."

"I know the reference."

"How?"

"I heard people talking about him when I was a kid, so I found a book of his plays at the public library. Each time I went there for several months, I'd read an act or two from one of his plays. I didn't like some of them. I didn't understand some of them, but I did like *The Merchant of Venice*. The two women were so clever and saved a man's life, and I wrote down the words to the speech one gave when she asked for that man's life to be spared." She shut her eyes and recited, "'The quality of mercy is not strained. It droppeth as the gentle rain from heaven upon the place beneath. It is twice blest: It blesseth him that gives and him that takes.' It is a beautiful example of what Jesus shared on the Mount when He said, 'Blessed are the merciful: for they shall obtain mercy.'"

He gave her a wry grin. "It sounds like you know the play and the reference and your Bible verses, so what don't you understand?"

"Why you would think that Laurene and Naomi feel that someone needs to be repaid for an unwise loan. Their birth *mamm* must have had her reasons for giving them up for adoption. As yours did." When he didn't give her a swift reply, she asked, "Don't you wonder about your birth parents?"

"Probably about as much as they wonder about me."

He walked past her, and she turned to stare at his back. Just when she thought she could guess the thoughts in Joel's head, she realized she didn't.

But his changing the subject again—this time with silence— let her understand his heart. It was infected by the thought that two sets of parents had no interest in whether he was alive or dead. There was nothing she could do to bring about a reconciliation with his birth parents unless it was discovered who and where they were. But on Saturday, she was going to find a way to mend the torn fabric of his adoptive family.

Whether he wanted her to or not.

Chapter Fourteen

The sample donation center had been set up in the red brick church's basement multipurpose room. Flags leaned against the industrial green wall in one corner. In another corner, two stacks of plastic chairs were stacked almost to the ceiling. A large raised dais at the far end of the room had one bright purple curtain closed and the other open enough to reveal tables and boxes and a stack of what Joel guessed were hymnals. A movie screen hung against its back wall.

In the center of the room, the donations were being collected. There was a general hushed atmosphere, showing everyone was aware of the importance of what they were doing. Lives could be saved. Lives could be changed. Nobody knew which one among the volunteer donors might be the perfect match for someone who needed their bone marrow to fight a deadly disease.

Everything was as Joel had anticipated. The room was filled with plenty of plain people as well as *Englischers*. The two groups were mingling as they waited to be called forward one by one to do paperwork or to have the inside of their cheek swabbed.

"What a crowd!" Grace said as she stepped off the lowest stair and moved to stand beside him. "This is a *wunderbaar* blessing for all of those who will be helped by the samples given today."

"*Danki* for coming," Laurene said as she paused beside Joel and Grace. Handing them each a sheet of paper, she hesitated before she added, wearing a strained expression, "*Gute mariye*, Joel. It's nice of you to come."

"How have you been?" What a trite question, but standing in line at an event aimed at saving her birth *mamm*'s life wasn't the place to start a long explanation about how he was sorry for treating her badly when they were kids.

"I'm *gut*. Adam told me you'd found a job and are staying in Bliss Valley for the foreseeable future."

He glanced at Grace to bring her into the conversation. And as a bulwark against the past? He was shocked at that thought, but hurried to say, "I'm working for Harold Coffman, doing some maintenance work on his farm. I hear you are studying so you can be baptized."

"I am." Without another word to him, she said, "I'm so glad to see you, Grace. The sign you hung up at the shop has brought in quite a few possible donors and helped spread the word through the plain communities, too."

Grace smiled. "I'm not surprised at the *wunderbaar* turnout. I had several of our quilters mention it when they came in over the past few days." Her smile became a playful grin as she hooked a thumb in his direction. "And I convinced Joel to come, too."

Laurene's face remained frozen in its practiced smile. "We appreciate everyone who's here today." She didn't say anything more as she continued along the line, but fired a glower at him before she spoke to the couple standing beyond Grace.

When Grace patted his arm but said nothing, Joel wondered if he'd been stupid to come to the event. Laurene had been as welcoming as a cactus. Not that he'd expected her to throw her arms around him and welcome him back and say that all was forgiven. He hadn't gotten that from Adam or Samuel. Still, he'd thought she would be a bit more sincere in her greeting.

And if she was so cool to him, how could he expect his sisters, if he saw them, to be more effusive?

This had been a bad decision. He was chasing a happy-ever-after ending that didn't exist. He'd lost the right to that when the judge hit his gavel after announcing Joel's sentence. All his hopes, all his plans…what *gut* were they when nobody would let him forget his mistakes?

Joel started to turn to leave when an *Englisch* minister, whom Grace whispered was Pastor Criss, stood and held up his hands. He was almost as tall and as lanky as a willow. His thick, black curls were cropped close to his skull like many of the prisoners Joel had encountered, but the smile on his tanned face made him very approachable.

"Before we begin," he said in a voice that seemed too deep for such a skinny man, "let us thank God for bringing us together today and praise Him for the lives we might save."

Joel bent his head as the pastor began his prayer. When Grace slipped her hand into his, holding it tightly, he struggled to pay attention to the minister's words. Fireworks were going off in his stomach, and a brass band seemed to have taken up residence in his head as he savored her warm skin against his palm. Her fingers were the perfect size to fit into his hand, and he would happily have held them for the rest of the afternoon. Who was he trying to fool? He'd happily hold them for as long as she'd let him.

But that couldn't be. He wasn't going to ruin her life along with his own. She was the epitome of kindness and generosity while he'd taken what he could out of life without regard for anyone else's feelings. Sometimes, not even his own.

When he dropped her fingers before the prayer came to an end, he sensed her confusion. He didn't look at her as everyone around him said, "Amen." Instead, he acted as if he were fascinated by the words on the page Laurene had given him. Everything on the paper blurred, but he refused to believe tears were filling his eyes as he came face-to-face with the truth he'd hoped never to confront.

Joel Beachy wasn't wanted in Bliss Valley. He…

A gasp burst out of him as a group of young plain women emerged from the draped side of the dais and stepped down. They were giggling as if they were scholars. He stared. He couldn't be mistaken, though more than ten years had passed since the last time he'd seen his sisters and heard them laughing together.

Grace's fingers wove through his again, startling him. Then he realized she'd reached out to him in compassion, not in passion. She'd known the sight of his sisters would be disconcerting.

When his oldest sister looked in his direction, her face lost its humor. She stiffened, then said something to their other sisters. Both nodded, but remained where they were as Rosemary walked toward him.

"Appreciate that she's making an effort," Grace murmured before she released his hand and moved past him to fill in a gap in the line.

He stayed where he was when Rosemary stopped in front of him, more than an arm's length away. He didn't want their first conversation in over a decade to be shouted across that distance, so he stepped forward. When she didn't skitter away, he was grateful, but he couldn't help noticing how she was balanced on her toes, ready to flee.

He needed to make the most of whatever time they had to speak. He hadn't seen any sign of their parents, but *Daed* would be furious if he discovered his oldest daughter talking to his only son.

Even knowing that, the first words out of Joel's mouth were a simple, "*Gute mariye*, Rosemary."

"What are you doing here?" she asked, her voice tight and tense.

"I'm volunteering to be a donor."

"Really?"

He was shocked she was surprised at his answer and thought he had an ulterior motive for coming to the church.

Before he could think of something to soothe her obvious disquiet, she said, "I guess this is neutral territory."

"You make it sound as if we're at war."

"Call it what you wish, but we've been separated because of your anger all these years."

"Not just mine."

"I don't want to talk about this now."

"Later? You could come over to—"

"I'm not coming to the Coffmans' farm and making them part of this, though you've already done so," Rosemary said, aiming an uncomfortable glance in Grace's direction.

"You're right," he replied, glad Grace was talking to one of the volunteers at a table and reaching for a pen to sign a form.

Drawing her into his family's drama was the last thing he wanted to do because he knew she'd be eager to help. She would say she'd mixed him up in her family's troubles, so it would be fair. She didn't know what she was talking about. Wyman Beachy had concealed his cruelty behind a jovial exterior he showed everyone except his son.

Rosemary walked away, and he groaned when he saw her go to Grace and speak to her. Even as he watched, Grace seemed to draw into herself as if her outer form was a protective wall between the real Grace and the rest of the world. The vibrant woman who'd pushed him to come to the event had vanished, and he guessed if she could have become invisible she would have as his sister walked away and one of the volunteers led Grace to where the sample would be taken.

What had Rosemary said to her?

Though Joel wanted to push ahead in the line and rush to Grace and demand an answer, he waited until it was his turn to go to the table. He didn't read what he assumed was a permission form before he signed it. The sooner he gave his sample, the sooner he could find out what had upset Grace.

"Ready?" asked a male technician as he picked up one of the packets and opened it. "Open wide so I can get a good sample."

Joel complied, and the whole process took seconds. He started to leave, but the technician said, "There's about a one in three hundred chance of you being matched to someone. Of course, it's much higher odds if we're talking about you matching a specific person." He glanced at the card Joel had filled out. "Are you a close relative to the person needing the donation?"

"I've never met her." He glanced toward where Grace was talking to Laurene. When he saw his sisters heading in that direction, he moved away from the table.

"One more thing," the technician said as he put the sample and the card in the bag and set it in a box with the other completed sets. "Though it's unlikely you'll be a match for the person needing the donation, that's okay. Once your sample is in our database, it'll be considered every time someone needs a donation." He handed Joel another card. "If you move or change your phone number— Do you have a phone?"

"A friend does." He pointed at the card in the plastic bag where he'd written the number of the phone in Grace's family's phone shack. How much longer was this going to take? "It's on there."

"Good. A lot of your Amish friends don't have phones. Not that it's a big problem, because we contact people when they're a potential match by mail. Make sure we've got your current address and phone number, though."

"I will." He didn't wait for the man to say anything else before he wove his way through the crowd to where Grace now stood by herself.

"Ready to go?" she asked with false cheer.

"Grace, what did Rosemary tell you?"

All attempts to hide what she was feeling vanished, and tears bubbled into her eyes. "You don't want to know."

"Tell me. Please."

She flinched when he said, "Please." Looking up at him, she said, "You're not going to like it."

"You didn't."

"No, I didn't." She raised her chin. "Rosemary says she intends to obey Eddie's edict and not let you come to the farm."

Another bubble of hope burst in his heart. He'd been so sure when Grace told him how Rosemary wanted to talk to him, and when his sister had come over to him herself, that somehow they would find common ground and close the chasm between them.

So sure.

But he'd been wrong.

"Was this made in Lancaster County?" asked the tall, gray-haired *Englisch* woman.

Grace didn't let her professional smile slip, even though this was the fourth customer that afternoon who'd asked the same question. "All our quilts are stitched here."

The woman frowned. "Was this completely made in this county?"

"*Ja.*"

"I've been hearing about quilt tops that are made overseas and then they're made into complete quilts here, so shops can say they're locally quilted."

Grace nodded. "I know what you're talking about, but our quilts are made in Lancaster County by plain quilters. Some were sewn by Amish women. Others are made by horse-and-buggy Mennonites. A few were pieced together and quilted by a group comprised of both Amish and Mennonites. The women sometimes come together for what we call a work frolic. You'd call it a quilting bee."

Grace was relieved when the woman nodded and asked to see one of the king-size quilts that was hanging on the rack at the left side of the shop. It was a double wedding ring quilt in pale shades of pink, blue and green. After examining every inch of it, the woman decided she needed to look at other shops before making a purchase.

Thanking her for stopping by, Grace held in her annoyed groan until the woman had left. One of the least favorite parts of her job was refolding the biggest quilts and placing them back on the rack. She glanced at the clock, glad to see it was almost closing time. Traffic had been brisk, though not as busy as last Saturday when the bone marrow sign-up had been held up the street. However, sales had been slow.

Tiffany wouldn't be happy, and when Tiffany wasn't happy, she made sure Grace wasn't either. It wouldn't be a *gut* time to ask for a raise, but first thing Monday morning, Grace must. The price of meat and staples had risen again at the market, and her pay was already strained when covering the cost of feeding six people. She didn't want to have to tell Joel that they could no longer afford to have him share their table, because the pittance *Daed* was paying him would leave him close to starving.

Closing up, she hitched Pearl to the buggy and headed home. She left the buggy doors open because the day remained as hot as midsummer. Not a wisp of breeze eased the heat. Pearl didn't step out as lively as he usually did, and she didn't push him to go faster.

Grace parked the buggy under a tree, led the horse out into the meadow and made sure the water trough was filled with cold water. Patting Pearl on the nose, she was about to head for the house when she heard shouts from the far side of the barn. She followed her curiosity around to the back and smiled when she saw her nephews splashing in the pond *Daed* had dug years ago to make sure there was nearby water in case of a fire.

In the shade of a full maple, Joel watched them. He looked more relaxed than she'd seen him since they'd gone to provide swabs as possible bone marrow donors. Had something changed? Had Rosemary—or Eddie!—decided to let Joel come to their place? Though Joel had remained tight-lipped about his plans, she'd felt a subtle shift in him. She wanted to urge him not to do something rash like leaving Bliss Valley again without trying to ease the wounds his last departure had caused.

Each time she'd tried to bring up the subject of his family, he changed it or acted as if he were too busy to talk. He'd done the gargantuan job of painting all the fencing along the lane and the main road with a speed and skill that made *Daed* smile. In the past two days, he'd painted the chicken coop and the garden shed. She'd decided to wait until he couldn't hide behind a paintbrush any longer, but now that she'd found him here with the boys...

"Looks like fun!" Grace said as she came within earshot.

"Want to join them?" Joel grinned and grabbed her arm, pretending he was going to shove her in.

"It's tempting."

"*Ja*, it is."

All of the sudden, she wondered if they were still talking about the pond. The glow in his light blue eyes created a sweet fire right beneath her heart. His hand on her arm softened, and his other rose toward her waist. A single step would bring her within the curve of his arm and to his lips, which were growing ever closer to hers.

A spray of water broke the moment, and Grace bit back her protest when Joel released her and called a warning to the boys before he bent to slap his hand on the water, splashing them. He got giggles in return.

She made sure by the time Joel was looking at her again, her face was composed and she wasn't gazing at him with the yearning of a kitten longing to be picked up and cuddled. Had she lost her mind to want his kiss when a few minutes ago she'd been thinking about how he seemed ready to leave? She'd been left once already. Why was she setting herself up to be hurt like that again?

When the boys scrambled out of the pond, she handed them the towels they'd brought with them. They ran back to the house, laughing.

She smiled. She'd spent so much time in the past week trying to figure out how to make her nephews feel at home. The boys alternated between being too loud and too quiet, too polite and too sharp, too full of energy and too lethargic. She wished they'd listen when she told them she understood the storm of emotions swirling like a tornado inside them, but they didn't know her well enough to heed her. She'd tried talking about their parents in a casual tone. That had seemed to work for a few days, but Brandon had gotten angry last night that she kept, as he put it, "harping on my dead *mamm* and *daed*."

His words had upset his sensitive younger brother, and Wesley had cried himself to sleep. Grace had offered to sit next to his bed. The little boy had started to agree before Brandon muttered something Grace didn't hear. She didn't have to hear it because she guessed what Brandon had said when Wesley asserted he was too old to have her sit there.

How she'd longed to say, "You're not being a *boppli* if you admit you need to be listened to when you're sad. Even grown-ups like to have someone nearby when they're upset."

Saying that might have made the situation worse.

"It's so *wunderbaar* to hear them being happy," Grace said, wishing she could help Joel as he'd helped her nephews. "I know their hearts have a long way to go to heal, but for a few minutes, they were happy kids playing in the water on a hot day. *Danki*, Joel."

"Brandon was picking on Wesley, and I told him to quit it. Brandon got huffy and stomped around. I said something about being hotheaded would never get him anywhere. When I suggested he needed to cool it, Wesley thought I meant in the pond." A smile came and went across his face. "How could I say no when Wesley was so excited?"

Joel had found a way to handle Brandon by taking him at face value. Scolding him when he was naughty and trying to teach him the right thing to do. Teasing him back and letting him have fun. Wesley, too.

She wanted to ask Joel how he'd learned to do that, but swallowed the questions. She didn't want to see him as stressed as he'd been for the past week since speaking with Rosemary.

Instead, she asked, "And, for once, Brandon went along with your idea of playing in the pond?"

"He acted as if he'd planned the whole thing."

Grace chuckled. "Fritz was like that, too. He'd tease someone until that person was in the mood to do something fun."

"I'm not sure this was the same. Brandon can be rough on his brother." Joel's face tightened. "Like my *daed* was rough on me, nitpicking everything I said or did. I didn't like it, and I don't want Wesley to have to endure that, too."

"I'm sorry you and your sisters had to go through that."

"Not my sisters. Just me."

She picked up the straw hats the boys had tossed aside before they jumped in the pond. "I don't understand."

"It's simple." His jaw tightened as he looked north and east in the direction of the Beachy farm. "My *daed* has always cared more about me being a mark on his reputation than anything else."

"Your sisters—"

"He doesn't find fault with everything they do." He laughed tersely. "Or, at least, he hasn't before now. On the other hand, he never expected them to be as perfect at everything they said and did as he did me."

"Why?"

"If I knew, I'd tell you. I don't know. Everything was fine before Rosemary was born." His gaze turned inward, and she guessed he was savoring whatever happy memories he had of his childhood. "*Daed* spent time with me, teaching me, teasing me, doing what a *gut daed* should do. All that changed when he realized there would be another *kind* in the family. A *kind* with his blood, not the *kind* of another man."

"That makes no sense. You were his son."

"His *adopted* son who needed to prove to everyone in the community he was as *gut* as the other kids. No, not as *gut*. Better."

Grace walked with Joel toward the house, collecting other discarded pieces of clothing and schoolbags as she went. Doing so allowed her to gather her thoughts into some semblance of order. "That makes even less sense, Joel. Why would your *daed* dote on you for six or seven years and then change? Could it have had more to do with you going to school than your sister's birth?"

"I've asked myself that at least a million times."

She arched her brows.

With an abrupt grin, he said, "All right, maybe not a million times, but a lot."

"You sounded like Brandon there for a minute."

"Guess he and his bad habits are rubbing off on me."

Grace laughed. Out loud and hard.

"What's so funny?" Joel asked.

"Everyone's warned me about not letting the boys be influenced by you."

"And now the situation is reversed." He smiled, genuinely smiled, for the first time in a week. "Who would have guessed?"

"Not me."

He bent to scoop up the boys' lunch coolers. "I'll clean these out after I wash the paint out of the brushes."

"*Danki.*" As he turned to walk away, she called, "*Danki* for everything. I know the boys and my folks appreciate your help as much as I do."

He paused, but didn't face her. When he continued walking toward the barn, she wondered if one of these days, he'd keep walking right out of Bliss Valley, trying to escape the pain that haunted him. She could have told him, if he'd asked, that if it'd been possible, she would have walked far, far from her memories.

Chapter Fifteen

When she stepped into Adam Hershberger's shop two days later, Grace was astonished to see Joel and Samuel also there. Joel had told her he needed to run some errands, but he hadn't said he was heading for Adam's.

She decided having him there was a *gut* thing. He could confirm what she wanted to discuss with their deacon before the situation got out of hand.

"*Gute mariye*, Grace," Adam called over the sound of metal grinding on metal. He reached out, flipped a switch and silence settled on the space.

It took Grace a moment to realize that because her ears were ringing. How did Adam tolerate the cacophony? She understood when he reached up and extracted a plug from each ear.

Grace greeted each of the men, making sure her gaze didn't linger longer on Joel than the others. It wasn't easy because he looked handsome with the light playing off the sharp planes of his face. But she wasn't there to enjoy a chat with the men.

She needed help.

"I'm here because of Brandon and Wesley," she said without a preamble.

Adam donned a quirky smile. "They're quite the imps, ain't so?"

"This isn't a joke." She stamped her foot.

All three men stared at her as if she'd turned the same purple as her dress.

Realizing she'd shocked them into silence with her uncharacteristic show of emotion, she knew she had to take her chance while she had it. "This morning, I came down to find the kitchen covered with partially thawed cookie dough from one end to the other."

"They made cookies?" Joel asked in surprise. "They brought toast and *kaffi* to me in the *dawdi haus*." He grimaced. "Not great *kaffi*, but *gut* enough to get me going. I thought it was nice of them to do that."

"Or a way," she retorted, "to keep you out of the kitchen so you didn't see the catastrophe they'd left."

"How did they get cookie dough everywhere?" Samuel asked.

"They decided the dough looked like a baseball, so they decided to take batting practice with a spatula." She rolled her eyes as the men struggled not to laugh. "I know it sounds funny, but *Mamm* was so upset I was afraid she would have one of her spells. *Daed* tried to comfort her, but he was shaking so hard he could hardly speak."

Joel's smile disappeared. "Did the boys apologize?"

"If you could call it an apology. I think they—especially Brandon—were more sorry they got caught than they'd done something to upset their grandparents." She raised her hands in the air. "I don't know what gets into them sometimes."

"They're boys," Adam said, grinning. "They're young boys whose emotions are so mixed up they can't think straight. It happens to most kids at one time or another, but they've had a trauma with losing their parents and losing their home."

"I understand that, Adam, but I'm beginning to think they need something I can't give them."

"I know what it's like to lose your parents as a *kind*." Adam's voice grew somber as he met her gaze. "There's nothing that makes you more bitter, and your world tilts out of your control."

"And when you lost your parents, what did you do, Adam?"

"I wept. I retreated from everyone. I was in everyone's face. I wanted nobody to see me at the same time I wanted to be the center of attention." He exchanged a look with Samuel and Joel. "And I acted out, knowing the best way to get everyone's attention was to do something outrageous. Then even outrageous wasn't enough. I wanted to make the whole world feel as bad as I did."

"As Brandon and Wesley do." Joel whacked his palm against his forehead. "Why didn't I see that before?"

"Maybe because you're too close," Adam replied.

"Or maybe," Samuel said in a tone as serious, "because you spent so much time wishing you were free from your parents."

When Joel gasped, Grace started to leap to his defense. He waved her to silence. "Samuel's right, Grace. You didn't know me then. He did, and he knows how I wished I'd never see my *daed* again."

She wanted to retort that wasn't true, but had to admit it was. Though Joel had lamented about not having a chance to speak with all his sisters as well as his *mamm*, and he wished that his conversation with Rosemary had been more pleasant, he hadn't mentioned once about talking to Wyman.

Lord, if You can use me to help bridge the gap between Joel and his daed*, I am here to be Your servant.* Though she knew God listened to every prayer, she wondered how He might answer that one.

Looking from one man to the next, she said, "Adam, Samuel, you both have *kinder.*"

"You've got kids, too?" Surprise heightened Joel's voice.

"You didn't know he and Naomi have three little ones?" Grace rolled her eyes again. "What do you guys talk about when you're hanging out here?"

"Farming," Samuel said.

"The weather," Adam added as he picked up a wrench and eyed the small engine on the table.

"Sports." Joel gave her a wink that sent a heated frisson of delight down her spine.

How could he make a one-word commonplace answer sound flirtatious?

"Can any of you be serious?" she asked. "You would have been serious if you'd had to scrape off the residue from chocolate chip cookie home runs for the past hour and a half. Wesley pulls to the left when he bats."

She wasn't sure which one of them started laughing at her earnest comment. Soon they were all laughing, and tears were blossoming in the corners of her eyes. She knuckled them away before they could tumble down her face, but each time she thought she had her laughter under control, she'd glance at Joel or one of his friends, and she'd dissolve into giggles all over again.

Adam was the first to overcome the waves of laughter. He set the wrench on the table and folded his arms in front of him. "You're right, Grace. The boys need help at this point. Help beyond what just one of us can give, so we need to work together. When you're a kid and something monumental happens, you don't know how to ask for help or even what to do with the help someone offers."

"So what do you suggest?" she asked. "You're both *daeds.*

You've got experience with *kinder* who have suffered losing a parent."

Joel's head jerked around to look at Samuel, then at Grace. She mouthed, *Later.* He nodded, but she could see he was frustrated that he knew so little about the lives of the men he'd once called his best friends.

"The twins are so young they don't have any memories of Marlin." Samuel added, "Marlin Ropp was their *daed*. Did you know him, Joel?"

"Not that I can recall. Was he from Bliss Valley?"

"He had a place just over the county line in Honey Brook."

"I wouldn't be surprised if the twins remember more about him than they're letting you guess." Adam arched his brows. "I'm speaking from experience. My daughter knows things about her *mamm* I never told her. She surprises me sometimes with her memories. They've enhanced my own."

"And Brandon and Wesley are older, so they have more memories," Grace said.

"Along with more of a sensation of loss." Joel shoved his hands in his pockets.

She was relieved he did because his words had been so laced with sorrow she had been ready to reach out and fold his fingers within hers to offer him some comfort.

"We need to find them something to bring them joy," she said, "without plastering the whole kitchen in cookie dough."

"How about getting everyone together for an outing?" Joel asked.

His friends for once didn't exchange a glance before they nodded.

Adam said, "I know Laurene enjoys any chance to spend time with Naomi and the *kinder*. The other day, she was saying she'd like to get to know Grace better."

"Samuel?" he prompted.

"It's a great idea. Be prepared for a lot of running around. Jesse and Jared haven't gotten the concept of sitting still yet."

"Nor has Mary Beth."

"We've got two built-in babysitters with Brandon and Wesley," Grace reminded them.

"Are they *gut* with little kids?"

"I guess we'll find out, ain't so?"

Adam gnawed on his lower lip, then said, "You'll be having church at your farm in two weeks, ain't so, Grace?"

"*Ja*, but—"

"That would be a great time to get together," Samuel hurried to say.

"After all, we'll all be there." Adam looked at Joel. "Ain't so?"

Instead of answering, Joel walked out of the shop.

Adam's face fell. "I'm sorry, Grace. I thought I might help him see that he could help himself at the same time he helped your nephews."

"It's not your fault." Samuel curled his fingers into a fist on the table. "I pushed too hard."

"It's nobody's fault." Grace went to the door and looked out to see Joel standing by a small pond edged with reeds. "Let me talk to him."

She wasn't surprised when both men nodded.

Joel raised his head as she approached, but said nothing.

"I'm not intruding, am I?" she asked.

"On what? My communion with nature?" He glanced upward. "Or with God?"

"You tell me. I don't want to intrude."

He snorted. "It sounds to me as if you're already intruding."

"I can go if—"

He stretched out an arm. "No, stay. I shouldn't be taking out my frustration on you."

"You don't want to get the *kinder* together?"

"That sounds like a great idea."

She sighed. "Just not on a church Sunday. You'd be welcome to join us, you know."

He pulled a piece of dried grass and rolled it between his fingers. "I appreciate it, but your opinions don't match everyone else's."

"They match more people's than you'd guess."

"But not enough."

"It's your *daed*, ain't so?"

She'd expected him to look away as he did each time she mentioned his family. Instead, his gaze remained steady. "Someone once said it better than I ever could. Hope springs eternal."

"Alexander Pope."

"Who?"

"Alexander Pope is the poet who first said that hope springs eternal." She smiled. "I read that at the library."

"You've read a lot of books at the library over the years."

"It stuck in my brain. I've heard people use that saying so many times, so it was fun to find out about its author."

"You are the most unusual plain woman I've ever met." He shook his head as a grin played across his lips. "No, that's wrong. You're the most unusual woman, either plain or *Englisch*, I've ever met."

"I'm going to assume that's a compliment."

His smile broadened. "You should. I meant it that way. You're a constant surprise."

"Do you trust me?"

His face grew rigid again, and she realized she might also have pushed him too far. But he needed to be shoved outside his comfort zone. No, his *discomfort* zone. He didn't like where he was, but he couldn't force himself to change. He needed a nudge to move in one direction or the other, toward a plain life or away from it. She wished she knew how to do that.

Then she realized she didn't need to be the one to do it. "Why don't you talk to Jonas?" she asked. "You found it easy to talk to him before."

"I needed help then."

"You need it now. To help you find your way back to God." She hesitated, then said, "No matter how much your *daed* is standing in your way."

Was Grace right? Did Joel need to meet everyone halfway instead of assuming they'd turn and walk away if he put out the slightest feeler to reconnect? He regarded her earnest face. She believed if he stepped forward one step, he wouldn't be knocked back two.

For Grace, faith seemed easy. How had she remained faithful when the person she'd loved most in the world had been taken away from her?

"We'll have the picnic for the kids," he said. "Just not on a church Sunday."

Her face revealed her disappointment. His hands closed at his sides. Disappointment! He'd rather have her spitting angry at him than looking as if he'd let her down…again.

How many times had he seen that same expression on his *daed*'s face after *Daed* had become so exacting? Years ago, Joel had been very excited to share the news about how well he'd done on a project at school or a skill he'd learned on the farm. Each time, *Daed* had regarded him as if he were an utter failure. Why had one of the other *kinder* received as high a mark? Why hadn't Joel been the best in the whole school? Why had Joel made so many mistakes before he mastered a skill on his own? Why hadn't he gotten it right the first time?

Each question had been like a separate lash, cutting into him with invisible wounds that never had a chance to heal. Soon it became easier not to share the news of a praised assignment or a task he could do with competence. He met *Daed*'s demands for updates with sullen silence in a battle of wills he couldn't afford to lose. If he did, any sense of self would have been pulverized beneath *Daed*'s unending expectation of excellence.

If he couldn't live up to his *daed*'s expectations, how could he ever live up to God's?

It was a question he wasn't any closer to answering than he had been the day he'd decided to leave Bliss Valley. The question had plagued him the day he'd walked out of prison and tried to figure out what he was going to do next. It ached through him today.

With *Daed*, it had seemed like a well-fought victory each time Joel defied him by not proving he was the best of the best. It was different now. He couldn't look at Grace because it hurt as if he'd swallowed a burning brand when he thought of disappointing her.

"I'll see you later," he mumbled and loped along the farm lane before she could respond.

Coward! Fool!

As he strode along the road leading toward the Coffmans' farm, he couldn't argue with the words bursting out of his own heart, but he wasn't willing to accept them either. They were words his *daed* had used, and Joel had been determined to prove them wrong. He needed to be as resolved to prove them wrong when they flitted about in his mind.

Lord, help me find a way to be the man You want me to be. The words came from his lacerated heart.

The prayer hadn't faded from his mind as Joel reached the Coffmans' house. Seeing Harold walking from the barn, he pushed aside his grim thoughts. He didn't need to dump them on the older man who was struggling with his cane to walk across the yard.

A blur of motion caught the corner of his eye, and Joel reacted before he even had a chance to see what it was. He jumped forward to get between it and Harold, not wanting the fragile man to be knocked over. Holding up his arms, he steeled himself for the impact.

When it came, he rocked back on his feet, almost stumbling into Grace's *daed*. He wrapped his arms around Brandon to keep the boy from falling backward. Wesley running into his brother helped keep all of them on their feet.

"What's your rush?" asked Harold, frowning as his fingers bleached with his tight grip on the top of his cane.

"Let me go!" shouted Brandon. "Let me go!"

Joel didn't release the boy, though Brandon wiggled like a hooked fish. "You heard your *grossdawdi*. Slow down before you end up hurting yourself or someone else."

"We've got to hide," Wesley cried, his eyes wide with fear.

"From what?" Joel made sure his voice remained stern.

Brandon clamped his lips closed, but Wesley glanced over his shoulder. When the younger boy started to answer, Brandon said, "Shut up! You're going to make it worse."

"Make what worse?" asked Harold. His words shook almost as much as his body.

Still holding on to Brandon, Joel said, "I can handle this, Harold, if you'd like."

The old man hesitated, then nodded. "I'll be in the kitchen having some *kaffi* and a cookie or two if you need me."

"Cookie?" asked Wesley, but didn't add more when his older brother glowered at him again.

Joel remained silent as Harold climbed the back steps with labored motions. When he saw how the boys were watching as well, he considered letting go of Brandon. His grip eased, and he felt Brandon tense to flee. He released one of the boy's arms, but held on to the other.

"What's going on?" he asked once the older man was inside the house and out of earshot.

"Nothing." Brandon's mutter was petulant.

"You're running awfully fast when nothing is chasing you."

"It's a nice day. It's fun to run."

Joel looked from the older boy to the younger one. He noticed Wesley was carrying a baseball bat.

"Playing ball?" Joel asked.

Brandon nodded, but Wesley continued to stare at his feet.

"Having fun?"

Another nod.

"It must be hard."

Brandon started to nod, then gave him a puzzled look. "What's hard?"

"Playing baseball without a ball."

Wesley burst into tears. "It was j-j-just an accident. We d-d-d-didn't mean to."

Joel bent toward the smaller boy. "What was an accident?"

"The w-w-w-window."

Draping his arm over the boy's trembling shoulders, he released Brandon. A single glance in the older boy's direction warned him to stay where he was. Joel was surprised when the boy obeyed, then realized with the truth out, Brandon didn't have any hope of keeping what had happened a secret.

"Accidents happen." Joel pulled out a dusty bandanna and handed it to Wesley to wipe his face. "I assume you apologized to the house's owner." In truth, he didn't assume any such thing, and from the guilty expressions on the two young faces, he knew he was right to be suspicious.

"Why do I have to say I'm sorry?" Brandon blinked back tears. "You never did, Joel." When Joel stared at him in astonishment, the boy raised his chin in feeble defiance. "We've heard all about what you did when you were a kid. You caused lots of trouble, and you've never said you were sorry for anything you did."

"You're wrong. I did say I was sorry."

"Not when you were a kid."

"No," he had to agree, "not when I was a kid, but since then, I've learned how vital it is for a man to own his mistakes and atone for them. Own and atone. Those are two important words that help define a man. Do you understand?"

"Ja," Wesley said first, surprising him. "It means we should have said we're sorry."

"It's not too late," Grace said from behind Joel.

He'd been so wrapped up in trying to reach the boys that he'd failed to notice her there. When she stepped forward and held out her hands, he resisted the longing to take them in his own. Instead, he waited for the boys each to take one. She aimed a silent question at him, and he nodded as he fell into step alongside them.

The boys led them to a neighboring house. The empty lot beside it showed signs of regular ball games because the grass was matted down, and there were bare spots where players had slid into the makeshift bases.

Walking up the drive of the *Englisch* house, Joel sensed the fear coming off Wesley like a heat wave. He remembered shaking in his own shoes on the few occasions he'd been caught and had to face the consequences. What he hadn't realized then was no amount of advice would ease the conversation that waited, so he remained silent. He led the way around a black pickup with a large motorcycle in the back and turned toward the front door of the flat-front brick house. Windows were open, and filmy curtains had slipped through to waft on the faint breeze.

"Go ahead," Joel ordered.

He waited while Brandon went up and knocked on the door before turning to Wesley. "Are you going to let your brother take the rap all on his own?"

The boy looked baffled. "You think I need to knock, too?"

"No," Joel replied, struggling not to smile. He should have guessed an eight-year-old Amish boy might not understand a phrase like "taking the rap." Pushing down his amusement, because one look at Grace's face reminded him there wasn't anything funny about the situation, he explained, "You don't need to knock on the door, but are you going to let Brandon take all the blame when he wasn't the only one involved?"

"I d-d-don't know."

Grace squatted in front of him, her skirt pooling around her. "You and Brandon aren't alone."

"You're here, *a-a-aenti.*"

"I am, and so is Joel, but I meant that with God, you are never alone. He knows how hard this is and how scared you are. But you know what?"

"What?"

"He's close, keeping you safe and reminding you'll never take a single step without Him being with you, watching over you."

Wesley nodded, but didn't move.

"If you want, I can go with you." Joel offered his hand to the little boy.

Wesley grabbed it and held it so hard Joel readjusted his own grip. The boy gulped as Joel walked with him and Grace toward the front door.

It opened as they approached. A wide *Englisch* man with tattoos on his forearms and the back of his hands barked, "What do you want?"

Then a real bark came from inside the house. Both boys

flinched, but Joel said, "We'd like to talk to you about your broken window."

The man appraised Joel, expecting to daunt him as he had the boys. Joel kept his expression calm and met the man's gaze when it returned to his face. In prison, he'd learned to get a fix on other people. Not their facades, but their true intentions. It had been a necessity to survive the vicious world of unrepentant criminals who had little to lose. Even after he'd found a group of other prisoners eager to turn their lives around and start anew beyond the walls, he'd needed those skills of pegging a person right away.

And that sense was telling him the man was more bark than bite, and his small brindled dog that was trying to get past him was more about wagging his tail than taking a chunk out of him or one of the boys.

"It was a-a-an a-a-accident," Wesley said with a courage that Joel admired. "W-w-we're s-s-sorry."

The man's face softened. "I appreciate that." He looked at Joel. "There were a bunch of kids playing next door. Nobody else has come to apologize. That's big of you boys."

Both Brandon and Wesley's shoulders rose at the praise. Joel listened as the man, who introduced himself as Herb Esbenshade, suggested the boys do some simple chores to help repay the cost of the window. When Grace arranged with her relieved nephews and Herb for the boys to return to begin those chores the next afternoon, Joel hoped this would be a *gut* lesson for both Brandon and Wesley.

He mentioned that to Grace as the boys ran ahead when they returned to the farm. "This might give them a new perspective about living with you and their grandparents."

"Don't count on it." Her voice remained bleak. "I stopped by the mailbox on my way home, and there was a note in it from their teacher at school. She wants to meet with me to-morrow. The boys have been causing trouble there."

"What sort of trouble?"

"She didn't say." She pulled a crumpled page out of her pocket and handed it to him.

He scanned the few words. It wasn't a request. It was a command for Grace or her parents to have a conference with the teacher the following afternoon after the scholars left. It wasn't even signed.

"I'll go with you," he said.

"You don't need to. They aren't your family."

He shook his head. "Your family has given me a job to do repairs around the farm, so maybe I can help you fix this. More than that, you've made me feel welcome. You know I'm familiar with about every way a kid can cause trouble, so let me go with you."

The relief on her face was almost identical to Wesley's when Joel offered to walk with the boy to Herb Esbenshade's door. "*Danki*, Joel. I appreciate it. I wasn't looking forward to handling this on my own."

"You would have done fine."

"I'm not so sure."

"I am. You'd fight a lion to do what's right for those boys. You're a great *aenti*."

When she stood on tiptoe and kissed his cheek before rushing after her nephews, he stood, frozen with shock. Not only that she'd kissed him, but how much he regretted she'd kissed his cheek and not his lips.

Chapter Sixteen

Time collapsed as Joel looked around the single classroom. Behind him, Grace herded her nephews into the small school. The building had been built from concrete block and stucco, and painted a pale tan that would handle both the summer sun and the winter cold without needing much maintenance. The single room had four rows of desks separated by an aisle. A few posters hung on the walls between the matching trio of windows on both sides. The blackboard was dusty.

It hadn't changed since he'd last been inside, though everything seemed smaller. He couldn't help thinking of the first day he'd arrived at the school, so thrilled to be counted among the scholars and sure he could master every lesson put in front of him so his *daed* would be proud. Within an hour, he'd discovered how much he *didn't* know as the other *kinder* spoke in English to their teacher. Joel hadn't had older brothers or sisters to teach him as they learned at school, and *Daed* had insisted only *Deitsch* be spoken in the house. Not knowing even the simplest phrases had led to laughter from the other scholars. Now he could see he should have laughed along with them, but he'd been hurt and anxious he wouldn't be able to keep up and be the best in his class as *Daed* had demanded.

Bertha Tice had overseen the school then, and she'd made every effort to help the newcomers. She'd been a beautiful young woman who'd seemed wondrous to Joel, and he'd wished he could grow up to be just like the kindhearted and wise teacher who had a smile for each scholar. Odd to realize Teacher Bertha had been younger then than Joel was now.

Then Teacher Bertha had married and been replaced by Millie Hausman, a widow who was neither kind nor wise and rarely smiled, either in school or outside it. At the same time, *Daed* had increased the pressure on Joel to try to achieve perfection. Joel had gone from looking forward to school to dreading it. Teacher Millie had no patience with the scholars, who wondered what they'd done wrong to deserve such a teacher. The older kids longed for Teacher Bertha to return while the younger ones grew despondent, fearing school would be an endless source of misery for them.

"There's nobody here," Wesley said.

"Let's go home." Brandon turned on his heel to head out the door, but a single glance from Grace halted him. "Are you sure it's today?"

"Are you sure it isn't?"

He gave an emoted sigh, then plopped down at one of the desks. "I'd rather be picking up trash so we can pay off that window than wait for Teacher Millie."

Teacher Millie?

Joel looked at Grace in astonishment. "Did you know Millie Hausman was still teaching here?"

"No. She was supposed to retire in the spring." Putting her arm around Wesley's shoulders, her eyes darkened with sympathy.

"Our new teacher is starting after Christmas," the little boy said.

"Until then," grumbled Brandon, "we're stuck with her."

"And she's stuck with you," Grace replied with an attempt at a smile. "You need to put yourself in her shoes."

Wesley's brow furrowed. "Her shoes are too big."

Joel faked a cough to hide his grin. The boy took everything literally. How was Grace going to explain this concept to him?

"When someone talks about putting themself in someone else's shoes," she said, "it doesn't mean putting on the shoes. It means thinking about how other person feels."

"How can you know that?" Brandon interjected in a snide tone.

Grace started to answer, but Joel said, "Let me."

"All right." A plea in her eyes for him to be gentle with the boy was one he wanted to tell her was unnecessary.

"Brandon," he said, "you spoke to your *aenti* in an impolite way."

"So?"

"So if I'd done that to my *daed*, I'd be on my way to a thrashing right now. You know how that would feel, ain't so?"

"My *daed* wouldn't have done that." Brandon scowled. "He was the best *daed* ever."

"That's not the point." Grace patted the boy's arm. When he flinched, she said, "You're thinking about it, ain't so? Thinking of how fearful Joel would have been when he was your age and did something that displeased his *daed*."

"*Ja.*"

"That's putting yourself in someone else's shoes. Thinking how you'd feel if you were that person."

As she continued to share the lesson with her nephews, Joel thought of a time when he'd received a severe scolding and spanking in front of the whole class. He'd asked *Mamm* why Teacher Millie had to be cruel. After all, Teacher Bertha had used kindness to instill a love of learning in the scholars. A minor misdemeanor was punished by writing an essay about why what the scholar had done was wrong instead of physical punishment that was both painful and humiliating.

Mamm's answer had been that God had put Teacher Millie into that position, and it wasn't for them to question God's will. Joel's argument that God loved His *kinder* and didn't want them to suffer led to *Mamm* giving him a hug and telling him never to forget that. Maybe by his example, she urged, he could teach his teacher.

Joel must have been an atrocious teacher, because Teacher Millie never grew less likely to slap a *kind* for something as simple as stumbling over an answer.

His breath caught as he looked at Wesley. Though the little boy stuttered less at home, he fell back on the habit when he was nervous. Joel couldn't imagine anyone more apt to make a *kind* nervous than Teacher Millie.

You're not a scholar any longer, he reminded himself as he squared his shoulders. *You don't have to be intimidated by her.*

Sympathy swept over him as Grace put a hand on each boy's shoulder and smiled. Her nephews had to endure Teacher Millie's sarcasm and icy stare. No wonder they'd sought any excuse to cause trouble.

The door at the rear of the room opened, and Teacher Millie walked in. Joel was astonished how little she'd changed. Her face would have been attractive if she smiled, but she wore the same wizened expression that made her lips tight and her eyes narrow. More gray laced through her hair in front of her *kapp*, but she wore an identical black dress and apron to the ones she'd had on every day he'd been in school.

Grace stepped forward. "*Danki* for sending me that note. We—"

"What are *you* doing here?" The older woman ignored her

and the boys as she aimed her scowl at Joel. "I thought you were gone for *gut*."

"I've returned." No emotion sifted through Joel's voice as he exerted every bit of his willpower to tamp down his feelings.

When Wesley clung to Grace's skirt as if he were a toddler, so many scenes rushed through Joel's head of Teacher Millie punishing him and the other scholars for not being intimidated by her cruel punishments that exceeded the mistake a *kind* had made. Even as he watched, the little boy stuck his thumb in his mouth and hid his face.

Grace glanced at Joel, and again a silent message passed between them. It was unnerving how easily he could read her thoughts. Right now, she wanted him to say nothing to Wesley. Chiding the boy for sucking his thumb would upset the sensitive *kind* more.

As if Grace had spoken aloud, Teacher Millie snapped, "Get your thumb out of your mouth, Wesley Coffman! Who knows where it's been?"

"I know," Brandon said. "It's been on his hand."

The older woman's mouth twisted. "It seems you two boys are picking up more bad habits because of your *aenti*'s bad choices. Some women shouldn't have *kinder* when they can't make the right decisions about them and their own lives."

When Grace opened her mouth to retort and then closed it, he touched her arm. She looked at him, and he hoped she could see the surprise—and respect—blossoming in his eyes. He understood her need to spit out words that, though they were true, would have been more humiliating for her than for Teacher Millie. She couldn't let herself lose her temper, adding more fuel to the fire the teacher liked to light under a defenseless *kind*.

Today might not be the only time she needed to defend her nephews from the cruel teacher. She must guard her words.

But he didn't. He could say what he'd been waiting for more than two decades to say. Yet, he must be as careful as Grace. He could handle the teacher's nasty barbs, but he didn't want to concentrate her unrelenting rage on the boys.

When no one else spoke, Teacher Millie lifted her chin and tried to look down her nose at them, something that was impossible when Joel stood almost a full head taller than the older woman.

Grace put her arms around both boys' shoulders again and drew a stiff Brandon closer to her. Joel noticed his hands had closed into fists, but he kept them at his sides. With a nod, Joel hoped he could convey how proud he was of Brandon for holding his tongue.

The teacher didn't do the same. In a snide tone, she said, "Now I understand why Fritz's boys are misbehaving. I couldn't figure it out because Fritz was polite, but it's you— you!—who's being such a bad influence on them, Joel Beachy."

Grace tried to interject, "He's not—"

Teacher Millie cut her off. "You don't know what you're talking about. You were a little girl when he convinced his friends to get into trouble."

"I know all about that," Grace replied.

The older woman ignored her. With her angry eyes focused on Joel, she said, "You aren't welcome in my school. Please leave."

Again Grace started to protest, but the slightest motion of Joel's fingers warned her to be silent.

"We will leave," he said, "as soon as you apologize to Grace."

"For what?"

"You know." He lifted his chin and gazed down at her. "You know very well, Millie. It was in the spring of Grace's first year at this school."

"I won't have you threatening me, Joel Beachy."

"I'm not threatening anyone. I'm stating the facts we all know. You can't have forgotten the day you kept Grace after school and what you had planned."

The old woman's face became an unhealthy crimson as the boys exchanged wary glances. He could almost hear their puzzled thoughts as they pondered what was going on. Grace looked as confused. How could that be? Didn't she remember?

"You don't know what you're talking about," Teacher Millie said with a dismissive sniff.

"Don't I?" Joel motioned toward the windows to the right. "You can't have forgotten the firecrackers that went off in the outhouse before you could put your plans into motion? You came rushing out, fearing the outhouse was going to burn down."

Teacher Millie's face tightened more, but she didn't answer.

"I set those off," he said. "It was the only way a kid could figure out how to make sure you didn't beat Grace black-and-blue because she got chalk dust on your dress."

Grace gasped and stared at him in horror. Had she been too young and too innocent to realize the peril she faced? He'd suffered those beatings and knew other kids had, too. Kids who were too terrified by the teacher's threats to say a word about her abuse to anyone, not even each other.

"That shouldn't be any surprise," the teacher snarled. "You were a hopeless case. I know how to raise *kinder* right."

"A *kind* raised with the chance to make a simple mistake without being brutally punished for it will be a *gut* and decent adult. Those who are whipped for the slightest misdeed will find ways to protect themselves."

"By ending up in jail?"

He shook his head as he gave her a smile so threatening she took a half step back. "No, you can't take credit for that, Millie. What you did was make me feel like the ends always justify the means. One of the bad lessons you impressed on us."

"Get out!"

"I will." He shook his head. "Someone should have reported you to the school board years ago, but you intimidated all of us so we wouldn't speak up. That's another bad lesson I got from you. If I'd spoken up when I should have…" He turned away and motioned to Grace and the boys. "*Komm mol.* Let's go."

He'd taken a single step when the teacher called his name. When he looked at her, she asked, "You aren't going to say anything to the school board, ain't so?"

He stopped himself from saying, "*Ja.*" Her face was gray, and he realized she was fearful of losing the reputation she'd never earned. *Hochmut* and hatred were all she had after her husband had died, and she'd held them as close as another woman would have a *kind.*

"You aren't going to strike any scholar ever again, ain't so?" he asked.

She stared at him for a long moment without answering. "No, I won't."

"I trust you are a woman of your word." He smiled at Wesley and Brandon who were listening with open mouths. "You need to keep in mind these *kinder* know if they come to me or Grace and tell us you've broken that pledge, we'll believe them."

No one else spoke as he held the door for Grace and her nephews. He closed the door behind them gently, though he'd longed to slam it. Teacher Millie had been as mean-spirited today as she'd been when he and Grace were among her scholars.

"Wow!" Wesley punched the air. "That was amazing, Joel! You told her!"

Brandon wasn't as ecstatic. "And she's going to make our lives miserable."

"No, she won't." Grace led them down the steps and toward the road. "You heard what she told Joel."

"And you believe she'll keep her word?" the boy fired back. Wesley made a soft moaning sound and grasped Joel's hand. Patting it, Joel said, "*Ja*, I believe she'll keep her word."

"Why?" Brandon wasn't ready to concede.

"Because she knows I'll keep mine."

Brandon considered his answer, then nodded. Without another word, he took off, running along the side of the road with Wesley trying to keep up.

Joel reached out and took Grace's hand, holding it between them where no passerby could see. He waited for her to pull away, but she didn't as he matched his steps to hers.

"Joel, I'm sorry," she said. "I shouldn't have let you come with us."

"You've got nothing to be sorry about, Grace." He squeezed her fingers. "You didn't know Millie Hausman was still teaching after all this time."

She stopped and faced him, holding his hand. His heart seemed to have forgotten how to beat as she said, "*Danki*, Joel. I'm confused about one thing."

"What's that?"

"I thought you said you didn't remember much about me from school?"

"Some things you can't forget, and I remembered *that* day."

"I never knew you were my hero that day."

"I didn't want to see anyone else suffer." *Especially you*, his erratic heart added. He didn't say the words aloud, because she'd think he was flirting with her. But the truth was, in spite of what he'd said to her, gentle-hearted Grace Coffman was one of the people in Bliss Valley he'd never been able to forget.

★ ★ ★

Grace knew the boys were trying the rest of the afternoon to make up for what had happened at the school. Though she'd assured Brandon and Wesley she appreciated their assertions that they wouldn't cause any further trouble at school—or at least until Teacher Millie retired once and for all—she had to wonder if they were making promises they couldn't keep. She also saw how the whole situation had upset her *mamm*.

"You should have told Joel to go to the school board." *Mamm* stamped around the kitchen, sounding like a runaway herd instead of one short woman. "If I'd had any idea how that woman was treating the scholars, I would have…" Her words ended in an unintelligible groan.

"Sit, *Mamm*," Grace urged, hoping it was frustration rather than her weak heart causing *Mamm* to stumble over her words. Guiding her *mamm* to the kitchen table, she was pulling out the chair when she heard a commotion from the lane.

"What is it?"

Grace pointed out the window where *Daed* was bringing the buggy to a stop. "*Daed*'s home."

The boys ran to their *grossdawdi*. Cheers erupted through the air as *Daed* pointed to the buggy's other door. Both boys ran around the vehicle, and Brandon flung the door open so hard Grace half expected it to fly off. As the whole buggy quivered, he pulled out a bright blue scooter. He handed it to Wesley and reached in again.

"Go ahead, Grace," *Mamm* said. "I'll be right behind you."

"We'll go together." She linked her arm through her *mamm*'s and walked onto the front porch.

By the time they reached the lane, Brandon had pulled out a vivid green scooter. It was smaller than the blue one, so he traded with Wesley. Both boys were grinning so broadly their faces strained to hold their expressions.

Shouting their thanks, they started pushing the scooters along the lane. They took a few minutes to learn how to make them go in a straight line and at a steady speed, but they were soon racing each other. Despite his shorter legs, Wesley pushed his scooter past his brother. They both managed to stop before they hit the buggy or Grace and her parents. With hoots, they spun the scooters around, pushed off and accelerated along the lane.

"They love them," *Daed* said with a pleased chuckle. "*Gut!* That will keep them busy so they don't look for mischief."

Mamm gave him a wry grin. "You don't really believe that, Harold. Boys and mischief go hand in hand."

"You worry too much, Saretta."

"And you look as if you could use a nice glass of lemonade and some of my date-nut cookies."

He chuckled. "You know I always need those."

"Go along," Grace said, making shooing motions. "I'll watch the boys to make sure they don't decide to try daredevil tricks on their first day with the scooters."

As her parents went to the house, Grace's smile didn't fade. She admired the love her parents shared. She'd always hoped she would have a love like that of her own. She'd believed that was possible until...

Her brow ruffled. Where was the familiar pain that suffused her whenever she thought of what might have been if Lamar hadn't been killed? There it was. In one small corner of her heart. It was faint, not the crippling pain it had been. When had that changed?

When Joel spoke about how he protected you so many years ago.

She'd been touched by his childish attempt to save her, though if her nephews ever used firecrackers in an enclosed space, she would be furious at their foolishness. In that moment, when Joel spoke of that day she'd forgotten, the bars imprisoning her heart in grief had loosened.

But what now?

As if answer to that question, another buggy came up the lane. Grace was glad to see that the scooters pulled over onto the grass to let the buggy pass before the boys resumed their fun.

The buggy stopped, and Adam jumped out. Without a greeting, he asked, "Grace, is Joel here?"

"I—I—I th-th-think so. He was going to be working on the old ice-ice-icehouse out by the tr-tr-tree l-l-line." Why was she stuttering while talking to Adam? She'd known him for years, but she'd never seen him wearing such a taut expression.

"I need to talk to him." The dark tension underlying Adam's voice sent a shiver down her spine. "And you."

"If you're worried about him helping at the farm, don't. He's been doing a great job." She frowned. "But you're not here to talk about that."

"No, I'm not. There's been an accident."

She pressed her hand over her heart that ached as it had the day she'd gotten the call from Montana. A parade of beloved faces flashed through her face, and she fought to draw in a breath.

"Who?" asked a deeper voice from behind her.

She whirled. "Joel!"

He flashed her a fleeting smile. "I heard the shouts from the boys, and I decided to see what the excitement was. But from looking at your face, Adam, I think that's going to have to wait. What's happened?"

Adam's face seemed to lengthen right before her eyes as he said, "Eddie Mishler didn't come home last night. This morning, Rosemary went to Jonas who contacted the police.

A search party was sent out. Eddie was found in the woods behind their barn."

"Dead?" Joel asked, his voice devoid of any emotion.

Grace grasped Joel's arm, which felt as hard and unresponsive as a statue's, as Adam said, "The police told me that it looked like he'd been shot by his own gun. They're guessing he must have tripped and fallen, and the gun went off."

She held her hand over her mouth to keep her horrified gasp from escaping. Somehow, she managed to ask, "Rosemary didn't find him, did she?"

"No," Adam said. "He was found by Calvin Hertzler. They're *gut* friends. *Were gut* friends." He looked at Joel. "I'm going to be asked by your *mamm*, Joel, so I might as well get the answer from you right now."

"Will I be coming to the viewing and the funeral?" He sighed, and she saw the pain in his eyes. "Before I answer that, I've got another question for you, Adam. If I go, will I be allowed in?"

Chapter Seventeen

Joel paced from the barn to the house and back. Not pacing so much as heading inside, then turning away from the kitchen door at the last minute. Would his presence at the viewing for Eddie Mishler be a comfort for Rosemary, or would it disrupt everything? Should he go?

There were so many reasons not to. He didn't want to be a hypocrite and pretend he'd liked the man. His family would be present, including *Daed*, and emotions would be high. The wrong word spoken could cause wounds that would never heal. Many of the *Leit* would be gathered to support the mourners, and he feared his presence would eclipse them. Not that anyone in the community would pelt him with questions or rumors—both true and false—about his recent past.

At least not in the house, but he guessed he would be the subject of a lot of speculation outside.

If you'd listened to Grace's advice and attended church, this wouldn't be as much of a problem now. The Leit would have had their chance to hypothesize why you're back and what will happen if you stay.

He was a stubborn fool, exactly as his *daed* had called him over and over. But it was too now late to play the "woulda/coulda/shoulda" game. Not that doing it had ever gotten him anywhere. He'd learned that after listing, day after day while he was behind bars, all the reasons he "woulda/coulda/shoulda" done things differently so he hadn't end up in prison.

Instead, he needed to think about the reasons he had to go to the wake today. There were two.

Rosemary and Grace.

Rosemary had been widowed only eight months after she was married, and Grace had to be thinking about losing her fiancé before they even had a chance to exchange their vows.

Daed would be there along with the rest of the family. Would they speak to Joel? Would they try to toss him out as Teacher Millie had? He hadn't had any trouble closing the door at the school, but he dreaded the idea of someone shutting him out of his family. Once and for all time.

If he stayed away, he could enjoy the fantasy that once upon an undefined time, he'd be part of his family again. No doors slammed and locked. No creating drama when his sister was in mourning.

Not going and being patient and letting his family come to him would have been the sensible decision, but something was drawing him toward the Mishler farm as if he were a yo-yo climbing its string.

Not something.

Some*one*.

Grace's face had displayed her dismay when he asked Adam if he'd be allowed to go into his own sister's house. That he had to ask the question hurt her as much as it'd hurt him. She cared about him. It would have been so simple to fall in love with her, but he couldn't. Not when his life was so messed up.

Knowing he couldn't put off changing into his best clothes

any longer if he wanted to go to the viewing with the Coffmans, Joel walked into the *dawdi haus*. A sound from the bedroom broke into his chaotic thoughts. Someone else was in
the *dawdi haus*. Who?

Pausing in the doorway, Joel was astonished to discover
Wesley lying on his belly and peering under the bed.

The boy jumped to his feet and gasped when he saw Joel.
Color rose up his cheeks, consuming his freckles.

"Did you lose something?" Joel asked in a neutral tone.

Wesley shook his head and stared at the floor.

"Did you want to talk to me about something?" He thought
of the times the boy had acted as if he were ready to open
up to him and Grace before Brandon shut him down with a
sharp comment.

"No." Wesley's voice was so soft Joel wasn't sure he'd heard
him speak.

"What can I do for you?"

For a moment, Wesley studied his best shoes. Raising his
head, he asked, "What happens when someone dies?"

Joel wanted to groan. He'd left himself open to such a question, but how was he going to answer a little boy who was
mourning his parents?

He sat on the bed, taking care not to wrinkle the clean
shirt and trousers Saretta had placed there. "Jesus says He is
the resurrection and the life."

"I know that. I heard that in Montana and here. But what
happens when someone dies?"

"What do you think happens?"

The boy didn't answer. Shuffling his feet on the floor, he
considered Joel's question. As one minute passed, then a second, Joel fought his impatience that urged him to jump in
and answer his own question.

Finally Wesley said, "I think you open your eyes and see

everyone you love who's already in heaven. They give you hugs and kisses and tell you how much they love you. They were ready for you to come there to join them because they've been watching over you every day of your life."

"I hope you're right." He was impressed by how much thought the boy had given to the subject.

"But does it hurt to die?"

"You're asking hard questions, Wesley," Joel said with a sad smile, "that men far smarter than I am have struggled with for thousands of years. All I can tell you is what I've seen. I was by my *grossdawdi*'s bedside when he died. He'd been in a lot of pain, and suddenly there was a smile on his face. His muscles had been fighting his anguish, and they relaxed as he was taking his last breaths. My *mamm* told me our souls don't take any pain with us into death. It made me feel better about my *grossdawdi*'s passing because I knew he wasn't suffering any longer. Not that I missed him any less."

"I miss my *mamm* and *daed*."

"I know you do. It's sad to have someone we love die. It's wrong to pretend otherwise."

"So it's okay to mope?"

"Mope?" He frowned. "Did someone use that word?"

"*Ja*. One of the girls at school said that I should be a big boy and stop moping." He faltered, then asked, "What's moping?"

"Nothing you need to worry about. Feel what you want to feel. What you *need* to feel. If someone gives you flak about it—"

Wesley ran out of the room. His best shoes thundered across the small living room and out the door.

What had Joel said to spook the *kind*? He'd been trying to convey empathy as Grace did with him. To judge by the boy's reaction, it was something she was far more skilled at doing than he was.

Why had Wesley come to him? The boy seemed to be growing closer to his grandparents. Harold and Saretta doted on their *kins-kinder*. He'd seen proof of that in many ways, the cookies Saretta baked for them, the time Harold spent with the boys and the new scooters. That affection was returned. Though Brandon always seemed to find out a way to evade being embraced, Wesley was happy to get as many hugs as he could.

So why had Wesley asked him the tough questions instead of his grandparents? Playing the conversation back through his mind, Joel realized the boy hadn't revealed why he'd been in the *dawdi haus*. With a sigh, Joel shook his head. It wasn't a discussion he wanted to have now.

Joel changed into the clean clothes he'd brought with him to Bliss Valley. He'd been wearing plain clothing to work around the farm, but didn't feel right about wearing broadfall trousers, a black vest and *mutze* coat to his brother-in-law's viewing. Church clothing was what the others would be wearing, but it felt too hypocritical for him to put on the outfit left by Saretta.

He checked his appearance in the small mirror over his dresser and ran his fingers through his hair. He needed a haircut. No, the *Englisch* version of him needed a haircut. For the plain part of him, his hair was too short and layered. He no longer was sure which aspect of himself he wanted to be. The *Englischer* had messed up his life beyond redemption. The places he'd applied for jobs had made that clear, even if he hadn't seen the suspicions on his parole officer's face and listened to Shriver's lectures about keeping his nose clean. The taint of jail clung to him like a skunk's reek on the grass at dawn and spread out to offend everyone he passed.

Except for Grace. She was ready to give him a second chance. *Give him enough rope to hang himself*, as *Daed* would have said.

Joel's hands clenched at his sides. *Daed* was going to be at Rosemary's house. The whole family would be. Would any of them welcome him, or would they wish he was in the coffin instead of Eddie? Ice slithered up his back.

"Snap out it," he growled to his reflection. "Be grateful for the blessings you've be given in the past few weeks. Be thoughtful of the loss Rosemary is dealing with."

He repeated those phrases to himself as he emerged from the *dawdi haus* to see Grace and her *daed* waiting beside the buggy. Grace held a casserole dish wrapped in a dish towel. Guessing Saretta was remaining at home with her *kins-kinder* who shouldn't attend another viewing so soon after their parents', Joel hurried to join them. He bent his head when Harold urged them to pray before they left for the Mishlers' farm.

Grace helped her *daed* into the buggy and onto the rear seat without any fanfare. When she started to speak as she put the casserole on the floor behind the front bench, she glanced at Joel and closed her mouth. He wasn't sure what she saw on his face that warned her to keep her thoughts to herself. Or maybe she'd guessed. She had an uncanny ability to gauge his feelings even before he was aware of them.

Other than to give him directions to his sister's farm, no one spoke during the ten minute drive. The buggy turned into the farm lane between a mailbox and a fieldstone building with a slate roof. The narrow road led to a farmhouse that looked comfortable in its setting. Porches sprouted from every angle of the structure that was half white clapboard and half fieldstone. A trio of trees shadowed the house and a small building made from the same stone as the house that wasn't far from the mailbox by the road. A tidy garden peeked around the right side of the house, lush and filled with vegetables ready to harvest.

Not a single one would go to waste. If Rosemary was too

distraught to take care of her house and the garden and the farm animals, members of the community would step up to assist. No one would offer help. People would simply come and do what needed to be done for as long as Rosemary couldn't handle things on her own.

"I've heard she's thinking of selling the herd," Grace said as she leaned toward him.

"That's too bad." He kept his gaze on the buggy in front of him so he didn't run the horse into it if the other driver came to a sudden stop.

"I know, but she should get a *gut* price for the cows. Unless..."

He slowed the horse to a stop as he looked at her for the first time since they'd left her folks' house. "Unless someone comes and takes care of them for her."

"*Ja.*"

"Great minds think alike."

A smile warmed her grief-lined face. "I'm glad to hear that, Joel."

"I'm not sure my help would be welcome."

"You don't know that."

He gave the reins a gentle ripple across the horse's back as the buggy in front of them moved forward a few feet. "I know what my *daed* will say."

"Then Wyman needs to take over tending to the cows himself, and we know how much he hates tending to livestock." She folded her arms in front of her.

Joel hadn't guessed he'd ever feel like laughing this afternoon, but he had to force his chuckles back into his gut. There would be enough scandalized glances in his direction. He didn't need to create more by being seen laughing at his brother-in-law's viewing.

But he appreciated how Grace had pegged *Daed* so succinctly. Joel had never understood why Wyman Beachy was a farmer. He hated every aspect of the work and had turned over as much as he could to his son as soon as Joel was ready. Even before, because Joel shouldn't have been working in the fields alone the summer after his first year of school. *Mamm* hadn't liked that, and she'd made excuses to come to check on him. However, like everything else in their house, she hadn't gainsaid a single order *Daed* gave.

A boy came forward to show them where to park the buggy near an oak tree. Joel didn't ask him to unhitch Pearl. When he saw the glances and a few outright stares aimed in his direction as he'd climbed out of the buggy, he doubted their visit would last long.

"It's a *gut* thing you're doing," Grace murmured as she stepped from the buggy.

"Do you need help with Harold?" he whispered. If he showed how much he appreciated her support, he might break down in clear view of those people who were judging him and finding fault with him before he opened his mouth.

"We'll be fine." She took his hand and gave it a quick squeeze before she turned to assist Harold to the ground. She picked up the casserole. With a motion of her head toward the house, she urged Joel to go ahead of them.

Though he would have preferred to jump in the buggy and set Pearl to his top speed heading anywhere but where they were, Joel walked to the front door of Rosemary's house. His feet weighed more with each step. That might have been a *gut* thing, because otherwise, he might have turned on his heel and hightailed it out of there.

The crowd on the porch parted as if he were Moses commanding the Red Sea. A few people started to speak their condolences, then stopped. Because they didn't know what to say or because they didn't want to get caught speaking to a man who'd been in prison?

Nodding to them as if they'd greeted him warmly, he went into the front room of the house. His sister's furniture had been moved out. Folding chairs were placed in rows near the bier where a simple plain coffin sat. The lid was closed, and Joel guessed the funeral director hadn't been able to conceal the damage done by the bullet that had killed Eddie.

Only about half of the chairs were occupied, but all the seats in the front row were taken. He recognized his sisters and *Mamm* who had claimed the chairs on either side of Rosemary who sat facing the center of the coffin. His heart tightened in pain as he imagined them stepping aside without speaking to him as the people had done on the porch.

His hopes of coming home and resurrecting his connections to his family…as dead and gone as Eddie.

"Let's offer our condolences," Grace said as she stepped up beside him. She didn't have the casserole, so she must have handed it off to someone else.

He nodded, not trusting his voice to speak. Stuffing his hands in his pockets, he frowned. Where was the pocket-watch cover? Guessing he hadn't switched it into the pocket in these trousers when he changed, he followed Grace.

He stopped as if he'd run into a wall when *Daed* emerged from another room and sat beside *Mamm*. Wyman Beachy had gained a lot of weight around his middle, and his shoulders were hunched as if he carried a barrel on each one. His steel-gray hair matched his thick beard, but his bushy eyebrows dominated his lined face. Ruts had been dug into his cheeks and around his mouth, which was turned down in a frown.

Joel noticed that in the moment before he was struck by the icy glare aimed in his direction. If Joel left now…

No, he wasn't going to be that scared boy who'd done everything to gain his *daed*'s love and approval until he realized it wasn't possible to win either.

As Joel joined Grace and Harold in the line of mourners inching forward to offer their prayers and their respects, *Daed* remained in his chair, his eyes focused on the coffin in front of him. He appeared to be deep in prayer, but Joel wasn't fooled. He saw *Daed*'s eyes cut to him. They widened before he lowered them again. Did Wyman believe his son would skip out like the coward he'd called him?

As the line inched forward, *Daed*'s eyes shifted toward him every few seconds. If his *daed* was waiting for Joel to come on his knees to beg his forgiveness, he was going to be waiting a long time.

When Harold paused to speak to *Daed*, Joel edged around him and went to where Rosemary sat with their sisters. A crumpled handkerchief was twisted in her hands. She looked up at him, her tearstained eyes widening. Had she thought he wouldn't come to be with her at such a time?

Such a time as this.

The phrase from the Book of Esther resonated through his head. Esther's uncle had chided her for thinking she was safe from the persecution of the Jews because she lived in the king's palace. Like Esther, Joel had been separated from his family, though his own actions had led to the estrangement.

"Joel," she whispered.

He was nearly knocked off his feet when she threw herself in his arms. She clutched him as she had when they were much younger, and he'd carried her on his back through the high grass or up a hillside her shorter legs couldn't manage.

Too many memories threatened to strangle him. Giving Rosemary a hug, he helped her sit down so her wobbly legs didn't leave her on the floor. He looked from her to *Mamm* who had aged far more than he'd guessed in the past ten years. He wondered how many of the wrinkles gouged in her face were because of him. Words of apology bubbled into his mouth, but he didn't say a single one as she came to her feet and walked away.

Was that it? Was she refusing even to talk to him?

Suddenly he felt no older than Wesley and wondering if it hurt to die. He wanted to shout that it must be easier to die than to live with the pain pressing down on him like a massive weight, threatening to halt his heart in between heartbeats.

When *Mamm* paused and looked over her shoulder, Grace came to his rescue yet again. "Go to her. She wants to talk to you. Alone." A single shift of her gaze toward *Daed* told him that again she'd read the situation better than he had.

Joel followed his *mamm* out a door and onto a side porch that was empty. He could hear voices from inside the house and from the front porch, but flower bushes edging the side porch made it a hidden haven cut off from the rest of the world.

Mamm faced him as he came out and waited while he shut the door. Its window would give her a view of anyone coming near enough to eavesdrop.

"It is *gut* to see you, son." *Mamm* put up her hands as if to offer him a hug, then lowered them. Even though there were two walls between them and *Daed*, it was as if *Daed* lurked behind her, guiding each motion as if she were a marionette.

"And to see you, *Mamm*." He smiled and saw her relax slightly. Had she thought he'd turn his back on her?

Then he thought of the letters she'd sent him after he first left Bliss Valley. Back then, he'd been irritated by each one because they'd been filled with pleas for him to return before he was lost to them forever. He could think of one poignant letter that was filled with reminiscences of his childhood when he and *Mamm* had spent long hours together, playing and cooking and cleaning the house. Those special times had come to an end when Rosemary was born, and *Daed* declared *Mamm* had babied him too long.

He's a boy, he could remember *Daed* pronouncing like some Old Testament prophet laying down the law, *and he should be doing boy things. Not following you around, Sharon. You've got a daughter now. Let me raise the boy the way he's supposed to be raised.*

Mamm hadn't protested, but Joel had seen emotions in her eyes he hadn't understood at the time. In retrospect, he recognized them as sadness and frustration. Why hadn't she protested *Daed*'s edicts?

Maybe she had in her quiet way. Just as she was talking to him now, she'd written letters to him. *Daed* must have prohibited any communication between the family and Joel. But she'd kept writing...

And he'd kept tearing each letter up into the tiniest possible pieces, venting his own frustration in a childish way. She'd given up writing when he hadn't replied or reappeared at their home. How he'd wished he could hear from her while he was in jail! He could have taken the initiative and sent her a note, but he wasn't sure if *Daed* would let her have it.

"Are you well?" *Mamm* asked.

"I am. You?"

"Not as spry as I used to be." She started to smile, then, after a quick glance past him, recomposed her face into a blank expression. "It is *gut* to see you looking so well."

"I am living at Harold Coffman's farm. They're making sure I'm well fed."

"I've heard that. Are you happy, son?"

Something stuck in his throat when she called him son. Not for one second during his life had she made him feel less loved because he hadn't come from her womb. It was a gift none of them had ever spoken of, but that silence didn't make it any less precious.

"I am," he replied. "I'm doing work I like, and the Coffmans treat me like family."

An expression he couldn't read slipped across her face and vanished before she said, "Wait here."

He didn't have time to protest before she slipped past him and into the house. He leaned against the porch railing. Looking up at the trees, he saw a few leaves had begun to don their autumn glory. Another year coming to an end, but for the first time in years, he could look forward to a new year as something more than another blank calendar where he marked each day as it passed. He'd counted down the days until he could be free. Now he was…at least partly.

"God, I could use some instructions on what to do now." He sighed.

The door opened, and he stood straighter when his two youngest sisters came onto the porch. Neither would meet his eyes at first, giving him a chance to see how they'd grown from being cute little girls into lovely women. He'd missed more than half of their lives, and he shouldn't have been surprised they acted as shy as if he were a complete stranger.

Alta was the middle daughter and the prettiest with her pale blond hair and a sense of style that even her plain dress couldn't conceal.

And Erma, the *boppli* of the family, who always wore her emotions openly.

"I'm glad you're back," Alta said, her voice cautious.

"*Ja.*" Erma nodded. "Even though I've got to admit I was wrong. When Rosemary told us she'd seen you at the quilt shop, I said you'd hightail it out of Bliss Valley before now."

"Why would you think that?" he asked.

"Because you were thinking about it when we saw you at the bone marrow event." She leaned against the railing and folded her arms in front of her. "You need to stay. At least for a little while longer. Rosemary is going to need all of us." She sighed. "I worry about her. She and Eddie are—were—

still newlyweds. I know she was hoping to announce by now to us that they were going to have a *boppli*." Tears rolled in fat drops down her cheeks. "Now that won't ever happen."

His sisters looked relieved when Joel said he assumed they had a lot to do to help with the many visitors coming to the viewing and he shouldn't keep them away from the callers. He knew most would be bringing a dish to share as Grace had. He was grateful Grace had remembered what he should have. He'd have to thank her later.

When Alta rushed into the house, Erma faced him with a frown. "I know I shouldn't say anything."

"The others have—"

"Short memories." Her mouth tightened. "They're so happy you're home they've forgotten what it was like while you were away."

"Maybe that's because it's easier."

"Not for me." She strode into the house.

Joel started to follow, but was waylaid by two little boys who ran up to him. They looked almost identical when they looked up at him. "Fun? Have fun?" He started to ask what they meant.

They darted away, and he watched them run to where Naomi was standing beside Samuel. Seeing the two of them together, with Naomi holding a *boppli* in her arms, made his head spin. Were the little boys their *kinder*, too? He could recall how Samuel had taken extra pleasure in finding ways to play pranks on Naomi. Had it been because, even back then, Samuel had had strong feelings for her? During the time between when they'd jumped the fence and the accident, his friend hadn't been serious about any *Englisch* woman. Had he been pining for Naomi all that time?

He looked in the opposite direction and saw Adam speaking with Rosemary's in-laws. Laurene stood beside him, her arm around the shoulders of Adam's four-year-old daughter.

Adam and Laurene...

Samuel and Naomi...

The impossible made possible by love. A pang cut through him. Was it possible for love to offer the same second chance to him?

He sighed. His friends had made most of their mistakes when they were foolish teens and should have known better. He had continued long after he'd become an adult and definitely had known better.

And now he was reaping what he'd sown.

Chapter Eighteen

The barn was quiet in the twilight when Grace entered. She drew in a deep breath, loving the scents of animals that once had lived beneath its roof along with hay and the remnants of the day's heat. How many evenings had she come into the barn as a *kind*, hoping to have some special time with her *daed*? While he'd strained the *millich* he'd collected from the cows, she'd perched on a stool and listened to stories of his own childhood. Like her, he'd been the youngest and had known that someday the family's farm would be his responsibility.

Tears clogged her eyes, blurring her vision as she thought of how impossible it would be for *Daed* to do the simple chores he once had handled with ease. No longer did she hear the soft low from a cow or the skittering when one of the barn cats chased something in the loft. The stanchions were silent because the cows didn't wait to be milked before heading out into the pasture to graze.

It shouldn't have changed. *Daed* should have been healthy, and Lamar should have been working side by side with him.

By now, she and Lamar would have had a family, maybe even a young son or daughter old enough to toddle behind him into the barn like she once had trailed after *Daed*.

"Do you need something?" Joel's voice cut through her memories and regrets.

She watched as he came along the concrete walkway between the two gutters. His steps were heavy.

"You must be tired," she said in reply.

"Why do you say that?" he asked as he leaned a push broom against a wooden post at the end of the stanchions. He lifted a stack of pails, then wincing, put them back on the floor and took the top two.

"What's wrong? You're only carrying a couple of pails at a time. Usually you lift far more than that."

Setting the pails on the concrete floor again, he stuck his hands into his pockets. She could see him opening and closing the fingers on his left hand. Had he injured himself somehow? She hadn't seen any sign of that while they were at Rosemary's house, but he'd disappeared for almost fifteen minutes after they'd arrived. Then, he'd gone outside and sat by the buggy until she and *Daed* returned. He hadn't said much on the way home, and he'd been as silent during supper.

"I'm fine," he said. "Are *you* all right?"

"Me? You're the one who lost a brother-in-law." She sat on a bale of hay that had been left near the milking parlor. "Even if there wasn't any love lost between you two, I know you are sad for your sister who lost her husband."

"But you lost the man you loved, too, Grace." He sat beside her on the bale. "Today had to have been tough for you."

"It was tough for everyone."

"Stop it!"

She flinched at the whiplash of his voice.

Instantly, he apologized, then lifted her hand so it was sandwiched between his. "You need to stop deflecting away anyone's concern for you. You take the time to reassure others you're aware of their troubles and you'd like to help. But if anyone offers to help you, you throw up barriers so high and so thick nobody can scale them."

"My troubles happened long ago. No one wants to hear about them now."

"I do."

She blinked, blinded by a flood of tears. She'd never imagined two little words would mean so much to her. Everybody else had accepted her claims that she'd come to terms with her pain.

Everybody except Joel.

"Tell me about him, Grace," he urged when she didn't answer.

"You don't remember him?"

"Not really. I know I should. There weren't more than twenty scholars in the school most of the time I was there."

"I'm not surprised you don't remember him. He was the kid nobody seemed to notice. He stood at the side of the games during recess. Back then, I thought he was as shy as I was. That changed when he had a growth spurt, and the girls were eager to keep him from being alone. Not that he ever seemed to have eyes for anyone but your sister."

"Which one?"

"Rosemary." Her brow knit as she added, "I heard some stories about him attending a lot of parties with both plain and *Englisch* kids when he was having his *rumspringa*, but I never heard of him walking out with anyone other than Rosemary."

"I didn't realize you and Rosemary had that loss in common."

She nodded and looked at where his fingers had curled around her own. "She assured me she and Lamar were never serious." Smiling sadly, she said, "She told me your *daed* was eager to see her married, so she hung out with Lamar."

"And Lamar was okay with it?"

"*Ja.* He said she was a *gut* friend, so why not help her? Especially when he was too shy to ask out the girl he was really interested in."

"You?"

"*Ja.* Finally he got up the nerve, as he said, and asked me to walk out with him. I'm glad he did. He was a fine man, Joel. You would have liked him." She sighed. "I wish you'd have had a chance to get to know Eddie Mishler better. It was clear he loved your sister with all his heart."

"You're talking about how he warned me away from her."

She nodded, and it was his turn to sigh.

"Maybe," he said, "under other circumstances, we might have been able to tolerate each other, but he couldn't look past the lies my *daed* fed him to see the truth."

"You don't know—"

"I do know, Grace." He patted their entwined fingers with his other hand. "I know my *daed* well, and I know the face he shows the world is different from the one he showed us." Waving aside her answer before she could give it, he said, "You've changed the subject. Why don't you ever mention Lamar?"

"It makes people uncomfortable when I talk about him, so I don't."

"But you want the boys to talk about their parents because you believe it'll help them."

"It will help them." She sighed. "It helped me to talk about Lamar sometimes."

"So talk about him."

"With you?"

"Why not? Tell me about him. I never knew the man, so I don't have any preconceived opinions. Tell me what he was like. Really like. Not only that he helped my sister, though that tells me you're right when you said I would have liked him."

"I don't know where to begin."

"What did he look like?"

She smiled. "That's a very *Englisch* question, Joel. What we look like on the outside isn't as important as what we are like inside."

"So what was wrong with him? Did he have four eyes? Ten toes on one foot and none on the other?"

"Don't be silly."

"I won't be silly if you'll tell me about him. He's so much a part of your life, but yet I know nothing about him."

For a long moment, she said nothing. How could she explain everything about Lamar in a few sentences?

Joel waited for her to answer. She was amazed. He was impatient and hated silence. Was it because it had been so quiet in his cell or so loud? She longed to ask that, to get to know *him* better, but he'd accuse her of evading talking about Lamar again. And maybe she was. It wasn't easy to sum up a whole life, even one cut short too soon, in a few words.

"Lamar was a *gut* man," she said, gazing straight ahead at the spot where she used to watch Lamar and *Daed* working with the herd. "He had a strong, *wunderbaar* faith, and lots of people believed God planned for him to be ordained one day. I was one of those who was certain of that."

"The life of an ordained man's wife isn't an easy one. Her husband is so busy with others' families he has far less time for his own."

"I knew that, and I was prepared to assume that life if Lamar was put into the lot and was chosen." She lowered her head and pulled her hand away from his. She clenched her fingers together. "But that wasn't God's plan for him or for me. Nobody ever found out how the bull got into the field, but it didn't matter. Lamar was dead, a *gut* man who should have had more time to spread his kindness through the community."

"And you were alone." He took her hands and drew them apart. Again he laced his fingers through the fingers of her left hand. Lifting her hand to his lips, he kissed her knuckles.

Her breath caught as sensations, powerful and explosive, swept over her like the leading edge of a fierce storm. His kisses were light and swift and *wunderbaar*.

Lowering her hand, he snagged her gaze as he said in a husky voice, "But you were never alone. You had the whole community around you." He curved his hand along her cheek, tilting her face toward his, so she couldn't let her eyes slide away. "But you didn't let their attempts to comfort you reach past those barriers, ain't so?"

"You don't understand, Joel."

"Then help me understand."

Coming to her feet, she wrapped her arms around herself as if trying to keep out a chill, but the cold was inside her. "Lamar saw me, Joel. Really saw me instead of dismissing me as a girl who couldn't string two words together when she was nervous. He didn't let me linger in the corner and watch the world go by. He drew me out of my corner and out of myself."

"The other guys then discovered what they'd overlooked with you."

She shrugged. "Maybe they did. Maybe they didn't. What mattered to me is that until Lamar came into my life, most of them treated me as if I were invisible."

"Then they were fools."

"Or had learned to overlook me." She gnawed her lower lip for a moment, then added, "Like you did when we were in school."

"I've tried to block out everything between those walls. Going back there was rough."

"No kidding." She tried to laugh, but the sound fell flat. "But I'll never forget how you protected me when I didn't realize I needed help."

He nodded, and his jaw tightened. Was he trying to keep from saying something? She was curious what it might be, but it was clear he didn't want the words to escape.

To help him get his emotions under control, she said, "I'm going to get the boys a calendar so they can mark off each day until they get a new teacher." When Joel flinched, she asked, "What's wrong?"

"Nothing. Just an old memory about a calendar I used to keep." She almost asked if it had been while he was in prison, but he forestalled her question when he stood and wiped his hands on his trousers. "My life has been on hold while I was in prison, but it sounds like yours has been, too. You haven't walked out with anyone since Lamar died?"

"No one asked me."

"None of the guys around here came calling after giving you a chance to mourn?"

"Several came, but they didn't return after that first visit." She raised her eyes to meet his. "Most likely because I didn't do anything to encourage them."

"Was that because you felt they should have seen you as you were earlier?" He took her hand and folded it between his much larger ones. "Who were you punishing for their mistakes, Grace? Them or you?"

She stared at him for a long minute, then realized she had no answer to give him. She spun and walked out of the barn. When he didn't follow, she wasn't sure whether to be grateful or to give in to the tears searing her eyes. Nothing was simple any longer.

★ ★ ★

Joel stepped out of the low-slung brick building that held the medical clinic just outside the village of Strasburg. A glance at the clock on the wall as he left warned him that he had to make a fifteen minute walk in less than ten minutes. Deciding to cut through a few backyards, he loped toward the road curving into town.

When he'd agreed to join Adam and Samuel for a pizza to make plans for the picnic to get the *kinder* together, he hadn't expected to find a voice mail for him on the phone in the shack by the road. He'd discovered it after attending the funeral for his brother-in-law two days ago. The message had been from the bone marrow registry.

Shocked, he'd wondered if he was a match for someone. The worker at the donation event had assured him, if he actually was a match, he'd be contacted by mail. So why the call? The male caller hadn't left many details. Just a number to call back as soon as possible.

When Joel had returned the call, the lady who answered couldn't give him any specifics beyond it was important for him to supply a blood sample to accompany his swab. She couldn't—or wouldn't—tell him if it was because he was a possible match for someone.

He'd thought about telling Grace and asking her advice, but she hadn't said more than a handful of words to him while she prepared the breakfast he'd had to skip and refused to meet his eyes. He was shocked she hadn't asked why he wasn't eating breakfast, but she didn't. Did she regret being so honest with him in the barn a few nights ago? Or was she trying to keep him from touching her? If she had any idea of how he'd longed to kiss her mouth instead of her fingers…

Shaking his head, he hurried along the road toward the pizza shop. He was starving, and the idea of pizza and a soda seemed as scrumptious as heaven-sent manna. He looked forward to seeing his friends, but once he returned to the farm, he needed to search some more for his *grossdawdi*'s watch cover. He'd checked throughout the house, careful not to let anyone know what he was looking for. Other people had called the cover a piece of junk, and he didn't want to hear that again.

You wouldn't from Grace, reminded the honest little voice in his head.

He knew that, but he didn't want to make a big deal about a lost watch cover when she was dealing with so many things. Harold had stumbled on his way into the house again, and the older man was nursing two scraped palms and a bruised knee. His Parkinson's often made it difficult to raise his toes high enough when he was walking. The tumbles seemed to be coming more often. Joel was glad Harold hadn't fallen during their trip to the livestock auction yesterday.

And to add to his frustration, nobody at the medical clinic had been able to answer his questions about the call from the bone marrow registry. The woman who had drawn his blood knew only that an order for the procedure had been sent to them.

Lost in thought, Joel almost bumped into a plain woman who was walking with her *kind*. He swallowed hard when he realized the two were Laurene and Adam's daughter. What was the girl's name?

"Step to the side, Mary Beth," Laurene said. "We can't hog the sidewalk."

"Danki," he said.

She stepped between him and the little girl, then looked disconcerted as if she couldn't believe her own instinctive motion.

"Sorry," he said. "I wasn't sneaking up on you."

Laurene gave him a smile, but she remained as flighty as a cat. "I didn't think that. You...you surprised me. That's all."

Joel knew she was trying to put the past behind her. After all, she'd fallen in love with his friend. She trusted Adam, but not Joel. Why should she trust him? He hadn't given her any reason to when they were kids, and he hadn't given her any reason to change her mind since his return to Bliss Valley.

"Laurene, can we talk for a moment?"

She hesitated, then urged Mary Beth to go into a nearby garden and look at the display of pumpkins among chrysanthemums that were yellow, orange and red.

He watched the little girl skip to the largest pumpkin and wrap her arms around it. Or try to. Her fingers missed touching by more than six inches.

His gaze returned to Laurene when she said, "All right, Joel. What do you want to say?"

"I owe you an amends. An apology."

"You're in AA?" Her mouth became a complete circle before she closed it.

"You know about Alcoholics Anonymous?"

She gave him a hint of a smile. "I spent fifteen years living as an *Englischer*. You'd be surprised what I've learned along the way."

"No, I wouldn't."

Her face became serious again. "No, I guess you wouldn't."

"I've been in AA since the car accident. I continued in prison, though I haven't been to a meeting since I came here."

"There's a group at the church where we had the blood donor drive. I saw a poster there."

He nodded, not wanting to admit he hadn't noticed much besides his sisters. He also didn't want to tell Laurene about being contacted by the bone marrow registry. Until he knew who would possibly be receiving his donation, he didn't want to get anyone's hopes up.

"I'll check it out," he said when he realized he had to say

something to acknowledge her kindness in mentioning the meetings at the church. "One of the things I learned at AA was that I can't start over until I deal with the mistakes I've made. That's why I want to tell you how I'm sorry for what happened years ago. I could give you a long list of the reasons why I was such a bully, but we both know that list doesn't matter anymore."

"Not to me, but does it still matter to you?"

He couldn't help recalling how Grace had said pretty much the same thing when she found him about to take vegetables from her garden. Did it still matter to him? He wished it didn't, but it did.

"I know," he said, "I can't move on in my recovery until I make amends to those I've hurt. The ones I've hurt most are you and Naomi and Adam and Samuel."

"And your family."

"I know."

Sympathy filled her eyes. "I've learned how hard the road back to feeling at home in Bliss Valley is, and it's got to be more difficult for you. My parents made the decision to jump the fence and took me along. But I had to come to the realization that, though they insisted I go with them, I could have returned as soon as I was an adult. I didn't, and I can't blame that choice on anyone but myself."

"But you came back?"

"Not of my own free will." She laughed. "Definitely not of my own free will. God decided when it was time for me to come back. He presented me with the opportunity to make the choice to stay or return to the *Englisch* world. It sounds as if He is doing the same for you, Joel."

He nodded, because he couldn't find words to say how he envied her such a clear-eyed faith.

As if he said that aloud, Laurene added, "If you think making that choice was easy, Joel, you're wrong."

"But you fell in love with Adam."

A sweet smile settled on her lips as her soon-to-be stepdaughter danced over to her and threw small arms around Laurene. "First I fell in love with this moppet. Mary Beth and I are besties, ain't so?"

"*Ja.* BFFs."

Joel laughed at hearing a plain *kind* using slang popular among *Englisch* preteens. When Laurene grinned, too, he was sure he saw her wariness fall away. He wasn't naive enough to believe it wouldn't return, but he would take each small step forward.

"Aren't you late?" Laurene asked. "Adam said he was meeting you and Samuel at noon, and it's nearly that."

With a wave to Mary Beth, he hurried along the street. He glanced at the quilt shop as he passed and saw Grace was busy with several customers. She didn't look his way, and he didn't want to distract her by lingering and admiring the gentle curve of her lips. Talk about distracting!

Joel laughed as he waited for the light to change. Crossing the street, he went into the pizza restaurant. Scents of cheese, basil and oregano met him as he entered. His stomach growled loudly, and Samuel and Adam, who sat near the door, laughed.

"Have you ordered yet?" he asked in lieu of a greeting.

"*Ja,*" Adam replied.

"The regular?"

Samuel grinned. "If you mean double pepperoni and double cheese, then *ja.*"

A woman at the counter called, "Number six."

"That's us." Adam started to rise.

"I'll get them," Joel said.

Going to the counter, he waited while the woman filled

three soda cups. He took them back to where his friends sat before returning to carry two large pies, paper plates and napkins to the table. Setting them in the center, he motioned for his friends to help themselves. His friends. He was glad he could think of them that way again. After all they'd been through for the past ten years, they could have been changed or become bitter. He glanced at Samuel as he sat and reached for a slice of his own. There had been a time when he would have announced to the whole world that he'd be glad never to see Samuel King again.

But he hadn't been angry at Samuel. He'd been angry at himself. Looking back, he guessed his friend had felt the same. However, they were too wrapped up in their cloaks of *hochmut* to admit the truth that they both were homesick and tired of wondering how their families were doing.

Coming home hadn't done much to help with that. While Samuel spoke of his siblings with great affection and enjoyed telling stories about his half sister Kari, who was planning on attending a nearby Mennonite school this fall, he hadn't spent any time with his *mamm* who couldn't forgive him for being born before she was married.

Joel wondered how long it would be before he had another chance to see one of his siblings or his *mamm*...or even *Daed*.

They ate in companionable silence for a few minutes. It seemed a precious gift to Joel that he could sit with his friends and not feel as if he needed to fill every moment with conversation. Quiet wasn't uncomfortable between them. It'd always been that way, and he hadn't known that sense of belonging and peace with anyone else.

Until Grace.

For once, he didn't argue with the exacting voice in his mind. He couldn't because what it said was true.

Joel put down his napkin and looked across the table. "Samuel, I've apologized to Adam and Laurene, and now I need to apologize to you."

"For what?" He took another bite of his pizza. "For taking more than your share of the cheese off this piece?"

He ignored his friend's jests and remained serious. "I need to apologize for what happened the night of the accident."

Samuel shook his head but lowered his pizza to his plate. "You didn't force me to drink that night, and you didn't force me behind the wheel."

"I could have stopped you."

"How? You could barely stand by the time we got to the car." He met Joel's eyes. "You wouldn't have been able to convince me to do anything I didn't want to do. I was such a fool I couldn't see my own foolishness." With a sigh, he added, "Well, there's one thing that's bothered me since the accident."

"What?"

"It doesn't matter that much."

"It must if you're bringing it up." He shifted his gaze to Adam, who gave him an encouraging nod. "Tell me, Samuel."

His friend traced an aimless pattern in the condensation on the table. Not looking up, he said, "All right. It seems petty after so many years, but I was upset you never came to the hospital to see how I was doing after the accident."

"I was there."

"You were?" He choked on the two words and had to grab his soda and take a deep swig to halt his coughing. When he could speak again, he asked, "You were there? When?"

"A day or two after the accident." He didn't want to admit he'd lost track of time as he'd faded in and out of consciousness in a cheap hotel room he'd rented when he didn't want to be found in his and Samuel's lousy apartment. He'd known he should have sought medical help himself, but he'd wanted to avoid questions, especially about contacting his family. The situation had been bad enough. Why make it worse by giving his *daed* more proof about what a worthless son Joel was and how he'd wasted his life?

"Really?" asked Samuel. "You were there?"

Joel grasped the edge of the table. When he tried to get his hands to loosen their death grip, they refused to obey him as images of Samuel burst from his memory.

The hospital had been eerily quiet at 4:00 a.m. that morning. Even the footsteps of the medical staff had been hushed along the terrazzo floors when Joel had emerged from a stairwell. The room he sought was on the seventh floor, but he hadn't wanted to use the elevator, which would have beeped to announce its arrival. The lady in the information booth had reminded Joel, when he stopped to check which floor Samuel was on, that visiting hours hadn't started for the day and he'd have to come back in five hours.

He'd thanked her, gone out the sliding doors where the darkness was beginning to thin and found a door near a delivery dock. Once inside, he'd considered, for a moment, grabbing a pair of scrubs from a peg. He hadn't because he hadn't been sure if the scrubs would draw attention to him if whoever wore them wasn't supposed to be on that floor or in that section. Besides, some part of him, a part he hadn't been able to quell, whispered stealing was a sin.

Glad for his dark hoodie and jeans, Joel had slipped along hallways that smelled of bleach and other disinfectants, reading the names on the whiteboard beside each door. He searched for more than fifteen minutes before he found one with "King" on it. But it wasn't Samuel. The man sleeping on the bed inside was more than a decade older.

Joel had kept searching and had almost given up hope when he saw another door with the name "King" written beside it. A single glance into the room told him he'd found Samuel.

The other bed was empty, a relief because Joel hadn't wanted another patient to wake up and alert the nurses.

He'd tiptoed in, scanning the monitors hanging by the bed. Samuel was still alive because his steady heartbeat had been displayed on one of the machines over his bed. Other numbers and symbols had been on the screen as well, but Joel hadn't known what they meant. His eyes had focused on the unchanging heartbeat pattern rippling across what looked like a small television.

That way Joel hadn't had to stare at his friend. The one look he'd taken when he'd come into the room had almost sent him staggering into the hall.

Lost in a swath of bandages, Samuel's face had been so bruised, swollen and distorted it no longer looked familiar. His right leg had been raised in traction and his right arm wrapped in a thick cast. The fingers on his left hand had the sheets in a death grip, a sure sign the medication dripping through the IVs wasn't easing his pain. Each breath he'd taken appeared to demand all the energy he had remaining.

Only a few days before the accident, Samuel had been bragging about how much weight he was lifting with some of the men they worked with on a building project. The week before, he'd won an impromptu race by scrambling up and over a fence surrounding the construction site.

Now he couldn't move, except for his left hand that clenched and unclenched the sheets in a steady rhythm that was unnerving. Each time Samuel loosened his grip, Joel had worried his friend was letting go of life, too.

Joel stayed until he heard a nurse coming toward the room. He'd wanted to pray, but couldn't. The words wouldn't come, or maybe he'd assumed God wouldn't listen to someone who'd turned his back on Him.

He'd known it was unlikely he'd be able to sneak into the

hospital again. There was a search for him. He'd heard that on a television at a diner, and he had been grateful neither of the people eating there nor the waitress had connected him to the news story about someone seen lurching away from the car that had crashed into a telephone pole. Even so, he'd quickly left the diner, keeping his hoodie over his head and his broken fingers hidden in a pocket.

A shudder ran through Joel now as he recalled the blinding pain when he'd clumsily splinted his own broken fingers. Other than his fingers, he'd suffered bruises and a few cuts. He released the table, flexing his fingers, which years later stiffened at the worst possible times.

Like when Grace had been curious why he hadn't lifted all the pails the night of the viewing for Eddie Mishler. He hadn't wanted to explain why, fearful of disappointing her as he had so many in his life.

"When did you come?" Samuel asked, allowing Joel to escape from layers of painful memories. Though he'd relived each horrible moment, only seconds had passed in real time.

"I snuck in a couple of days after the accident. Before dawn when the nurses were changing shifts. I hoped nobody would pay any attention to me." He clasped his hands and let them hang between his knees. "You looked awful. You were covered with bandages and in traction and connected to all sorts of IVs and machines. I could hardly bear to look at you."

"I have looked better." Samuel's attempt at humor fell flat.

Adam reached across the table and put a steadying hand on Samuel's shoulder. Staying silent, Adam looked from Samuel to Joel. He didn't need to say anything.

Joel understood. Others had told him suppressing bitter memories would keep him from healing and putting his past behind him. He'd tried. *God, You know how hard I've tried.* But each time he'd failed, backing away before confronting the worst he'd seen and heard and done.

As if Joel had said all that aloud, Adam gestured with his chin. It was a clear command to fill the silence left by Samuel's attempt to lighten the tension.

Joel looked at Samuel. It was as if he were seeing him for the first time since returning to Bliss Valley. He didn't let his eyes shy away from Samuel's right side, which had endured so much damage. Samuel had accepted what had happened to him. Why couldn't Joel?

"You didn't see me, Samuel," Joel said. "You were asleep."

"I wasn't. I was somewhere between sleep and being awake. You stood at the foot of the bed, ain't so? Then you took one step around to my right before turning and walking away. Is that right?"

"Ja."

"All these years, I thought it was a dream, a way to give myself some comfort that my friend hadn't abandoned me."

"I did abandon you. I could have stayed and made sure you were going to be okay, but I didn't stay once I knew you were alive." He didn't feel the need to add he'd been hiding from the authorities. Samuel must have guessed that. As for Adam learning the truth, it wasn't important any longer.

"I probably would have done the same," Samuel said.

"I'm not so sure about that."

Samuel shook his head. "I am. Both of us made mistakes then. Mistakes we aren't proud of now." He lowered his eyes. "Or even then."

Adam put a hand on Samuel's arm, then did the same to Joel. When they were younger, Adam had often done that to calm them down so they didn't run off half-cocked and get themselves in more trouble. It was a shock to recall that. From the moment Joel had heard Adam had been put into the lot as a possible deacon, he wondered how even three people in the district could consider Adam a *gut* candidate. But Joel had been the one who'd failed to see the truth. Adam had had, even when they were kids, the insight and the yearning to help that a *gut* deacon needed.

"Tell me," Samuel went on. "You made a strange sound, ain't so? Not quite talking to me, but not quite talking to yourself either."

"You heard that?"

"I did, but I wasn't sure what you said. That's why I always questioned if it was a dream. If it had been, I would have dreamed words I could understand. Were you asking me something?"

"No." He looked at his clasped hands. "I was yelling under my breath. I was angry at God for not keeping you from being hurt." His lips tugged in a wry grin. "I wanted to tell Him how furious I was He'd let the accident happen, but I also didn't want to alert anyone I was there. So I was shouting in a whisper."

"You've always done things the hard way." Adam's chuckle was kind.

"Always," he agreed.

Strong emotion clamped around Joel, making it impossible for him to speak without risking his voice breaking like a teen's. Then he realized, as he looked from Adam to Samuel, words weren't necessary. Years ago, they'd been so in tune with each other they could do one of their pranks without speaking. Now...

Now it was something deeper. A connection he'd taken for granted then, never guessing how lost he'd feel when it was gone. He and Samuel and Adam were like a three-legged stool. With one of them missing, the other two were unsteady. It'd been like that since they'd become friends.

Samuel leaned forward. "I know you're angry with God, Joel, but I've come to realize He saved my life that night. He gave us every chance to return to Him, but we kept turning away as we drove headlong along the road to self-destruction. The accident and my long recovery gave me time to realize how long God had been trying to get my attention."

"He could have found another way." He opened and closed his stiff fingers again. "I haven't been able to figure out why He let that accident happen."

"God didn't let it happen, Joel." Samuel hit the table so hard soda splashed out of their cups, but nobody paid the dark pools any attention. "*I* made it happen."

Adam added, "God doesn't dictate our choices. He gave us free will to make them ourselves. It's our choice whether we make them with Him or without Him." He put his hand on Joel's arm. "God has forgiven you, Joel. When are you going to forgive yourself?"

Chapter Nineteen

Grace was sure she must have heard Joel wrong that evening when the family gathered at the table in the kitchen. As she put a platter with sliced roast beef in front of *Mamm*, she asked, "Joel, did you say you're joining us for worship on Sunday?"

"I thought I might." He served himself a generous portion of the mashed potatoes before spooning a matching serving on *Daed*'s plate.

Grace wanted to thank Joel for assisting him, but that would embarrass her *daed*. He was less steady tonight than usual. He'd stumbled and fallen again coming up the back steps that afternoon. When *Mamm* and Grace had tried to help him, he'd waved them off, saying he didn't need them hovering over him. Joel made it seem like it was the most natural thing in the world that he helped serve Wesley and then did the same thing for *Daed*.

Joel put the bowl on the table. As he took the next bowl from Brandon, he ladled out brown gravy onto his plate and onto *Daed*'s. Was he being nice or trying to avoid meeting her eyes?

"I assume you could use help setting up the benches for the service," he added when no one spoke through their shock at his announcement.

"I'm going to help," Wesley said, puffing out his chest.

Grace smiled. "*Ja*, you are, and I'm glad you are. Brandon is, too."

Her older nephew muttered something that she knew better than to ask him to repeat. How many times had she prayed that God would reach into Brandon's heart and open it to see she and his grandparents wanted the best for him? She'd lost count.

Sitting at the table, she concentrated on putting food on her plate, though her appetite had vanished. She didn't want anyone, especially Joel, to see how his simple words had thrilled her. That he was attending the service wasn't an announcement he planned to stay in Bliss Valley, but it signaled a change.

Somehow she managed to eat a few bites before the end of the meal. She sent her parents into the living room to relax while she gathered the dishes and put them in the sink. For once, she didn't wash them right away. Instead, she wandered outdoors to where Joel was playing catch with the boys.

She leaned on the porch post and watched them in the lengthening shadows. The air had a touch of fall in it, warning she might soon be sorry she hadn't brought a shawl with her. Wrapping her arms around herself, she smiled as she heard the boys' excited shouts.

Joel glanced over his shoulder when Wesley pointed at her. "Are you finished with the dishes already?"

"The dishes are soaking." She walked to where they were playing. "It'll make cleaning them later easier."

Tossing the ball to Brandon, Joel said, "I need to talk to your *aenti*."

Brandon made smooching sounds. Joel laughed, but Grace felt heat climbing her cheeks. Grateful for the shadows, she knew she'd be smart not to say anything.

Joel led her around the house toward the lane. As they emerged from under the trees, she asked, "What happened to your arm?"

"I got called in by the bone marrow registry," he said, glancing down at the small bandage on the inside of his right elbow, "to donate some blood. They won't tell me if there's someone out there for whom I'm a possible match, but I'm assuming so."

She clapped her hands with glee. "What a blessing that would be, Joel!"

"I never thought of myself as a blessing for someone else."

Her smile vanished. "Enough of that! Your life isn't the same it was even a few weeks ago. You could feel sorry for yourself when you didn't have a job or food or a roof over your head. Now you've got all of those in addition to seeing your family and friends."

He strode over the fence. She was torn between leaving him alone to feel sorry for himself and spending a few more minutes with him. The quartet of calves he had bought with an advance on his wages from *Daed* would be delivered in the morning. Once the calves arrived, he'd be as busy as any parent with quadruplets. They would need to have their food intake monitored and be kept from getting into trouble or injured.

"I'm sorry," she said as she went to stand beside him. "That was uncalled-for."

"I've been whining for years, blaming everyone for my troubles. It's gotten to be habit." He gave her a crooked grin. "I now blame myself for my troubles, but I'm still whining. *Danki* for calling me on it. If I keep being reminded of my shortcomings, I may be able to overcome them."

"Is that why you changed your mind about coming on Sunday?"

"No, that was because of something Adam asked me."

She waited for him to go on, but he didn't. In spite of her curiosity about Adam's question that had triggered such a change, she said nothing.

An excited squeal came from the yard, and Grace looked over her shoulder to where Wesley and Brandon were rushing after the ball rolling toward the porch. Wesley got to it first and held it up before running back toward where they'd been playing catch.

Beside her, Joel chuckled. When she asked what was funny, he said, "It looks like they've learned their lesson about playing too close to a house."

"They have. For now at least. I was surprised how willing they were to go and do chores to pay for the window until I found out that they got a big piece of cake each day after finishing their work. And then *Mamm* gives them cookies because she's proud of them doing as they'd agreed. Wesley doesn't always take them, but Brandon does and asks for more."

"And they eat a full meal every night." He chuckled. "They must have a black hole inside them the way they pack food away."

"Growing boys."

"Growing boys who will come to see how blessed they are to have ended up in your care."

"We are the ones who've been blessed. Having them here is a joy I hadn't expected, though it's been challenging becoming an instant *mamm*." Her face blanched. "*Ach*, I didn't realize how that would sound. I'm not happy my brother and his wife died."

"No one would think that, Grace. We've seen how much you've mourned their loss."

"I hate that word."

"What word?"

"Loss. It's a nice, comfortable word that lets us avoid talking about our pain when someone dies. They aren't lost. They are, as they always were, in God's hand."

"I think people use loss because they feel as if they've lost any more opportunities to spend time with the one who's died."

"Do you ever wonder if your birth parents are alive or dead?"

"No, I never had any questions about them." He gave a snort. "Why would I want to deal with another *mamm* and another *daed* when I have had enough problems with the ones who raised me?"

"So Laurene and Naomi finding their birth *mamm* doesn't pique your curiosity about your own?"

"No. I'm happy for them, but I want to bury my past, not dig into it."

"But what we are comes from what we've been."

"I agree. However, I don't have to hold up a mirror to my mistakes every day. Nor do I want to sit and go through that long list before I fall asleep every night."

"Do you do that?"

"I have, but I know there's nothing I can do to change what has already happened."

"What if you could? If you could turn back time, would you change anything?"

He laughed. "Are you kidding? I'd change *everything*. I'd tell the angry kid I was he was on a one-way trip to disaster. To start being thankful for what was right in his life and forget about the rest."

"All of us would like to go back to our teen years so we could reassure ourselves the problems that seemed insurmountable then will seem less important than a hill of beans." She put her hand over his on the rail. "I'm glad you're coming to services on Sunday, Joel. Whatever Adam asked you was what you needed to hear."

"*Ja*, but you've inspired me, too, Grace. I would be lying if I didn't admit that."

"But?"

He chuckled. "Give me a chance to take a breath before I also admit I've come to realize how most of the holes in my soul can be filled by acknowledging I've been a fool to turn my back on God when He never turned His back on me."

"You've inspired me, too."

"Me?" He made a funny face at her.

She laughed. "*Ja.*"

"I hope I haven't inspired you to take up a life of crime."

"No. You've inspired me to look at my life and what's important in it and to be grateful." Raising her hand, she cupped his cheek as he had hers. "*Danki*, Joel."

When he faced her, his arm slipped around her as he drew her closer. He held her, gazing into her face. She knew if she wanted to, she could slip out of his arms and he wouldn't hold her against her will. But she didn't want to edge away. She wanted to be where she was, within his arms as her heart thudded so loudly he must be able to hear it. He lowered his face toward hers.

"Grace?" he whispered.

"Kiss me."

"You don't have to ask me twice."

With tender mastery, he teased her lips to surrender to his. When her hands slid up and around his shoulders, he explored her lips as if it was the most precious journey he would ever make. She forgot everyone and everything when he caressed her back.

As he released her, he gave her an enticing grin. "Well, maybe you can ask me twice…if you'd like to do that again."

"Kiss me."

Her giggle vanished into the storm of sensation that swept over her when he pulled her close again. A warning burst through her head, a warning that nothing had changed, that he might not be staying in Bliss Valley, that she might be setting herself up for a broken heart all over again.

She didn't listen. There would be time enough for regrets later. For now, she wanted to savor his kiss so she could remember it if he left her and Bliss Valley.

That had been unexpected.

Joel's head felt ready to explode each time he thought about how Grace had asked him to kiss her. Not once, but several times. He wondered if they'd still be standing by the fence if Wesley hadn't come over in tears to ask her to patch the hand he'd cut when he dove to catch a ball. Though she'd reverted to the caring *aenti*, he hadn't missed how she'd looked back at him with longing in her eyes as she hurried the boy into the house.

That look had stayed with him all night as he gave up on trying to sleep. What would have been the purpose of sleeping when he was living the sweetest dream he could imagine?

During breakfast, while he'd gulped *kaffi* as if it were the only thing to keep him alive—which wasn't far from the truth when he was short a night's sleep—he'd watched her smile at her family. She'd served them a delicious breakfast, as she did each day. She urged her nephews not to be late for school, as she did each day. She smiled as she refilled his cup…but not as she did each day. There was something more scintillating, more alluring, more conspiratorial in her smile when their gazes collided and held.

He'd hoped for a moment alone with her, but she'd been

busy with her morning chores, and the loud rumble of a truck in the lane had announced the arrival of the four black calves he'd bought at the livestock auction.

The older man almost beat him out of the house. Only the steps slowed Harold enough so Joel could reach the truck before he did. The calves were bawling and frightened, but calmed down when he put them in a small pen in the barn where he'd keep them for the first few days.

Harold had outlined a long list of supplies Joel would need. Telling Joel to take the open wagon into town to get them, he shooed Joel toward the door.

Thanking him for his advice, Joel had obeyed. He'd paused in the doorway to see Harold stretching over the railing to pat the head of the runt of the group.

"I think your name is going to be Big Boy," Grace's *daed* had cooed as if talking to a human *boppli*. "You'll show them when you grow, ain't so?"

Now, after Joel had loaded those supplies in the back of the Coffmans' wagon, making sure they wouldn't shift when he went down the hill toward the farm, he walked toward the front. He couldn't wait to get back to the farm. He needed to get to know the calves and maybe steal a moment—and a kiss—with Grace.

"Joel? Joel Beachy, is that you?" asked a man who came from the other side of the wagon.

He froze. Impossible. It couldn't be…but it was! He stared at a once-familiar face.

"Ross," he said in his coldest tone.

The other man's reaction to the ice dripping from that single word was a quick blink and a wavering of his smile. What had Ross Elborough expected? For Joel to welcome him with a big hug? It wasn't as if he and Joel had ever been friends. In fact, Joel didn't know if Ross was the man's real name or an alias he used when running errands for the drug dealers who'd tossed a few bucks Ross's way to risk his life on tasks they didn't want to chance doing themselves.

In addition, Joel had suspicions Ross had secured a plea deal the night he'd been with Joel in the car where drugs had been found. That had included pointing the finger at Joel. Though Ross hadn't testified against Joel in court, the prosecutor had possessed information that must have been shared by Ross in an effort to keep himself out of jail.

"I'd heard you got out," Ross said with his usual smile that managed to be snide and charming at the same time.

As he had each time his path had crossed Ross's, Joel had to wonder why Ross tried to look like some bit player in an old black-and-white mobster movie. Those movies had been favorites of Joel's and Samuel's after they jumped the fence. The hokey dialogue and plots had provided hours of laughter. That had been before he'd met Ross who tried to emulate those gangsters. Even today when it was once again hot and humid, Ross had on a dark worsted suit that was shiny from wear on the collar and elbows with a black shirt and a dark, narrow tie. Sweat trickled from beneath his wool fedora and emphasized that he was in need of a shave.

And a shower, Joel realized when Ross stepped closer and whispered, "I need to talk to you, Beachy. Business. Important business."

It took every ounce of Joel's willpower not to roll his eyes. No Hollywood hack could come up with lines as trite and stale as what Ross considered sparkling conversation.

"What are you doing here?" Joel asked. Maybe if he played along with Ross's big, bad gangster game, he'd find a way to convince the other man to leave him alone.

"You should know." He pulled a strand of grass from the side of the parking lot and chewed on it.

"If I knew, I wouldn't be asking."

Joel didn't wait for Ross's trite reply. Instead, he checked Pearl before continuing around to the driver's side of the wagon. He reached for the reins to climb in.

Thick fingers clamped on his left wrist. Without a word, Joel twisted his arm, breaking the hold on him. His calves needed the milk supplements and the other supplies, and he didn't know what the hot sun would do to the containers. He couldn't linger and listen to Ross's jabber, even if he wanted to.

Which he didn't.

But Joel had forgotten how annoying the other man could be. Ross reached out and grabbed his arm, slamming him up against the side of the wagon. Pain raced along his ribs. Shocked, Joel shook his head to clear his eyes and yanked his arm out of Ross's grip. His fingers curled into a fist, but he forced them to open again.

Ross snickered. "I'd heard you'd become one of the passes-on-fists."

Passes-on-fists? What was Ross talking about? The answer came as Joel rolled the phrase around in his mind.

Pacifist. That was what Ross meant.

Joel almost laughed, but halted when Ross leaned toward him; the shorter man's own hand was clenched in a tight fist. Too low for anyone else to hear, Ross said, "I didn't believe it, but I guess it's true. Not that it matters. I'm no passes-on-fist."

"What do you want, Ross?"

The other man glanced around the almost empty parking lot, then snarled, "I want my money."

"I don't have any of your money."

Ross rubbed the backs of his fingers across his chin in a pose he believed made him look tougher. That might have worked when they were kids. Did he still think it gave him a threatening air?

"Sure you do, Beachy. You had it in your car."

"So it's gone."

"You spent it?"

Tired of the absurd conversation, Joel said, "Face it, Ross! If there was any money in that car, it would have been confiscated by the cops. They searched every cavity in it."

The other man cursed, then, as if a light switch had been flipped, he grinned. "Well, we could make more."

"I'm making a *gut* living now."

"*Gut?* You look like these backward fools, and now you're talking like them."

"You know I was raised Amish."

"Yeah, yeah, I heard that." He grimaced. "But that was in the past. Why are you dressed like one of them now?"

Joel wished for the words to put an end to the conversation. No, he didn't wish. He *prayed* for the words he needed.

A warmth swept over him, a feeling of belonging he'd thought he'd never experience again. He wasn't wearing a costume as Ross was. Perhaps he had been when he first put on broadfall trousers and suspenders, but he couldn't think of the last time he'd wondered why he was wearing clothes he'd vowed never to don again.

"What do you want, Ross? I mean, I know you want your money, but I've already told you I don't have it." If he tried to explain what he was thinking to the other man, Ross would belittle everything he said.

"Money, man. I need money." He kicked an empty cigarette packet across the parking lot. "I need it bad."

Sympathy swarmed over Joel. For the first time, he noticed the dark crescents under Ross's eyes, and the lines in his face. His skin seemed to hang off his bones, a sure sign he was ingesting more drugs than food.

"If you need a place to stay or something to eat, I can help."

"I don't need handouts. I need money. Real money." He glanced away and then back at Joel. "Look, I know a guy who—"

"Knows a guy," he said. "I know the routine. Maybe even your guy knows a guy who knows a guy."

"You know the routine, so are you in?"

"In on some deal you want me to bankroll while you ruin more kids' lives? No."

"C'mon, Joel. You can't want to stay in this sleepy town."

"Borough. Strasburg is a borough."

"What does that matter?" His brows dropped toward each other. "Hey, are you making fun of me?"

"No, I wouldn't ever do that." Joel would be stupid to push Ross too far. The man's temper was always simmering below the surface. Though it took a lot of prodding, when it exploded, Ross showed a level of violence and indifference to someone else's suffering that was dangerous for anybody within reach. Joel had seen Ross knock a much bigger man unconscious with a single blow. It had required three men to pull Ross off the senseless man.

"You've always been my boy."

"I'm not any longer." He clapped the shorter man on the shoulder. "I'm going to be late for feeding my calves, so I'd better go."

"You can't leave!"

"I can, and I am." He edged past Ross.

Though Ross didn't reach out and grab his arm, Joel didn't relax his guard until he climbed in the wagon and reached for the reins. His hands were trembling. He gave Pearl the signal to get going as he fought not to look over his shoulder. He didn't want to lead Ross to the Coffmans' farm.

He snuck a glance as he looked both ways before pulling out of the parking lot. Ross was on his cell phone and walking in the opposite direction. A car pulled up beside him and Ross got in. They sped off without coming near the wagon.

Everything about Ross brought back the thunderstorm of memories, each scene of his fall from grace as brightly lit as if lightning flashed. The horrifying scene of the accident, the decisions he'd made in the aftermath in an effort to prove he was worthless, hitting rock bottom as he heard the judge's gavel echo in the courtroom and in his heart. So many moments in prison when he'd lambasted himself for his poor decisions, and the nights before he slept when his *daed*'s voice had derided him as a failure.

But he wasn't that man any longer. He was trying to find his way back to the right way to live his life.

Leaning forward, he put his forehead on his clenched fists. *I want to say* danki, *Lord, for Your never giving up on me, even when I was ready to give up on myself.* Danki *for showing me I don't have to make the same mistakes over and over.*

The prayer was simple and from his heart. Had it been that easy all along? Just opening his heart and reaching out to God? Even someone like him who'd taken such a fall from grace?

He raised his head as he frowned. *Fall from grace?* That phrase seemed to be running through his thoughts too often.

If he was returning to his faith, was that a fall toward grace? Or was it as simple as he was falling *for* Grace?

She was at the core of the changes in his life. It would be so easy to give in to his heart's longing, but he had too many amends to make before he could let her entangle her life with his.

He'd begun, and he had to keep going. He needed to look into the AA meetings at the church and keep a lifeline open to God to safeguard his sobriety. For the first time in his life, he couldn't let himself give up or focus on taking the easy way out. Losing Grace would be too high a price to pay.

Chapter Twenty

Opening her eyes, Grace looked out her bedroom window on Sunday morning. The faint hint of color to the east marked the coming of dawn. A few weeks ago, the sun would have been over the horizon by this time, but summer had come to an end.

The turning of the seasons always made her happy and sad. She looked forward to autumn with the leaves changing color and the air losing its humidity, and the cool evenings when the stars were so bright it appeared as if the sky were a dark pool she could explore.

This was what peace felt like. She'd forgotten how it was possible to draw in a breath without it shuddering against her lungs as she tried to restrain her stress from exploding around her. Her muscles didn't ache from tension.

But this wasn't just any church Sunday. It was the church Sunday when Joel was returning to worship with them. She'd seen how pleased her parents were when he asked if he could join them, but they'd acted as if it were the most ordinary thing in the world. Last night, Wesley had been so excited he'd almost forgotten to eat his dessert.

Almost.

She smiled, grateful for the chance to witness Joel's first steps toward reconciliation with the community.

And for his kisses.

She rolled onto her back and stared at the ceiling. They hadn't had a chance to share another kiss since the night by the fence. Joel had been busy with his new calves.

A smile slipped along her lips. Joel talked about the calves as other men talked about their *bopplin*. He was worried about how much they were getting to eat, and he and *Daed* discussed when to turn them out into the pasture with as much detail and precision as if they were launching a mission to the moon. They'd even drawn the boys into their conversations, teaching them.

Pushing herself up to sit, she wrapped her arms around her knees and leaned her chin on them. There would be a youth singing tonight at a farm on the other side of the district. Though she and Joel would be the oldest participants, they could use the singing as an excuse to drive to and from the farm. Alone in the buggy, out on an autumn night beneath the stars, they could share more kisses.

A heated shiver skittered along her, settling around her heart. She couldn't remember the last time she'd been eager to participate in something beyond work and her family. Joel had said how much having her in his life had changed him.

It seemed that he was changing her in ways she hadn't even realized.

For the better.

The voice of doubt whispered in her mind. Was she wrong to trust him when he said he'd changed? That he was thinking about staying? That working with *Daed* and the calves was a dream come true? She prayed not, because she didn't want to have to try to piece her heart back together again.

Everything was as it'd always been on a church Sunday when Joel was a boy...and everything was different. Instead of loitering off to one side with Adam and Samuel, trying to come up with ways to avoid attending the service or finding an excuse to slip out, he stood in the midst of the district's men. Most were farmers, so he listened to what they had to say about raising calves. Not much because the conversations revolved around the best price for their harvested crops.

He looked for his friends. Samuel was talking with Dale Hershberger, Adam's younger cousin, who was working with Samuel at his father-in-law's buggy repair shop. Adam was inside the house with the ordained men.

The other men didn't ignore him. In fact, most of them had nodded a greeting as he approached the side of the barn door where the men were gathered. A single glance toward the house warned him of the danger of letting his gaze linger there. Not only were his sisters gathered in a tight circle, but Grace sat on the porch steps with her nephews, listening to whatever they were telling her.

"Don't stare," he warned himself under his breath, but his gaze kept slipping toward her. The warmth of her smile, the way she used her hands like a pair of birds to emphasize what she was saying, how she gave the boys a hug while laughing along with them. He wanted to commit every aspect of her to a special place in his memory.

Just in case.

Just in case his world turned inside out again. He'd been sure he'd put the last ten years behind him when he found a home on the Coffmans' farm, but Ross's appearance had thrown him. His past lurked out of sight, ready to pounce. He couldn't let it hurt Grace and her family.

At the thought of family, he wondered when and how he should approach Rosemary to ask if she wanted his help with her herd. He hoped there would be time after the service to talk with her...if she'd talk to him.

Brandon ran across the drive toward him. "Grace says I can go in with the men if it's okay with you."

He waited for the boy to reach him before he replied, "It's okay with me, but you can't decide you'd rather sit with her in the middle of our worship."

Wrinkling his nose, Brandon said, "I don't want to sit with the women. I'm not a *boppli*. I'm a big boy."

"Just like the littlest calf?"

"It's a silly name. The calf isn't even a boy. It's a girl!"

"I think your *grossdawdi* likes silly names, the sillier the better. Didn't I hear him calling you Marlon the other day?"

The boy rolled his eyes. "*Ja*. When I asked him why, he laughed and said I'd find out one day."

Joel almost said he'd guessed Harold had chosen the name because Brandon and Brando were so close, but then he'd have to explain to the youngster who Marlon Brando was. Besides, he didn't want to interfere in the game between a boy and his *grossdawdi*. His own *grossdawdi* had enjoyed teasing him, too, and Joel had treasured every minute of it. He suspected Brandon, in spite of his grimace, was enjoying the jests, too.

As they lined up to go into the Coffmans' barn, Brandon edged next to Joel. He put his hand on the boy's shoulder and waited for their turn to enter. The oldest men went in first. Looking along the line ahead of him, he saw his *daed*, glowering at him as he had at the viewing and the funeral.

"Does he think he can burn a hole right through me if he stares long enough?" Joel grumbled. "I know he thinks he's superior to the rest of us, but he's not some superhero with laser vision."

"Give him some time," Samuel murmured from behind him. "It's got to be a shock that his son has returned to Bliss Valley and hasn't come to beg his forgiveness."

"It's no shock." Joel's voice was taut. "He knows I won't ever beg. I'm too much like him that way."

Samuel gave him a sad nod, but didn't say anything more as the line moved forward.

Joel sat between Brandon and Samuel. His heart ached when he saw Rosemary join their sisters in the middle row with the other *maedals*. She was no longer a married woman, but a widow. Why was she sitting with the single women? When Erma put her hand on Rosemary's shoulder in silent solace, he saw tears glistening in his sisters' eyes. Wishing he had the words to ease their grief, he folded his hands and bent his head.

Some sense that seemed to go beyond his regular five urged him to look up as Grace came in with Wesley. They sat behind Naomi and her two little boys who looked like twins. They must be the *kinder* Samuel had spoken of. She turned to place a *boppli* in Grace's arms while she bent to speak with the boys.

Through the long service, and he'd forgotten how uncomfortable it could be to sit on a narrow, backless bench for three hours, his eyes kept cutting to Grace. She continued to hold Naomi's *boppli*, feeding it and burping it while Naomi got up several times to take one boy or the other out.

By the final blessing, Joel had Brandon's head on his lap as the boy snored. His own legs were asleep, so numb he knew they were going to send bolts of pain along each nerve as they awoke. He gently shook the boy, who roused with a snort so loud it echoed across the barn's main floor.

Brandon jumped up and ran to join the other *kinder*. Joel

got up more slowly, feeling as tentative and unsteady as Harold when his deadened feet wobbled beneath him.

"Are you okay?" asked Naomi, startling him because he hadn't expected her to come to his rescue.

"Feet went to sleep." He shook one leg, then the other, wincing.

"Fun!" cried one of the little boys beside Naomi. He began to wiggle his own leg.

"These are my twins. Jared and Jesse." Her tone was tentative. Did she wonder if she still needed to be prepared for him to do something appalling so he and his friends could enjoy a laugh?

No, that couldn't be. She'd forgiven Samuel enough to agree to be his wife, so she must have put aside her anger at him and Adam.

Then he realized what made her falter. What *mamm*—plain or *Englisch*—would want her *kinder* spending time with a man who'd spent years in prison? No matter what Samuel had done, and he'd done plenty of things wrong in the *Leit*'s eyes, he hadn't been arrested and convicted.

"I know what you're thinking," Naomi said so her words wouldn't reach the men who were rearranging the benches for the midday meal, "but it's not that."

"It's not what?" He was amazed she was continuing the conversation. She used to scoot away if he came within an arm's length of her.

"I don't judge you for what you've done. That's not my place. It's God's, but you've made it no secret you don't know whether you're staying here and committing to a plain life or if you're going to leave again. I don't want my boys to get attached to you and then you're gone. They don't understand why their *daed* left them."

Joel hesitated, then said, "I'm sorry he's gone. Was he ill for long?"

"No, he died in a fight."

Shocked, he blurted, "What a stupid thing to do!"

She sighed. "I don't usually put it that bluntly, Joel."

"You should. Your boys need to learn everyone is capable of making mistakes, even their parents. Don't expect them to be perfect, or they'll do everything in their power to prove they're not."

"Is that what you did?"

He nodded. "I thought that was pretty obvious."

"It is now. Back then…" She took a deep breath and released it. "It's better not to talk about back then." Looking past him, she smiled. "Grace, *danki* for watching the *boppli*."

"My pleasure," she said as she handed the tiny girl to Naomi. "You've got your hands full and more."

"*Ja*, the twins thought it would be more *fun* to sit with me today instead of Samuel. I've been hoping to talk to you about working with a few of us to make a quilt for next year's Bliss Valley Volunteer Fire Department's mud sale."

"I would love to help. Let me know what you need. People, fabric, whatever."

"The more the merrier, as they say." Naomi grinned. "If we have too many people to work on a single quilt, we'll make a second one to donate."

"Have you selected your pattern?"

Joel left her to talk to Naomi about quilting and colors and which thread would be best. How had he failed to notice how much Grace loved quilting and quilters? There always was a warm glow within her, but it grew stronger when she spoke of quilts. Was that why she stayed at the shop and put up with Tiffany's temper tantrums? She depended on the money to help her family, but there were other jobs she could have gotten.

He reached for a bench to carry it to where the men were working, but halted when he heard the sound of automobile tires on the farm lane. Turning his head, he looked out the door to see a police car come to a stop in the barnyard.

An abrupt silence fell on everyone in the barn when the car door opened and a state trooper stepped out. *Mamms* gathered their *kinder* closer to their skirts. *Daeds* moved to stand with their families. Though no plain man would raise his hand against someone else, the men would take the brunt of any attack upon themselves to protect their wives and *kinder*.

Adam pushed his way to the front of the *Leit* and walked out of the barn with a quiet ease that belied the tension inside it. "Can I help you, Officer?" His voice was steady. Far steadier than Joel guessed his own would have been.

"I'm sorry to interrupt," said the officer.

"We just finished our service."

The officer looked at his cell phone, then asked, "You're Deacon Hershberger, right?"

"Adam Hershberger, *ja*."

"I am Trooper Eric Knox with the Pennsylvania State Police. I need to speak with one of your parishioners."

Adam didn't correct the police officer and explain they didn't use the term "parishioners." Instead, he asked, "Which one?"

"Joel Beachy."

The trooper's answer didn't surprise Joel...or anyone else, he guessed.

Not giving Adam time to reply, Joel stepped forward. "I'm Joel Beachy."

The policeman eyed him up and down, then motioned with his head for Joel to come with him toward his patrol car. Feeling the eyes of the *Leit* slicing into his nape, Joel was glad he couldn't see their faces.

Most especially, he was glad he couldn't see Grace's. How he wished he could have kept this part of his life from seeping into his new life, the one he wanted to spend with her! The Amish lived separately, and his presence in her life would bring the outside world in time and again.

The officer reached into the car and pulled out a sheet of paper. It was a photograph, and he moved it so everyone who'd emerged from the barn could see it. "Do you recognize this man?"

Joel swallowed hard. If he told the truth, the words might condemn him right away. He cut his eyes toward where Grace stood between her nephews. Young Wesley's face was as pasty white as uncooked bread dough. When he turned it against Grace's apron, she bent to lean her cheek against the top of his head. However, her gaze remained focused on Joel.

"Beachy," demanded the policeman, "answer my question."

"*Ja*... Yes, I recognize that man."

"What's his name?"

"He's got a bunch of names, but I think his real name is Lewis Philbrick."

"Do you know where he is?"

Joel's jaw tightened as he held back the words he hadn't used since he returned to Bliss Valley. "I know where I wish he was, but I'm sure he's alive and well if you're asking questions about him."

"Have you seen him?"

"No. Not since before I was sent to prison." He thought about mentioning how he'd encountered Ross, one of Philbrick's gofers, but he wouldn't throw the man under the bus as Ross had him.

"That's odd, because he had something he says belongs to

you." The officer glanced at the *Leit*, then said, "You'd better come with me."

"Where?"

"To the station on Route 30 to answer some questions, including why Philbrick had something he claims is yours."

"Philbrick is there?" He couldn't imagine the drug dealer walking into a police station of his own free will.

"No. Someone dropped off this item along with a note." Sympathy darkened the policeman's eyes as he said, "I don't think you want to discuss this in front of these people. Do you?"

"No."

The worshippers had gathered in a half circle with his *daed* at the center of the arc. He heard his *daed* grumble something. Wyman Beachy wouldn't believe his son wasn't involved with the drug dealer. He'd never thought anything but the worst about Joel.

His gaze was caught by his friends, and he saw their worry. Because they feared for him, or were they troubled at the idea he might still be selling drugs?

I never was! How he longed to shout those words to his friends, to his family, to the cop...to Grace.

At the thought of her name, he couldn't halt himself from looking in her direction. What he saw startled him and at the same time heartened him. She stood with her arms around her nephews, but she was holding her head high. Even as he watched, she raised her right hand and gave him a thumbs-up. The motion dampened his frustration and his fear that a suspicion of something he hadn't done could send him to prison.

"All right." The trooper raised his voice as he said, "Let's go."

"No!" shouted Wesley as he darted toward the trooper, his small hands clenched with fury. "No, you can't take Joel!

He didn't do anything wrong! I know he didn't. I can't lose him, too!"

Wesley's words pierced Joel like a serrated knife, twisting in his heart. The *kind* was accepting his parents weren't coming back. Now, after daring to trust Joel, Wesley was afraid of losing someone else he cared about. He heard a groan and realized it'd come from his own throat. He could never regret taking the boy under his wing, but he almost wished he hadn't because he hated the idea of causing more pain and grief for the boys.

Grace ran forward and wrapped an arm around Wesley. Keeping him back before he struck the trooper, she bent and whispered against his hair to calm him. He wiggled, trying to escape her, but she slipped her other arm around him and tightened her hold. She molded her own body around his, offering him a cocoon to shield him from the reality of what was right in front of his eyes.

"It'll be all right," she said. "The policeman wants to talk to Joel."

"No!" he cried. "Don't take him. Take me instead!"

The trooper frowned as he glanced from Joel to the boy. "Why would I do that, young man?"

"Because I've seen that man."

Gasps came from every direction, and Harold pushed forward along with Brandon. They wore identical expressions of fear.

Grace squatted in front of Wesley and smoothed his hair back from his tearstained face. "*Liebling*, where did you see that man?"

"On the road home from school."

Even the trooper looked dismayed by that information. He put his hand on Grace's shoulder and motioned for her to get up. She did, and he stepped in front of the boy. Holding out the photo, he said, "Take a good look, young man. It's important you don't make a mistake."

Wesley glanced at the photo. "It's the man I saw. Are you here to talk to Joel because of the cover from his *grossdawdi's* pocket watch? Joel didn't give it to that bad man."

"How do you know?" Joel asked, hoping Wesley wasn't about to spin a wild tale in an effort to protect him.

"Because I took it first."

"You took Joel's watch cover without telling him?" asked Grace, and he could hear the sorrow in her voice.

He didn't have to look at her to know what was on her face. She believed *she* had failed by not being a better example for the boys. Did she think Wesley's mistake had anything to do with her? She was doing the best she could with the *kinder*.

Two more large tears rolled down Wesley's pudgy cheeks. "*Ja*. I'm sorry, Joel. I know I shouldn't have, but I wanted to show it to my friends at school."

"You took it the day I found you in the *dawdi haus*, ain't so?"

Wesley nodded, miserable, as he repeated, "I wanted to show it to my friends."

"But if you took it to show your friends, how did Lewis Philbrick—the man in the photo—get it? Did you lose it somewhere?"

The little boy shook his head as he rubbed his knuckles against his eyes. More tears tumbled down his face.

"Wesley?" Grace prompted. "If you dropped it, it's okay. Tell us what happened."

"I didn't lose it."

"*Gut,*" she said. "I didn't think you did, because you're so conscientious of your own things and everyone else's."

He nodded, but didn't speak.

Again she squatted in front of the boy, so she had to look up into Wesley's eyes. Putting her hands on his elbows, she asked, "Do you know how Lewis Philbrick got Joel's *gross-dawdi*'s watch cover?"

Again Wesley nodded, even as he seemed to shrink into himself.

"It's all right," she said, not shifting her gaze away from the boy's tear-filled eyes. "You can tell me and Joel and the officer. We want the same thing. For you to be safe."

"And Joel, too?"

She glanced at Joel, and he was almost knocked off his feet by the strength of her gaze. "*Ja.* Tell us, Wesley."

Joel couldn't keep from curling his fingers into his palms as the *kind* spoke of Lewis Philbrick stopping his car and talking to Wesley when the boy was on his way to school. At first, Philbrick had asked for directions; then he asked Wesley to show him how to get to his destination. The little boy had refused, so Philbrick had driven off.

He returned when Wesley was on his way home from school. Though the brothers were supposed to walk together, Brandon had decided to send Wesley on ahead while he enjoyed a few more innings of baseball with his new friends. Again Philbrick tried to engage Wesley in a conversation, asking the boy about the watch cover he had been tossing from hand to hand as he walked along the road.

"He said he was your friend, Joel, and asked me to show him the watch cover." Wesley choked out the words. "He said you used to live in his house. That's where he said he'd found your *grossdawdi*'s watch."

"Is that possible?" Grace asked.

"Anything is possible." Joel wished his heart hadn't leaped at the thought of having all the pieces of his *grossdawdi*'s watch again. He couldn't help imagine sitting and opening it with Grace's nephews the way his *grossdawdi* had shared it with him. But Philbrick probably had been lying. He did that as easily as he betrayed anyone in his path. "Go on, Wesley. What happened then?"

"He told me if I gave him the watch cover, he'd put the pieces back together and bring it to you as a special surprise. I thought you'd like that surprise." He looked over his shoulder at Harold, then to Grace. "I thought about what Grace said to Brandon and me about putting myself in someone else's shoes and trying to think about what they would want. I knew if I were in your shoes, I'd want to get back something my *grossdawdi* gave me."

"So you gave it to him." There was no need to make it a question.

Wesley ducked his head and chewed on his lower lip. "I'm sorry, Joel. Don't be mad at me."

When Joel saw the shock and dismay on the faces around him, including on the trooper's, it took every ounce of self-control not to push past the police officer, Grace, the boys, everyone. He wanted to find the fastest vehicle he could get his hands on and race to where Philbrick was holed up like some slithering snake. Only this time, it wouldn't be the drug dealer who'd be striking as he had when he sent his henchman to make sure Joel went to prison for crimes he hadn't committed.

But he had no idea where Philbrick was holed up. Even if he had known, confronting the crook that way wasn't what he wanted to do. He needed to trust the police and God to bring Philbrick to justice.

He bent and gave the boy a quick hug. "I'm not mad at you, Wesley. You were being the *gut* and trusting boy I hope you always can be." He stood and took a steadying breath. "All right, Officer. Let's go."

"Why does he have to go?" Brandon cried. "Wesley explained everything."

"It's okay," Joel replied, hoping it was. "I'll be back soon."

Grace grasped his hand and squeezed it before he got into the car. Something disgusting seemed to be crawling along his skin as he thought of the first time he'd sat in the back of a patrol car. He'd never guessed he'd end up in prison, paying for someone else's crime.

As the trooper turned the car and headed down the farm lane, Joel looked back to see Grace and her family huddled together. His eyes focused on her anguished face.

What had he been thinking to kiss her as he had? She deserved a *gut* man in her life, not one sullied by crime and criminals. He bowed his head asking her forgiveness and God's for bringing such darkness into her life.

God could be showing him that he didn't belong in Bliss Valley any longer. He should leave...unless he was given one strong reason to stay. A reason that had nothing to do with how he'd fallen in love with Grace, because he didn't want to leave her mourning another man who'd vanished from her life.

Chapter Twenty-One

"Grace?"

Raising her head and leaving her prayer unfinished, Grace looked across the living room to where Wesley stood. She motioned for him to join her on the bench by the unlit stove. When he sat beside her, she put her arm around his slender shoulders. They were quivering so hard she could hear his teeth gnashing.

"Joel isn't back yet," she whispered.

The *kind* deflated like a puffball someone had stepped on. "It's my fault."

Brandon burst into the room. Standing with his hands on his hips, he cried, "No, it's not your fault! Tell him, *Aenti* Grace. It's not his fault."

"But I gave that bad man Joel's *grossdawdi*'s watch cover, and now the police have taken him away." Wesley wiped his nose on his arm.

Grace stretched to pull a tissue out of the box her *mamm* left on a table. Handing it to the boy, she said, "Listen to your brother. Brandon is right. Your only mistake, Wesley, was talking to that man. Didn't you see Joel's face when you said that? He wasn't upset with you. He was angry at that man because he put you in danger."

He shook his head, looking more wretched, which she hadn't believed was possible.

She framed his freckled face with her hands. "Now listen to me, Wesley Coffman! What do you think would have happened if you hadn't given that Philbrick man the watch cover?"

He didn't answer.

Turning to his brother who appeared on the edge of tears, she asked, "What do you think would have happened, Brandon?"

"I don't know," he mumbled.

"I know," she said, making sure her voice held no trace of doubt.

Wesley raised his head. "You do? What would have happened?"

"One of two things. Either that horrible man would have snatched the watch cover from you." She shuddered as she imagined the boy being overwhelmed by the man who hadn't cared who was hurt in his plan to frame Joel. "Or he would have found another way to cause trouble for Joel."

"Or he would have snatched you and the watch cover." Brandon's eyes twinkled with excitement. "Then *Grossdawdi* would have been contacted to pay a ransom for you. It would have been in the newspaper, and *everybody* would have been talking about it."

"But what if *Grossdawdi* couldn't pay the ransom?" Wesley's lips trembled again.

Annoyed at Brandon for making his little brother more upset, she said, "Well, we could always have traded that bad man something to get you back. Maybe your brother."

When Brandon gasped, Grace winked at Wesley who began to giggle. The little boy threw his arms around her and pressed his damp cheek to her face. She hugged him, then looked past him to where Brandon wore his shock. Holding out her arm to him, she was amazed—and grateful—when he let her pull him into their embrace.

She wasn't sure how long they would have remained like that, taking comfort from one another, if the front door hadn't opened. Raising her head as the boys looked over their shoulders, she heard Wesley yell, "Joel!"

The little boy ran to him, blubbering out apologies, as she drank in the sight of Joel. His face was drawn, giving him a haggard expression. His shoulders were bent as if he'd carried the house to Strasburg and back. But he smiled as he scooped up the little boy as if Wesley were no more than a toddler. Wesley's laugh rang through the house when Joel set him on his feet.

Grace stood as her parents came into the living room to see what was going on. They greeted Joel as if he'd been gone for a year instead of a few hours. Even Brandon grinned and began to ask dozens of questions about what had happened at the police station.

"We got the facts straight," Joel said, but Grace knew it had been more than that when she caught sight of the gray shadows underlining his eyes.

"Did you get your watch cover back?" asked Wesley.

"Not yet. The police are keeping it as evidence."

"But you didn't do anything wrong!"

Grace put her hands on her nephew's shoulders. "I'm sure that's not why they're holding on to it."

"She's right," Joel added. "They think it might help them with another potential crime. Apparently, they believe that someone may be trying to set-up Philbrick by suggesting to the police that he's here in the area so they can nab him. The cops want to check the watch cover and the note for any clues that will lead them to him."

"So you're helping the police?" Brandon asked, amazed.

"It's Wesley who's helped them." He ruffled the little boy's hair, then turned to reassure her parents everything was all right, and he was, too.

Grace waited for Joel to do the same with her, but he seemed to find every excuse not to look in her direction or speak to her. While she got the boys calmed down with a story from their *mamm*'s Bible and listened to their prayers before tucking them into bed, he spoke with her parents. She came downstairs, and *Mamm* and *Daed* sought their own night's sleep.

As soon as they went into their bedroom, Joel said, "Well, it's been a long day, and I need to check the calves."

"They're fed and bedded down," she replied. "*Daed* and I saw to that."

"I didn't mean for you to do my chores."

"I know, but *Daed* enjoyed it."

"Enjoyed watching you tend to them, ain't so?" He glanced toward the back door. Was he trying to find an excuse to put an end to their conversation?

"I was glad to do it. Joel—"

Again he looked toward the door. "You must be exhausted. It's been a long day with having the service here...and all."

"If you want to go, say so. Don't act like one of the boys trying to sneak around to avoid talking to me."

He pulled in a deep breath and let it out in a long sigh. "Is it that obvious?"

"Only to anyone with eyes in their head. What happened at the police station?"

"What I told you. Lots of questions. When they realized I was telling the truth and Philbrick had probably stalked your

nephews in an effort to get something on me, they [...]
in my parole officer who asked all the same questions. Th[...]
didn't have any reason to hold me, so I was released."

She frowned at how he recited the facts with a cool dispassion that contrasted with the anger that kept his hands fisted at his sides. "So how are you doing?"

"I'll be fine."

"Really? You may have fooled my family with your attempts to make light of what happened today, but don't do that with me. Be honest with how you feel. Let those who judge you go ahead and do it. They're going to do it anyhow." She closed the distance between them and put a hand on his tensed arm. "We're imperfect humans, Joel. We make mistakes and do things that we wish we hadn't and don't do things we wish we had."

"Some of us are more imperfect than others."

"I'm not sure that's true. Either way, it matters how we right our mistakes."

He stepped away. "I'm glad you said that, Grace. I've had a lot of time to think today, and one thing is clear to me. I don't belong in Bliss Valley. I should never have come here, and that's one mistake I can rectify."

"You're leaving?" Her fingers went to her lips as she recalled his on them. How could he kiss her and then walk away?

"Once I can sell the calves, I'll go. It'll be best for everyone." He turned to walk toward the back door.

She knew she should let him go, but her own feet were moving before she could halt them. Blocking his way, she demanded, "When did *you* get to be the one who decides what's best for everyone?"

"I won't ruin your lives any longer. As long as I stay here, the taint of my past stains you and your family and my family."

"But what if I say I love you?"

"Then I'll say you're going to have to get over it." His voice softened. "I'm sorry, Grace, but believe me. This is for the best." He pushed past her and went out the door.

This time she didn't try to stop him or her tears.

The next two days went so slowly Joel wanted to scream out his frustration. He avoided Grace, which left a hole in his day. So many times he thought about what he wanted to say to her or recalled a joke he knew would bring forth her musical laugh.

He tried to stay away from the rest of the Coffmans as well. He couldn't miss the puzzled expressions on the boys' faces when he saw them across the yard before they went to school. It told him they—most especially Wesley—were wondering what they'd done to upset Joel. Trying to explain to them would have led to a farewell he didn't want to make. Better that he finish up his business and leave Bliss Valley without prolonged goodbyes.

For the past two nights, he'd eaten soup out of cans. It couldn't compare with Grace's cooking, but what he missed more was the sense of family he'd enjoyed around the Coffmans' table. He'd thrown away his previous family in anger. Now he was losing another one, because he needed to do the right thing and protect them at the cost of denying his heart its most precious wish.

How empty his life would be! Without Grace's smile, her teasing wit, her bright eyes and her gentle heart, his days would have no flavors, no sweet aromas, no happy glow.

He sighed as he reached for another can of the horrible tasting soup. He halted when he heard a soft rap on the door. His heart leaped in his chest as he whirled to throw it open, praying it was Grace.

Joel stared. "Laurene, Naomi, what are you doing here?"

"We need to talk to you." Laurene frowned. "Aren't you going to ask us in, or will you make us stand out here in the rain?"

"Of course." He'd felt so grim he hadn't noticed the day was as gray.

The two women came in, and he motioned for them to take a seat on the worn sofa.

"I don't think either of us feels like sitting," Naomi said. "Why didn't you tell us?"

"Tell you what?"

Laurene frowned. "Didn't you hear from the bone marrow registry?"

"I did. They asked me to give a blood sample. That was the day I met you and Adam's daughter in Strasburg."

The two women looked at each other, then at him as Laurene asked, "Didn't you get a letter from them? Just in the past day or two?"

His eyes shifted toward the stack of mail on the table. Someone had brought it in from the mailbox, but he hadn't bothered with it. The only mail he ever received were flyers from local stores and offers for credit cards and used cars.

Naomi stretched across the table and pulled out a white envelope. She slapped it into his hand. "A letter like this one."

He stared at the return address with the logo from the registry. Opening it, he scanned the request for him to contact the bone marrow registry. He was a potential match for Naomi and Laurene's birth *mamm*? What were the chances of that?

One in three hundred, he recalled the technician saying.

No, that was not the chance of being a match for their birth *mamm*. The odds of that, he'd been told, were astronomical.

"Well?" asked Laurene.

"Well what?"

"Are you willing to donate?"

"How can you ask that?" he asked. "Of course, I'm willing to donate. No matter what you think of me, I'm not so awful that I would turn my back on a woman whose life might depend on this transplant."

"She didn't mean—"

Laurene interrupted by putting her hand on Naomi's arm. "*Ja*, I did mean what I asked. Donating is, as we were told at the collection event, voluntary. I had to ask."

"As I would have," Joel replied, "if our situations were reversed. You don't have any reason to trust me."

"Just one. You could save our birth *mamm*'s life."

"Her life is in God's hands. All I can do is offer a donation."

The two women smiled. How had everybody in Bliss Valley failed to see what was now so obvious? The two women didn't look the same, but so many of their motions and expressions were identical. Laurene had a way of raising her eyebrows like Naomi did, and both smiled as if joy was bursting out of them.

"What happens next?" he asked.

"Your marrow is harvested and put in our *mamm*. Her own will have been destroyed so the new marrow can grow to fight her cancer." Naomi hesitated, then added, "At least, that's how I understand it."

"Me, too." Laurene blinked as her eyes filled with tears. "There isn't any danger to you. They'll use general anesthesia, but the chances of a bad reaction to it is small. You'll be in and out of the hospital, we've been told, with a single night's stay. There's one more thing. Gina Marie would like to meet you."

"Why?"

"Must you question everything, Joel?" Naomi rolled her eyes. "You always did that in school, but we're adults now."

"And that was an adult question. I'm curious why she wants to meet me. From what I was told, a lot of the time, the donor doesn't even know the name of the person receiving the donation."

"She wants to tell you how grateful she is."

Again, he looked from one woman to the other. More than fifteen years had passed since the three of them had been in school together, but in some ways, nothing had changed. Laurene and Naomi were presenting a united front when speaking with him, fearing what he'd say.

"I'm glad I can donate," he said.

"Then you won't mind meeting her?" Naomi blinked back tears. "It would mean so much to her, Joel, to be able to express her gratitude in person."

Before he could reply, Laurene jumped in to say, "And Gina Marie is willing to come to the Coffmans' farm with her attorney."

"Attorney?"

"You should have guessed there would be paperwork if you agreed to donate."

He gave a terse chuckle. "You're right. I should have guessed, but why is her lawyer coming to the farm? Most lawyers I know don't like to do business outside their offices."

"Grace suggested you might be more comfortable here," Naomi said. "She thought you'd had enough interactions with lawyers in their offices already."

"Grace? She knows I'm a match?"

"I saw her this morning in Strasburg," Laurene said, "and I mentioned it to her. I was surprised when she didn't know, which is why Naomi and I decided to come here to make sure you'd received the letter."

He found his own eyes filling with unexpected tears. He blinked hard as they grew cumbersome, threatening to fall and shame him. If *Daed* saw... His jaw hardened. *Daed* was as vindictive about his son showing emotion as any hardened inmate.

"Why do you sound surprised?" Laurene asked with the forthrightness she'd acquired during her time among *Englisch-ers*. "She cares a lot about you."

"I know."

"Then you should know," Naomi interjected, "she'll do whatever she can for those she cares about."

"I know that, too."

Laurene asked again, "So why did you sound surprised?"

Sure he was being tag-teamed, he wondered how many more body slams he could take before he tumbled face-first to the ground. *Be honest with how you feel. Let those who judge you go ahead and do it. They're going to do it anyhow.*

"Not surprised. Relieved." Now that was the truth. He was relieved he could do something to help a woman who would die without his donation. He was relieved he didn't have to go and sit in another cold, impersonal, overdecorated attorney's office. Looking at the sisters, he added, "Very relieved. When can we do this?"

Naomi threw her arms around him and sobbed against his neck. "*Danki, danki,* Joel. You don't know what a gift you've given us."

He patted her back clumsily, unsure what else to say. Was this the answer God had sent for his prayer of having another *gut* reason to stay in Bliss Valley? To help a dying woman?

If it was, as far as Joel was concerned, it was too late. He couldn't stay and destroy Grace's life.

Grace stamped past the remnants of her garden the next Saturday afternoon. Soon she'd be pulling out the low fencing and letting the rabbits and other animals feast on the remnants. They would come in droves to finish off the vines and leaves.

How she wished she had something that would draw in her nephews with such ease! She'd thought the boys had given up their skittish ways, but they'd vanished as if they'd never set foot on the farm. Where could they have gotten to now?

Going into the barn, she saw her *daed* currying Pearl.

"*Daed*, have you seen the boys?"

He looked up. He kept the brush against the horse, so his tremors wouldn't make it impossible for him to get it in the right position again. Joel had suggested he try that, and *Daed* had listened.

So many changes Joel had brought into their lives, but now he was determined to leave. The bone marrow donation would delay him a few weeks; then he'd be gone.

"Not since dinner," he replied. "Something I can help with?"

"No, but *danki*." Not wanting to worry him, she said, "I'll find them so they can finish the chores I have for them before supper."

"*Gut*. Boys should be kept busy so they stay out of mischief."

Oh, how she hoped they hadn't already found it. Since the incident with the baseball through Herb Esbenshade's window, the boys had been conscientious about letting her know where they were going and when they'd be home. Though she'd begun to wonder if they were being honest with her. She'd noticed how Wesley didn't look her in the eyes when they spoke of where they were going.

"Wesley is here," came Joel's voice from the shadows at the far side of the barn.

Torn between wanting to race away so she didn't have to face the man who had thrown her love back in her face and needing to make sure the boys were okay, she lifted her chin and squared her shoulders. For her nephews, she could talk with Joel for a few minutes.

"*D-d-danki*, J-J-Joel." She shut her mouth before she could

306 A Search for Redemption

stutter over more words. Hating the habit that showed up whenever she was uncertain, she looked at the boy standing beside him.

Wesley wouldn't meet her eyes. He shuffled his feet and laced his fingers together. His pose made it clear he wanted to be anywhere but there.

Putting her arm around his shoulders, she steered him out of the barn and toward the back porch. He plopped down on a step and stared at the grass.

"Do you know where Brandon is, Wesley?" she asked, though she wanted to say she comprehended how he felt. She didn't want to be there with Joel, who'd followed them from the barn.

Her nephew nodded.

"Where is he?"

"Not telling." He folded his arms in front of him. "Brandon says anyone who snitches—"

"Gets stitches. I know, I know." She took a deep breath and tried to push the irritation out of her voice.

"He told me not to tell."

"About what?"

Wesley hung his head. "I can't tell."

"Then let me guess," Joel said. "Brandon hasn't been going over to the Esbenshade house to help pay for the window."

The boy's head snapped up. "How did you know?"

Grace was wondering the same thing, but didn't ask when Joel gave his head a slight shake. He'd made a guess, and it'd been a *gut* one. How could she have failed to see the truth?

"Where does he go when he's supposed to be at Herb's?" Joel frowned. "And what about you?"

"I went!" the little boy asserted. "After all, it was my fault. I threw the ball Brandon hit through the window."

Wanting to roll her eyes at the logic Brandon had used to

persuade his younger brother to do the work they both were supposed to do, Grace said, "Tell us the truth, Wesley. All of it. I'm not asking you to snitch. I'm asking you to tell me where he is. *Grossmammi* is worried about him." She sat on a step that was lower than where he was perched. "I'm worried as well."

"Me, too." His eyes filled as he whispered, "What if something happens to Brandon? What if he's left me too?"

"He wouldn't leave you." The words came out automatically, but she knew they were true. Brandon might convince his brother to handle the mess they'd both been part of, but he would have been the first to jump in if something endangered his little brother.

"Everyone else has."

"I know, Wesley." She put a consoling hand on his knee. "I know how you feel." She didn't look at Joel, but was aware of him standing behind her, listening to every word. "It's sad when people leave us. We must continue loving them as we did when they were with us."

"Brandon said he'll be okay," the boy persisted, "but what if he isn't? *Mamm* and *Daed* told us they'd be okay, too."

"Tell us where he is," Joel interjected. "We'll get him and make sure he's okay."

She closed her eyes, but couldn't shut out the pain Joel's easy offer created deep within her. He was acting as if he'd never spoken of leaving Bliss Valley...and her. She pushed aside the hurt. Now wasn't the time to think about that. She had to make sure Brandon was safe.

"Where is he, Wesley?" she asked again. "Do you know where he went?"

"*Ja*," he said.

"Where?"

"I'll show you."

She grabbed his hand and almost yanked him to his feet.

When he told her they'd need the buggy, Joel ran toward the barn. He came back out leading Pearl and hitched him to the buggy.

Daed followed with his unsteady steps. "What's going on?"

Again Grace was caught between two things she wanted to do. She wanted to reassure her *daed*, but she didn't want him to worry while they were gone. So she convinced Wesley to tell her right then where his brother had gone. She hid her surprise when he said Brandon had gone to the lumberyard. What was he doing there?

Knowing that asking questions would be wasting time they needed to get the boy, she said, "*Daed*, we'll be right back."

"All right." He glanced at the back steps, and a strange expression crossed his face.

Wesley must have seen it, too, because he said, "You go. I'll help *Grossdawdi*."

She wiped away a sudden tear when he went to assist *Daed* onto the porch. Wesley waved to them as he opened the door so his *grossdawdi* didn't have to struggle with closing his trembling hand around the knob.

"Let's go," Joel said, tossing her the reins. "You know where to go, ain't so?"

"*Ja.*"

That was the last word either of them spoke until they reached the lumberyard at the edge of Strasburg. Large trucks moved among the stacks of lumber and building supplies. A salesman came out with a smile to ask how he could help. His smile was replaced with a frown when she said they were looking for her nephew.

"The kids like to play hide-and-seek in the yard," he grumbled. "It's not a problem until one of them decides to try to climb the lumber. A collapse could kill them."

"Can we look around?" Joel asked.

"Yeah, but be careful. I've got a half dozen guys working in the yard. There's machinery everywhere, and they're not used to looking out for people except in the samples area."

Grace half hoped Joel would suggest they split up to explore, but nodded when he urged her to come with him. Minutes passed, and she realized what a huge job was ahead of them. If Brandon remained in one place, they might find him by going up and down the aisles between the supplies, but they couldn't assume that would happen. They kept walking and walking with no sign of the boy.

Joel took her arm and motioned for her to stop. He put a finger to his lips, then tapped his ear.

She strained to hear what he must have. Her heartbeat seemed too loud in her ears, blocking every sound.

Then she heard a young voice. She couldn't pick out the words, but she recognized the voice.

Brandon!

Rushing to where her nephew stood beside a stack of boards, she slid to a stop when she realized he was talking to one of the lumberyard's employees. The man who was close to her *daed*'s age was listening as Brandon explained something, using his hands and pointing to a piece of paper he held.

"Brandon!" She ran to him. "We've been looking everywhere for you."

"Is this your boy?" asked the *Englischer*.

"*Ja.* I'm sorry he's bothering you."

The man grinned. "He's no bother. He's a good kid. See you later, Brandon. We'll figure out how to get you what you want." With a nod toward Grace, he walked toward the store.

Before she could ask Brandon why the *Englischer* seemed to know him so well, Joel stormed past her. His voice was honed to such an edge that Grace flinched along with Brandon when he asked, "What were you thinking running off like that,

Brandon? Don't you know how worried you've made every-one? You know the rules. You don't leave the farm without telling someone where you're going."

"I told Wesley where I was going." He stuck out his chin.

"He wouldn't tell us where you were at first."

"Not my problem." He hooked a thumb in the direction of the farm. "You need to yell at him for that. Not me."

Grace hurried to speak to halt Joel's retort. "He thinks you're going to get hurt, and he'll be on his own."

Brandon looked skyward as if praying for patience. "He's a kid. He doesn't understand anything."

Not wanting to remind Brandon his brother was only two years younger than he was, Grace noticed Joel about to make another demand. She put up her hand to silence him and asked, "What are you doing here, Brandon?"

"I work here."

She shook her head. "No, that's impossible. They can't hire someone your age. It's against the law."

"It would be if they were paying me. I've been doing er-rands, getting stuff for customers. In return, they're going to let me have the wood I need."

"You've been here instead of paying back Herb Esben-shade?" Joel's voice remained sharp.

"Wesley's handling that. We discussed it and worked it out. He'd go there to do chores, and I'd come here, so I could get wood."

"Why?" she asked, unable to figure out the reasoning of two young boys.

"I want to build ramps on the front and back porches for *Grossdawdi*." His demeanor changed, and he gave her a shy smile so unlike his usual superior expression she was shocked. She understood she was seeing into his heart when he said, "It'll help you, too, because he's depending on you to get into the house. Maybe this way, he won't fall so often. I don't like seeing him with scabs on his hands."

She shouldn't have been surprised the boy had noticed. Tears prickled at the back of her eyes as she realized sometime, she wasn't sure when, Brandon had begun to let his life move forward again, daring to let his heart care about his *grossdawdi*. She wanted to hug him and thank him for being so kind and for showing her it was possible to live after losing someone so dear. She didn't because it would embarrass the boy. Instead, she smiled and nodded.

He brightened, and she guessed he'd gotten the message she hadn't spoken. Fritz hadn't been the most demonstrative one in the family. In fact, though he'd been fun-loving and playful as well as hardworking, he'd seldom shown any affection with hugs. That was what Brandon and Wesley were accustomed to, and she had to remember and respect that.

Just as she respected Brandon for caring about his *grossdawdi* and finding a solution she should have. She *would* have if she hadn't been so caught up in her attraction to Joel. Well, that was over now. He'd made that clear with his plans to hightail it out of Bliss Valley, so her focus needed to be on her family.

"We'll handle it from here, Joel," she said, not looking in his direction.

"I can—"

Unable to forget how his words had whipped at her nephew like his announcement he was leaving had her, she said, "You've done enough. *Danki* for helping me find Brandon, but now it's time we learned to do things on our own." Every word she spoke closed the door to her heart again more securely. It had only begun to open in the wake of Lamar's death when she'd met Joel.

She would make sure it would never be opened again.

Chapter Twenty-Two

"Where is she?" Joel went to the window and peered again at the gathering clouds before glancing at the clock on the mantel. It was almost three o'clock, and Gina Marie and another of her daughters, one she'd raised herself, should be arriving within a half hour.

Laurene said, "Gina Marie—"

"I'm not talking about her. Where's Grace?"

Both Laurene and Naomi shrugged in unison. He hadn't known Grace would be coming home for this meeting with their birth *mamm* until Naomi mentioned it after she arrived. He'd assumed Grace would be busy at the quilt shop and would wait for Harold and Saretta to pick her up at day's end after visiting friends south near Quarryville. The boys had volunteered to stay after school to play ball with their friends, leaving the house to him for the meeting.

"She said she'd be here," Naomi replied.

"I'm amazed she didn't say anything to you about it," Laurene added. "She said she'd be glad to be here for us."

For you, not for me, he wanted to say, but he didn't. That would be petty, when Grace had offered not only her home, but her time to help ease what was an uncomfortable, stilted meeting.

"But it's not like Grace to be late." Laurene went to look out another window and flinched when the distant shriek of an emergency vehicle filled the quiet afternoon, followed by a roll of thunder.

"You're right." He strode into the kitchen and snatched his hat off the peg beside where Harold's had been hanging.

"Where are you going?" Laurene grabbed his sleeve, jerking back her hand when he turned with a scowl. Was she afraid of him? Still? Her face was as colorless as it had been when they'd been scholars.

Lord, I thought I'd changed from that angry kind. Have I been fooling myself? Guide me to find the right words to show Laurene and Naomi I'm not that boy any longer.

"You can't leave now," she said, her voice unsteady.

"I don't want Grace walking home in this storm."

Laurene and Naomi exchanged an uneasy glance before Naomi said, "You're right."

"Go!" urged her twin. "Take my buggy. Sparks is easy to drive, and he's quick. You can get there and back in half an hour, ain't so?"

"A little bit longer, but I hope I'll meet her along the way." He paused in the doorway. "Tell your *mamm* I'll be here as soon as I can."

The women nodded before he shut the door and ran past the partially finished ramp he had been working on with Brandon and Wesley. They had built one at the back already and equipped it with solar lights so it could be used after dark. Harold was able to go up and down with an ease that surprised everyone. Joel hoped the one in front would be done before he had to go to the hospital to make the donation.

Or did he? If the front ramp wasn't finished, it would give him an excuse to stay longer and hope that he could figure out some way to salvage the disaster he'd made of his life. He couldn't forget how Grace's face had fallen when he said he was leaving Bliss Valley for *gut*. No, not for *gut*. Forever. There couldn't be anything *gut* about leaving Grace who had looked inside Joel and seen the potential for him to become a better man. He wished he could discern the same.

Joel didn't slow until he reached Laurene's buggy by the lane. The gusting wind spit raindrops at him. He pulled on the door to slide it back. As he was stepping inside, he heard his name called.

He glanced out, expecting to see a car with Gina Marie and her lawyer coming up the lane. Instead, Brandon and Wesley ran toward him.

"Where are you going?" Brandon asked.

"To get your *aenti*. Your *grossdawdi* took her buggy, so she walked to work this morning. I don't want her to get caught in the storm." He frowned. "I thought you were staying at school to play ball."

Another rumble of thunder answered him.

Brandon said, "You're not going without me."

"Without us." Wesley stuck out his chest in what he clearly thought was an assertive pose.

Under any other circumstances, Joel might have laughed at the boys' determination to insist on him taking them with him. Or would he have? When he saw the fear hidden behind their demanding tones, he realized how worried they were about their *aenti*. As worried as he was, and with *gut* reason. Their parents had disappeared out of their lives without warning, and they didn't want to lose Grace as well. Seeing how Brandon rubbed his hands together, Joel guessed the boy wouldn't be so ready to wander off on his own again because he was beginning to understand how others felt.

Holding out his hands, he said, "All right. Let's go."

He was astonished when both boys grabbed his hands. They must be more worried about their *aenti* than they were letting on.

As he was.

Grace forced herself not to look at the clock on the wall behind the cash register as more thunder exploded overhead. She knew she was going to be late for the important meeting with Laurene and Naomi's *mamm* and Joel. Oh, how she hated being late! Especially today when walking home in the storm would delay her longer, but she refused to shift her feet toward the door.

Instead, she listened while Tiffany paced back and forth in front of the counter, listing everything she believed Grace had done wrong since she'd started work at the shop five years before. Grace acted as if she were paying attention as she rearranged the display quilts on the center table after showing them to a customer who had decided on the first one she'd seen. Tiffany was outraged because Grace had gone against her expressed orders and had paid each of the quilters whose quilts had sold more than a month ago.

"I made myself clear," Tiffany shouted. "You know the rules."

When her boss took a breath for her next rant, Grace said, "I do know the rules. The rules you set state our quilters should be paid within thirty days of the sale of their consigned quilts. I did that."

"You know that's not the way we've done things."

"It's what it says in the agreements you created."

Tiffany gave an inelegant snort, which was almost lost beneath thunder cracking along the street. "Those terms aren't carved in stone. The quilters know our expansion to a second store will mean a bigger market for their work and a temporary slowdown on payments."

"It hasn't been temporary." She glanced toward the street. It hadn't begun to rain yet, but lightning flashed, followed by more thunder.

"Whose side are you on?"

Grace continued folding the last quilt as the door to the street opened. Though she was curious who was out in such weather, she didn't look. This conversation was long overdue, and she refused to let it be interrupted. "I didn't know there were sides, Tiffany."

"Of course, there are sides, and you need to figure out which side you're on. The quilters or mine." She laughed. "You think those quilters are your friends, but they're using you."

"You're wrong about that."

"We're going to have different quilters soon."

"What do you mean?"

"I mean, I've made deals with other quilters who make real plain quilts, not those with the outlandish quilting and appliqué."

Comprehension hit her like a fist, painful and infuriating. "You're talking about the quilts the Hmong quilters make. Pepper and her *mamm* and *grossmammi*, ain't so?" She flung a hand toward the discount rack. "You moved their quilts there so they'd make less money, ain't so?"

"It's my store, and I make the rules. You know how many questions we get about whether the quilts are made in Lancaster County by plain artisans. I've got a reputation to keep."

"Your reputation is that you're slow paying your quilters. They're not going to put up with it much longer."

"That won't be your problem." Tiffany's voice took on that arrogant tone that suggested she knew more than anyone else. "Take a moment to think about it, Grace, and you'll have your answer. After all, you need this job."

Grace recognized the footsteps behind her, but didn't turn. What were Joel and her nephews doing there? Had the time for the meeting with Gina Marie been changed? She didn't want to look away and let her boss believe Grace was conceding the argument.

As Grace always did.

She couldn't let Tiffany think that she was backing down.

As Grace always did.

Tiffany was assuming Grace would tuck her tail between her legs and give in.

As Grace always did.

Tiffany was certain Grace would never stand up to her ultimatums or do anything that would threaten her job.

As Grace always did.

But Tiffany was wrong. As she often was, though nobody seemed willing to tell her that.

Until today.

"Tiffany, you need to pay the quilters as you've agreed to." Grace flinched as hail struck the front windows.

"Don't preach to me."

"I'm not." Grace placed the quilt on the top of the pile and smoothed it with a loving hand. It was one of Rosemary's, and she wondered when her friend would make another with such vibrant colors. Working with bright shades wasn't easy when in the depths of mourning. Grace knew that too well. "I don't need to. You know the difference between what's right and what's wrong."

"This conversation isn't going anywhere. I've got work to do. So do you."

"Tiffany, you started the stories about Pepper and the other Hmong quilters, ain't so?"

"You can't prove that."

"I don't have to. Missy Garnier mentioned when she was in here earlier with her tour group that you'd told her to be careful about foreign quilts because they were of inferior quality." Grace hadn't wanted to believe Tiffany would stoop so low. "You know Pepper's quilts aren't poorly made. In fact, they're some of the best ones we sell. Why would you want to stop selling them when they're popular with our customers?"

"Because you push your friends' quilts on our customers and ignore the rest." She faltered as the sky opened, and rain hit the building so hard it sounded like innumerable tiny hammers.

"You know that's not true." Grace's eyes widened. "You don't want to stop selling the quilts Pepper and her family make. You want to destroy her reputation. Why?" She answered her own question. "You don't want her consigning her quilts to anyone else, but you also don't want to pay her fairly. When she started to make a fuss because you refused to pay her on time, you found another way to attack her."

"You don't know what you're t-t-talking about." Tiffany's voice wobbled as if she'd been infected with Grace's nervous stutter. "You don't know anything about running a successful business."

"I know how *not* to run one. You can't be successful by cheating your suppliers. Others are going to realize what's going on."

"How? Are you going to blab to everyone?"

Grace shook her head, wondering how Tiffany could have failed to see the real person Grace was after years of working together. Then Grace realized she couldn't fault Tiffany for that. Grace had held back so much of herself, afraid of letting her real self shine.

"I'm not the only person who's figured this out," she said.

"There's nothing to 'figure out.'" Tiffany made air quotes with her fingers. "Other than what you're going to do now that you're fired."

Grace waited for the sickening dismay that had sunk through her each time she'd imagined Tiffany speaking those words. The feeling didn't come. Instead, there was a loosening inside her as if iron bands, wrought after years of holding in her true feelings, broke. For the first time in longer than she could remember, she felt free. She didn't feel she needed to try to be someone she wasn't. She wasn't Tiffany's sycophantic servant, so afraid of losing her job she let one wrong after another slide.

"If that's the way you want it—" Grace began.

"It is."

"All right." The rain drummed against the windows, but the room was otherwise silent. "Do you have my final check ready, or should I stop back tomorrow?"

Tiffany frowned. "Your final check?"

"I worked last week and half of this one. You'll find my time card in its usual place."

"Why should I pay you when you're walking off the job and leaving me in the lurch?"

Had Tiffany forgotten that she'd fired Grace just moments ago? Not wanting to point that out and infuriate her former boss more, Grace said quietly, "Because I worked those hours."

"So what?"

"I wouldn't want your business to suffer if it was learned you weren't paying your employee and your contractors what they were due."

"That sounds like a threat."

Grace shook her head. "I don't mean it as a threat. I love this shop, Tiffany. I love it so much I've excused your behavior for too long." She ignored her soon-to-be former boss's sharp intake of breath. "You're an excellent businesswoman, so I know you'll see the wisdom of doing the right thing."

For a long minute, Tiffany tried to intimidate her with a baleful stare, but Grace wasn't the first one to look away. Tiffany snapped, "Wait here!" She stamped into the back room. The sound of papers being tossed in a dozen directions drifted out.

Joel stepped forward with the boys, who had remained quiet through the whole conversation. Their eyes were almost as round as their open mouths, but they didn't make a sound. Neither did Joel. He gave her a thumbs-up. Wesley did the same, followed by Brandon who gave her a shy smile as well.

She guessed the boys had no idea what was going on, that they were copying Joel. It didn't matter. She appreciated their support. All their support. She was happy to have this pleasant moment to remember after Joel left.

Tiffany stormed into the front of the store, her brows as low as the thunderheads. She held out a folded check to Grace. "Here you go. Now get out of *my* store."

"*Danki.*" Grace turned to leave, then paused. Opening the check, she looked at the total. It was right, she was glad to see. She didn't want to have to argue with Tiffany again. "*Komm mol*, boys. Let's go."

"That's right," snarled Tiffany. "I don't want any thieves in here. You remember that, Joel Beachy."

With a beatific smile, he said, "I will, and if I ever encounter any thieves, I'll give them a heads-up you are particular about your clientele."

Grace bit her lower lip to keep from giggling and motioned

for the boys to remain quiet. It was futile. The laugh burst out of her before she was able to close the front door behind them.

The rain had stopped as quickly as it had started, leaving puddles in every depression and the smell of wet asphalt heavy in the air. She leaned against the door, shaking with her amusement as well as relief that the confrontation she'd avoided for so long had come and gone.

"*Aenti* Grace," Wesley said, tugging on her apron, "people are looking at you."

She tousled his hair as she stood straighter and wiped tears from the corners of her eyes. People? She saw an *Englisch* couple in front of the ice cream shop across the street. They were staring, but was it because she was laughing or because of her plain clothing? She didn't care. To her nephew, she said, "I'm glad."

"You are?" both boys asked at the same time, then grinned at each other.

"*Ja*. It does people *gut* to see someone who's happy. When they're happy, too, it reminds them it's okay to show it. If they're not happy, maybe seeing someone else's joy brings a memory of a time when they weren't sad."

"That's why," Brandon said with amazement, "you tell us it's important for us to share how we're feeling."

"*Ja*." With a grin, she ruffled his hair as she had his younger brother. For once, he didn't complain. "Being honest about how we feel can help others as well as ourselves. God wants us to be open with one another as we are with Him. We're family, and we should share the happy times and the ones that aren't happy."

"Listen to your *aenti*," Joel said. "You can learn a lot from her. I have."

She longed to reach up and touch his face, though they stood on a public street corner. But she didn't. She was staying in Bliss Valley. He was leaving once he'd made his bone marrow donation.

At that thought, she gasped. "You're supposed to be meeting Laurene and Naomi's birth *mamm*, Joel. What are you doing here?"

"I came to get you. They said you were going to be there, and we got worried when you didn't arrive." He looked up as thunder sounded, but farther away. "I didn't want you walking home in a thunderstorm, so I came to get you so you could be there to support Laurene and Naomi as you said you would."

She didn't correct him and say she wanted to be there foremost for him, because that would risk opening herself to more pain. "I wanted to be. Then Tiffany—"

"I get it. You were superb in there, you know?"

"I almost lost my temper. A couple of times."

"But you didn't."

"No." This wasn't how she'd imagined they would talk when or if he stopped acting as if he'd already said a final goodbye. She changed the subject.

"Komm mol," he said with a strained smile. "I borrowed Laurene's buggy. Her horse likes to step out, so we'll get us to your house in record time."

She took Wesley's hand, motioned to Brandon and hurried around the side of the building to the parking lot. She bumped into Joel as he halted.

"What's *he* doing here?" Joel's voice was hard.

"Who?" She couldn't see around him.

"My parole officer."

Bending, she told the boys to get into the buggy. She thought they might protest, but they nodded, shooting uneasy glances in Ronald Shriver's direction as he stepped out of his car. Unable to halt herself, she gripped Joel's arm. It tensed beneath her fingers until she could have been holding onto a steel bar.

"Grace, isn't it?" the parole officer asked without any greeting.

"*Ja.*"

"I need to speak with Beachy." He cleared his throat. "With Joel."

"Go ahead." She couldn't believe her own temerity.

Both men stared at her, but she refused to quail. Joel lived on her family's farm, so she would defend him against whatever Ronald Shriver accused him of today.

With a shrug, the parole officer said, "I was on my way to see you, Beachy. I wanted to let you know the rumors about you being involved in a drug deal have been traced back to their source. Your name has been cleared."

"Who started the rumors?" Joel asked, showing no surprise or appreciation at the man's words.

"You know I can't tell you that." He held on to the edge of the car door. "Let's leave it that someone mistook what someone else said and added two and two and got seven."

"So I'm no longer under suspicion."

"Not for this incident."

Grace bit her lip to keep herself from giving voice to the protests flooding out from her heart. She despised how Joel had been assumed to be at the center of someone else's attempted crime. Or even for crimes that hadn't yet happened.

As if he heard her thoughts, Joel cupped her elbow in a request for her to remain silent. His gaze never left the other man's face as he asked, "For another incident?"

"You sound like you're suffering from guilt, Beachy."

"We all have things we regret, but my regrets have nothing to do with any crimes."

"Glad to hear that." He frowned. "Are you staying in Strasburg?"

"He has to." When Ronald Shriver's eyes shifted toward Grace, she added, "He needs to stay here until the bone marrow donation is complete."

"Bone marrow donation?" The parole officer's brows shot upward. "Are you sick, Beachy?"

"No."

"Then—"

Again Grace spoke up. "Joel is the donor for a woman who's got non-Hodgkin's lymphoma."

The parole officer arched a single eyebrow, then nodded. "Keep your nose clean, Beachy, or you'll end up back in jail. Neither of us want that to happen."

"Really?" Grace clapped her hand over her mouth, but it was too late. The word had escaped.

"Really," the parole officer said. "I don't like to see my guys back in jail. It means both of us have made mistakes." He released the door. "And I don't like making mistakes." As he turned to get in the car, he paused. "Oh, Beachy, this is yours."

Light flashed on something the parole officer flipped in the air. Joel caught it and gasped. His *grossdawdi*'s watch cover.

"We don't need it any longer," said the parole officer.

"What about the watch that goes with it?" Joel asked. "Philbrick told Wesley that..." He halted himself. "Never mind. Philbrick was just lying again."

"Glad to see you've finally wised up to that snake and his games, Beachy. There might be hope for you after all." With a two-fingered salute, he added, "Let me know when the surgery is scheduled, so we can talk about your plans for after it."

Joel nodded, but stared down at the thin gold lid in his hand as the car drove away.

"You got it back," Grace said. "*Danki* to You, God."

"*Ja.*" He tossed the watch cover into the air and caught it before putting it in his pocket. "Well, that proves I should have listened to Adam right from the beginning. He said to trust that God would watch over me."

"Adam has been a gift to the *Leit* with his kindness and *gut* advice." She guessed her eyes were twinkling like his when she added, "*Gut*, practical advice. And you know how I like practical advice."

"I know you like to give it."

"I take it, too." She regarded him from the corners of her eyes. She couldn't believe they were sparring with words as they once had. Did that mean he'd changed his mind about leaving? She ached to ask, but her courage deserted her as it hadn't when she stood up to Tiffany and Ronald Shriver. "When I hear *gut*, practical advice."

"Like what you've given me."

"And like what you've sometimes accepted."

"When my pride didn't get in the way of my common sense." As they walked to the buggy where the boys were waiting impatiently, he said, "Adam told me God had already forgiven me."

"I believe that, too. As I believe the *Leit* will forgive you and invite you back into our community whenever you're ready to ask for forgiveness."

"Not all of them."

She climbed into the buggy. She waited while he showed the boys the watch lid and smiled when Wesley flung his arms around Joel and gave him an excited hug.

"Boys, we can't be late for the meeting," she said. "Let's have a celebration later."

"What kind of celebration?" asked the always detail-oriented Brandon.

"Why don't you two come up with some ideas?"

As the boys bent their heads to discuss what sort of party they'd like to have that night, she waited until Joel had driven the buggy out onto the road heading south. She lowered her voice as she said, as if there had been no break, "Joel, your *daed* must accept the rules of our *Ordnung*, too. For generations, the *Leit* has welcomed back those who ask for forgiveness. One man, lost in his own bitterness, cannot change that."

"He thinks he can have everything his way."

"He's wrong."

When he didn't reply, she knew he didn't believe her. No matter how much he wanted to.

Wyman Beachy had driven his son away from Bliss Valley once. It looked like he was going to do it again.

And Grace had no idea how to change that.

Chapter Twenty-Three

A large black car was parked in the driveway. From the back seat of the buggy, the boys exclaimed about how shiny it was and asked Joel what gadgets he thought were inside. He wasn't surprised at their knowledge of cars. At their ages, he'd been fascinated with them, too. Though he wanted to warn them not to be led astray by the trappings of the *Englisch* world, he knew nothing he said would make a difference unless they were wiser than he'd been.

Grace sent the boys to the barn to play with the calves, then walked with Joel toward the house.

Laurene met them at the door. "They're here," she said needlessly.

Joel looked across the room to where a woman who was little more than fragile flesh stretched over bones sat on the sofa. A surgical mask covered the lower half of her face. Her hair must have fallen out because she wore a brightly patterned turban. Pain from her cancer had carved deep canyons in her face, but he guessed she once had been attractive.

Sitting beside her was an *Englisch* woman with bright purple streaks in her hair and glasses with vivid green and rhinestone frames. She looked to be several years younger than Laurene and Naomi, but he noticed a similarity in the shapes of their faces. Was she their half sister?

Behind them, standing as silent as a pillar, was a tall *Englischer*. His black hair was streaked with silver at the temples. He wore a tailored suit that Joel guessed had a fancy designer label. That must be the attorney. Joel fought to keep from walking—no, running—away, not wanting to be in the room with a lawyer.

You agreed to this meeting, he reminded himself. *You knew a lawyer would be here, and this isn't the incompetent fool who did more damage than help your case.*

The older woman's eyes smiled, but the younger one frowned at him, shifting toward the woman he guessed was Gina Marie. The motion was protective, and a warning he'd be sorry if he did anything to cause her more pain.

"I'm Joel Beachy," he said when everyone else remained silent. "They tell me our bone marrows are a match."

His words sounded awkward and uncertain, even in his own ears. By his side, Grace gave his arm a quick squeeze. He appreciated her trying to bolster him, but he couldn't remember a time when he'd ever felt so nervous and uncertain. Not even when he'd gone before the parole board to ask to be let out on *gut* behavior.

"So glad to meet you at last, Joel," the older woman said. "I'm Gina Marie Tinniswood, as I'm sure you've guessed. This is my daughter, Skylar Lopez." She gestured toward the woman with the green glasses, then motioned toward the man behind the sofa. "This is Charles Satterfield, the attorney who helped me find my other daughters, Laurene and Naomi."

She glanced toward the twins, then at Grace. "I'm assuming you're our hostess."

Grace smiled. "I am. I will leave you to discuss—"

"No, no, don't leave," Gina Marie said. "I want to thank you for your kindness in offering your home to us. Please stay. My daughters have told me a little about you and how you convinced Joel to come to the bone marrow volunteer sign-up. If it hadn't been for you, we wouldn't be here today."

A pretty flush climbed Grace's cheeks. "It didn't take much to convince Joel to participate."

"I'm glad to hear that." Gina Marie's eyes crinkled with another smile. "Even so, please stay because I'd like to get to know you better, too."

"If you wish…"

"I do." Looking at Joel, she said, "Sit down, son, so we can get to know each other a bit before we meet again at the hospital." She patted the cushion beside her. "Here."

He complied, aware of everyone's eyes on him. His own gaze cut toward Grace. The strength she'd revealed when facing her boss continued to shine in her eyes. When he'd first met her, he'd thought she was a gentle spirit, as easily bruised as a fresh peach. He'd been wrong. She was as strong as the foundation holding this house, doing what she must for those around her without any pomp or most people noticing her. She'd stood up to the storms that had lashed her. She'd lost her fiancé and her oldest brother and his wife. She'd brought two angry, scared boys into a household that already taxed her with the needs of her parents. She defended friends and their work against a woman who wanted to cheat them.

For him, she'd held up a mirror so he couldn't hide from the truth. Not to be cruel, but to help him. The mirror had been in her eyes as she convinced him to believe he was how she saw him, broken but not irreparable. Hurt but eager to heal. Lost among those who yearned to find him. Filled with rage, but eager to rediscover love.

Even more, she'd seen into his heart and showed him how to let it trust again. She led him to accept that not everyone was worthy of trust or would be open to trusting him again… and that was all right. Doing his best to be the man he was meant to be was all anyone could ask of him.

And when he told her he was leaving, she'd been courageous enough to divulge the love she held for him in her heart. He doubted he could have been that brave.

"You look uncomfortable, Joel," Gina Marie said. "You're sitting as stiffly as a man on his way to the gallows."

He didn't want to explain his thoughts, so he said, "I don't want to bump into you. You look fragile."

"I am, but I know you're being careful, son. You can't know how grateful I am that you were willing to meet me here."

"Better than in your lawyer's office."

Her laugh was strong coming from her frail form. "Yes, the girls explained that to me. I'm sorry you've had such a tough time."

"I brought it on myself." Again his gaze moved toward Grace, and he saw tears seeping from her eyes. He'd tell her that the words felt liberating. He wasn't guilty of the crime that had sent him to jail, but if he'd lived the life God had laid out for him, he wouldn't have been in the wrong place at the wrong time.

"As someone who's made more than my share of mistakes," Gina Marie said, "I know the strength it takes to say that. It sounds as if you've grown through your experiences, son, rather than let them define you."

He flinched.

"What's wrong?" she asked.

"You keep calling me son, and you should know that you're better off that I'm not your son."

"Why?"

"I've been a big disappointment to my parents." He tried to smile, but failed.

"Impossible."

"Quite possible." He couldn't figure out why the conversation had taken this turn. He'd thought the only thing Gina Marie would want to discuss was how soon he could donate his bone marrow so she could receive it. "My *mamm* and *daed*— My mother's heart was broken when I was sent to jail. As for my father, nothing I ever did met his expectations."

"You're talking about your adoptive parents."

"*Ja.* I don't know anything about my birth parents."

"You never searched for them?" She looked past him to Laurene and Naomi. "I can understand why they didn't. After all, they had no idea they were adopted until earlier this year. But you've known you were adopted all your life, right?"

"*Ja*, but I never felt the need to search." His mouth twisted in an ironic grin. "I was disappointment enough to the parents I knew, so I didn't feel it was right to walk back into the lives of my birth parents. I figured I was better off not knowing anything about them."

"So you've never been curious?" Gina Marie asked.

"I guess I was, but that was when I was a kid, and I didn't have access to a computer or any other way to find them. Later, I was wrapped up in too many other things, running away from my life."

"Running to what?"

"That was always the question." He was amazed how easy it was to talk to her. She was a stranger who'd never met the person he'd been, only the man he was now. "But I never looked, so I don't know anything about my birth parents."

Gina Marie took his hand in her trembling fingers. "I do." Raising her other hand, she put it against his cheek. "I do, son." Her voice broke as she whispered, "My son."

He looked from her to Grace whose eyes were wide with astonishment. Suddenly he wanted nothing more than to have Grace put her slender arms around him and offer him the haven of her touch. His head was spinning, and he almost reached up to grab it and make sure it didn't fly away. The last time he'd felt like this was when the judge pronounced his sentence. He hadn't been able to believe what he was hearing then…and he couldn't now.

"Your son?" he choked out. "I don't understand."

Skylar, who hadn't said a word up until now, put a cautioning hand on her *mamm*'s shoulder. "You had twin girls. We know that. I don't understand what you're talking about either."

"Neither do I," Laurene said as she edged closer to Naomi. "Are you saying you had another baby you gave up for adoption? Before us or after?"

Gina Marie's sparkling eyes hinted at the dynamic woman she must have been before cancer and chemo ravaged her. "At the same time."

"But we're twins. We're not…" Laurene groped for a nearby chair and clutched the back.

"Triplets?" gasped Grace. "Laurene and Naomi aren't twins? They and Joel…?" She choked on her astonishment as she looked at him.

Again silence dropped on the room, and he stood as he said, "There's got to be a mistake."

Gina Marie shook her head. "DNA doesn't lie. Part of the blood test we requested was for a DNA test to confirm the compatibility of our bone marrow. It showed unexpected results."

"Mom," Skylar said gently, "you're confused. Remember? The doctor said your new medicine could cause confusion. You had twins."

"That's what I thought, too."

Joel glanced at Grace. Was Gina Marie's mind compromised by the many drugs she must have taken during chemo? He drew his hands away and got up as Skylar continued to plead with her *mamm* to listen and accept the truth.

Naomi put her arm around her twin's shoulders. "But you were there, Gina Marie. You know how many *bopplin* you had."

"I was given drugs to help with the labor, and I was ill after you were born. The doctors kept me sedated because I had so many complications. When Vikki, the midwife who attended me during the birth before I had to go to the hospital because of complications, told me I'd had twins, I didn't have any reason not to believe her. After all, I couldn't imagine anyone lying about something like that."

"But she did," Grace said into the stunned silence.

"Yes, she did." The older woman's mouth pursed so sharply he could see the motion beneath her mask. "She lied about everything, including the fact she'd collected money from Laurene's and Naomi's parents, which was supposed to help pay my medical bills. She kept it and vanished, taking all information about where my babies were with her. She later died, we have learned." Her face softened. "But she did do one thing I asked. She placed you with Amish families in Bliss Valley. I'd told her I wanted my children to be raised Amish because their father was a plain man."

"Our *daed* was Amish?" Joel asked in amazement. When Laurene and Naomi—*his sisters!*—reached out to take his hands, he realized they must have known that important fact already. How much else did he have to learn about a past he'd never wanted to explore? "And you're my sisters? When I think of what I said and did to you... All I can say is I hope you can forgive me."

"Brothers always pick on their sisters." Laurene gave him a smile tinged with tears. "So, though we didn't know, it seems like we acted more like siblings than we imagined."

"No brother treats his sisters like I did."

"But you aren't that kid any longer." She raised her eyes to meet his. "All of us have been changed by what's happened to us since then. I'd like to start over as brother and sisters, Joel."

He glanced at Naomi, who nodded, too choked up to speak.

"I'd like that, too," he said.

Turning, he saw Grace wiping away tears. He longed to hold her close so she could help him make sense of his upended life. He took a step toward her when Gina Marie spoke again.

"When Naomi and Laurene suggested a bone marrow donor sign-up, none of us realized that God would do far more than bring me help to fight my cancer. He brought my son home to me."

A knock sounded on the door, and Joel wasn't the only one who flinched as the outside world barged in on them.

Grace opened the door. Before she could speak, his *daed* burst in. "What is going on here? I got a message to come over here, but it didn't say what was going on." He scowled. "If you dragged me over here to persuade me to forgive my son, you're wasting—"

"Wyman!" Gina Marie tried to get to her feet and failed.

Joel stepped forward and put his hand under her elbow to assist her. The motion allowed him to stand between her—his birth *mamm!*—and his unpredictable *daed*. What would *Daed* do when he discovered Joel's birth *mamm* had found him?

Then he realized what Gina Marie had said. She'd called *Daed* by his given name. How...?

"You know him?" asked Skylar, her brow wrinkled with her confusion.

"Yes, I do." Gina Marie stared at him as if seeing someone who'd come back from the dead. "Wyman and I dated thirty years ago."

Joel's head whipped around. His *daed* had gone out with an *Englisch* woman? Wait! His stomach clenched. Thirty years ago *Daed* had been married. Did his *mamm* know? His adopted *mamm*! Everything was growing more confusing by the moment. When Grace slipped her hand into his, he held on to it so he didn't get sucked down into the eddy that swirled around them.

For once, *Daed* didn't bluster out an answer. His gaze went from one person to the next around the room, and he cowered like a trapped animal.

"Wyman, it's not like you to be silent, though you cut me off without another word after I told you I was pregnant," Gina Marie said with more gentleness than antipathy. "With your children."

Joel lurched as if someone had smashed something heavy against his chest. He heard Laurene and Naomi—*his sisters!*—gasp and saw the lawyer's eyes narrow as they focused on his *daed*.

"Do you want to sit, Joel?" Grace asked from beside him.

"No, but *danki*." He gave her a quick smile, then turned to *Daed*. "Is what she's saying true?"

For a moment, he saw his *daed* debate whether to be honest or not. Joel wasn't sure which he'd choose. Wyman Beachy had always preached following the rules. He insisted his son follow the straightest and narrowest of the straight and narrow paths while he was hiding an affair that had left a woman pregnant.

"*Ja*," *Daed* said. "It's true."

"But you and *Mamm* legally adopted me, ain't so?"

"*Ja*, we did, but that doesn't change the truth. You were first my son by birth. Later, you became my son by adoption."

"I don't understand. If I'm your birth son, why did you adopt me?"

Gina Marie said quietly, "Wyman, tell him the truth. There have been too many lies for too many years." When he hesitated, she added, "If you don't tell them, I will."

"You know the truth?" *Daed* asked.

"Enough so I can guess the rest. When my midwife, Vikki, discovered we'd had a son, she went to you to see if you wanted him. She flattered your virility for having a son even as she extorted money from you when she sold you your own child."

"She said the money was to keep quiet about our agreement."

"Ten thousand dollars would buy a lifetime of silence, wouldn't it?"

"How did you know how much it was?" *Daed*'s face grew even paler.

Joel had heard enough about the past. He needed to know about the present. "Does *Mamm* know the truth?"

Daed nodded with an abrupt return of his arrogant nonchalance that revealed to Joel that *Daed* was sure he could handle the situation and come out the winner. Winner? Did *Daed* believe this was some sort of contest? It was life, and a person needed to own his mistakes and atone for them. That was a hard lesson Joel had to learn, but he had.

Had his *daed*?

"Your *mamm* does now," *Daed* said. "Somehow she found out the truth after you jumped the fence. She wouldn't explain how she learned about Gina Marie and me, but agreed not to tell you if you ever came back to Bliss Valley."

Joel stepped toward his *daed*. "You lied. You lied to me." He swept out his arm. "You lied to everyone."

"I never lied. I simply didn't tell the truth."

"You're splitting hairs."

Daed shrugged, as self-assured and self-satisfied as ever, but Joel had caught the unexpected emotion glowing in his eyes for a single heartbeat before *Daed* masked it. His *daed* was filled with fear and uncertainty.

Was Wyman Beachy scared that the far-from-fun house of mirrors he'd created to baffle his son and the rest of the community was about to shatter? The shards crashed around their feet, revealing the truth that could no longer be distorted by reflection upon reflection upon endless reflection.

"You had an affair while you were married," Joel said.

"Being married was something he didn't bother to mention to my mother," Skylar interjected, glaring at *Daed*. "Not even when he dropped her like a hot potato after he found out she was going to have his baby." She laughed sharply. "His three babies."

"Three?" he choked out.

Gina Marie sat on the sofa, clearly having run out of energy. Grace rushed into the kitchen and returned with a glass of water. His *mamm*—his birth *mamm*—took it from her with whispered thanks.

Knowing Gina Marie couldn't handle much more, Joel said, "I think we should discuss this out on the porch, *Daed*."

"I don't have anything more to say," *Daed* retorted.

"*Gut*, because the rest of us do, dear old dad," Laurene said with a furious expression almost identical to her half sister Skylar's.

Wyman's eyes widened. "You two...?"

"You catch on quick." Venom dripped from her voice. "Don't worry. We don't expect anything from you." She turned her back on him, and Naomi did the same as they walked toward Gina Marie.

Joel hurried to their sides. "I'll talk to him, but don't let his mistakes create a stain of hatred and anger on your souls."

Naomi sighed. "You've really changed, Joel. You've gotten wiser. I'm sorry I didn't see that before now."

"I don't want you to endure the frustration and pain I have for so long."

"*Danki.*"

Going back to where his *daed* stood, staring at Gina Marie and her daughters surrounding her with love, Joel opened the door. He said nothing as Wyman walked out. Joel followed and closed the door.

"Do you want to explain?" Joel asked. "You had triplets with a woman who isn't your wife? Have you ever asked for forgiveness for that?"

"I asked God."

"But not the *Leit*. You spent my whole childhood lambasting me for failing to meet some artificial, unobtainable standards you'd set because I had to be the best in the eyes of the *Leit*, the very people you spent years deceiving."

"I didn't want you to make the same mistakes I did." He walked toward the partially built ramp and stared at it.

To avoid looking at his son? "You didn't need to worry about that. I made all my own mistakes on my own."

Daed turned to him, obviously amazed Joel hadn't hurled back another accusation. "They're saying you were wrongly convicted."

"I was. However, the fact is that the drugs were in my car, even though they weren't mine. I should have known the risks when I hung around with those guys. I knew what and who they were." He sighed. "If I hadn't gotten caught that day, it would have been another. God showed His love when I turned my back on Him, and I'm alive. Others weren't shown such mercy."

A buggy slowed to a stop by the black car. It wasn't the Coffmans' because Pearl didn't pull it. A solid black horse shook its mane as the buggy's door slid aside.

Joel heard his *daed* gasp when *Mamm* emerged. She paused to look at the car, then crossed the yard and climbed the steps.

"What are you doing here?" *Daed* asked.

"I wanted to meet the woman who will have my son's bone marrow."

"*Mamm,*" Joel began.

She raised a hand to halt him. "I know who Gina Marie Tinniswood is, Joel." With a sad smile, she said, "I know you're concerned for me, and I love you all the more for it, but don't worry. I believe it's a blessing you've found each other during her time of greatest need. You're giving her a stupendous gift. I hope you have many years to get to know each other better."

His throat closed around the clump of emotion filling it. He couldn't imagine how much love it took for her to stand to the side and watch another woman claim him as her son. *Mamm* had raised him, had been his haven when *Daed* erupted with fury, had written to him daily for months after he left Bliss Valley. She'd never given up on him and never loved him less than the daughters she'd given birth to.

"*Mamm,* my love for you hasn't ever changed. Not ever."

"I know."

"It won't change now."

"I know." She gave him a gentle smile. "You fret too much about things you have no control over, Joel. The things we know with our hearts are always the truth."

"When did you know he was my birth *daed*?" He glanced at his *daed* who was skulking toward the family buggy.

Wyman Beachy wouldn't want to face anyone now. Would he push aside his *hochmut* and get to know his "new" *kinder* better? Only *Daed* could answer that. *Mamm* was right. Joel fretted about too many things he couldn't control, but one thing he could control. He could be the man he believed God wished him to be.

"I suspected for years." She tugged his growing hair. "You two look so much alike I would have had to have my eyes closed for thirty years not to notice. When I saw you at Eddie's funeral, I began to suspect Wyman hadn't been honest with me about why he was so eager to adopt you. I've known about his affair with your birth *mamm* for quite a while now."

"How?"

"Secrets don't stay secrets forever." She smiled sadly. "Someone he unwisely trusted revealed the truth to me. I didn't want to believe it, but I don't think your birth *mamm* was the only one he broke his marriage vows with. Your sisters..." She sighed. "They don't know what I've just told you."

"I won't tell them." He didn't add that the choice was hers, and he would respect whatever she decided. "I'm sorry, *Mamm*. But why didn't you say something?"

"What *gut* would that have done? It wouldn't have helped you when you and your *daed* were already at odds. I saw how much you despised his stubborn ways and how it comforted you when you believed you wouldn't turn out as he did." She gave him a tremulous smile. "Will you introduce me to your other *mamm*?"

He stared at her for a long moment. How had he failed to see the strength within his *mamm*? She'd lived quietly in the background, protecting her *kinder* and trying to help ease their ways through life. Like never before, he wished he still had the letters she'd written him, letters filled with a love that had never faltered.

But he didn't need them, he realized. He now knew the truth about her amazing warmth and love, which had sustained her through years of her husband's philandering and her son's descent into ever more disastrous decisions and consequences.

"Ja." He opened the door and ushered her inside where everyone turned to look at them.

Mamm went forward to be introduced to Gina Marie. The floorboards beneath his feet seemed as unsteady as shifting sand. He had to grasp on to one part of his life, a part he knew he'd never want to let go of.

But which one? Even as the question popped into his head, his gaze focused on Grace. He'd messed up everything in his life. Could he repair the mistake he'd made with her? He prayed it wasn't too late.

"How are you doing?" Grace asked when Joel looked in her direction.

"I'm confused."

She put her hand on his arm, hoping her touch would convey what she wasn't sure how to say. The regret and sorrow in his voice told her what she already knew about him. Joel was working to find his way back to God in spite of all the roadblocks in his way.

"I'm not surprised." She tipped his face toward hers so she could look into his eyes. "But I know you'll handle this as you have so much else. I've learned from you, Joel, it's possible to start over as I've learned doing the right thing may not always end up the way I've hoped."

"What we hope for may not be what God has planned for us." He touched her cheek, and she leaned into his caress.

"God's surprises turn out to be exactly what we need and what we wanted in the depths of our hearts."

"Even getting fired?"

"I've wanted to have a shop of my own where I can work with quilters and treat them the way they should be treated." She smiled. "Now I'll have my chance."

He took her hand and drew her through the kitchen and onto the back porch. Once they were alone, he said, "You can run a shop of your own and take care of your parents and your nephews."

"You didn't make it a question."

"It wasn't. I'm sure you can do anything you put your mind to." He ran the back of his fingers along her cheek and cupped her chin. "You're a tigress, Grace. You'll take care of your family, no matter what."

"Life can be too short, and I don't want to miss a moment I can have with them."

"And will you take care of me?"

"Me take care of you? It seems you've been taking care of all of us, Joel. You're bringing the farm back to life, and that has brought so much joy to *Daed*. *Mamm* has mentioned that, despite his tremors, since you brought the calves to the farm, his steps are lighter than they've been in years. He's already planning what to plant in the spring."

"That wasn't what I meant."

"Then you need to say what you mean." She knew her words were blunt, but she didn't dare to believe her heart, which was clamoring for him to speak as candidly.

"I vowed I'd never be like my *daed*."

"You aren't."

"But I am. I kept telling myself I didn't care about anything to do with a plain life. I acted as if I was invincible and as if I knew everything. I've lied to myself just as *Daed* has lied to himself."

"No, you lost your way, Joel, and now you've found your way back home."

He hung his head. "But I judged Brandon since he got here as my *daed* judged me. Instead of giving him the benefit of the doubt, I acted like prosecutor, judge and jury without waiting for a single fact to come to light."

"Most people would have jumped to the same conclusion and been shocked to discover why he was at the lumberyard."

"Most people? Maybe, but not you. You always see the best in anyone." He lifted his eyes to meet her gaze. "Even in me when I was questioning if there was anything *gut* left inside me."

"There was. There is!"

"I pray you're right. I can't spend the rest of my life hiding from the truth as *Daed* has."

"I am right. Trust me."

He folded her hands between his. "I do trust you, Grace. I trust you enough that I'll admit something I seldom do. You're right, and I'm wrong."

"About what?"

Instead of answering, he pulled her to him and pressed his mouth to hers. Startled, she stiffened in shock for a moment, then softened against him. *Don't let this be our last kiss*, she prayed as she savored the caress of his lips.

He drew back far enough to whisper, "Let me stay with you, Grace. Let me love you. Let me stay by your side as we walk God's path together. You've mentioned you might love me. I pray that you do because I love you. *Ich liebe dich.* Let me show you how I love you every day of the rest of our lives."

"But you're leaving Bliss Valley, ain't so?" Saying the words pierced her heart.

"I asked God to give me one *gut* reason to stay. One reason beyond your love because I didn't trust myself not to botch up your life as I did mine."

"And God gave that reason to you?" She searched his face, praying he would speak the answer her heart needed to hear.

"*Ja.* I need to stay here and help my *daed* come to terms with his mistakes as I've had to do with mine."

"What if he never does?"

He gave her the lazy smile she adored. "Then I'll have to stay here forever. Will you marry me, Grace?"

"*Ja,*" she breathed, thrilled at the words she'd come to believe he'd never speak.

She brought his lips back to hers. It wouldn't be their last kiss. It would be only one of so many to come.

The back door opened, and Laurene peeked out. "Gina Marie— Oh!"

"Meet your future sister-in-law," Joel said.

"Joel, announcements are supposed to wait until they're published during a church service," his sister chided.

"When has Joel ever done things like anyone else?" Grace asked, unable to keep from smiling.

Laurene laughed, then said, "Gina Marie and Skylar and the lawyer are about to leave. I thought you'd want to see her off."

"We'll be right in," Joel said, his hands tightening on Grace's arms. When the door closed, he bent toward her again.

"We shouldn't delay your *mamm,*" Grace said.

He brushed his lips across hers again and whispered, "There's always time for giving you a quick kiss, Grace, and there always will be."

"I'm glad." She longed to pull his arms back around her so she could explore every inch of his lips, but she reached for the doorknob.

As she opened the door to walk through with him, as they'd walk through so many doors in the years to come, he said, "Me, too."

Epilogue

One month later...

Adam and Laurene sat in the *eck*, the corner where the tables came together to allow them to see all their guests. Conversations buzzed along the long tables, and guests went to speak to the newlyweds and Mary Beth who sat between her *daed* and her new *mamm*. There was a lot of teasing and laughter between Laurene and Adam and their guests.

Grace wondered if she'd look as radiant on the day she married Joel. It wouldn't be for at least ten months, because he needed to take baptismal classes so he could become a full member of the *Leit*. He'd already spent hours closeted away with Adam, Jonas and the two ministers while he offered up a list of his mistakes and worked with them toward forgiveness. After each session, he had stood a bit taller as more of his burdens fell away. He'd gone for a few AA meetings at the church in Strasburg as well, finding another community there that helped him move forward.

Her parents had been delighted with the news she was going to marry Joel, but her nephews had been even more ecstatic. The boys continued to have tough days when tears came easily as they mourned their parents. Those days were fewer and fewer, and they both trailed after Joel as he worked with his rapidly growing calves. Brandon was already pestering Joel to allow him to get a calf of his own to raise, and Joel had agreed…once school was out next summer.

Last month, all five of them had offered their opinions when Grace looked at a building not far from the farm that she hoped would be the perfect place for her own quilt shop. Already, most of the quilters she'd worked with had let her know they'd be working solely for her once she opened her doors. As soon as she'd signed the contract on the building that had been a small general store, her nephews and Joel had begun fixing it up. She wanted to throw open the doors in time for the Christmas shopping season.

"What do you think?" Laurene's question broke into Grace's thoughts.

"About what?" She saw Adam was talking to some of their guests by the corner table.

"Having some payback time with our little brother." Laurene giggled along with Naomi. Both of them had been delighted to learn Joel was likely the youngest of the triplets, because the midwife had hidden him from Gina Marie. Laurene and Naomi were determined not to let him forget it. Drawing Grace over to stand with them, she added, "You're marrying into this family. You need to be part of this prank."

Grace held up her hands and laughed. "I would have to lose my mind to get in the middle of a feud that's been going on for almost twenty years."

"And any of us would be foolish," Joel said as he came to

stand beside them, "to mess with my sisters. But I'm fore-warned, Laurene. You won't catch me off guard."

"Oh, a challenge. I love a challenge." Motioning to her sister, she said, "Let's devise something particularly fun. Something with spiders maybe."

"I hate spiders," he replied with a grimace. "They freak me out with all their legs and gooey webs."

"I know." With more giggles, the sisters walked away.

Grace frowned. "You don't hate spiders, Joel. I saw you carry one outside the barn and set it free."

"You know that, and I know that." He hooked a thumb over his shoulder. "But they don't."

She laughed as she strolled toward the front yard with him where the boys were playing on a tire swing with Adam's daughter, Mary Beth, and Naomi's twins.

"It was a beautiful day, ain't so?" she asked as he took her hand.

"It was, but our wedding will be even more *wunderbaar.*"

"I hope you're right. You can never tell with a wedding. So many things can go wrong, but those make for fun stories later."

"Nothing has turned out as I thought it would," he said.

"When has life ever been what we assumed it would be?"

"When I prayed for a loving woman to share my life with, and I met you."

She laughed as they paused to watch the *kinder* playing, her nephews making sure each younger *kind* had a turn and being extra careful with the toddler twins who kept shouting, "Fun, fun, fun!"

"When you met me," she said, "all you had on your mind was getting out of the rain."

"And I found the sunshine." He looked toward the porch where his birth *mamm* sat and chatted with *Grossdawdi* Ephraim and Naomi's *daed* who had to take it easy after his stroke earlier in the summer. His adopted *mamm* had come to the wedding, but his *daed* hadn't.

Joel's sisters had been furious at how their *daed* had forced Joel out of their lives for so many years because Wyman couldn't face his own mistakes. They had vowed they would find a way to forgive their *daed* when he was willing to admit his sins before the *Leit* and ask for forgiveness, but repairing trust would require much more time. Wyman realized that, which was why he was having his own sessions with the ordained men to come to terms with years of lies that had nearly destroyed his family.

But Joel had taken his cue from his birth *mamm*. Gina Marie had forgiven his *daed* for abandoning her, because he'd given her a *wunderbaar* gift. Three amazing *kinder* who were once again part of her life. If Gina Marie could forgive *Daed*, Joel knew he must, too. Grace was so glad Joel's residual anger had faded as he'd gotten to know his birth *mamm* better. She saw little aspects of his personality in Gina Marie, and that delighted her, especially when she saw both of his *mamms* talking together, sharing stories of Joel.

Grace smiled when she heard Gina Marie's laugh from the porch. It was cheerful, even when muffled by the mask she wore to give her weakened immune system a chance to recover.

That's the word the *doktor* used. Recover. In Grace's opinion, it was one of the finest words in the English language. Though Gina Marie remained fragile and had months of recovery ahead of her, Joel's *mamm* could look forward to a future with all of her *kinder*. And he could look forward to spending time with the *mamm* he'd never known he had…as well as with the one who'd raised him and loved him from the first time he was placed in her arms.

"God sent you into my life," Grace said, "when I thought I couldn't be happy ever again. He knew what I needed, and that was His grace."

He brought her to face him, then locked his fingers together behind her back. "No, the grace He brought into my life is you, Grace. You saved me from myself and reminded me God didn't make a mistake when He set me off on the path He created for me. For that and for you, I'll be grateful every day of my life."

"Your life in Bliss Valley?" she teased.

"In Bliss Valley and, more important, with you."

Not caring who might see, he bent to kiss her. Cheers came from where the *kinder* played and from the front porch, but she barely noticed as she answered the yearning in his kiss with her own.

★ ★ ★ ★ ★

If you liked this story from Jo Ann Brown, check out her previous books in the Secrets of Bliss Valley series:

A Wish for Home
A Promise of Forgiveness

Available from Love Inspired!

Find more great reads at www.LoveInspired.com.

LOVE INSPIRED

Stories to uplift and inspire

Fall in love with Love Inspired—
inspirational and uplifting stories of faith
and hope. Find strength and comfort in
the bonds of friendship and community.
Revel in the warmth of possibility and the
promise of new beginnings.

Sign up for the Love Inspired newsletter
at **LoveInspired.com** to be the first
to find out about upcoming titles,
special promotions and exclusive content.

CONNECT WITH US AT:

 Facebook.com/LoveInspiredBooks

Twitter.com/LoveInspiredBks

LISOCIAL2021TR

**IF YOU ENJOYED THIS BOOK
WE THINK YOU WILL ALSO LOVE**

LOVE INSPIRED
INSPIRATIONAL ROMANCE

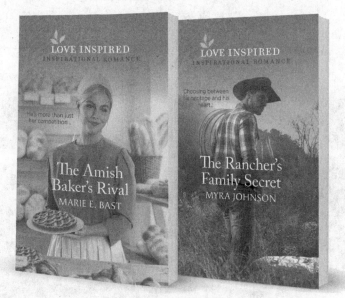

Uplifting stories of faith, forgiveness and hope.

Fall in love with stories where faith helps
guide you through life's challenges, and discover
the promise of a new beginning.

6 NEW BOOKS AVAILABLE EVERY MONTH!

LIXSERIES2021TR

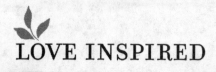